Please Come to Boston

a novel

Gary Goldstein

HADLEIGH HOUSE
PUBLISHING

Hadleigh House Publishing
Minneapolis, MN
www.hadleighhouse.com

ISBN-979-8-9850576-8-3
ISBN-979-8-9850576-9-0 (ebook)
LCCN: 2024903712

Also by Gary Goldstein

THE LAST BIRTHDAY PARTY

"Goldstein's crackling wit makes his debut novel an absolute joy. Come for the frothy plot and zippy writing, stay for the heartfelt storytelling and deliciously satisfying ending. A refreshing and uplifting read! – Susan Walter, author of *Good as Dead*

"A novel so real I kept expecting one of the characters to text me. You will think about *The Last Birthday Party* long after the final page." – W. Bruce Cameron, #1 *New York Times* best-selling author of *A Dog's Purpose*

"An achingly funny love letter to midlife in all its anxiety, anguish, and awe. I loved it." – David Dean Bottrell, author of *Working Actor*

"Brisk, funny, and wise, with a keen eye for the absurdities of L.A. living, in a city of constant reinvention, Gary Goldstein has written a warm, appealing, and heartfelt coming-of-middle-age story." – Mark Sarvas, American Book Award-winning author of *Memento Park*

THE MOTHER I NEVER HAD

"There are so many surprises and joys in this beautiful, human, well-told, emotionally rich story, that you won't want it to end."
– Iris Rainer Dart, best-selling author of *Beaches*

"A highly pleasurable read with a lovable main character at its center . . . The author also gives us a fine-tuned exploration of what family means . . . in this treasure of a novel. – Elyssa Friedland, author of *Jackpot Summer*

"Goldstein has crafted a 'what if?' tale that's as poignant and profound as it is propulsive. An evocative journey of love, loss, and discovery." – Darin Strauss, award-winning author of *Half a Life* and *The Queen of Tuesday*

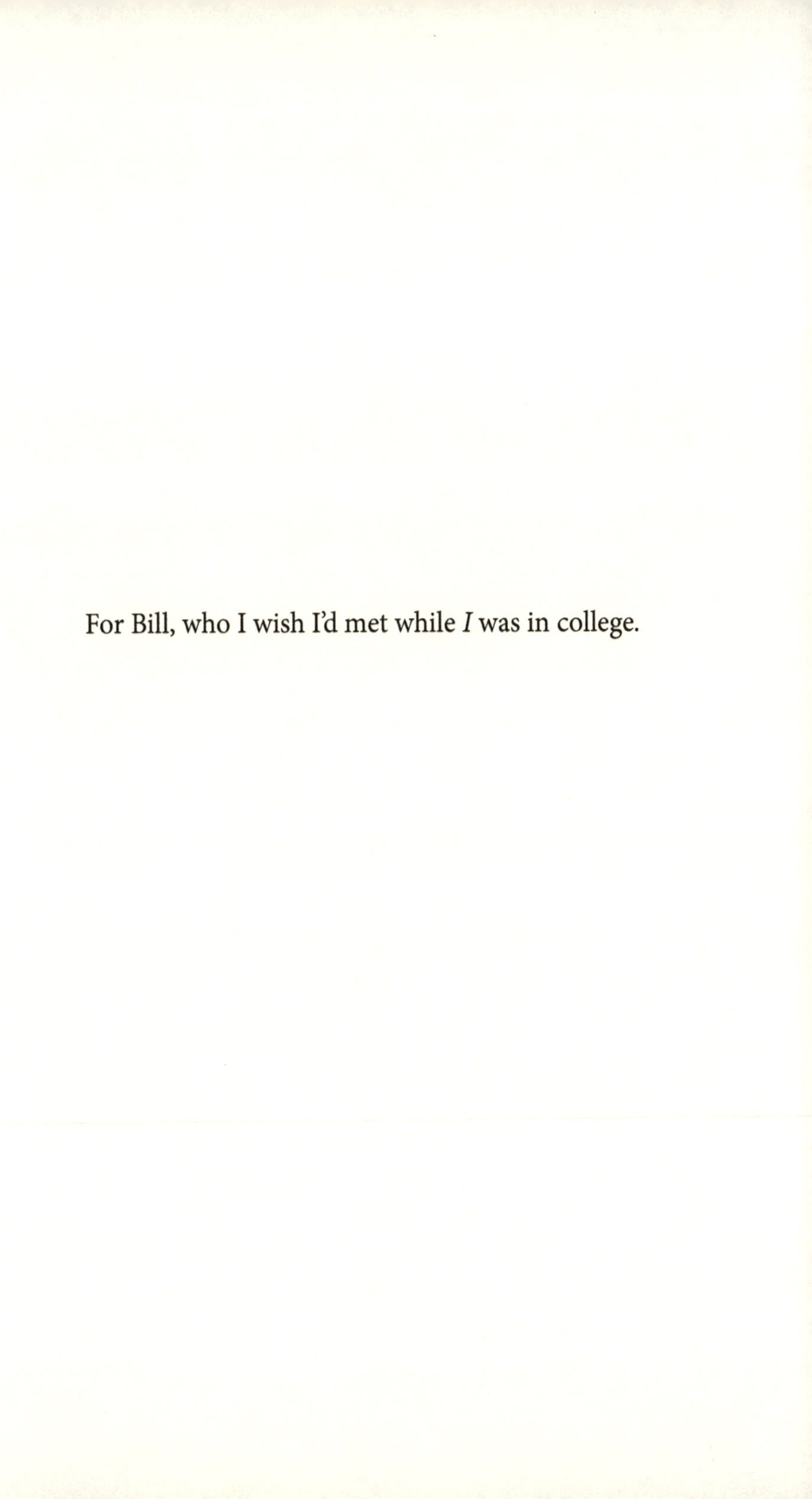

For Bill, who I wish I'd met while *I* was in college.

"It takes courage to grow up
and become who you really are."
— E. E. Cummings

ONE

Today

NICK'S HEART QUAKED in time with the pounding of his feet as he sped across the scenic riverbank. Not because of any great physical strain—not yet, anyway—but the alarming, needling, stranger-than-fiction thought that today's meeting could upend everything. All over again. An eternity later.

Still, Nick learned that when it came to romance, in all its various shapes and forms, you could never really make an accurate prediction. About yourself or anyone else. Yet here he was, back where the whole life-altering thing began that Labor Day weekend so long ago. Coming up on a shocking *fifty years* long ago. That's five-o, folks.

Nick always dug the fall weather, its crispness and clarity, the breezy exhilaration it offered upon opening a window, exiting a building, or sweating in the sun. So, it couldn't have been a better time to go for a bracing run along the Charles River, his nervous energy aside.

As he pushed on, Nick finally felt his pulse steady and his mind relax as he traversed the wide paved path that split the grassy esplanade. He was surprised at the ease with which he jogged, oddly less enervated now than when he was first introduced to running—that is, purposefully running—as a college freshman.

Sure, he'd been exercising in one form or another ever since. He even participated in the occasional 5K charity run. Nick had given up a weekly hoops game with friends (age-appropriate friends who'd aged as appropriately as he had) only a few years ago after one of his pals, Ramón, announced he was having a knee replacement. Worse, another friend, Doug, had a near-fatal heart attack. In truth, they'd all been hitting that court cement for far too long, even though, as time went on, they took it easier and easier on each other, playing more for enjoyment than for any real competitive satisfaction.

It's the same reason Nick stopped skiing and rarely engaged these days in any sport riskier than pickleball or tennis. (He'd never had the patience for golf, so it's doubtful he'd find it now.) He mostly focused on more "controllable" activities like weight training, power walking, and, like now, some stop-and-go jogging. He was in pretty decent shape for a guy his age, though he'd be lying if he said he wasn't always waiting for the other athletic shoe to drop. That was the thing about getting older—it could feel as if you were racing against an imaginary clock. Sometimes not so imaginary.

And there it was again: the anxiety. Or maybe something else just as unsettling—or even worse. As he stared out at the Charles's sun-kissed, gently choppy waves, the Harvard Bridge in the distance, and the familiar-unfamiliar collection of buildings flanking the river, a wave of nostalgia swept through Nick with such force it knocked the wind out of him. Gasping with the intensity of a panic attack (and not just a racing head—and heart), he dropped onto the first bench that appeared, like a mirage, thankfully just a few yards ahead.

Shit, was this what Doug's heart attack felt like? Nick waited for the notorious chest and arm pain to hit as he struggled to catch his breath and focus his hazy vision.

"Hey, man, you OK?" Nick was so disoriented he hadn't even realized someone was sitting next to him.

Nick turned and eyed his bench mate, a rangy teenager in jeans, black T-shirt, and a Chinese symbol tattooed on his forearm.

Although given how fuzzy things were looking, it could've been an image of Elvis. Then again, why would a kid his age have Elvis Presley's face tattooed on him for all time?

"Yeah, I just got a little dizzy," Nick finally answered. His vision slowly cleared, and his breathing found its normal rhythm. "Thanks for asking, though."

"You sure? You still look kinda shaky."

"No, I'm cool," Nick assured him, though he had to clench his right fist to mask its residual tremor. He wondered what just happened. Was it about today's reunion, the reunion he'd so quickly and happily agreed to? Traveled so many miles for? Had been feeling so warm and optimistic about—until he didn't?

As if to reassure himself that he was, in fact, "cool," Nick gathered his steam and asked, "What does your tattoo mean?"

The teen looked at his arm as if he'd never seen it before. "What, this? It's the Chinese symbol for happiness."

"Ah. So kind of a good luck charm?"

"We'll see about that. I just started college, so . . ."

Nick studied him, surprised. He thought this was just some high school kid ditching algebra. *Did I look that young when I started college?* "Where do you go?"

"Emerson." The freshman hooked a thumb up over his shoulder toward the school's Boylston Street campus.

Nick pointed to himself. "BU." Then, as if it needed clarification: "I mean, I *went* to BU. A long time ago."

Now it was the kid's turn to study Nick. "How long?"

"Let's just say I could have gone there with your grandparents." It sounded glib but it was the startling truth. Nick could see the calculator clacking away in the boy's head.

"Did you like it? I mean, do you remember?"

"Do I *remember?*" *Christ, how old were this kid's grandparents, anyway?*

"Sorry, that was dumb, I meant—"

"Honestly? Like it was yesterday." Maybe not exactly yesterday, but, at least at the moment, Nick's college days were a lot more vivid than, say, what he did last weekend. And, over the next few days, were bound to get even more vivid. "And yeah, BU was great. Not all the time, of course—we're talking four years. But on balance? Yeah." And because Nick felt like he should say something wise: "It's what you make of it."

The student vacantly rubbed his forearm as if summoning the tattoo to life. "My dad says college is just a way to pass time until you become an adult."

"Sounds a little cynical to me."

"My dad can be a dick. But he's paying my way, so not that much of a dick, I guess. I just don't want to fuck up."

"You mean, prove him right?"

"No, I mean have nothing to show for four years of school, no job when I graduate, then have to move back in with my parents and work at Starbucks." He adjusted the backward Yankees cap on his head, sighed with the entire weight of the world, and gazed out at the river.

"Maybe you should just take it, like, a month at a time. Enjoy yourself a little. This should be the best time of your life." Nick rolled his shoulders and felt his energy flooding back.

"Was it yours?"

Nick studied this boy, his taut skin, bright teeth, dark scruff (so many years before the flecks of gray would appear), and hopeful posture. He saw nothing of himself in him. And maybe everything. Nick looked away.

A mild wind came up as if beckoning Nick back to the running path. He turned to the student, who was clearly awaiting an answer. An answer Nick could not conclusively give. Still, what would Nick have wanted someone to tell *him*?

"Truth is, if I could snap my fingers and be back there, back to square one—day one—I'd do it in a heartbeat." And maybe it was true. Or true enough.

He extended a hand. "Nick."

"Tyler," the boy said, responding with a surprisingly firm hand-shake. Maybe this Tyler would be OK after all. And maybe Nick would be, too.

He was steady once again, strong and focused, his sneakered feet planted firmly on the running path. Ready to take on whatever this singular, long-awaited day might have in store.

And with that, Nick allowed the sweet breeze to sweep him up and send him back onto the jogging trail, the Art Deco swoop of the Hatch Shell amphitheater looming invitingly in the distance. Just like he remembered it.

TWO

1975

THE ELEVATOR DOOR opened onto the fourteenth floor and Nicky, waiting for a ride down, found himself facing his future. Not that he had the slightest inkling of that at the time. He was pretty far away from any deep self-knowledge just then, not to mention the presumption that the sturdy-looking guy in the cutoff jeans-shorts and shrewdly fitting Boston University T-shirt standing in the elevator would have any use for—much less any interest in—a puny freshman like Nicky. Well, puny compared to this big, smiley, white-toothed dude holding open the door who, it turned out, was an orientation leader for the dorm that Nicky had just moved into. The three, eighteen-story towers known as "700," for its address of 700 Commonwealth Avenue, were also known as "the Zoo," for reasons Nicky would soon learn (and not just because some wise guy once painted a tail on the "7" over the dorm entrance and the "Z" kind of stuck). But "Joe Hello," as Nicky would nickname his spirited welcomer, was friendly to every campus newbie that day, so, y'know, nothing personal.

And maybe, at that very moment, it wasn't. At all.

"Come on in, the water's fine," joked Joe O., as it was written on the name badge stuck above his left pec.

Nicky had no idea how to respond to that, though a simple "Ha!" would have sufficed. Sure, he was happy—OK, thrilled—to be starting college in a big city like Boston and leaving small-town Long Island behind. But Nicky was also feeling nervous and self-conscious and a little lonely. Maybe it was because his parents had just left to drive back to New York (was it his imagination, or did they seem in a rush?); his roommate, a freshman from Pittsburgh named Monty (really?), had yet to arrive; and he didn't know anyone else among the swarm of students streaming into the mega-dorm and setting up shop for the next nine months. Except now, apparently, this Joe O. person. Who was still smiling, awaiting a clever rejoinder from Nicky as he held open the elevator doors.

"Uh, thanks," was about as much as Nicky could muster as he stepped into the elevator, its flat metal walls painted a Band-Aid beige. Or seemingly repainted, if the scratchings and scrawlings peeking through the gloss were any indication. *Was that a cock and balls?*

"Joe O'Rourke," Joe O. said, thrusting out a quarterback-sized hand as the door rolled shut. "Dorm orientation leader," he added brightly, giving the nametag a hearty slap. "Welcome to BU!"

"I'm Nicky. Nick," he corrected himself, having vowed to dump the "y" as soon as he crossed the Massachusetts border. It didn't make him feel any older or more mature. In fact, he felt around twelve as he took in Joe's sinewy arms and shadowy stubble. He didn't mean to stare, there was just nowhere else to look.

"Need a hand with anything, bud, or are you all moved in?" Joe asked as the elevator rumbled in its descent.

"Uh, no, I think I'm set. Just going down to get my mailbox key."

"Cool. Anything comes up, you let me know. That's what I'm here for." Joe patted his nametag again. "I'm on 10C," he added, for the tenth floor, C Tower.

"14A," Nicky answered, pointing to himself, though the response was probably obvious.

"Right," Joe confirmed with a slight leer. "The new coed floor. Lucky you, huh?"

Before Nicky could respond, the elevator stopped at the eighth floor and another apparent freshman (the look was unmistakable) entered with her mother (also unmistakable). Joe gave both attractive women a conspicuous once-over. They smiled back. Nicky felt like wallpaper.

"Going down, ladies?" Joe asked as if the phrase *double entendre* had yet to be invented.

"Lobby, please," the younger woman answered, eyes lingering on the hunky orientation leader.

"I got it," chirped Nicky as he pressed "4" on the button panel. The girl reminded him of Laurie from *The Partridge Family*. He suddenly felt chivalrous. Joe beamed at him.

"Thanks, Nicky."

"Nick."

"Right." Joe shot him an indulgent wink, as if to say, *You're not "Nick" yet*. He gave Nicky a not-so-subtle nod in the female freshman's direction, with a slight eyebrow raise. Nicky hoped neither she nor her mother, both quietly facing the door, caught Joe's gesture. Still, in the interest of camaraderie, Nicky returned his orientation leader's well-intentioned smirk—*Yes, she's cute, even if I can't formulate any words right now*—and the elevator doors mercifully slid open.

"Have a great day, ladies!" Joe enthused, flashing those pearly whites, as the women exited into the dorm lobby. The mom turned and winked at Joe. But the Susan Dey lookalike, perhaps mortified by her more sociable mother, just kept going, head up and shoulders tight.

Nicky, watching this all play out, forgot he was supposed to leave as well. Or was he simply stuck in Joe's gravitational pull?

Joe, clearly familiar with dazed freshmen, slapped his big hand against the elevator door, holding it open for Nick. "This is you, bud. Lobby."

Nicky snapped to. "Right, thanks. Sorry. I'm a little . . . spaced out, I guess." Overwhelmed was more like it, not that he would have copped to such a decidedly newbie emotion in front of his confidence-oozing elevator host.

"Well, hustle up," Joe said. "Maybe you can run into that honey who was just in here. And I don't mean the mom, though she wasn't too bad herself." He grinned at Nicky like the cat who was about to eat the canary. Or maybe something less violent and more pleasurable.

Nicky struck a casual pose as the elevator threatened to close; Joe slapped the door back. "Yeah, she looks like Laurie Partridge," said Nicky. It hardly committed him to seeking her out but at least acknowledged her comeliness.

Joe noodled that until Nicky's reference sunk in. The cat-canary look resurfaced as he leaned into Nicky. "I'll leave you with this, friend: You like this lady, pounce. A week from now, they'll be lining up for her." Joe raised an eyebrow. "And I might be at the head of that line."

"Yeah, OK. Thanks, Joe," Nicky said, backing out of the elevator, a feeling in his gut he wouldn't be able to identify for a while to come.

NICKY DIDN'T REQUEST anything specific in a roommate when he filled out BU's lengthy housing form since there were no boxes to check for No Assholes or No Lunatics. He did, however, request a coed floor, figuring it might prove more interesting than living with forty other guys. Plus, it might feel more like real life: He grew up with two younger sisters and an older brother—not to mention a mother and father—so cohabitation for Nicky had always been a fifty-fifty gender split. His parents, never ones to err on the side of progressiveness, were dubious about the dorm arrangement. That it was the first time BU had ever offered this option rang a few warning bells for Stevie and Rose DeMarco, who both felt there was something "unnatural" about this kind of male-female proximity. Meanwhile, Nicky's older brother, Richie, dubbed the setup "totally natural" and Stevie and Rose somehow stopped sweating their younger son's housing preference. (Richie, though a mere eleven months older than Nicky, had magical, eldest-child powers over their parents; Nicky knew he would owe him one. Or six.)

But before Nicky could judge if he'd made the right selection of dorm floor, he first had to learn if he'd shit the bed by playing roommate roulette. He had no idea what to expect of Monty from Pittsburgh but it sure wasn't what he found when he returned to room 1406, mail key and a free weekly newspaper called *Boston After Dark* in hand. (He never did spot Laurie Partridge—or her mom—in the lobby amid its noisy mob of kids and parents.)

"Monty Rosenman," announced Nicky's new roommate, right hand extended to shake, a smoldering Marlboro in the other. Inexplicably, for a Jewish guy from the Squirrel Hill area of Pittsburgh, Monty looked like a cowboy: sturdy jeans, a plaid Western shirt (top two snaps undone), and worn-in Western boots. A rawhide necklace completed the incongruous picture. Something decidedly country played on a serious-looking turntable Monty had hooked up in Nicky's brief absence.

"Nicky DeMarco—uh, Nick," he corrected. "Hey." As they shook hands, sizing each other up, Nicky took in the plume of smoke swirling around their heads.

"Guess you didn't check the No Smokers box, huh?" said Monty, taking a long drag of his cigarette. Nicky had secretly smoked for a while in tenth grade but it didn't take, plus his father—once said secret was out—threatened beheading, so that was that.

"Guess not," Nicky answered, having no memory of that choice on the housing form. He noticed Monty's beard was full and neatly trimmed (maybe he was only part cowboy) and that he had the kind of floppy, uncomplicated hair that Nicky, he of the unruly waves and curls, envied in other guys. (Women occasionally said they wished they had Nicky's hair, not a plus in his book.)

"Is it going to be a problem?" Monty asked with a vague edge as he began to fill the closet on his side of their compact, cinder block-walled room. He stashed away three more pairs of worn cowboy boots plus a pair of white Keds that looked brand new.

This was where the rubber always met the road for Nicky.

He too often defaulted to no when the answer was decidedly yes. And "Sure, why not?" when "Fuck no, not on your life" was the more appropriate response. Being a rebel rarely worked out for Nicky (see: cigarette smoking) and he usually caved, sublimated, and/or kept the peace. Like now.

"Nah, that's OK," he said with a blithe wave of his hand through the Marlboro smoke. Then: "Hey, what's this music, anyway?" As in, *What's this irritating crap that I have the feeling I'll be stuck listening to way too much?*

Monty grabbed an album cover, presenting it proudly. It read: *Jerry Jeff Walker*. Beneath was a portrait of a morose-looking guy in a beard and cowboy hat. "Ever heard him?" Nicky shook his head. "Wrote 'Mr. Bojangles.' I've got all his albums," Monty informed him with a head tilt toward an orange crate of LPs, adding, "Trust me, he'll grow on you."

Like mold, Nick thought but nodded noncommittally. "I'm more of a rock 'n' roll guy, myself."

"Yeah? Who do you like?" Monty was now hanging what looked like ten of the same Western shirts in his closet.

Nicky sensed no one he would name would satisfy anyone who listened to this Jerry character. "Rolling Stones, Elton John . . . Bachman-Turner Overdrive. Lotsa stuff."

Monty turned from the closet, narrowing his gaze at Nicky. "Bachman-Turner Overdrive?"

"Yeah, y'know: 'Let It Ride,' 'Taking Care of Business' . . ."

"I know who they are. They're just kind of shit, that's all." It was said without disdain or judgment, just opinion, as Monty hung the last of his snap-happy shirts. Still, the response gave Nicky pause about his new roommate. Not that he had an option.

Instead of getting weird or defensive, Nicky decided to unpack as well, a silence settling in between them as they each made their half a home. It only caused Nicky to miss his real home more, a shock considering how much he'd been itching to leave it.

Filling his dresser drawers, as Monty sang along to Jerry Jeff, Nicky thought about Joe Hello. About how effortlessly charismatic he appeared, how comfortable with himself and everyone around him he seemed. And how Monty, in his own sort of posey way, also gave off a self-confidence that Nicky had yet to master—or even begin to approach.

Staring in the mirror that hung over his dresser—at his defiant, coffee-brown hair; wide, dark eyes; slightly gap-toothed smile; and sizable Roman nose (*thanks, Pop!*)—he wondered what it would take to start truly believing in himself in this alien, potential-oozing environment. What would be the cowboy hat, Western shirt, and honky-tonk music that *he'd* embrace to become his authentic self? Then again, what *was* his authentic self? The uncertain boy he'd left back on Long Island or the burgeoning man he'd uncover in Boston?

THREE

BY THE END of the day, every room on floor 14A was occupied with its designated pairs of roommates: mostly excited, wide-eyed freshmen with a handful of more relaxed sophomores in the mix. Nicky felt something decidedly electric in the air as students rotated in and out of each other's rooms to say hello, working overtime to prove their likability or coolness. That it was the first time that coed floors existed at BU brought an extra intoxication to these encounters; it wasn't so much sexual as it was liberating, like they were part of some grand experiment. It shouldn't have felt like such a big deal, but it did.

The instant group conviviality took Nicky's anxiety down quite a few notches, even if he had trouble remembering people's names (*Were there really three Julies?*) and hometowns (he was only one of two Long Islanders, which made everyone else feel kind of exotic). Then there was the matter of folks' majors and who was living with whom—and in which of the floor's twenty or so rooms. But considering that, at first, Nicky was called everything from Ricky to Billy to Barry, clearly everyone was having recall issues. Not that it mattered; that late afternoon was like an impromptu party for a bunch of strangers who wouldn't stay that way for long. (A joint that quietly made its way around aided in the loosening-up factor.)

It also gave Nicky a chance to observe Monty with others, to see if his first impression of him might have been a bit rash. So the guy dressed like a cowpoke and seemed a little arrogant, was that really so bad? And the smoking thing wasn't a personality issue as much as, what, a not-uncommon lifestyle choice? (Nicky noticed that Monty passed on toking the doobie, which was interesting.) To his credit, Monty didn't distance himself from Nicky but rather introduced him to others as if the two were childhood pals. Then again, Nicky eventually noticed, that was only in front of the women, around whom Monty mustered an impressive charisma; he already seemed to have captivated a shapely earth-mother type named Sabrina.

"Hi, Nicky," he heard from behind him as he chatted in the hallway with fellow Long Islander Shelley, a wavy-tressed redhead whose piercing New York accent made Nicky's telltale Nassau County cadence sound like the King's English. He turned around to find himself facing the Laurie Partridge lookalike. It took a moment to place her.

She helped him: "It's Lori. From the elevator?"

"Oh, right, hi. Wait, your name is *Laurie*? Like . . . Partridge?" Nicky hoped that didn't sound like he'd been talking—or thinking—about her, which he hadn't since returning from the lobby.

"Yeah, I know, I get that all the time," she said. "Well, more when the show was still on but . . . yeah. Though I spell it the normal way."

"How did *she* spell it?"

"The abnormal way." Lori smiled playfully, as if Nicky should've known that.

He thought she seemed much friendlier than when they first met, which, in truth, wasn't much of a meeting. Maybe she'd just been annoyed at her mother. Whatever, Nicky definitely felt less tongue-tied around her now. Still, he wondered what she was doing there.

"I thought you lived on eight?" Nicky asked, spotting Monty snaking toward them from the far end of the hallway. Lori looked blankly at Nicky. He clarified, "I mean, that was where you got on the elevator." If he was trying to impress her, in any way, he wasn't hacking it.

"Oh, I was just saying hi to a friend on eight. We went to high school together."

"Yeah? Where?"

"New Jersey."

He pointed to himself. "Long Island. Franklin Square."

"Never heard of it."

"You're not missing much."

"Ever hear of Cherry Hill?"

Nicky thought about lying but didn't see the point. "Actually, no."

"It's a nice place, but I'm glad to be away. It was kind of a tough summer."

Before Nicky could ask what she meant, Monty was standing next to them, scoping Lori out like some museum artifact. "Stairway to Heaven" started blaring from a nearby room. Nicky never liked the song, thought Led Zeppelin was ridiculously overrated. He could only imagine what his roommate thought of the group.

Monty threw an arm around Nicky and beamed at Lori. "I see you've met my main man here." Nicky was now scrunched between Monty and the corridor wall.

Lori eyed Monty, took in his Western getup, which now included a turquoise and silver arrowhead hanging from his neck on a length of rawhide. "Yeah, but I haven't met *you*," she answered. Lori narrowed her gaze, pretended to think, and said, "Wait—don't tell me: Clint Eastwood."

Nicky suppressed a grin. He decided he liked this Lori; she didn't seem to buy into Monty's bullshit like that Sabrina chick.

Monty unwrapped his arm from Nicky's shoulder, looking a bit thrown by her coolly mocking tone. He ran his fingers through his sleek locks (Nicky would soon realize that was Monty's "move"), and slapped on a cocky grin. "No, but I wish I had his bank account," he retorted. Lori was silent, as if still wondering about this guy.

Nicky figured what the hell and threw him a lifeline. "Lori, Monty. Monty, Lori." He flipped his fingers between the two and they nodded at each other, Monty more enthusiastically than Lori. "Monty's my roommate," Nicky added in case Lori *did* think he was Monty's "main man," whatever that was supposed to mean.

Monty sang along with the Zep, working his way through their puzzling lyrics. This betrayal of his purported musical allegiance was clearly for Lori's benefit but, from the cool look on her face, he needn't have strained his voice.

"Ugh, I fucking hate 'Stairway to Heaven,'" she declared as if reading Nicky's mind. "It's like the world's most overplayed slow-dance song."

"Yeah, and what the hell are you supposed to do when it starts rocking out?" Nicky added. "Just stand there and stare at your date?" He flashed back on dancing with date slash chem lab partner Maria Moss at junior prom. Which gloomily reminded him of what did—or didn't—happen afterward. (Let's just say no Bunsen burners ignited.)

"And don't get me started on 'Colour My World,'" said Lori. "*So predictable.*"

Monty, not to be left out, jumped in with a verbal U-turn. "Well, rock's not really my thing, anyway."

"He likes Johnny Walker," offered Nicky. *Wait, was that the singer's name?*

Lori perked up. "The scotch?"

Monty barely suppressed an eye roll. "*Jerry Jeff* Walker," he informed Lori. "He's the best. I'll play him for you sometime."

Before Lori could respond, Sabrina drifted up, all floral-patched jeans and scoop-neck leotard top. Lori gave her a little wave. "Have you guys met *my* roommate?" she asked Nicky and Monty. Without waiting for an answer, Lori made quick introductions, though Nicky knew Monty had already met—and put the moves on—the lovely Sabrina. Lori quickly learned that, too.

"Monty, I'd love to hear that album you told me about," Sabrina said, without a hint of coyness. Nicky and Lori traded a quick look, noting Monty's apparent pickup line—one that Sabrina had apparently picked up on.

Monty lit up like a neon sign. "What about now?"

Nicky and Lori watched their roommates walk off together, past other alliances being formed in that buzzing hallway.

"You may not understand this," Lori told Nicky, "but there's something kinda sexy about that guy. Physically, anyway."

"Monty?" Nicky may have sounded incredulous, but at some level he maybe got it.

"Don't get me wrong, he's not *my* type. Not that I really know what my type is anymore. I thought I knew, but . . ." Lori trailed off. There was clearly more than she cared to get into. She brightened. "Hey, I'm starving, wanna go eat? I think the dining hall opens at five."

Nicky wondered if he was supposed to wait for Monty—why, he had no idea—but he was hungry, too. He checked his watch. "5:05. Let's go." "Sister Golden Hair" by America wafted out of another room. He pointed in the direction of the music. "This is more my speed."

Lori nodded in agreement, smiled her Susan Dey smile: warm and just a tad mysterious. "I like you," she announced. "Let's be really good friends, OK?"

FOUR

THE WAY NICKY saw it, Lori likely had a more immediate romantic interest in Monty than him, her "type" notwithstanding. Ten minutes and she had already put Nicky in the friend zone—out loud, unequivocal. He was flattered, sure. She obviously saw something she liked about him—and vice versa. Not that he was competing with his roommate (except maybe for floor space) or looking for love, sex, or even a date at that very moment. After all, he just got there.

And talk about not being sure of your type. By all rights, someone like Lori should have been his type—any guy's type, really. *What did that orientation leader say? A week from now, they'll be lining up for her?* She was undeniably pretty and seemed bright and funny. And yet, more than anything, Nicky was just relieved to make his first friend at college without even trying. Wherever it went, well, that was gravy. Or was he just deluding himself and being self-protective? Times like this, Nicky wished he could unplug his mind and sail without a rudder.

The dining hall at 700 was a vast, multiroom affair with several lengthy food bays manned by work-study students. There were also two salad bars plus four self-serve drink stations. A sign at the entrance read: Take What You Eat but Eat What You Take, which Nicky found confusing.

"I think it means don't waste food," said Lori as they handed their ID cards to a door monitor. "It's all-you-can-eat." Inside, as they grabbed trays and silverware, she told Nicky about the phenomenon called the Freshman 15, which was how many pounds the average student tended to gain their first year of college.

"Considering I lost fifteen pounds before coming here, no way am I putting it back on," she asserted. Lori examined a tureen of saucy lasagna, opting for a broiled chicken breast instead. Nicky, eager to actually gain some weight on his skinny frame, took the lasagna *and* the chicken before following Lori to the salad bar.

As Nicky watched Lori sparingly top a green salad with low-fat dressing, he tried to imagine her fifteen pounds heavier and couldn't quite get there. He figured there must be a story behind it. Donna, the older of his two sisters, was always trying to lose weight—mostly unsuccessfully—so Nicky knew how tough and complicated it could be. (Which isn't to say he and his brother, Richie, hadn't mercilessly teased her about her fad diets.)

They spread out at a table for four near one of the drink stations as the dining hall quickly filled with a swirl of buoyant, hungry students, many of whom, like Nicky, seemed like awkward newcomers finding their way. As he and Lori dug into their food (though the lasagna wasn't Nicky's mom's, it wasn't half-bad), she expanded on some of the biographical data she'd hinted at in the 14A hallway. Nicky learned that her summer was difficult because, in June, her parents announced their divorce after twenty years of marriage. She attributed some of her weight gain to the attendant anxiety: as an only child, she was often stuck in the middle of their split. Then, in July, Lori broke up with her high school boyfriend, Joshua, who decided—categorically and without her input—that monogamy would be impossible once they were in college (more angst, more weight gain). Finally, in August, she got a little obsessed trying to shed the extra pounds and landed in the emergency room (she refused to elaborate; Nicky's mind spun). She was enrolled in CLA though knew most people thought liberal arts studies were for people who had no idea what they wanted to do with their lives. But she wanted to be a psychologist (she'd decided over the summer) and saw this as a good first step. Nicky didn't know enough about it to agree or disagree and simply nodded along in general support.

"You're a good listener," Lori announced between bites of chicken. Nicky noticed she peeled the skin off before eating it.

He responded with a thank you but didn't know what he did that was so special. All he did was listen and not interrupt her. Maybe that was the point.

"OK, tell me all about you," Lori continued with a genuine interest that impressed Nicky. He studied her: At first, he'd thought she looked like Susan Dey around the eyes, but he now saw their mouths were similar. Maybe the hairstyles too, though most girls (he realized he needed to start calling them women) had that parted-in-the-middle, straight-to-the-shoulders thing going on. On closer examination, Lori may have even been better looking than the actress.

But before Nicky could tell Lori his story, orientation leader Joe appeared, meal tray in hand, looming over their table, a sparkly smile on his face.

"Hey, you two. I see you found each other." He shot Nicky a sly wink. Lori may or may not have noticed, though she was definitely checking him out.

"Hi, again," Lori said, glancing at the name badge still stuck to his T-shirt, "uh, Joe."

"Lori and I are on the same floor," Nicky felt obliged to explain to Joe, who had no visible reaction to the Lori-Laurie coincidence nor that he'd picked her and her mom up on eight, not fourteen. He'd likely met a lot of freshmen on a lot of floors that day.

"Well, isn't that convenient?" Joe said with a grin. "The beauty of coed floors." Nicky could have sworn Joe laser-gazed at Lori at the word "beauty." Then, to Nicky and Lori, he enthused, "Welcome to the dining hall: the see-and-be-seen, beating heart of 700 Comm Ave!" That was the first, but certainly not the last, time Nicky would hear the expansive street referred to in its informal, two-syllable form.

"Want to join us?" Lori asked Joe, her voice turning huskier.

Joe assessed Nicky and Lori and the table's empty chairs, then nodded across the cafeteria. "Thanks, but I've gotta hang out with the other orientation leaders. At least tonight. Some other time, OK?" And with another toothy smile, he moved off. Nicky felt disappointed, though he wasn't sure why.

"I can totally tell you that guy's story," Lori said devilishly as she speared an orange slice off her fruit salad.

"Why, do you know him?" Nicky had just assumed they'd met today.

"No, but, c'mon, just look at him." She took a deep breath. "OK: captain of at least one high school sports team a year. I'd peg him more for soccer than football. Wrestling, possibly. Baseball, definitely. Too cool to run for class president, but whoever he supports ends up winning. Dates less than you'd think, doesn't give it away to just anyone, but gets around, maybe older women, too. Makes whoever he's with feel like the only person who exists—until he moves off to the next person. Youngest of three brothers and the favorite son, but his older brothers worship *him* instead of the other way around. Business major because he thinks that's what's expected of him, but he'll switch to SPC for his last two years because someone once told him he'd make a good sportscaster. He'll end up modeling athletic wear instead, then start working for his father-in-law's international shipping business, which he'll pretend to enjoy but secretly hate. That is, until he can take it over." Lori stabbed another forkful of fruit. "Shall I go on?" She chewed a pineapple wedge with a self-satisfied smirk.

Nicky realized he hadn't drawn a breath since the start of Lori's monologue. "Wow," he said, expelling air. "Do you have ESP or something?"

"Just an acute observer of humanity." She raised an eyebrow. "Or maybe just an observer of cute humans." Her gaze drifted off in the vague direction of Joe—or the Joes of the world. Which didn't seem to include Nicky. Lori caught herself, pointed at him.

"Yeah, you too, Nicky."

He could feel himself flush. "Thanks. And . . . I'm trying to go with 'Nick.'"

She shook her head. "Yeah, I know, I heard that today in the elevator. But I think you're a Nicky. It's endearing. You've got plenty of time to be an asshole."

Nicky stared into his chocolate pudding, unsure how to respond. *Endearing*, he thought. That felt like *friends*. Like *nice*. Like *I don't want to fuck this guy, just tell him about my problems with other guys.* An hour ago, he was OK with not having to think about Lori romantically—not right out of the gate, anyway. But now, one brief square of lasagna later, he wanted to at least be in the running.

He looked up, struck a wry tone. "Trust me, I can be as much of an asshole as anyone."

"And trust *me*," Lori countered, "if I thought that was true for even a second, we wouldn't be beginning this great friendship."

He looked around and saw a bunch of familiar faces from their floor, trays in hand, searching for open tables. He turned back to Lori, leaning in. "OK then, tell me *my* story. Like you told me Joe's."

She eyeballed Nicky. "Something tells me it's not so clear cut. Besides, I wouldn't want to be glib with you. I'd rather discover it for myself. Or, you can tell *me*. Anything."

What was there to tell? He was just another semi-ambitious guy from Long Island entering BU's School of Management. (His father's choice, not Nicky's. But if that's what it took to get to Boston, so be it.) He wasn't particularly special or unusual. Or was he? Did Lori know something he didn't? He suddenly felt a little intimidated, a little . . . naked.

Before Nicky had time to assemble his thoughts, Monty and Sabrina appeared at their table. "Is this a private party or can anyone join?" asked Monty, placing his meal tray down before Nicky or Lori could respond. Sabrina followed suit.

"Sure, of course, join us," Lori said.

Nicky noticed that Monty, the good cowboy that he was, had taken the sliced beef, while Sabrina's plates were filled with only salad and vegetables.

"Oh, I'm a vegetarian," she said, aware of Nicky's gaze.

"For now," Monty tossed off as he scarfed a piece of meat. There was something proprietary to his response that seemed to fly over Sabrina's head, but, Nicky could tell, not Lori's.

He also noticed that Sabrina was wearing a different top than before—a loose peasant blouse that only added to her ethereal look—and that Monty had ditched the arrowhead necklace. And was that pinkish blotch on his neck what it looked like? No wonder those two were the last down for dinner. Boy, Monty worked fast.

Nicky rose and crossed to the nearby beverage station. As he was unsuccessfully attempting to navigate the giant coffee dispenser, Joe sidled up, sticking an empty cup beneath its spout.

"Gotta turn the spigot to the right and press down," he said, demonstrating. The blackish brew dribbled into the cup. "Easy-peasy."

Nicky offered his thanks, then made sure to pull the cup away before it overflowed. Joe nodded approvingly as he placed his own cup under the spout.

"Guess I'm at the back of the line now," he said with a knowing grin. Joe filled his cup without even looking as he kept his eyes trained on Nicky.

"What do you mean?" Nicky asked, sugaring his coffee. Joe gestured in Lori's direction and waggled his eyebrows. "Oh, right," said Nicky. "We'll see. I mean, we just met and all."

Joe assessed him. "Playing it cool, huh?" he asked, giving Nicky far more credit—and cred—than he deserved. "OK. That works sometimes. Not exactly my style but, hey, *you're* sitting with her and I'm not." A wink and, "Not yet, anyway."

Nicky watched Joe move off, with his wide shoulders and top-of-the-world walk, and felt a surge that was at once vaguely recognizable and completely alien. He quickly shook it off and returned to the table as Monty was comparing folk singers Emmylou Harris with

Buffy Sainte-Marie, both of whom were news to Nicky. Sabrina seemed rapt.

"We'll continue our talk later," Lori promised Nicky in a quiet aside as Monty held forth.

Nicky sent Lori an appreciative smile, swallowed some coffee, and half-listened to his roommate's opinionated ramblings. He had a feeling there'd be many more to come.

FIVE

What a difference a week made.

A mere seven days later, Nicky felt like he'd been living in Boston, roaming the BU campus, and inhabiting that chaotic wonderland called 700 for a kind of mini-lifetime. It amazed him how quickly he'd settled into big-city college life and the whirlwind of people, places, and things that made up his new daily existence. Lori said she sometimes felt like she'd stepped into one of those old kaleidoscope toys, hit with a dazzling new formation of sight and sound every time she left her dorm room.

There was so much to absorb, observe, try, savor, choose, consider, decipher, like, and dislike. At times, seemingly all at once. Class schedules, meal schedules, study schedules, study spaces, living spaces, social spaces; his classmates' and floormates' names, backgrounds, personalities, goals, strengths, weaknesses, tolerance levels, senses of humor—or lack thereof—and openness to him as a potential friend, ally, study partner, colleague, and, as the case may be, romantic or sexual mate (though he was still feeling a bit arm's length about all that). Sharing such close quarters with someone as different as Monty had its own learning curve. It was one that got a bit easier each day, especially as Nicky became able to distinguish the guy's less appealing bullshit from his more engaging authenticity (though, so far, the ratio was about two to one: bullshit). Nicky, counter to his usual style, found himself standing his ground more with Monty, who generally acquiesced to his requests: *Could you blow your smoke out the window? Could we have a Jerry Jeff-free hour? Could you give me some notice when you plan to lock yourself in our room with Sabrina?* In turn, Nicky adjusted his ways for Monty, who, it was turning out, was kind of a neat freak and asked—OK, demanded—that Nicky not leave his shit all over the room, stash his dirty laundry out of sight, and make his "damn fucking bed" before leaving for the day. Nicky knew it wouldn't kill him to be less of a slob, particularly since his mother (thankfully) wasn't there to pick up after him.

Monty also showered and groomed himself (his beard alone was near-surgically maintained) more than anyone Nicky had ever seen and that included his mom and sisters. He attended to his boot collection with paternal care, pressed his Western shirts with a travel iron (talk about a new-fangled sort of cowboy), and seemed to brush his teeth a dozen times a day (once for each cigarette smoked?). Monty even kept his beloved record albums dust-free with a special cloth and cleaning solution, claiming it preserved their sound. Which only mattered if, unlike Nicky, you liked their sound to begin with.

Nicky had to admit that Monty always looked pretty pulled together without it seeming like it took all that effort, which was maybe the desired effect. As a result, Nicky started spending a bit more time in the mirror, though wasn't always sure what he was looking for. Should he grow some facial hair? To be determined.

In short order, the people of 14A broke down into two camps. While, so far, most everyone was either extra-friendly or friendly enough, only about half of the residents formed a kind of unit, with the rest largely going their own way or looking elsewhere for social connection. Without meaning to—or maybe it was just college's natural order of selection—Nicky landed in the group of floormates who hung out together, if not all at once, in various pairs, trios, quartets, and handfuls as their needs, schedules, and responsibilities allowed. There was always someone to do something with if you wanted; no one was ever forced to be alone or feel alienated.

It surprised Nicky how much he seemed to enjoy being part of this accidental "in-crowd," and was equally amazed at how easily he was accepted by the others. It was so different from junior high and high school which, to Nicky, had always felt like a revolving popularity contest, one whose caste system of jocks, brains, creatives, stoners, fuck-offs, lookers, and budding criminals practically divided kids into their own separate countries with unpassable borders and high bars of entry. Nicky never fully fell into one group or another, often palled around with other categorical orphans (perhaps a class unto itself?) or those who chose to break the rules and escape their pack, even if just temporarily. He wasn't ignored or ostracized by the members of the different cliques, but wasn't necessarily embraced by them either; he was allowed to coexist if not comingle. He got used to it, muddled along, and never tried to become something he wasn't to fit into a slot—partly for lack of interest and partly because he didn't really know how.

The 14A bunch seemed like more of a come-as-you-are party, an eclectic band of folks thrown together by chance and drawn to each other for reasons that seemed just as haphazard. Or maybe there was no real reason at all beyond that they were there.

He and Lori, however, continued their burgeoning friendship apart from the others and had already spent quite a few late-night hours recapping their lives and attempting to solve world problems. One time, sitting on her bed, they almost kissed but didn't get there. They were awkwardly silent right after it happened—or actually didn't—until Lori, who'd made the first move, seemed to figure it warranted at least a mention.

"I hope that wasn't weird," she said, scooching back on the mattress, giving them distance. "I didn't mean to start and then stop."

"Yeah, it's OK," Nicky assured her. "I wasn't sure you actually *were* starting."

"You have a nice mouth," Lori added with an apologetic shrug.

He did? Nicky, surprised, wanted to say that *she* was the one with the nice mouth—the nice Susan Dey-ish mouth—but let her words hang there. He felt as if he'd somehow disappointed her, even if she was the one who'd shyly pulled away before they could connect. He would have kissed her, even if it meant upending their "friend" status (would it have?), but he also wasn't going to push it.

"Thanks, no one's ever said that before," Nicky told her.

"Well, now someone has." Lori studied him some more. "I like your hands, too."

He spread his hands out in front of him, took a look, had no idea. "These things? What about them?"

"I don't know," she said, getting up to turn over the Cat Stevens album—*Teaser and the Firecat*—that had just ended. "They look soft and strong at the same time. Gentle yet protective."

Now he was getting *really* self-conscious. "You can tell all that just by looking?"

Lori let the stereo needle drop on side two. "Just my opinion. But maybe because I know you a little now. Or maybe I'm mixing up your hands with your personality."

Soft and strong at the same time. That gave Nicky something to think about. Was he more out of touch with who he was than he realized? Cat Stevens's mellow voice filled the air.

"And you don't bite your nails like half the guys I know," Lori added. "To me, you can be the hottest man alive but if you have nubby fingers, it's over. Gross."

That seemed a little harsh to Nicky who, nonetheless, happily examined his intact cuticles. "Did Joshua bite his nails?" he asked about Lori's ex.

"Joshua was perfect. Until he wasn't," she answered cryptically, leaving it there.

Lori returned to the bed and gazed at Nicky. He stared back. They seemed stuck for further conversation; a first. So he leaned in and planted one. Their kiss was brief, warm, experimental. More exploration than heat. Seeing what was what. She tasted like orange

Life Savers. Nicky pulled back, eyed Lori. She looked inscrutable, like whatever she said or did next might set a path that she—they—couldn't reverse. Or maybe that's what Nicky was thinking about his own next action.

Suddenly, like the sun breaking through (even if it was night), an amused smile crossed those Laurie Partridge lips. Nicky could feel his heart rate steady. He smiled back.

"Was that OK?" Nicky asked.

"You mean the kiss itself or the fact that you did it?"

Nicky didn't know how to answer, didn't know what she wanted to hear. It was hard enough knowing what to even feel himself. He stared at a poster neatly taped to the cinder block wall above her bed: a reprint of the poem "Desiderata." He read the first words—*Go placidly amid the noise and the haste*—then turned back to Lori. She looked exposed, vulnerable, not her usual assured self.

"Well, you sort of gave me the idea, so . . ." Nicky trailed off. He'd kiss her again if she asked. *Would she ask?*

Lori pulled her long hair behind her head, exposing her delicate ears. A pair of small gold hoops hung from the lobes. "I *did* give you the idea, didn't I?" She let her hair fall back to her shoulders. "It wasn't the worst idea, though, was it?"

A thought hit Nicky: *What would Monty do?* Monty, who wasted no time taking what he wanted, who didn't seem to worry much about the consequences—or maybe even think about them to begin with. Nicky knew the answer to his question so he leaned back into Lori and kissed her again. Longer, deeper, more purposefully this time. He realized he hadn't kissed a girl like that in more time than he wanted to admit, even to—especially to—himself. Eyes closed, he pressed himself into Lori, who was kissing him back with, he estimated, equal fervor, and let his hand gently wander below her neckline. He waited for her to stop him as he traveled south but she just kept up her part of the kissing and raked a hand through his mop of hair.

Before things got any more heated, Lori pulled away from Nicky, leaping up off the bed and catching her breath. Her face was flushed and her eyes moist. Nicky gazed up at her, wondering if this was the end of their brief friendship or the start of a new phase. *Shit*, thought Nicky, *now I've really done it.*

"I may not be the greatest kisser, but it's never made a girl cry before," he joked, which only made Lori's tears flow in earnest. She tried to push through a smile but couldn't get there. Nicky didn't know what to do, felt like the ground was opening up beneath him. This was the last time he'd pretend he was Monty. He didn't even really like Monty. Why would he copy him in any way? He felt like such an idiot.

Lori sat back on the bed, wiping at her eyes, trying to compose herself. "No, you're a really good kisser," she managed through her residual sobs. "I just . . ." Lori wiped her eyes with the back of her palms and swallowed hard.

"Just what? Think that we shouldn't have kissed? Or that we *should* have?" Awaiting Lori's response, Nicky gazed at Sabrina's lava lamp, glowing atop her desk, with its floating pink blobs. They moved almost in time to Cat Stevens's leisurely vocals.

"No," she answered, "just that I really miss Joshua. Kissing you reminded me of him. He did the same kind of thing with his tongue."

Nicky had no idea what he did with his tongue but thought it best not to ask. Although he did have one pressing question: "So you kissed *me* because you missed *him*?"

"Actually, it was the other way around. More or less, I guess." Lori paused, gathered her thoughts. "Just when I think I'm over the creep, I realize I'm not. Which is just so ridiculous."

"It's not ridiculous. It's how you feel. The two of you obviously had something. For a long time." Which, Nicky could've added, was more than he'd had, never dating anyone for more than a month or so, never getting into serious boyfriend-girlfriend territory. Not that it ever bothered him all that much, but he knew he had work to do on the romantic front. And tonight, for a moment anyway, seemed like kind of a next step toward that. Or not.

Lori rose, crossed to her dresser, and grabbed a tissue. She looked in the mirror as she blew her nose. "That's sweet of you to say, Nicky.

Someone is going to be really lucky to have you as a boyfriend one day."

It was like the needle just slid across *Teaser and the Firecat*, letting out a scratchy, scene-stopping screech. *What the hell?* Nicky wasn't sure he'd heard right. Who was she talking about? Who was this other person who'd be "lucky" to end up with Nicky? What about Lori? Was this her way of saying it would never be her? How did she know? And wasn't she the one to start all this? He realized nothing had changed from that first moment she'd said "Let's be really good friends."

Lori rejoined Nicky and took his hand. "Thank you," she said. "And I'm sorry if I seem confused right now. I didn't mean to drag you into it."

It's a little late for that, he thought, but instead squeezed her hand. "Hey, isn't that what friends are for?"

Monty sure wouldn't have said that. Fucking Monty.

SIX

Their first Saturday night together, a group from 14A—Nicky, Lori, Monty, Sabrina, Shelley (she of the honking Long Island accent), budding journalist Ken (he'd answer questions with questions), and musical theatre geek Chuck (he'd answer questions with Broadway show lyrics)—went out to the movies. It took about an hour to agree on a film: Nicky wanted to see *Jaws* again; Monty a double feature of porn hits *Deep Throat* and *The Devil in Miss Jones*, but Shelley said "Oh, my Gawd, I would *dzye!*" so that was that. They finally decided on a detective mystery with Robert Mitchum called *Farewell, My Lovely*, then piled onto a noisy trolley (hereafter known to Nicky as "the T"), which ferried them downtown to the cavernous Cinema 57.

The seven of them streamed into an open row about halfway down the theater's floral-carpeted aisle and settled in with their various drinks and snacks. Nicky, a giant box of Sno-Caps in hand, was the last one seated, which left Lori and her Diet Pepsi to his right and two empty chairs on his left. From down the row, Nicky could hear the others comparing the last movies they'd seen, with Monty and

Ken loudly arguing the merits of *Nashville*—Ken called it a "masterpiece," Monty said he had his "head up his ass." They went on to disagree about *The Day of the Locust* (Monty was a thumbs-up, Ken thumbs-down). Chuck, to no one's surprise, was a fan of the *Funny Girl* sequel, *Funny Lady* (he was the only one who'd seen it—or cared to), while Shelley found *The Return of the Pink Panther* "hysterical" and snorted out a guffaw in confirmation.

"What was the last movie you liked?" Lori asked Nicky between sips of soda. "Aside from *Jaws*. Which scared the shit out of me, by the way. Even more than *The Exorcist* because it was real."

"You *do* know the shark was mechanical, right?" Nicky answered.

"Yeah, wise guy, I got that part," she crinkled her eyes. "I meant sharks are real—in real life. So's the beach and the ocean and being eaten alive."

Nicky popped a couple of Sno-Caps. "So you're saying you don't think you can be possessed by the devil? Like that's not a real thing?"

He watched Lori as she thought that one through, brow furrowed, nibbling at her lower lip. In the days since their unexpected-though-maybe-not-entirely-total-surprise kiss, neither of them brought up what had happened and no further attempt to canoodle was made. They quickly fell back into fast-friendship mode with Lori opening up more about her relationship with Joshua than Nicky really cared to hear (including how often she and her ex had sex: fourteen times, But who's counting?). This Joshua sounded like a dick who totally didn't deserve someone as awesome as Lori, and it bugged Nicky that she still seemed to be carrying a torch for the guy, regardless of whether Nicky was going to be the object of her affections—if that was truly even his goal (a moot point now, it seemed).

The Joshua thing reconfirmed what Nicky's brother had told him a few years back: that girls liked guys who were jerks—or at least dudes who didn't make it easy on them. Nicky blew Richie off at the time given that his brother had had the same girlfriend since ninth grade—the co-pea in his pod, Franny Meyers—who Richie, for all his sarcasm and bravado, always treated like the goddess she was and, as far as Nicky could see, hardly ever challenged. So what did Richie know about what women really wanted? Plenty, Nicky now realized, considering the A+ girlfriend Richie snagged and the fact that Nicky never had a ton of game around the opposite sex. (Despite Richie's older-wiser encouragement, any dating Nicky *did* do in high school always felt more random than part of any master plan, a cycle he was now determined to break.)

Still, Nicky found himself flashing on his and Lori's lip-lock what felt like a thousand times since that heated moment—and that included this very second as she quickly mulled her belief in the demonic. No one had ever told him he was "a really good kisser," which, who knows, maybe took a certain level of confidence or lack of an agenda by the kissee to declare (unlike, say, his ill-fated junior prom date, Maria Moss). Or maybe it was just a statement of fact. Either way, it had given Nicky a charge he never knew he needed.

"Here's my take: exorcisms are a real thing but what they're try-ing to exorcise is not," Lori declared as chatter down the row turned to the merits of Al Pacino, whose new movie, *Dog Day Afternoon*, was about to come out. Lori looked at Nicky with full self-satisfac-tion as if she'd just arrived at the meaning of life. He had to admit she looked adorable in the theater's preshow half-light.

Before Nicky could respond, he felt a tap on his shoulder and heard, "Are these two taken?" He turned to see, of all people, Joe Hello standing there with a giant soda cup, a tub of popcorn, and a tallish, rather fetching woman at his side. Joe looked as surprised to see Nicky as Nicky did to see Joe, out of context as they both were. "Hey, bud!" Joe exclaimed. "Whaddya know?"

Here's what Nicky knew: Once again, the sight of Joe gave him that stab in his stomach and the sudden bonus of a dry throat. The reaction was confusing and inexplicable, and it freaked Nicky out. He forced cool and croaked out, "Hey, Joe. Yeah, these two are open." Nicky indicated the seats to his left as Lori looked on, eyes widening in recognition.

Joe met her gaze and there went his light-up-a-room smile. "Wow, Nicky *and* Lori. Together again. I love it." Joe's date gave Nicky and Lori an indifferent once-over.

"We're actually here with a bunch of folks from our floor," Lori attempted to clarify, a bit too quickly for Nicky's comfort.

As Joe plopped down next to Nicky and his companion took the aisle seat to his left, Joe hooked a thumb toward her. "By the way, guys, this is Rebecca. She's in SFA." At this point the rest of the 14A group had stopped yakking and was gazing in their direction, wondering what they were missing.

Lori now gave Rebecca the once-over, though with more genuine interest. "Are you going to be an actress?" she asked, in response to the School of Fine Arts reference.

"I'm already an actress," Rebecca said with a world-weary edge that ended all further questioning. She stuck a hand in Joe's popcorn box and stared at the darkened movie screen.

Joe sent Nicky and Lori a sly look that read: *Yeah, she's a handful, but I'm getting some later so whatever*. He followed with a happy slap on Nicky's thigh. "Funny running into you, huh? I mean, do you even know anything about this movie?"

Nicky shrugged, reclaiming his voice. "Not really. *I* wanted to see *Jaws* again."

"Yeah? Me, too! But Rebecca heard good things, so here we are." Joe leaned into him just enough for Nicky to take in the familiar whiff of aftershave. "You want to catch *Jaws* again?" he asked. "Let me know, we'll go." Joe put an arm around Rebecca as the house lights went down.

"She's a peach," Lori whispered drolly to Nicky, though her eyes were trained on Joe.

"No, she's an *actress*," Nicky countered. Lori returned her gaze to Nicky with an impish smile. She squeezed his arm and faced front as a coming attraction began for something called *The Rocky Horror Picture Show*.

Aramis, thought Nicky, as a bunch of zany images filled the screen. *Joe's aftershave*. Just like Mr. Silver, Nicky's twelfth-grade English teacher, used to wear. That Nicky recalled that factoid—or even knew it to begin with—gave him pause. He glanced at Joe, whose arm was no longer around his date, and wondered what was going through his mind. If anything.

Nicky concentrated on the movie screen—and his Sno-Caps—the best he could.

THE NINE OF THEM huddled in the theater lobby debating the ending of the film, which some found confusing, though most agreed the movie itself was just OK. Mystery fan—and self-appointed intellectual—Ken liked it the most, well-versed enough about star Robert Mitchum to contend he made a perfect Philip Marlowe; no one knew enough to argue. Shelley liked the old cars and clothes but thought it got boring. Musical fan Chuck was more intrigued by that *Rocky Horror* preview; Monty said it looked like a piece of shit; Sabrina thought it looked like a blast. Rebecca said nothing, just vacantly watched folks line up for the 9:40 p.m. show. Nicky thought she seemed taller—but no friendlier—in the bright lights of the lobby. Meanwhile, Joe looked his usual chipper, relaxed self, hanging easily with the group instead of bolting with the actress.

"Let's go get drinks," Lori announced.

"Yeah, lots of drinks," said Chuck, eyes glinting behind his thick aviator glasses.

"Excellent idea!" enthused Joe. This surprised them all, especially Rebecca, who looked like she was doing everyone a favor just by existing. Joe turned to her. "Wanna go?"

She thought about it and shrugged. "One drink."

"I've heard that before," Monty said to no one in particular.

A few T-stops, a ten-minute walk, and one soaring elevator ride later, they were taking up a row of pushed-together tables in the back of a cocktail lounge called the Penthouse, which sat high atop a Holiday Inn in the shadow of Mass General Hospital. The idea was Joe's, who warned the others that the place was kind of touristy but served stiff drinks, had a decent live Top 40 band, dance floor, and killer views of Boston. Oh, and no cover. He was right on all fronts. Which isn't to say Joe didn't get pushback from Monty and Ken (Rebecca silently sneered) when he first suggested the spot; it didn't sound cool and collegey—because it wasn't. But the others were game and the majority won. Besides, there was something about Joe that was so easy and convincing that you wanted to believe him—believe *in* him. At least that's how Nicky was starting to see it as he tried to figure out what exactly was drawing him to the guy.

The lounge was noisy and full and not as touristy as billed ("Really, aren't we *all* tourists?" Lori pointedly asked Monty when he initially griped), even if Nicky and his group were probably the youngest and most underdressed ones there. The combo—a drummer, bass player, and keyboardist—banged out an impressive cover of the disco hit "That's the Way (I Like It)" as folks boogied on a shiny, smallish dance floor in the middle of the room. Monty had a "shoot me now" look on his face, but Nicky soon noticed his roommate vaguely bobbing his head to the infectious beat. Lori blissfully shook her arms above her head, life-of-the-party style. Meantime, a cheerful server named Penny took their drink orders but not before apologetically carding each and every one of them. Except for Rebecca who charmingly told Penny she was "Twenty-one fucking years old," which seemed to surprise everyone, maybe even Joe, if his wide-eyed look were any clue.

"See, told you he probably liked older women," Lori whispered to Nicky, who now got why Rebecca seemed less than thrilled to be around so many freshmen.

Still, one round of colorful cocktails later—four margaritas, three tequila sunrises, a Harvey Wallbanger for Nicky (because he liked the name), and a piña colada for Monty (because *that's* what a cowboy might drink?)—and the group was on the dance floor cutting it up to a particularly rocking rendition of "When Will I Be Loved?"

Lori and Shelley gleefully sang-screamed along with the song as the nine of them—including a loosened-up Rebecca—ended up dancing en masse given the uneven male-female ratio.

At one point, Nicky found himself nose-to-nose with an ebullient Joe as they bobbed and lurched with the crowd. Joe flashed one of his shiny grins as he gave Nicky's shoulder a friendly pound. Maybe it was the alcohol or the burst of social joy he was feeling, but an ease took over and Nicky's stomach stayed perfectly intact. Nicky returned the smile *and* the shoulder pound and, for the first time, felt more on par with his magnetic orientation leader. Maybe he *would* take him up on his offer to see *Jaws* again.

"OK, people, so how about we slow it up a little?" The band's bass player purred into his mic. A few groans from the amped crowd, while a handful of other folks hung on the dance floor awaiting the next tune. Nicky and the group were on their way back to their table when the combo played the familiar opening bars to "Please Come to Boston." Lori excitedly grabbed Nicky's hand and pulled him back toward the dance floor.

"C'mon, dance with me? Please?" she pled. "You won't believe this, but this song was on the radio when I got my BU acceptance letter. It was so weird—but in a good way!"

Nicky said he believed her (why wouldn't he?) and promptly found himself in a slow dance with his new best friend. He could fake a fast dance (as he just had) but slow was a commitment—and an awkward one to boot, at least for him. But Lori being Lori made it easy for him to simply cozy up to her, draping her arms around his neck and swaying to the wistful number. She pressed herself against Nicky as they circled the dance floor, only one of three couples braving the song, and he could feel himself, well, rising to the occasion. Strange, he thought, that he hadn't during their brief make-out session, though his dick clearly had a mind of its own. Growing up, he might pop a boner riding the school bus or cuddling their neighbor's beagle, but not while, say, ogling his brother's *Playboy* stash. Well, not without some manual assistance. Then other times—there it was. He read somewhere it was best not to think about it, which seemed like the surefire way *to* think about it.

Nicky glanced over Lori's shoulder and across the lounge to see their group ordering another round of drinks. Only Joe's gaze was pinned to the dance floor, watching him and Lori dance, a warm if calculating smile on his face. Nicky looked away.

"I didn't tell you, I talked to Joshua last night," Lori said as they rocked back and forth.

"What for?" Nicky answered with a proprietary edge.

"You sound a little hostile."

"Sorry. I thought he made you unhappy."

"He did. Does. I don't know. I think he was checking up to see if I'd met anyone yet."

"Has *he*?"

"I don't think he would've called if he had. Anyway, we didn't talk long. Not about anything important, just . . . stuff. End of story."

"Good. As long as he didn't make you cry or anything."

Lori paused. "You're the sweetest. You know that?" And she left a thank-you kiss on his cheek as the song—and their dance—ended.

"OK, MAN, I'M confused!" Joe's voice boomed in the echoey bathroom. Nicky was so startled by Joe's noisy arrival he nearly splashed the guy's jeans when he spun from the urinal to face him. Nicky, as casually as the moment would allow, faced front again and finished his business as Joe unfurled at the adjacent urinal.

"Confused how?" a confused Nicky asked. He zipped and, avoiding Joe's gaze, darted to the sink. The calm he'd felt around him on the dance floor was vanishing in real time.

"Are you and Laurie Partridge together or not?"

Nicky stared in the mirror as he soaped his hands, thought again about growing a beard. Or at least a mustache. He knew he was stalling answering Joe, who was now washing up at the sink next to him.

"It's Lori *Conover*, and we've just become . . . really good friends."

"How 'good'? Because she looked pretty into you on the dance floor." Joe splashed water on his face, turning to Nicky with his glistening mug. "And you for her."

Nicky's heartbeat quickened as he eyed Joe's damp, dimpled face. Residual traces of his Aramis hit the air. "Yeah, I don't know," Nicky managed. "Hard to say."

They both grabbed for the paper towels. Joe snapped back his hand, and let Nicky go first. "Not sure I get that, and I'm sorry to hear it, but . . . are you OK if I ask her out?"

It's not like Joe hadn't warned Nicky, virtually from the moment they met, so his interest in Lori was no great shock. Yet Nicky felt protective of her—but also protective of himself. He figured if someone as charming and great-looking and self-assured as Joe started seeing Lori, what chance would a guy like Nicky ever have with her again? They'd be friends forever—which was the way things were going anyway. Still, something was holding him back from pushing the issue, from making Lori see him the way she once saw Joshua—only better. Maybe he feared losing her forever friendship if they tanked romantically. Maybe he didn't want to disappoint her. Maybe he should just shut the fuck up and stop overthinking it all like an idiot.

On the other hand, what made Nicky think Lori would even date Joe? She'd never shown any interest beyond making up that life story about him, which, let's face it, wasn't all that flattering. Lori also never mentioned that she found him attractive. *Monty, yes, but Joe, no? Really?* Though Nicky did remember the way Lori looked at Joe that first day in the elevator. She definitely liked what she saw—whether she said so or not. That much Nicky knew.

"Thanks, but you don't need my permission. Go for it if you want," Nicky finally answered, trying to sound cool and worldly. "But what about Rebecca?"

"What about her? She's sexy, but she's kind of a snob. Don't you think?" Hands dried, he made for the door.

Nicky followed. "Yeah. A sexy snob. Definitely."

"Still, I wouldn't throw her out of bed," Joe said as they exited to the lounge, which was rocking out with the band to "Long Train Runnin.'"

Before they reached the table, Joe clapped Nicky's shoulder. "Thanks for the assist, pal, you're awesome," he said, adding, "*Jaws.* Wednesday night. On me."

Nicky nodded, gave him a thumbs-up. Then wondered if he'd just made a big mistake.

SEVEN

TODAY

IT WAS CRAZY that Nick hadn't been back to Boston in all the decades since he graduated from college. How was that even possible? Especially considering all the lesser places he _had_ gone for his career as a marketing exec since the 1980s. Yet except for a brief overnight stay in 1990 thanks to a missed flight connection en route to London—and little time to explore beyond the airport Hilton's lobby bar—he'd never returned to the city that helped kick off his adult life. Maybe his absence was a more conscious choice than he'd realized, a stealthy effort to keep the place—and those dizzying days of discovery—frozen in time. Because, really, who could ever predict just which memories, unwanted or otherwise, a revisit might dredge up?

Still, no time like the present. And here Nick was, sweaty and tired, yet exhilarated by his river run, his little nostalgia attack now a blip on the morning's radar. Though he wondered what that Tyler kid must have thought of him, this wiry, gray-haired, older guy freaking out on a jogging path. What Nick was doing there—was doing in Boston altogether—was such an involved story, that no amount of explanation for his unnerved reaction would have sufficed. Not that it was any of Tyler's business; he seemed far too worried about his whole-life-ahead-of-him present to care much about some random stranger's ancient past. At least that's how Nick would have felt some fifty years ago, would have considered anything outside his navel-gazing collegiate cocoon irrelevant, especially that momentous first semester of university life. He could remember barely listening to his family's chatter during their weekly Sunday night phone calls, his parents and sisters (no Richie, he was away at SUNY Buffalo) relating events so mundane and disconnected to Nick's new world they might as well have been speaking in tongues. How he wished he could talk to his long-gone parents now; he'd hang on their every word.

Nick reversed course and made his way back up the Esplanade toward his hotel, surprised to see so many people on the riverbank—walking, biking, jogging, sunning, meandering—on a weekday morning. He never remembered it being so packed those many mornings he'd first gone running there. Of course, he may have been so focused on gaining speed and stamina and keeping up with (and, OK, impressing) his hale jogging partner that he didn't notice much beyond the grassy paths stretching out in front of him. Though for all Nick staunchly claimed to recall about his college years, he wondered if, over time, he'd confused or conflated a few— More than a few?—of those mental snapshots. He didn't think so, but his memories were sure to be tested this weekend.

Nick turned off the Esplanade, crossed busy Storrow Drive, and walked over the Dartmouth Street Footbridge to leafy Beacon Street, with its rows of Victorian- and Edwardian-inspired brownstones and their tiny, tidy front yards. And there it was, number 283, the building he'd lived in for a year after he graduated from BU until he figured out what he wanted to do with his life—and with whom. (It took longer than the year but that's all the time he could afford to spend exploring.) His apartment was a roomy one-bedroom with a bay window facing Beacon Street and, if you looked through a crack between the buildings across the street, you could catch a glimpse of the Charles River. The rent? $250 a month. Last he'd perused Apartments.com, comparable spots were $3,250. But, inflation aside, the place was hopefully a lot nicer now than it was in 1979, with its flimsy door locks, wonky plumbing, and sporadic mouse visits. No matter, it bought Nick time away from his family and any other biased influences to start getting his shit together.

He studied the building a moment, then moved off down the street. It looked largely the same as it had so long ago, except for the tonier cars that lined the curbs and the loftier elm and maple trees that shaded the homes and sidewalks. Nick had walked anywhere and everywhere back then, a habit that started in college and continued through that single year he lived in Boston as a full-fledged adult. Sure, he took the T and the occasional bus for longer hauls, but much of the city was so easy to traverse by foot that, as a penny-pinching student and graduate, he'd happily save the twenty-five-cent transit fare and hoof it instead. *Twenty-five cents. Damn!* he thought. *We didn't know when we had it good. Do we ever?*

From all that walking, Nick got to know the town inside and out, and it amazed him how easily he was finding his way around now—a lifetime or two later. Was it a case of the more things change, the more they stay the same? He wondered if, by the end of the weekend, he'd be able to apply that mantra to people as well.

EIGHT

1975

IF NICKY WASN'T feeling conflicted enough about Lori, he made the mistake of talking it over with Monty in the wee hours after they'd all returned from their Saturday night outing.

"No offense, but I would've never matched you with her, anyway," Monty said in the darkness as they each struggled to fall asleep, wired from the booze (they all kind of lost count) and the residual party energy.

"What makes you say *that*?" Nicky asked, offended, even if he knew what Monty meant.

Monty sat up, switched on a small light over his bed. "Just that Lori's kind of a live wire. In a good way! But I picture you with someone . . . quieter."

"Y'mean, boring?"

"What? No! More reserved. Like you."

Nicky was hating this conversation. Now he sat up, facing his roommate. "Oh, then someone like, I don't know . . . Sabrina?"

Monty's eyes bore into Nicky. "No, man, not Sabrina," he said acidly. As if Nicky would try to steal his girlfriend. Monty reached behind him for his Marlboros, tapped one out of the pack. "And don't let her hippy-dippy thing fool you. That chick's a force of nature."

Nicky assumed he meant in bed but didn't want any of what he was sure would be the far too explicit details.

Monty felt around for his lighter. He pulled off his covers and got out of bed to grab it off the dresser, bare-assed as the day he was born because Monty slept naked (of course he did). It startled Nicky, even if it wasn't the first time he'd seen him in the buff; the guy paraded around like that a lot. Whatever, Nicky wished he had half of Monty's balls. Speaking of which, he tried not to stare, but for a smallish guy (Nicky was no giant but he was taller than Monty), he had what seemed like a biggish dick. That is, at least compared to Nicky's and most of those he'd pretended not to glimpse in the high school gym showers. Monty also had a smooth thatch of dark hair that fanned out across his compact torso; unlike Nicky whose chest was home to a handful of curly sprigs. He was starting to get what Lori had said, that there was something attractive about Monty. And it was making Nicky uncomfortable. Monty sat back atop his bed, thankfully threw the blanket over himself, and lit his cigarette.

"Anyway, nothing wrong with the friend thing—if that's what you want," Monty said, puffing out a few smoke rings.

"Who says that's what I want?"

"Well, that's what Lori told Sabrina."

"Lori and Sabrina talked about it?!"

"They're roommates. Roommates talk," Monty said, wagging a finger between him and Nicky. "Obviously."

"Well, for the record—and do me a favor, don't repeat any of this to Sabrina—but it was basically Lori's idea." Nicky waved away a plume of smoke that had drifted over.

"Whatever, it's not a big deal, dude. There are a million chicks out there. Go find one that wants *you*." Monty stuck a hand under his blanket and scratched his balls.

"Just like that?"

"Yeah, just like that. Don't be such a pussy."

Leave it to his stupid roommate to bring down such an up night.

Monty stubbed out his cigarette in a paper ashtray. "Hey, I'm on your side," he said tersely, in his version of an apology. He snapped off the light. "I'm going to sleep."

Nicky lay in bed, wide awake, as Monty began to lightly snore from across the room. Maybe he *was* boring, maybe he *was* a pussy, or maybe he was OK and just needed to trust himself more. All he *did* know was that he should probably think twice before telling Monty anything.

Nicky found himself flashing on Monty's dick and chest and could feel a stirring in his shorts that forced him to think instead about slow dancing with Lori and how nice her arms felt around him as he gently pressed into her. And he kept that enticing image firmly in mind as, under the covers, he grabbed hold and proceeded to quietly take care of business.

"IF YOU WANT to go out with him, you should go out with him," Nicky told Lori a few days later at the George Sherman Student Union, where they'd met up after their morning classes for lunch at the goofily named PsycheDeli.

"That's not exactly a ringing endorsement," Lori said as she bit into her tuna on rye. "I was hoping for at least a little more guidance. I mean, you know him better than I do."

"Not by much," Nicky answered, wondering what he really knew about Joe beyond his hearty personality and imposing exterior.

As Nicky expected after that night at the Penthouse, Joe had asked Lori on a date. Unlike Nicky, who would have over-rehearsed his request and planned out the exact right moment to ask someone out, Joe had casually brought it up when he ran into Lori at the dorm mailboxes. Nicky hadn't mentioned anything to Lori about Joe's interest, unsure what the purpose would be other than seeming like a gossip or cementing his role as Lori's sounding board about other guys—a role he decidedly did not want. Joe had also never asked for his help, no "Put in a good word for me, would you, bud?" So, in that sense, he didn't want to betray his confidence, not that

Joe had asked for secrecy either. Anyway, as far as Nicky could see, this was between Lori and Joe. Not to mention that Nicky still had mixed feelings about not fighting Joe—or any other smitten suitor—for Lori's romantic attention, may the best man win.

"He suggested going to listen to music at this bar called Brandy's," Lori said. "It's up Comm Ave, past West Campus." She peeled off the top layer of rye bread and started eating her sandwich openfaced.

"Is there dancing?" Nicky wanted to know, imagining her slow dancing with Joe, tucked into his broad shoulder. It made him feel weird.

"I don't know, I didn't ask. He said it's cool, in a basement or something. Definitely not like the place we went Saturday night."

Nicky stayed quiet, focused on his roast beef sandwich. It was on a soft roll the lunch lady called a bulkie, even though it looked like a plain old Kaiser roll. Must be a Boston thing.

"So, what did you tell him?" asked Nicky with badly feigned disinterest.

Lori crunched on a pickle. "That I'd let him know."

Wow, if someone Nicky asked out said they'd "let him know," he'd be mortified. He'd had girls flat-out say no (well, "no, thank you"), which was bad enough. But to keep him hanging? Somehow that seemed way worse.

"I'll bet he wasn't expecting that," said Nicky as he squeezed extra ketchup onto his sandwich. "How did he react?"

"Impressively, actually. Just smiled that big smile of his, wrote his phone number on my hand, and said to call whenever. Couldn't have been sweeter about it." She showed Nicky her open palm with Joe's faded digits on it.

"Smooth move," he said, taking a mental note.

Through a mouthful of tuna, Lori added, "I don't think I ever realized quite how attractive he is. Don't you think he's attractive?"

OK, how does a guy tell a girl he likes that, yeah, another guy *is* attractive without sounding like he'd rather date the guy? It didn't matter because before Nicky could weigh in, Lori decided, "What the hell, I'll say yes. If nothing else it'll get my mind off Joshua."

Something that Nicky's presence clearly wasn't doing. He hoped that thought didn't register on his unshaven face. (Three days into a mustache, and he wasn't feeling optimistic.)

"You'll have a good time. Joe seems like a fun guy," Nicky assured her as he took a gulp of 7-Up. He looked away as a few folks from his Econ 101 class sat down two tables over. One of them gave Nicky a tentative wave as if she knew him from somewhere she couldn't identify.

"Hey, come *with* us!" Lori bubbled, eyes wide with wonder and hope—and maybe a touch of mischief.

Nicky nearly choked on his soda. "On your date? Why in the world would I do that?"

"I don't know, if I'm not having a good time with Joe at least I will with you."

Was she fucking serious? "And you don't think he would mind just a little bit?" God knows Nicky would be pissed if his date showed up with a friend, male *or* female. The night would be over before it began.

"Well, if he does mind, maybe he's not that much fun after all. And it's not like he doesn't know—and like—the both of us." Lori stopped, rethought that part. "I mean, I assume he likes me." She looked beseechingly at Nicky as she started the second half of her sandwich.

"Absolutely not," he told her, putting an end to the discussion.

She considered Nicky. "Maybe *you're* not that much fun after all," she said accusingly. But her playful smile betrayed her.

Nicky relaxed. "Just go, enjoy yourself, tell me about it after." He didn't mean to default to confidante mode and hid his annoyance in his sandwich.

"Or—we could double," Lori offered. "I've done that with a lot of my friends on their first dates, just in case they sucked—or the guy planned on getting handsy."

He sent her a dubious look over his bulkie. "Are you worried about Joe getting handsy?"

She offered a shy grin as if that were the *opposite* of what she was worried about. "No, he seems kind of gentlemanly. In a big, happy jock kind of way."

For a fleeting moment, the idea of a double date appealed to Nicky, at least as a more natural way to hang out with Lori *and* Joe. Then, of course, reality set in. "Who would I even ask?"

"I'm sure you could dig someone up."

"Uh, you have to *know* someone to dig them up." He wanted to add that he'd only been at BU for ten days—most of which he'd spent with Lori—so give him a break. But that hadn't stopped others like Monty, and now maybe Lori, from pairing off, so it wasn't the best excuse.

"I know one person who'd be thrilled to go with you," Lori said with a devilish look as she pushed aside her sandwich plate.

"Yeah, who?"

She paused for dramatic effect. Or maybe because she knew how Nicky would react. "Shelley."

"Shelley who?" he asked. Lori's droll look and raised eyebrow said it all. "Y'mean, Shelley on our floor?" Lori nodded enthusiastically like it was the world's greatest development. Which it wasn't. "How do *you* know?" Nicky asked, though the answer was embarrassingly clear.

"At the Penthouse? In the ladies' room? She told me she'd like to 'eat you up with a spoon.' That's a direct quote." Lori waved her spoon at Nicky for emphasis, then dipped it in a dish of lime Jell-O.

"She must have been drunk," Nicky said.

"Not *that* drunk," Lori retorted and swallowed a Jell-O cube.

It was the story of Nicky's life (one of them, anyhow): The girls he was into didn't know he was alive, and the ones he had no interest in wanted to eat him up with a spoon. How he'd ever had any dates at all was a miracle.

"I'm flattered, but no," Nicky said, starting on his chocolate pudding. Shelley was nice enough—they'd even danced together once Saturday night—and he didn't want to say anything bad about her because he didn't want Lori to think anything bad about *him*. But a whole evening glued to Shelley with her squinty gaze, foghorn voice, and giddy exuberance was just too much to contemplate, even to make Lori happy.

Christ, he realized, now he had to see Shelley every day at the dorm knowing she wanted to jump his bones. Was he *supposed* to know? Either way, it filled him with dread.

Lori eyed Nicky pensively, as if she were trying to conjure a way to sell him on Shelley, but seemed to come up blank. "What if I found you someone else?" she finally asked.

Nicky was quickly losing his patience with this discussion. Lori's question just hung there. She quietly ate her Jell-O. Nicky sighed.

Lori studied his face. "Are you growing a mustache?"

"Does this mean we're done talking about your date?"

She matched his sigh. "I think so."

He drew a finger circle around his bristly face and shrugged. "I don't know what I'm doing." That much was obvious.

NINE

LORI AND JOE had their date. The next night. The night Joe had invited Nicky to see *Jaws*. Which he'd obviously forgotten about. Though Nicky hadn't. He didn't take it personally, just wished Joe would have acknowledged the double booking and set another time to go with Nicky. He didn't bring it up to Lori, didn't want her to think it mattered to him. He didn't know that it *did* matter until Lori told him that she'd accepted Joe's invite—and for when. It left him feeling a little wounded. No wonder Monty called him a pussy.

"A weeknight?" asked Nicky, thinking it was kind of unceremonious for a first date with someone of Lori's caliber. Maybe he had overestimated Joe's savoir-faire. Or maybe Nicky didn't know shit about spontaneity. Or women.

"It's actually good," Lori told Nicky. "Doesn't give me any time to change my mind."

"Why would you change your mind?" he asked, perhaps a bit too emphatically.

Translation: What didn't Lori see in Joe that Nicky did? Or maybe, he realized, it was the other way around.

They were sitting on the floor of Lori's room sharing a doobie. Sabrina was gone, across the hall with Monty, studying. Which Nicky took to mean "studying." He hadn't sat on Lori's bed with her since their kiss. Which they'd never mentioned again. At least not in so many words.

"It occurred to me that Joe's, like, a foot taller than me," Lori said, taking a healthy toke on the joint.

"That would make him like six-six," he estimated. Nicky was five-eight and Lori a few inches shorter. She wasn't quite what you'd call willowy, but she also wasn't petite. Joe was maybe six feet tall. Six-one, max. Of which Nicky reminded her.

"Well, he seems a lot taller than that." She handed Nicky the joint, which he sat with for a moment. He was feeling a bit lightheaded.

"He makes a big appearance," offered Nicky, whatever that meant.

"He has really nice arms. Like a rower."

"I haven't noticed," Nicky lied. He took another hit.

"Think he's a rower?" Lori wondered.

OK, thought Nicky, *enough talking about other guys*. Why did he keep getting sucked into these conversations? "How would I know?"

"I don't know, I'm just asking. Jeez, I'm not asking if you know how big his thing is." She grabbed a roach clip, sucked out the last of the joint. Handed it to Nicky.

He waved her off. Was feeling stoned enough and didn't need to loosen his lips more. "His *thing*?" Nicky asked, realizing what she'd just said and exploding into laughter. Lori guffawed, which made Nicky cackle even more and, in a chain reaction, the two of them roared so long and so hard, they could barely catch their breath. They rolled around the floor like a couple of blitzed hyenas.

Fortunately, they forgot what they'd even been talking about and split a hunk of icebox cake Lori had smuggled out of the dining hall that night, her diet be damned.

IT WASN'T LORI, but Joe who first told Nicky about their evening out. Though Lori said she'd check in with Nicky when they got back from Brandy's, she still hadn't returned by the time he went to bed. It was just as well; Nicky didn't want it to seem like he was waiting up for all the gory details—which he was and also wasn't. Besides, he had an early class the next day and needed the sleep. There was no sign of Lori in the morning as Nicky waited for the elevator, nor in the dining hall when he entered for breakfast. But when he grabbed a table to scarf down his Cheerios before heading out for psych class, Joe plopped down in the chair across from him with a cup of coffee. He looked ready to take on the day, in running shorts, sneakers, and a hooded BU sweatshirt.

"Hey, just wanted to say thanks," Joe said, as he gulped coffee. Nicky noticed that he grasped the cup around its mouth—not by its handle—which struck him as particularly masculine. He'd have to see how Monty held his.

"Thanks for what?" Nicky asked, playing dumb even if he could guess where this was going.

"For encouraging Lori to go out with me."

Nicky had to think about that one. "Is that what I did?"

"I don't know, but that's what Lori said." He rolled his shoulders and rotated his neck like he was warming up for something. "You run?"

"Only away from things," Nicky joked. As if on cue, he spotted Shelley enter the dining room. She looked over and gave him a full-arm wave so emphatic she almost knocked some guy's breakfast tray from his hands.

"Oh, my Gawd, I am so *saw-ry!*" a mortified Shelley told her would-be victim, loudly enough that it reverberated across the dining hall. She skittered off toward the food bays.

Nicky returned his attention to Joe, who had pulled off his sweatshirt to reveal a clingy T-shirt and his wide rower's arms. Nicky sensed that jolt in his stomach again. "Do *you* row?" he asked Joe, who looked at him oddly. "I mean—run?" Nicky felt like he was back with him that first day in the elevator. He vacuumed up the rest of his Cheerios.

"Yep. Along the Charles," Joe said. "You should come."

"I'd probably hold you back. I'm not real fast or anything." That wasn't true; Nicky was weirdly fast. Almost always finished in the top five whenever he ran the track in his high school gym class. (He usually had to puke after, so it was kind of a mixed blessing.) So why was he being so damn self-effacing?

Joe took another slug of coffee. "It's not about speed, it's about stamina. Unless you're competing, then it's about both. Anyway, it's a great way to clear your head and get out in the fresh air." He flashed a sparkly grin. "We're cooped up inside those lecture halls enough, right?"

The thought of running with Joe was all kinds of appealing, but Nicky wondered if a few days from now he'd forget that he even asked—as he had about seeing *Jaws*.

Then Joe the mind reader put down his cup and said, "And don't think I forgot about going to *Jaws*. I know I said Wednesday night, but I wanted to strike while the iron was hot with Lori, y'know?" He shrugged bashfully. "I kinda couldn't wait to go out with her."

"Sure, yeah. Of course," Nicky tossed off in casual agreement. "Actually, I forgot all about the *Jaws* thing till now." If Joe believed that, Nicky might have an acting career ahead of him. Out of the corner of his eye, he could see Shelley steering herself toward a table. Thankfully, she stopped before she reached Nicky's and sat herself down with one of the Julies from their floor. (Nicky still couldn't differentiate between them; he needed to work on that.)

Joe pushed aside his coffee cup and leaned into Nicky. There was that fucking Aramis again. "So, what *did* you say? To Lori, I mean. About going out with me?" He raised a quizzical eyebrow, but couldn't hold back a smile.

Just then, Nicky realized that as much as he didn't want to talk about other guys with Lori he also didn't want to talk about Lori with other guys. Specifically, the one currently breathing into his face. But he'd been evasive enough, so he threw Joe a bone. "I told her that you seemed like a fun guy." Joe took that in, looked impressed. Maybe even grateful.

"Well, we definitely had fun. A ton of it," Joe said with a puckish grin as he proceeded to tick off the high points of the night: Brandy's was "a blast," this band called the Holy Craps was "awesome," Lori "looked way better than Susan Dey," they made out a little riding back on the T and again in the 700 elevators, and talked about some "cool stuff." Throughout his buoyant recap, he looked and sounded like a kid with a new toy. It made Nicky squirm.

"Did you know her dad's plane was shot down in World War II?" Joe asked, his gray-green eyes still wide. "Spent almost an entire day in the ocean waiting to be rescued!"

Nicky didn't know that, didn't know anything about Lori's dad beyond his name, which was Ralph. Or maybe Randolph. Wait . . . Rodney? *Relax, it's not a contest*, Nicky thought. He glanced across the way, spotted Shelley and whichever Julie eyeing him from their table, then engaging in a giggly whisper. He so wished Lori had never mentioned that Shelley liked him.

"Anyway," Joe continued, "I can't wait to do it again."

"Go out with Lori?" Nicky asked like a dunce.

Joe leveled his gaze. "No, see the Holy Craps a second time." He broke into another smile. "I know it was only one date but . . . I don't know, I'm feeling really optimistic about this. And not just because she's such a babe."

Nicky gulped down the last of his coffee, then grabbed his tray and rose. "Gotta get to class. Have a good run." He nodded at Joe, who looked disappointed that Nicky was leaving.

"I'm gonna get you out on the Charles, you'll see!" Joe brightly called after him. "Gonna run your ass off!"

Nicky turned and gave Joe a thumbs-up, which couldn't have looked or felt dorkier. On the plus side, he did manage to elude Shelley as he exited, which felt like a small triumph.

SURPRISINGLY, LORI WASN'T as gaga as Joe was about their night out. Nicky didn't even talk to her till late afternoon when they ran into each other at Mugar Library; she was walking in as he was walking out. He wondered if she'd been avoiding him all day—or at least not going out of her way to find him to share the dirt. It seemed strange, but, in truth, Nicky had heard enough about the date from Joe that morning to satisfy his curiosity. Sparks flew! It was a match made in heaven! Good for them!

Except maybe it wasn't.

Nicky had followed Lori back into the library to talk—loudly whisper, actually—as they stood in a narrow aisle between the world history stacks. She wore embroidered flared jeans, a ropy sash belt, and a purplish paisley blouse that, upon inspection, showed no sign of a bra beneath. Nicky thought she looked particularly beautiful framed against the towering bookshelves.

The long and the short of it was that Joe wasn't Joshua. Maybe Nicky wasn't either but that didn't seem to be a factor—*the* factor—between him and Lori. She had fun with Joe, as Nicky predicted (he didn't want to tell her it was just a guess), and it wasn't like she didn't find him super attractive, which she did. But he felt like a stranger. Which, Nicky reminded her, may have been because he was.

"We just got here. Who are you going to go out with who's not basically a stranger?" he asked with more logic than was likely appreciated.

"*You're* not," Lori answered, her mouth forming a little pout.

"Really? I don't even know your father's name."

"It's Burt. Burton. And what difference does *that* make?"

Burt? Where the hell did he get Ralph and Rodney from? "You might be missing the point."

"The point is: You want me to like Joe because you like Joe and you like me. And that's really sweet of you, but I don't know, maybe I'm not ready for anyone right now." She wistfully eyed Nicky as if to say that included him.

Nicky didn't get it. What kind of hold did this Joshua creep have over her? He'd seen pictures of him and, at least in Nicky's estimation, he was pretty average looking. Plus, it sounded like he'd made it clear to Lori that they were done—with no evidence of backtracking. Maybe it was like what Richie had told him: play hard to get and they'll want you more. That still seemed so twisted. Did Lori even *want* the guy back? Her answer surprised Nicky.

"No," she admitted. "And that's what makes it even more fucked up." Her eyes began to brim. "Bottom line, Nicky: be careful who you lose your virginity to." She flashed a wan smile as a tear trickled down her cheek.

Nicky reflexively matched her smile until he realized what she'd just confirmed: Joshua was her first (Nicky had figured as much), and she assumed Nicky was a virgin. OK, it didn't take Sherlock Holmes, but it also seemed presumptuous on her part—was it really that obvious? *Now* what was he supposed to do? Dispute the embarrassing and unnerving truth or say nothing and let her think what she wanted? Anyway, wasn't this conversation supposed to be about *her*?

"Well, you obviously liked Joe enough to fool around with him," he pointed out. He wanted to jam those words back into his mouth the second he said them. Lori stared glassily at him. Nicky had vowed that he wouldn't tell her about his talk that morning with Joe. He so didn't want to get in the middle of any of it, which was exactly what he was doing. He was about to apologize—or something—when Lori's lips curled into a sly smile.

"Do you want to know if you're a better kisser than he is?"

From beyond the stacks, there was a forceful shush, followed by "Take it outside, would you?" It thankfully prevented Nicky from having to answer Lori's question, something, of course, he wanted to know—but not necessarily hear. How did his life get so deliciously complicated in just a few short weeks?

Back outside, standing in front of the library, Lori revealed that she'd probably go out with Joe again if he asked ("He'll ask," Nicky assured her), and that she needed to hop the train out of Joshua-ville for good because it was messing her up. Any further discussion of Nicky's virginity, kissing ability, or how he knew Lori had made out with Joe were all left behind in the world history stacks.

"Joe wants me to go running with him some morning," Nicky told Lori, apropos of nothing (or maybe more than he thought), as they crossed the Comm Ave trolley tracks toward the 700 entrance.

"Yeah? He's a total jock, y'know. Turns out I had the whole high school soccer-wrestling-baseball thing right. Except he only made captain twice. Oh, and he *does* have two brothers—but he's the oldest, not the youngest." Lori's enthusiasm for the guy seemed almost tangibly visible. Even she looked surprised.

Nicky held open the dorm door for Lori. "See, he's not such a stranger after all."

She smiled. "You know who's the stranger? Joshua's the stranger."

"Exactly!" Nicky heartily agreed as he followed Lori through the door. He didn't know what prompted her sudden turnaround—maybe Joe *was* an amazing kisser—but he was happy to see her happy. Or at least trying to put Joshua behind her. Nicky hoped it would last.

TEN

"**WHAT ARE YOU** doing up so early?" Monty mumbled as he rolled over in his bed.

Nicky, dressed in what he hoped would pass for running gear, was sitting on his desk chair, tying his new Adidas, which he'd bought the day before on a trip downtown to Filene's department store. Yeah, the sneaks looked ghostly white and screamed rookie runner, but his worn-out Converse were a nonstarter. As it was, he figured he'd feel self-conscious enough jogging with Joe; he didn't need to worry about what were on his feet.

"Going running," Nicky informed Monty. He rose from the chair and grabbed his ID and room key off his dresser.

"What the hell for?" Monty threw the blanket over his head.

"Ever hear of exercise?" Nicky said as if he'd created the concept. He checked his look in the mirror: his mustache had finally started taking shape. It was filling in better than he expected, even if it was a shade lighter than the thick curls and waves atop his head.

Monty muttered something from under the covers that sounded like, "Yeah, I get plenty of it from fucking," which was, in fact, exactly what he said.

It was sunny but cool that morning by the Charles River, a Boston landmark that, strangely, Nicky could see clearly from his fourteenth-floor dorm window but had yet to experience up close. Even stranger, it was only a few blocks off campus and, in some ways, a part of the campus. Maybe it was because Nicky had never been the outdoorsy type per se—like forests and lakes and mountains outdoorsy—that he hadn't thought to explore the riverfront. Oh, he thought about it like: it was there, he'd get to it. Like visiting Fenway Park or Bunker Hill, which were also on his list. Who had time when you were still trying to remember which buildings your classes were in, which trolley line to take where (and the city's map in general), how to work the damn coffee machine in the dining hall (which he still hadn't fully mastered), and to call your parents, who seemed as far away as the moon after just a few short weeks? Not to mention keeping up with your mountain of coursework, which took up way more time than those peppy college brochures ever came close to revealing.

Nicky met Joe in front of 700 and followed him up Comm Ave for a block, but not before Joe gave Nicky's shiny new Adidas a jokey wolf whistle. They hung a left on a side street that led to a footbridge zigzagging over noisy Storrow Drive. It dropped them on the Charles River Esplanade, a wide, grassy area that gave way to what seemed like an endless ribbon of running and biking paths, all overlooking the vast waterway. Nicky thought it was a hell of a lot more impressive than from his dorm window. Between the dazzling view, the brisk gusts off the water, and the folks zipping past on cycle and foot, he felt a rare surge of energy, promise, and, yes, self-assurance. That Joe complimented him on his facial hair ("That 'stache is really starting to happen!") was the cherry on the confidence cake.

Nicky was ready to run but Joe, responsible coach that he was, made Nicky join him on the grass first for a round of stretching exercises. "You don't want to pull a hammy!" Joe warned with his usual, ingratiating smile. Nicky, never the best at following directions (he wasn't a rebel, just not always that coordinated), dutifully copied Joe's movements, most of which involved elongating each of his limbs until he felt pain. Which was a lot sooner for Nicky than Joe, who, for a big guy, was surprisingly flexible.

"Just takes practice," Joe affably explained. He directed Nicky to sit opposite him, legs extended, heels flat against his. "Now grab my hands and push hard against my feet," Joe said, as they locked fingers and pressed their sneaker soles together. Nicky could feel two things: his "hammys" getting a good, painful stretch, and the strength and warmth of Joe's intertwined hands. The sudden sense of connection sent that familiar rush through Nicky's belly and up his spine. He locked eyes with Joe for a flash, then reflexively pulled away. He leaped up, rolled his neck (isn't that what *Joe* did?), and pretended he was itching to get going.

Joe looked up at Nicky, grinned, and got to his feet. "OK, tiger, let's hit it."

Tiger? Coming from anyone else, that might've sounded corny, embarrassingly so. From Joe, it felt like a verbal arm around the shoulder. Nicky relaxed, ready to run like the wind—or at least a stiff breeze. Hopefully, no upchuck would be involved.

As they took off along the river's edge, Nicky's first thought was that he wanted to impress Joe. Maybe not impress him, exactly, but at minimum prove a worthy jogging partner. Someone who could keep up with him and maybe even give him, well, a run for his money. Someone Joe would take seriously, consider an equal, and not just some naïve freshman who needed an ongoing orientation leader. And then, as Nicky could feel his lungs filling and his heart hammering from his increasing speed, it dawned on him: He wanted Joe to be his friend. His pal, his buddy. And not the way Lori was any of those things—because that had its own set of complications. But more like his old Franklin Square friends: Wally and Brad and Pins (Fred Pinsky hated his real name). Guys he could just hang around with, no reaching for conversation or being something he wasn't; no judgment or suspicion. Not the way he felt with the exhausting Monty or the overeager Chuck or the opinionated Ken, though maybe he just didn't know them well enough yet. (He was pretty sure he knew all he needed to of Monty.)

Still, he felt things around Joe—things he tried not to ponder but couldn't quite ignore—that he never did with Wally or Brad or Pins, and he wasn't sure how well that boded for actual friendship. He wasn't sure how well that boded for a lot of things. Or if it meant anything at all.

Either Nicky wasn't as fast as he was in gym class or Joe was extra fleet on his feet but, after a short time pounding the path, he found himself struggling to keep pace. He didn't want to fall behind, so he kept pushing along, a smile slapped on his reddening face to match Joe's joyful, wind-in-his-hair expression. And that's when Nicky, breath now coming in ragged spurts, glanced at the river for a split second, only to trip on a slick patch of grass and fall into a sprawling azalea bush.

It took Joe a beat to realize Nicky was no longer at his side. He couldn't help but guffaw as he doubled back and extended a hand to pull up his prone—and mortified—running mate. "What the hell are you doing in *there*?" Joe asked as he helped Nicky out of the shrub and back onto his feet.

"I'm really into plants, didn't I tell you?" Nicky managed to joke even if he felt like the world's biggest idiot. That newfound confidence he'd been feeling? Out the window.

"Well, you were definitely 'into' that one, that's for sure!" He gave Nicky's shoulder a fraternal clap.

Nicky kept a forced smile going as he swept leaves off his T-shirt and sweatpants, his heart rate recalibrating. Despite the fall, his Adidas still looked blindingly clean.

Joe studied him. "Why were you running so fast?"

"Was I?" Nicky asked with feigned innocence, then admitted, "I mean, I was just trying to keep up."

"That's cool, but you don't have to try so hard. Run at your own pace. Remember what I said: It's not about speed, it's about stamina. Gotta build up to it."

Nicky nodded. He wasn't sure if his spill was due to speed or distraction, but either way, it required no further discussion. He wanted Joe as a friend he could be himself around, right? Well, maybe this was as good a time as any to start. He just had to figure out who he truly was. As Joe bent down to retie a sneaker lace, Nicky watched a row team whooshing down the Charles. They looked so graceful, so unified. The phrase "poetry in motion" came to mind, though Nicky realized he'd never really known what that meant until just then.

"OK, no more stunts, pal!" Joe ordered as he jogged off, waving Nicky after him. Nicky took a deep breath and fell in line with Joe, who seemed to be running a tad slower now—Or was it Nicky's imagination? Either way, Nicky felt himself moving at a more comfortable pace, even if puking was not completely off the table.

"How often do you run?" Nicky huffed out as they passed Kenmore Square on their right, the humongous, red-white-and-blue Citgo oil company neon sign looming above it all.

"Two, three times a week. That's the goal, anyway. I try to lift a coupla times a week, too."

"Lift?"

Joe eyed him, suppressed a grin. "A piano, the occasional station wagon. Y'know."

If Nicky wasn't in motion, he would have slapped his forehead. "Oh, y'mean weights. Like at a gym." *No, like at a frickin' bakery. Jeez.* Nicky noticed how straight Joe's back was as he ran, head high, shoulders level. He tried to adjust himself accordingly but still felt short in comparison. Though, he guessed, not as short as Lori must've felt—especially when she and Joe kissed. *Lori.* Joe hadn't mentioned her at all yet that morning. Interesting.

"Ever been to Case Gym? On West Campus?" Joe asked, voice clear and steady, unlike Nicky's, which seemed to bounce along with his legs.

"Nope. Never been to West Campus altogether." Nicky made it sound like it was West Virginia. In truth, it was only a few T-stops up Comm Ave from the main campus.

"Great weight room. *And* a Universal machine. You should check it out." Joe slowed up, then stopped, hovering in place. "Take a break, tiger!" he called after Nicky who continued to run ahead.

Nicky gladly put the brakes on. It was perfect timing: He wasn't sure how much longer he'd be able to go on even at the reduced speed. He wondered if Joe knew that and had called time-out for Nicky's benefit. He caught his breath and trotted back to Joe, who was back on the grass stretching.

"Think you can make it to the Harvard Bridge?" Joe asked, one leg kicked behind his back, right arm arcing over his head.

Nicky couldn't mask his alarm. "All the way to Cambridge?" From where they were, the famed university had to be at least a few miles away. Did that mean running back to BU as well? Christ, what had he gotten himself into?

Joe let out a warm chuckle. "You've gotta work on your Beantown geography, son. The Harvard Bridge isn't *at* Harvard, it's just up there," he nodded into the distance, "at Mass Ave."

Nicky eyed the nearby bridge, relieved. "Yeah, I can definitely make it there." At least he hoped he could. He shot Joe a competitive grin. "Can you?"

Joe hopped up, gave a confident shrug. "Piece of cake. But don't get all cocky, pal. Like I said, it's not a race." Then, with a wink, "Not yet." And he jogged off, Nicky promptly at his side.

They didn't talk much more as they ran toward Massachusetts Avenue, the sun quickly warming up the morning. They briefly rested again when they reached the bridge, walking in wide circles, hands on hips. Nicky wanted to ask Joe if he always took breaks like that but held back. He didn't want to hear, even in jest, "No, only when I run with rookies like you." He posed what he considered a less leading question. Or was it?

"Do you usually run alone or with someone else?"

"Who wants to know?" he joked, an eyebrow raised.

"The *Boston Globe*," Nicky retorted. "They're taking a survey."

Joe gave one of his deep chortles. "Well, in that case, yeah, usually it's just me, myself, and I. I like the focus, the concentration," he explained. Eyes fixed on Nicky, he added, "But sometimes it's good to have company."

Nicky felt his stomach flip and goosebumps blaze up his arms. Staring back at Joe, with his ropy arms and persuasive smile, little

Nicky DeMarco from Franklin Square, New York, had a certain brain-bending thought for the first time in complete and total earnest. And he had no idea what the fuck he was supposed to do about it. Nothing seemed like the best and only solution.

Joe did finally bring up Lori as they finished their run and dragged their asses—well, Nicky dragged his, Joe looked coolly invigorated—across the Storrow Drive footbridge back to Comm Ave.

"So, I'm gonna ask Lori out again. I'm thinking somewhere nicer this time. A decent restaurant or something. Wine, candlelight, soft music. Set the stage."

"Set the stage? For what?" It may have sounded like another dumb question but Nicky knew just what he was asking. He felt like a dad grilling his teen daughter's hot rod-driving date. Still, not to seem uncool, Nicky sent Joe a wry, just-giving-you-shit look.

But Joe looked slightly put off. "Hey, it's not what you're thinking. Not yet, anyway. I just want to make a good impression, show a little class."

"Well, I don't know about the 'class' part, but I think you've already passed the good impression test." *You have with her* and *me,* Nicky wanted to say, but kept his trap shut.

Joe considered that. "Do you know what kind of food she likes?" he asked, with a lot less game than Nicky would have guessed for a guy so seemingly attuned to women. But something in Joe's look suggested that he thought Lori was extra special—and didn't want to blow it no matter how much of a catch *he* may be.

"I'm sure she'll appreciate anywhere you take her," Nicky answered. "But she may not eat a ton. She kind of watches herself." Nicky wanted to slap himself. He didn't mean to leak anything too personal about Lori. He needed to start saying "I don't know"—to both of them. But Joe seemed unfazed, glad to have any kind of inside track.

"A shape like hers? She doesn't need to count calories," Joe said. "But, hey, thanks for the heads-up."

They started walking down Comm Ave toward the dorm. The concrete campus was in full morning swing now as students streamed down the street, peeling off to one building or another for their first class of the day. Nicky's classes didn't start until eleven; he might even try to grab a quick nap. He hoped Monty would already be gone.

They stayed quiet the rest of the way as Joe seemed lost in thought, probably brainstorming the perfect restaurant. Nicky wouldn't admit it to anyone but himself, but he was a little envious. Maybe more than a little.

ELEVEN

NICKY STASHED THE rattling feelings he'd had during his run with Joe in some deep, unreachable corner of his brain. But they didn't exactly disappear the way he expected. If anything, they triggered a bunch of other memories that Nicky also thought he'd tucked away for good. Things he'd dismissed as just part of a horny teen's daily sensory overload. Things he never connected to anything more far-reaching than isolated moments of . . . What? Admiration? Aspiration? Who could take that stuff any more seriously than those random school-bus boners? Still, why did this feel different? And, maybe even more importantly, why now? Why *him*?

Lori seemed extra interested in Nicky's river run with Joe, peppering Nicky with questions about his "new jogging buddy." Not only did Nicky want to avoid talking, much less thinking, about Joe, but he wanted to do better about staying out of Lori and Joe's budding connection. If not, before he knew it, he'd be telling Lori that Joe was going to ask her out again and that Nicky had spilled the beans on her food intake. Which is exactly what happened as, back between the stacks at Mugar Library that night, Lori wore him down for details. But instead of being annoyed that Nicky mentioned her weight issue, Lori was charmed.

"Aw, honey, that was so sweet of you. To look out for me like that," she gushed, in the hushed tones they reserved for library chitchat. "You're the best." She gave Nicky a little hug and extra squeeze with a guilelessness that was so heart swelling he wondered, once again, why the hell they were just friends.

And then he thought about Joe and naked Monty and buff high school wrestling star Larry Marquez, who used to give Nicky a two-fingered, "How's it going?" wave as he'd strut past him in trig class on the way to his seat—and how it kinda made Nicky's day. He shook the images—and whatever they did or didn't mean—out of mind and tried to be interested in what Lori was telling him about her condescending creative writing professor and the C+ he'd just given her on her first paper.

"Maybe, in this case, it stands for 'creative plus,'" Nicky joked, trying to cheer her up.

"See," Lori said, her face brightening again, "that's why I love you."

Oh, that's *why*, Nicky thought with an inner eye roll.

Sure enough, a few days later, Joe asked Lori out again for that Saturday night. He had apparently settled on a spot on Mass Ave called the Newbury Steak House, which didn't sound particularly healthy or like a candles-and-soft-music place, but Nicky assumed Joe knew what he was doing. Lori seemed excited about it, and she was already trying to figure out what to wear. Fortunately, she didn't ask Nicky's opinion about that, at least not yet. Meanwhile, Joe left a note on Nicky and Monty's erasable door pad asking if Nicky wanted to run the next morning. Much as he wanted to hit the Esplanade again, Nicky found himself telling Joe he couldn't make it when they bumped into each other later at dinner. One look at Joe in his snug Izod polo shirt, and he decided some distance from the guy would be best. Joe shrugged, said "Another time, I hope," and left for the food bays.

Nicky returned to his dinner table where Manhattanites Chuck and Ken were comparing the merits—and demerits—of the *New*

York Times, *New York Magazine*, the *New Yorker*, and *New Times* magazine. Nicky had nothing to contribute except that he thought Long Island's *Newsday* had a great sports section. Chuck and Ken, stumped for a response, resumed their scholarly debate. Nicky focused on his baked schrod and thought about Joe's arms and Lori's mouth and the next day's econ test he had to cram for.

"Why would that Joe guy want to be friends with you?" asked Monty later as Nicky erased Joe's running invite off their message board. "Not a slam," he qualified, "just curious."

Nicky reentered their room and closed the door behind him. "Why *wouldn't* he want to be friends with me? I'm a friendly person," he countered, slightly stung, even if part of him understood the question. *OK, maybe not* that *friendly*. He plopped down in his desk chair and opened his econ textbook.

Monty slipped a Jerry Jeff album on his turntable and dropped the needle on side one. "Well, he's older and, I don't know, you guys seem really different." He stood over the stereo and blissfully bobbed his head in time with the first track, something about the Salvation Army. Or at least that's what Nicky thought he heard; the songs all sounded the same to him.

Nicky swung around in his chair and tried not to sound defensive. "Maybe Joe and I are more alike than you think," he said, knowing that wasn't true. "I mean, has every friend you've ever had been just like you?" *How many fake Jewish cowboys with crummy taste in music who smoke too much are there in Pittsburgh, anyway?* Nicky wanted to add.

Monty sat on his bed, mulled Nicky's question as he lit a cigarette. "No, I guess not." He took a deep drag. "But it's like . . . Do you think he's just being nice to you to get next to Lori?"

Nicky thought that was kind of a shitty thing to say and told Monty so. Monty shrugged innocently, awaiting Nicky's answer. "He already *got* next to Lori. He doesn't need me," Nicky told him. "Besides, we're not really friends, we just kind of know each other." That seemed about as good an explanation as any. He turned back to his textbook, hoping Monty would get the hint and end it there.

His silence made Nicky hopeful. *Fuck, I am so not prepared for this test*, Nicky thought as he stared at his econ book.

"Hey, do you know what Jerry Jeff's real name is?" Monty finally asked.

"Abraham Lincoln," Nicky answered without looking up.

Monty ignored the sarcasm. "Ronald Clyde Crosby," he said proudly, as if he'd christened—or maybe rechristened—the singer himself.

"Is there a point here, Monty? Otherwise, I really need to study."

"Yeah, there's a point," Monty answered curtly but was interrupted by a gentle knock at the door. Just as well, Nicky didn't want to hear his "point"—if there actually were one.

Nicky eyed Monty. "Expecting someone?" But he could guess the rest.

Monty stubbed out his cigarette, took a hit of Binaca, and made for the door. Sabrina was standing there, looking her usual sexy, serene self in a flowy, tie-dyed blouse and ceramic dove necklace. Nicky didn't know much about women's clothes but wondered if Sabrina's look was already past its prime. He kind of liked that she didn't seem to care. As did, apparently, Monty, who clearly appreciated a personal fashion statement.

Monty kissed Sabrina hello, making a show of it, Nicky presumed, at least partially for his benefit. Nicky also knew it was his cue to exit. He still couldn't get Monty to give him some notice when he needed the room to himself. (Was that a control thing on Monty's part—or Nicky's?) He stood, econ text in one hand, notebook and pens in the other, and started for the door.

"Lori's in our room, if you want to study there," Sabrina sweetly informed Nicky as she sat on the bed. Monty joined her, stroking her long, chestnut blond hair. Nicky was amazed at how Monty instantly transformed around her: from prickly to puppy dog. She was a good influence on him. It made Nicky wonder what kind of influence *he* would need—and could be.

When Nicky knocked on Lori's door, she answered it in tears, phone cradled between head and shoulder, in mid-conversation.

She angrily mouthed "Joshua" in response to Nicky's startled look, then snorted back a sad wad of phlegm.

"No. No, no, no!" Lori shouted into the phone. "*You* were the one who wanted to see other people, not me!" She rolled her soggy eyes at Nicky.

With a sympathetic look, he backed away, mouthed "I'll talk to you later," and closed the door behind him. Nicky was confused: What happened to "*Joshua's* the stranger!" or whatever else Lori seemed to be telling herself to get over the jerk? And wasn't dating Joe an exciting enough prospect to push past any residual thoughts of him? There was obviously more to the Lori-Joshua puzzle than Nicky knew. As he rounded the hallway corner en route to the elevators, he walked headfirst into Shelley, clutching a stack of textbooks—which flew out of her arms and onto the floor.

"Oh, my Gawd, Nicky! I'm *so* sorry, you must think I'm such a klutz!" she said, scrambling to retrieve the books. Nicky wondered why that sounded so familiar and then recalled Shelley's near-collision with that guy's breakfast tray in the dining hall.

Nicky bent down to help gather her books and, as they rose in unison, their heads clonked. They were both stunned—eye-to-eye, mouth-to-mouth, like in some corny movie when the shy couple is finally forced together. They each stood embarrassed, self-conscious, staring at the floor, then up at each other. Up close like that, Nicky noticed what sparkly blue eyes she had (no squint this time!) and her smooth, rosy skin. She smelled nice, like cookies. And her breasts looked way larger beneath her stretchy turtleneck than Nicky remembered. (Had he ever even really noticed them?) Weirdly—or not—he was getting hard.

"I was just going down to the lounge to study," Nicky told Shelley.

"I just came from there," she said, as if destiny were shining upon them.

The elevator arrived, strangely unbidden. It hovered behind them empty, expectant. "I should go," Nicky said as he edged away, his dick now at full mast.

Shelley gazed at him, sensing if not his exact state of arousal, then maybe some one-time . . . opening. "You're welcome to study in my room. The lounge was pretty packed, y'know?" Before Nicky could decline, she added, "And Julie's out of town overnight, so . . ." Her Long Island accent suddenly didn't sound quite so jarring. More like familiar, comforting.

"Which Julie's your roommate again?" asked Nicky, considering her invite.

"Elkins. But I'm actually closer to Julie Pressman," she answered. "Not to be confused with Julie Ohanian," Shelley clarified about 14A's third Julie. That made her giggle—but sweetly, not annoyingly.

Before Nicky knew it, he was in Shelley's brightly decorated room (so much purple!), rolling around with her on her lilac-patterned bedspread. They kissed frantically, exploring each other's mouths with curiosity and gusto. Nicky was startled by his eager reaction to someone he'd been keeping at arm's length. The hot pot Shelley had plugged in to make them tea—her kind offer that had gotten Nicky over her threshold (not that he ever drank tea)—was burbling in the background.

"I should unplug that thing," Shelley murmured between tongue swabs.

"Leave it," Nicky ordered as his right hand traveled under her turtleneck, fingers grazing her bra. He felt like he was back in high school, seeing how far he could get with a girl, whether he really wanted to or not. The difference now was that he had a more willing participant—and for some reason, he felt more motivated. But why exactly?

He shut his mind off and pressed forward, his hand moving under Shelley's surprisingly pliable bra and making contact with the smooth flesh beneath. She groaned as they kissed, but, Nicky noticed, seemed more restrained than usual, certainly less vocal. Maybe, he thought, she was nervous or afraid of blowing it with him. He hoped that wasn't true—it embarrassed him to think he could affect someone that way. (Even if, when it came to romance, the shoe was usually on the other foot.) Their kissing and groping and rolling about continued until Nicky, caught up in the moment, tried to push Shelley's entire sweater up over her head. Their lips still locked, she grabbed his hands and pushed the sweater back down, murmuring something in the vicinity of "No way, buster." Nicky complied and busied his hands elsewhere, but felt his will—and the lump in his jeans—vanishing. Shelley seemed to slow down along with him until she pulled back and gave him a wistful look.

"Sorry for the mixed signals," she said, catching her breath, "but I really just wanted to talk. To get to know you better. I hope you understand." *Tawk. Unduh-standt.*

I thought you wanted to 'eat me up with a spoon'? Nicky wanted to ask. "Well, I guess we both know each other a *little* better now," he joked as his heartbeat settled.

Shelley smiled appreciatively and disentangled herself from Nicky. "Well, that's good, right?" she asked, rising off the bed to unplug the gurgling hot pot. "Wanna cup?" she asked, with a hopeful look.

"I don't really like tea," Nicky answered. "Reminds me of being at home sick."

"And see, *that's* what I like about it!" She giggled. "I'm such a freak, I know."

Nicky sat up, wondering if he should go. He still had all that studying to do. He watched Shelley prepare her tea and suddenly had no desire to move. "Got anything else in the hot beverage department?" he asked.

She pulled out a box of Swiss Miss and waved it at Nicky. "You like hot chocolate?"

"Now you're talking."

And talking is what they did. For about an hour until Nicky knew that if he didn't study till at least midnight, he'd surely flunk his econ exam (*Mom, Dad, guess what?*). They chatted mostly about Long Island—Shelley was from semi-upscale North Woodmere (*Wood-me-uh*), a few towns over from Franklin Square—and their mutual memories of growing up there. It was clear from the way she mooned over places like Green Acres Mall, Jones Beach, Valley Stream State Park, Nathan's Famous Hot Dogs, and the Grant Park ice rink that she missed her home turf a lot more than Nicky did, which may have explained her sentimentality about sick-day cups of tea. Shelley also apologized again for putting the brakes on their make-out session and if she'd led him on, but that she didn't move that fast, even though she did like Nicky "tons." Nicky was starting to get the "friends" vibe once again though this time was more relieved and less confused than when it happened with Lori.

For Nicky's part, he played it cool, as if sometimes he scored, sometimes he didn't, and he didn't take it personally (*Ha!*). He thought it was best not to reveal that, before that night, he'd had no interest like that in Shelley, and that the reason he went for it just now was because his dick, which was reacting in alarming ways lately, was pointing in her direction, and he needed to do some serious testing of its selection process. Oh, and it wouldn't have hurt to lose his virginity with someone nice and unexpectedly attractive—and get it the hell over with. He did, however, tell her that she was a good kisser because (a) she was and (b) he knew how good it had felt when *he* was told that—So why not? Shelley got all shy and self-conscious and returned the compliment. Another guy might have taken that as a cue to go back for seconds, but Nicky left awkward enough alone.

A second cup of cocoa later, he was in the 700 study lounge, head swimming in such thrilling economic theories as opportunity cost, resource allocation, competition, and scarcity, while all he really wanted to do was have another make-out session. But not necessarily, he realized, with either Lori *or* Shelley.

TWELVE

IT TURNED OUT that Shelley didn't want to just be friendly floormates with Nicky. She thought he was still totally "spoon"-worthy—or so she told Lori (Did she really think Lori wouldn't report back to Nicky? Or maybe that was the point)—but wasn't ready to "give herself over to him" just yet. She was a lot more careful and self-protective than her bubbly personality might imply. At least that was budding psychologist Lori's take. Still, Lori was damn surprised that Nicky and Shelley had "a moment." But not as surprised as Nicky—and he told Lori so. He also told her to please not repeat anything he said to her about Shelley *to* Shelley and Lori gave him a dry look that read: *How stupid do you think I am?*

All this by way of explaining how Nicky ended up back in Shelley's room and, this time, sticking *both* hands under her bra and then getting a hand job. How did this happen? Well, it was the result of a kind of perfect storm of events. Lori's looming dinner date with Joe left Nicky feeling particularly antsy. He hadn't seen or talked to Joe in the days since he'd turned down his offer to go running again and was feeling a vague (or maybe not so vague) void. Nicky could have easily found him and picked up where they left off. After all, Joe had no clue about his effect on Nicky and probably hadn't thought twice about him since. But Nicky, who had thought about Joe lots more than twice, still felt some inner need to keep him physically at bay.

Still, when he did get to eyeball Joe again when he arrived that Saturday night to pick up Lori, he was glad to see him and, it seemed, vice versa.

"Where you been hiding, bud?" Joe jovially asked when he bumped into Nicky at the 14A elevators. He was wearing a patterned, collared shirt under a navy wool crewneck, tan chinos, and beige desert boots. To Nicky, he looked kind of preppy but also completely comfortable and even cool. Like he knew just what to wear and how to wear it for maximum Joe Hello effect. Unlike Nicky, who would have changed six times before leaving his room for a date—and still been unsure if he'd gotten it right.

"Nowhere, been right here," Nicky answered as casually as he could, despite his increasing pulse rate—and the stirring waft of Joe's liberally applied Aramis. "You here for Lori?" he asked like a dunce because who *else* would he have been there all handsome and pulled together and scented up for?

"Yep, second date." Joe sent Nicky a playful wink. "But I guess you knew that already."

Before Nicky could answer, Lori appeared, looking quite gorgeous in a shortish print dress, high leather boots, and waist-length leather jacket, hair artfully tousled. "What are you two boys yakking about?" she asked coyly.

Joe's eyes turned silver-dollar-sized as he took her in. "We're talking about *you*," he answered approvingly. "You look fantastic," he added and gave her a peck on the cheek. Lori blushed, returned the compliment, and they bid Nicky goodnight as they disappeared into an arriving elevator.

Nicky suddenly felt like the loneliest guy on the planet. Maybe he'd take Chuck and Ken up on their offer to go see *Dog Day Afternoon*, though he wasn't sure if he was up for their embattled dissection of it that was sure to follow. (Those two annoyingly debated everything, from old TV shows to the best—and worst—dining hall dishes.) Meantime, all three Julies, who'd apparently bonded over their shared name, were going to Katy's, one of the dance clubs in Kenmore Square. They were looking for guys to join them so they wouldn't have to dance alone, at least at first. But Nicky had said a flat no when they'd asked, so it'd be too weird to change his mind now—not that he wanted to go. Monty might've been up for a drink at the Dugout, the campus dive bar just up the street (they'd gone a few times and Monty had been tolerable), but he had already vanished into the night with Sabrina. Nicky could take advantage of some rare alone time in his room to study or to call Wally or Brad or Pins. Though if they were around to answer their dorm-room phones on a Saturday night they'd probably be as down as he was—and who needed that? He could check in with his parents, but that'd bust open a rat's nest of questions starting with "What's wrong?" so forget it.

After an hour alone in his room zoning out to an old episode of *Mission: Impossible* rerunning on some snowy UHF channel, Nicky tucked in his shirt and crossed the hall. He knocked on Shelley's door, startled when she opened it. She was in a baggy Peanuts T-shirt, pink sweatpants, hair up in a knot, big round glasses, with a thick text-book in hand. Nicky wondered if this was a mistake.

"Oh, my Gawd, Nicky! I look terrible!" Shelley shrieked. "I shouldn't have opened the door! Go away!" She nervous-giggled. "No, I'm kidding!" She sobered, eyed him. "Wait, is something wrong? Aside from how I look?"

Shelley didn't look bad at all, Nicky thought, still surprised at how much he'd underrated her appeal. And there was something to be said for the fact that it was *her* door he knocked on for company. Or was it just because he was bored or anxious and he figured she'd be glad to see him—If she was even in her room on a Saturday night? Which she was, working on a paper for her Introduction to Human Development class. WVBF-FM, a local Top 40 station that announced its call letters with a toilet flush, was playing on her radio. Nicky liked that she wasn't too cool to listen to a song like "Feelings," which was on in all its awfulness.

"Nope, nothing wrong," he answered, still hovering in the doorway. "I just . . . I don't know, I wanted to see who was around."

"I'm around. Obviously," Shelley said, removing her glasses. "The Julies asked me to go clubbing, but I thought I'd feel like a fifth wheel." Nicky was about to say that she couldn't be a "fifth wheel" if she was the fourth person in a group, but didn't want to sound like some kind of word nerd. "Wanna come in?" she asked, unclipping her hair, shaking it out, and letting it fall to her shoulders.

Nicky didn't know much about body language but that hair thing was a pretty smooth move. So, with a mental shrug, he found himself back in the purple room and back on Shelley's bed, kinda turned on and copping those two-handed feels. Shelley was more proactive than before, grinding against him and letting him explore more freely—up to a point.

"I think you know I like you," Shelley said, unlocking her lips from Nicky's. "But I can't, y'know . . . do it with just anybody. I'm not saying you're just anybody but I—"

"It's OK, really. I'm cool," Nicky said, sitting up and getting a sort of déjà vu feeling about the moment—but in a useful sense. It struck him that maybe Shelley was a virgin, too, and that she might get attached if Nicky was her first. For several key and probably misguided reasons, Nicky wasn't worried about the reverse being true, but he *was* concerned about leading Shelley on in any way. That would be wrong—and complicated. Still, that Shelley ended up giving Nicky a hand job through his jeans a few short, overheated minutes later showed an astounding lack of resolve on both of their parts and did little to clarify Nicky's confused state. He was also now a sticky mess and Shelley got quiet again.

"I know people usually go out and *then* come back and fool around," Nicky said, rising off the bed, "but . . . do you feel like going for a drink or something?"

As Shelley thought about that, Nicky wasn't sure if she was going to laugh or cry but ended up doing neither. "Give me ten minutes to change, OK?"

Nicky said to make it twenty, took a quick shower, and, in short order, they were walking into the lights of Kenmore Square in search of a semi-decent watering hole. Nothing jumped out so they kept going up Comm Ave until, just past Mass Ave, they reached a Polynesian restaurant called Aku Aku and Shelley got jazzed about the prospect of a mai tai.

"I got sick on one last year at my cousin's wedding—though it might've been the Long Island iced teas I drank before," she explained in a bad sell job that somehow didn't dampen her enthusiasm.

As they entered and looked for a table in the restaurant's gaudy tiki bar, eyes adjusting to the dim lighting, they saw a familiar twosome chatting brightly over colorful cocktails. Nicky spotted the pair first and thought of exiting before they saw him and Shelley, but he didn't move fast enough.

"Nicky?!" Lori exclaimed as she looked up from her umbrella drink. "And Shelley?"

"Wow, hey guys!" Joe enthused with his best orientation-leader energy. "What are you two doing here?"

Lori shot Nicky a curious grin. "Yeah, what are you two doing here?" She left off the word "together," but it was implicit.

"Following you!" Shelley joked with a loud chuckle. Nicky hoped no one actually thought that was true and shrank back a step.

But Nicky's discomfort was short lived as Joe nimbly pulled two chairs up to their little table and made room for Nicky and Shelley to join them. It was a classy move, and Nicky thought Lori looked relieved to have the company. He and Shelley ordered the requisite mai tais (Nicky had never had one, but when in Polynesia . . .) and toasted Lori and Joe's now-half-empty glasses when their tall, bright-orange drinks promptly arrived.

Explanations were quickly made: After a tasty dinner at the Newbury Steak House ("It had, like, the best salad bar!" Lori gushed; Joe had plainly scored points on his restaurant choice), Joe brought Lori to nearby Aku Aku for a nightcap. Shelley, with appreciated, if thinly veiled discretion, jumped from Nicky's door knock directly to their walk up Comm Ave on bar patrol. Nicky could see Lori filling in the blanks; Joe seemed to take it all at face value.

As the conversation continued and the mai tais kicked in, Nicky thought he noticed a few key things. First, Shelley became extra chatty and flirty around Joe. Meantime, Joe, probably used to the effect he had on women, stayed his usual warm and genial self, showing polite interest in Shelley without losing focus on Lori. This wasn't to say he didn't send Nicky the occasional smile or fraternal wink over his refilled cocktail (a sex on the beach, as it turned out), whatever their purpose. Lori, on her second rum punch by now, seemed unfazed by Shelley, whom she liked and apparently felt no threat from—as she shouldn't have.

For Nicky's part, he felt surprisingly relaxed and glad they'd run into Lori and Joe; the weirdness he first feared never materialized. Maybe for now it was OK to have a bunch of unreconciled feelings about the folks in his little universe—as well as about himself. Still, he found himself hanging on a few too many of Joe's words (he told a harrowing story about his cousin's years-back tour in Vietnam) and staring at both the small cleft in Joe's square jaw and the way his light-brown hair fell in neat, even layers, casually dipping across his forehead. Nicky forced himself to look away before Lori, Shelley, or, God forbid, Joe, caught the direction of his gaze. Moments later, though, Nicky noticed Joe studying *him*, a smile spreading across his face.

"I'm liking the mustache, Nicky," he said as he finished off his second drink. "Looking good, pal."

So much for Nicky's relaxed state, even with that mai tai. Sure, it was OK for *him* to eyeball everyone else, but he didn't want to be the center of any of *their* attention. Not right now. He mumbled "Thanks" and chewed on the pineapple wedge clipped to his glass.

Lori weighed in. "I didn't think I'd like it, because I'll always love the Nicky I met on day one," she effused. "But I have to admit, it's working." She added a warm smile and Nicky melted a bit. He checked Joe's face for any proprietary reaction but there was none.

"It tickles," Shelley murmured into her mai tai, just loud enough for Nicky to hear and, it seemed, the others, who may have pretended they didn't. Nicky swallowed the rest of his cocktail and was about to change the subject until Joe changed it for him.

"So, mustache man, when are we running again? You keep avoiding me, I'll start taking it personally." There was something about his expression, easy as it was, that made Nicky wonder if he wasn't completely joking. The last thing Nicky wanted was to offend him.

"How about Monday morning?" Nicky found himself asking, then realized: "But can you go after nine? I have an eight o'clock class."

Joe grinned, a bit glassy-eyed, and said, "It's a date." Which Nicky found an odd, if slightly thrilling choice of words.

THIRTEEN

OCTOBER BROUGHT WITH it cooler temperatures, the start of foliage season, and increasingly shorter days. Though it wasn't so different from autumn on Long Island, Nicky found himself far more aware of the changes around him and was enjoying the brisker weather and the sweaters and jackets he wore in bulky layers. He even bought himself a navy pea coat that Joe, who swore by his, helped him pick out at an Army Navy store in Cambridge, where they landed after jogging one morning all the way up Mass Ave. (Truth: they only got as far as the MIT campus, then took the T into Harvard Square.)

It had been just a few weeks since Nicky and Shelley's impromptu double date with Lori and Joe, a night that ended better for the latter couple than the former even if the former had more sex that night than the latter. That is, if you want to consider the denim-sheathed hand job that Nicky received "sex." (Nicky chose to, but more for morale than authenticity's sake.) When they returned to 700 from Aku Aku, Lori followed Joe back to his room on 10C—a coveted corner single that he'd nabbed in a one-time lottery situation—while

Nicky and Shelley returned to 14A, but called it a night because both of their roommates had also returned. Not that Nicky needed to spend more time with Shelley—nor, apparently, she with him. (She would later tell Lori that as much as she liked Nicky, she didn't think the feeling was mutual—or at least mutual enough. She was right, it wasn't. But it wasn't her fault. Not really.) Monty and Sabrina, who'd just had a fight over his constant smoking, ended their evening early and Monty actually seemed happy to see Nicky when he rolled in just after midnight. Monty was, natch, sitting there smoking a cigarette.

As for Lori and Joe, they stayed up all night talking and kissing and doing some other first- and second-base things, but the evening was, as Lori was clear to point out, "fluid-free." So, for what it was worth (the answer: not much), Nicky and Shelley beat them on that front. That said, Lori emerged from Joe's room at 5:00 a.m. less equivocal about him than she'd been. "I'd be an idiot not to be into him," she told Nicky the next day. "I think he's really a beautiful guy—inside and out." Which, after Nicky thought about it, wasn't quite the stamp of approval it may have first seemed—like she was talking herself into a relationship. No matter, Lori and Joe saw a lot of each other after that and finally "did the deed" two nights ago.

"It was lovely," Lori reported back, which sounded to Nicky like what she might have said about sex with *him*, not someone she was really hot about. Still, that she offered no further details was (mostly) fine by Nicky, and he didn't press her because he didn't need anything else to horn him up. He also wondered if Joe would mention it to him the next time they were together—they had a run planned in a couple of days.

Since the night at Aku Aku, Nicky and Joe had jogged the Esplanade four times, including that jaunt to Cambridge. Nicky was amazed at the stamina he'd built up and how much more flexible he felt with every stretching session. Joe switched up those exercises each time, but somehow, always included the one where they locked hands and pressed soles. It still sent a flush through Nicky, but he no longer backed away. He tried instead to enjoy the moment, whatever it meant.

Nicky didn't know if Joe was becoming the kind of friend he was hoping for—or if it was even possible. Sure, Joe couldn't have been more fun, encouraging, or easygoing; they joked around a lot and gave each other shit. They'd started talking about more personal, serious things, too. (Joe told him about his dad's near-fatal heart attack a few years before; Nicky talked about his parents' marital rough patch awhile back.) Still, the complicated, more "forbidden" feelings Joe continued to bring out in Nicky kept him too on guard, too self-conscious to fully be himself with the guy. Ultimately, Nicky knew he needed to knock Joe off the imaginary pedestal he'd placed him on so he could feel on more even footing. Or maybe it would just come in time.

"So, I guess you heard—about Lori and me," Joe said as they headed out on the Esplanade that overcast morning.

Was Nicky supposed to know? Had Joe wanted him to know? Did Lori want Joe to know that Nicky knew? Nicky could play dumb with the best of them. "Heard what?"

"She didn't tell you?" Joe asked. *Was that disappointment in his voice?*

"She tells me lots of things—but not *every*thing. Can you be more specific?"

"Well, I guess you could say we took things to the next level."

"Yeah? Wow, cool. How was it?"

"Pretty fucking special, in *my* book," Joe said, with a mix of pride and wonder. *At least he didn't say "lovely,"* Nicky thought.

He glanced at Joe, happily bobbing alongside him. Joe had a faraway look like he was replaying the highlights. Maybe he was. Nicky wanted to explain so many things to him just then: about Lori, about why Joe was sleeping with her and *he* wasn't, about how good—yet also how strange—Joe made Nicky feel, about the hand job Shelley gave him, and how, if he was being totally honest, he thought not only about her silky breasts and soft lips when he was about to come but also Joe's strong forearms and big shoulders. But, of course, Nicky said nothing, just looked straight ahead and tried to avoid falling into any bushes.

A row team blazed across the river on their left. Nicky found himself picking up the pace, almost in time with them, but the rowers sped quickly past. They made it look so easy, but Nicky knew it wasn't—that nothing was. That everything that mattered took work and discipline and focus and good luck and even better timing. And it was up to you to make your life happen. His father tried to tell him that once, in his own ham-fisted way. But Nicky shined him on, thought it sounded like rah-rah, World War II–era bullshit (lance corporal Steven J. DeMarco saw action in Japan and, thankfully, lived to talk about it—which he did a lot). A few years after his dad's lecture, he was seeing the world a little differently. Maybe he needed to tell Corporal DeMarco he was right after all.

"What about *you*?" Joe asked Nicky when they took a break to regain their steam. "When are you going to find *your* Lori?"

I found my Lori, Nicky wanted to say, *and I let her choose you.* "I don't know, maybe she'll find *me*," Nicky said with a wan smile. Joe probably wasn't the best person to have this discussion with, all things considered. Not that it wasn't fair of him to ask. Nicky dropped to the ground to stretch; Joe joined him.

"I thought something was going on with you and Shelley," Joe said as he reached for his toes. "She seems fun."

"She is. She's nice. We messed around a little, but . . . I don't see it happening." Nicky felt guilty that he let Shelley down. She deserved someone better—or at least more enthusiastic.

"She's got nice tits," Joe said with authority. "I'll give her that."

"If you like big ones, yeah."

Joe eyed Nicky like he'd just landed from Mars. "Who doesn't like big ones?"

"Lori's aren't that big." Nicky had no idea where he was going with this.

"That doesn't mean they're not perfect."

"Lori's great," Nicky said, hoping that would cover it. He was getting in over his head here. He jumped up and did a few leg lunges, just like Joe had taught him. Joe looked up with a quizzical look.

"So then, what—you're an ass man? A leg man?" Did Joe mean that Lori had a good ass and nice legs? (She did.) Or was he just asking in general? Nicky really needed to change the subject.

"I'm an equal opportunity admirer, how's that?" If Nicky didn't realize just how appropriate that comment was, Joe certainly didn't. Still, because Nicky always wanted to impress him, he added, "But, yeah, tits, ass, legs . . . I like 'em all."

Joe rose, flashing his sunny grin. "There you go!" He resumed running position, fixing his gaze on Nicky. "She's out there, bud, trust me."

Maybe he was right, Nicky thought, maybe he just needed to find the right girl and all these other thrilling and troubling thoughts would fade away. Maybe Lori, for all her wonderfulness, wasn't really a match for him. Shelley, too. Same for all the first dates and prom dates and fleeting flirtations in high school that peaked early, petered out, or hit dead ends. There was a phrase he'd once heard, probably from some teacher: "nature abhors a vacuum." He wasn't exactly sure what it meant, but it sounded about right for his present, slightly derailed train of thought. *Fill the vacuum and all will be well.*

"Yep, I'm sure she is," Nicky finally responded, giving his words a bright spin, as they fell back into line with each other. The clouds darkened, and a chilly wind whipped up. Rain couldn't be far behind.

"My two cents? You've got more going on than you think," Joe told him.

"What do you mean?"

"That you could probably get any woman you want," he said, picking up the pace. Nicky shot him a dubious look. "OK, maybe not *any* woman. I mean, Linda Ronstadt walks through the door, she's not gonna be looking for you—*or* me."

"What about Susan Dey?"

"Who needs her when we have Lori?"

"*You* have Lori."

"So do you. Just in a different way." A wink. "We're both lucky devils." Nicky didn't know how to respond to that, much less the idea that he could get any woman he wanted—or might want any woman he could get. "Anyway," Joe added, "just trust yourself, okay? And, when in doubt, remember: you grew yourself a pretty cool mustache."

Nick nodded, appreciative, as he worked to keep up with Joe—running-wise, anyway. The rowers were now sculling back in the other direction. Or maybe it was another team. Nicky could watch them all day. Maybe he should take up rowing. If only to build up his forearms. He felt a raindrop. And then a bunch more.

"Wanna keep going?" Joe asked as folks on the Esplanade began to scatter.

"That a challenge?" Nicky answered with a wet, raised eyebrow.

"Only if you want it to be!"

What Nicky *didn't* want was his time with Joe to end so soon, so he gleefully doubled down. "Don't be a pussy, O'Rourke!" Nicky yelled, as if channeling Monty, then raced on ahead with a cackle.

"Takes one to know one, DeMarco!" Joe called. He sped up and passed Nicky, flashing a middle finger as he ran into the rain.

Maybe they *could* have the kind of friendship Nicky hoped for. He just had to keep kicking at that pedestal.

FOURTEEN

TODAY

THOUGH NICK HAD awoken early that morning and easily made his way out for a long and satisfying run, he felt a jolt of jet lag when he returned to his room at the stately Lenox Hotel. He'd arrived from LA yesterday afternoon and immediately attempted, as he did when traveling coast to coast, to convert to Eastern time. This meant, of course, that while the clock may have read 11:00 p.m. when he climbed into his Boston bed, it was still only 8:00 p.m. in his California body. Which, strangely, didn't stop Nick from instantly conking out and enjoying eight uninterrupted hours of sleep. Still, he knew from experience that the second night in a new time zone was harder to adjust to than the first. And, with what he was bound to have pinballing around his head after today's "adventure," any kind of proper sleep might be doubly hard to come by.

Nick had a few hours before he had to leave for his lunch date. He knew he'd need at least an hour to get ready—shower, shave, blow dry, get dressed, change clothes several times (fortunately he brought limited choices), and study the restaurant's online menu—which left him an hour to squeeze in a suddenly much-needed nap. He looked out the window of his ninth-floor corner room, high above Boylston Street, with its view of the iconic Prudential Tower and the many newer (as in, newer since the 1970s) buildings around it. Beyond the Pru sat Kenmore Square and, just past that, the BU campus, which Nick would be visiting soon. He'd looked at recent photos of the school online and though he hoped, for sentimentality's sake, things would look about the same, time had definitely marched on. Still, he was sure he'd find his way around like he'd never left. He set his alarm for ten forty-five (really seven forty-five LA time—*OK, stop that!*), lay back on the cushy king mattress, and shut his eyes.

But he didn't fall right to sleep. He thought about his brief meltdown by the Charles, the anxious kid whose bench he shared, the anxious kid *he* once was, and the anxious older man he could sometimes be. Nick thought about how strange but comforting, how thrilling but mind bending it was to be in Boston again so many decades later. How there was so much water under so many bridges, so much time well spent and squandered, so many people whose lives he crossed and affected and was affected by. And how all of those people—friends, enemies, loved ones, coworkers, strangers— were still on the planet or long gone; taken too soon or granted rich, full, and happy lives.

Nick thought about the twisty, unexpected paths that he'd taken in work and relationships and love and family and where they ultimately brought him—here, at this moment, to this city, to this room, to this bed. And, once again, how today's reunion could either topple Nick's comfortably ordered world or leave it virtually untouched; just another in an endless line of memories—good, bad, and indifferent—that he'd carry into his future and store away for safekeeping. Shit, it was no wonder he couldn't get to sleep.

But sleep he finally did, and it came with a dream. A dream that found him and Lori and Joe—looking like they did in college, though the time was now—rowing a boat together on the Charles. The sky was dark, the water choppy, and sporadic blocks of ice would appear that they'd push away with their oars. But because there was an uneven number of rowers, they couldn't keep their boat balanced, and it threatened to tip over. Dream Nick offered to jump out and swim to the Esplanade so Lori and Joe could row alone and safely reach their destination. But Lori left the boat instead, swam away, and Nick and Joe spent the rest of the dream trying to find her—and couldn't. Nick woke up in a sweat and, for a second, thought he was still in LA until he realized where he was and why he was there. And maybe why he'd had that particular dream.

Nick got out of bed, padded to the well-appointed bathroom, and stared in the mirror over the sink. The lighting seemed especially bright or maybe his eyes had become more sensitive lately. On the other hand, his overall vision hadn't changed in ages—perfect in one eye, slightly less so in the other—not counting those bug-like floaters that showed up one day in his sightline and refused to leave. All in all, Nick thought he looked pretty OK for a man his age (maybe even for someone a bit younger), still rocking a decent head of hair (those willful curls and waves of his youth became tamer over the years), lines and creases kept in check by good moisturizers and SPF 50 sunscreen, his five-eight frame still fairly lean and toned (if you didn't look too closely). Still, he noticed darkish circles and slight bags under his eyes. Were they there in LA or the result of jet lag?

Whatever, no one was expecting him to look like it was 1975—or even 2005. Least of all Nick. And, in the end, despite all the effort, what difference did that make? It was who he was inside that counted. Who he was to his son, siblings, nieces, nephews, cousins, friends, and cohorts. And maybe who he would be—*could* be—to the next person he might fall in love with. If anyone was still out there for him. It took him a long time, a lifetime really, to learn some of the most important, yet most basic lessons. That education began in earnest that first semester of college; morals and patterns and codes and messages that, whether he knew it then or not, would lay the groundwork for so many of his future choices and interactions. And, even at sixty-eight years old (*Jesus, seriously?*), it seemed as if he were still learning every day. Would it ever end?

Nick could only imagine what new life lessons might come his way in less than two hours.

FIFTEEN

1975

MUCH AS NICKY had been wary of being around Joe too much, of the sophomore's mere presence tapping something hidden and disturbing in him, he found that the time they were now spending together—running, chatting when Joe visited Lori, the occasional dining hall meal—was way more enjoyable than unnerving. Joe seemed to want Nicky as a friend, to go out of his way to engage him in activity and conversation, and to treat him like one of the guys. It gave Nicky a new and subtle kind of self-assurance that started seeping into other corners of his daily college life, not the least of which included his classes.

Joe, like Nicky, was a business major, but unlike Nicky, had a well-honed work ethic that placed studying over partying, and responsibility over recreation. You wouldn't necessarily know it, given how much "recreation" Joe seemed to indulge in, though rarely before hitting the books. He was also a quick study, had a knack for numbers, and knew how to prioritize (he called it "putting the lima beans before the lamb chops"). He was also at BU on a partial scholarship, so good grades were a driving force: his dad, a no-nonsense Cincinnati police detective, would gladly send his son to cheaper—and closer—Ohio State instead. (Joe won that fight but it came with strings: a minimum 3.5 GPA.) With a bit of tutoring and the benefit of having taken a few of the same classes the year before, Joe helped Nicky improve his test and paper scores—and maybe even his appreciation for the courses. So, for Nicky, it was a win-win. What, he wondered, was Joe getting from *him* to warrant that extra effort?

"He's a generous guy; he likes helping people," said Lori.

She and Nicky were sitting in a back booth at Deli Haus, a cozy, greasy spoon–style eatery in Kenmore Square that the two had begun to frequent after 10:00 p.m. They'd eat cheap fried or scrambled eggs and toast and drink countless cups of coffee that somehow never kept them awake when they'd go to bed several hours later.

"Or maybe it's kind of a big brother thing," she added, nibbling on a slice of dry rye toast. "He's been a big brother his whole life; it's probably just a habit. A good habit, wouldn't you say?"

"I'm not complaining, believe me," Nicky said as he swallowed a forkful of eggs. "But I feel like maybe I should be doing something in return." He also thought about his real big brother, Richie, and how he needed to be nicer to him; how they'd been so stupidly competitive and prickly with each other for so long. Nicky vowed to give him a call in Buffalo over the weekend.

"Anyway, buy Joe a beer next time you're out and call it even," said Lori. "He likes you, dude. He told me so. Said he 'connects' with you."

"He said that?" Even if Nicky had been feeling that, it was heartening to hear it from someone else.

He wished he could talk to Lori—talk to anyone, in fact—about the other way Joe affected him. He had tried to put those feelings into so many little compartments that he could believe they didn't even exist. But they did, and Nicky still didn't have a clue how to reconcile them. He kept going back to the right-girl-is-all-it'll-take theory but hadn't been doing a lot to find that "right girl"—short of just keeping his eyes open. Even so, it wasn't like many other guys around him, aside from Monty and Joe, seemed to be having much luck in the dating department. (Oh, there *was* a sophomore on 14A, Terrence, an aloof Brit with a Rod Stewart shag and collection of tight pants, who Nicky found in the men's bathroom one morning balling some chick in a shower stall. Though he didn't know if they were exactly . . . dating.) No matter, Nicky figured it was only October and anything could happen that semester.

"I'm still your best friend, though, right?" Lori wanted to know as she sprinkled a Sweet'N Low into her coffee refill. She looked at Nicky with the puppy dog eyes she seemed to save for her most vulnerable moments. He wondered where that was coming from.

"Why would you even ask that?"

"Well, guys like having guy friends," she said. "It's a fact." Was that Lori's way of saying she was envious of him—and/or of Joe? Nicky was familiar with the emotion.

"Sure, but I've always had girl friends, too—y'know, friends that were girls," Nicky said to make her feel better, though it wasn't true. He'd been friend*ly* with a few girls in high school but not what you'd call friends. In any case, however you defined their relationship, he'd be lost without Lori. Which he told her.

Tears welled in her eyes. She wiped them with a paper napkin. "I love you for saying that," she said with a sniffle. "I think you know I feel the same."

He'd hoped so, but once again, it was nice to hear it said out loud. Yet something told Nicky a deeper issue was at work. He took a stab and gingerly asked, "Have you talked to Joshua lately?"

Lori studied Nicky, her eyes filling again. "What are you, psychic?" She managed a smile and busied herself with her eggs. Nicky shrugged (apparently, he *was* psychic) and waited for her to elaborate. Lori looked up from her plate, sighed, and answered. "He called a few hours ago, in fact. He is *such* a fuckhead." But her conflicted look told Nicky that the fuckhead still wasn't a total goner.

Nicky pushed aside his plate. "I still don't get it. What *is* it with you and this guy? He's been terrible to you. He makes you miserable. Why do you spend even five seconds thinking about him anymore?"

And, because Nicky was on a roll, couldn't stop himself from adding, "Plus you have this great, hot boyfriend who thinks you're amazing. It's like, what do you want?!"

Yikes, did he just call Joe hot? He reflexively looked away and buried his face in his coffee cup. Maybe she didn't hear that.

She did. "You think Joe is *hot*?" Lori asked, sounding more curious—as in taking-a-poll curious—than surprised by Nicky's use of the word.

Nicky feigned blasé. "Yeah, he's a good-looking guy. I don't think you need *me* to tell you that." He took a gulp of coffee, then struck the most masculine pose he could think of. (It involved leaning against his seat back, stretching his arm across the top of the bench, and sneering. He was sure he looked ridiculous.)

Five guys and one woman, all dressed like costume-party versions of a failed garage-rock band, noisily entered and crossed to a nearby table. Nicky guessed they'd come from—or were going to—the Rathskeller (aka the Rat), a grungy bar and music club up the street. The woman, with her raccoon eyes, dangly skull-and-crossbones earrings, and jet-black hair topped with a man's fedora, shot Nicky a sly wink and a naughty tongue wag as she took her seat. Lori caught that action.

"Look at you, drawing 'em like flies," she said with a grin. "Must be the mustache."

"Yeah, that's because they're so rare," Nicky joked. He counted eight across Deli Haus alone, and that didn't include those on Fedora's "bandmates."

"Well, whatever, she's got good taste," said Lori.

"I'm sure she was just screwing with me, but thanks." Nicky drained his coffee cup, eyeballed Lori. "Speaking of taste—*bad* taste—you didn't answer me. Once and for all, why are you still so hung up on your stupid ex?"

Lori slumped in her seat. "Joshua's a lot of things, but stupid's not one of them," she finally said. "I mean, he goes to Princeton."

"There's all kinds of stupid, y'know." Nicky wasn't sure why he was pressing this. Much as he tried, it seemed impossible to avoid discussions of Lori's love life—especially with Joe in the picture. "Like him dumping you, for example," he continued pressing.

"Actually? He's now having second thoughts about that."

"What, the Princeton princesses not falling at his feet?"

Silence, then: "He wants us to get back together," Lori said to her hands.

"Are you shitting me?" Nicky said so loudly that Fedora turned around to look.

Lori looked up with a twisted half-smile. "I shit you not. Wants to come up to visit this weekend."

If this were a cartoon, steam would have been coming out of Nicky's ears. "And what did *you* say?"

"What do you think I said?"

"I don't know, but I hope it included the phrase 'go fuck yourself.'"

Lori didn't answer. She looked tired, restless. "Let's get out of here, OK?"

Walking back to 700, Lori revealed that she told Joshua not to come to Boston, that she didn't want to see him, and was happily dating someone else.

"'Someone bigger and stronger and lots nicer than you,' I said, which I'm sure totally pissed him off," added Lori.

"Poor baby," said Nicky. They broke into a song parody called "Please *Don't* Come to Boston," which made them both laugh so much they couldn't finish the first stanza.

When they calmed down, Lori finished her Joshua story: "Anyway, he said that he made a big mistake and wasn't going to give up on me. The. End."

"I sure as hell hope so," said Nicky. "He's not worthy of you."

"Like Joe?"

What was that, a test? "Yeah, like Joe. I think you're both very worthy of each other," he answered.

"And where do *you* fit in?" Lori asked as they passed Aegean Fare, a popular, late-night Greek place that Nicky had been wanting to try.

"How do you mean?"

"I *mean*, how do we all fit in together?"

Nicky still didn't get it. "I don't know, we're all friends. What else?"

Lori wore that same look of mischief and wonder as when she'd invited Nicky out on her first date with Joe. But as she was about to answer, she got diverted by a display in the window of New England Music City. It was for a new record album called *Born to Run* by someone named Bruce Springsteen. Nicky thought he'd heard of him in passing. Or maybe he was mixing him up with someone else. Lori gazed excitedly into the window.

"Let's go in," she said, "I want to get the album. Joe loves this guy. He's from South Jersey, just like me!"

"Joe is from Ohio."

"Not Joe, dummy! Bruce Springsteen!" She grabbed Nicky's hand and pulled him into the store. Lori enthused about the singer—Joe had played her this new record as well as parts of his first two albums—as they worked their way toward the rock 'n' roll bins. "He's pretty amazing. Sings these really big, heartfelt songs. Very intense and poetic. Damn cute, too."

Nicky didn't know how "cute" he was, at least from his album cover, though he did notice the guy had a mop of wavy curls, not unlike Nicky's, so there was that. Unfortunately, *Born to Run* was sold out, so they left empty handed. On the way out, though, Lori spotted a hand-lettered sign over the checkout counter: "Springsteen tickets still available!" It turned out he had a show in Boston a week from Friday. What were the chances?

Lori looked shocked. "I can't believe that Joe didn't mention anything!"

"Maybe he didn't know," Nicky guessed.

"Whatever—we should go! The three of us! It'll be a blast!"

Nicky had to do some quick mental calculus before responding. If they went, it's not like it would be an actual, formal date for Lori and Joe. Concerts were, by nature, communal events, right? And Nicky was closer to Joe now—and to Lori—so it wouldn't be so weird. It *could* be a blast. And Nicky assumed he'd like the music. If Lori wanted to know how the three of them fit together (and the question definitely intrigued Nicky), this could be a way to answer that. Maybe they could be a kind of trio after all. Of course, Joe would have to agree. But, first things first.

"Let's do it!" said Nicky as they exited the store.

"Yes!" Lori yelled to the sky. "I'll talk to Joe and we'll get tickets."

But the next day, when she told Joe the plan, he was a step ahead of her. He'd already picked up tickets for them as a surprise, which was why he'd never brought up the concert. He was going to wait till the night before to tell her. The even bigger surprise was that he'd also grabbed a ticket for Nicky: He wanted to introduce him to his new music idol. He was happy when he heard Nicky was in. As was Nicky when he heard the news. He couldn't wait for next week.

To PRIME NICKY for the big night, Joe invited him to his room to listen to his Springsteen albums. "The better you know the music, the more you'll like the concert," Joe told him with inarguable logic. Nicky's first impulse was to pass. Being alone with Joe in his small, single room seemed a little too intimate for the way Nicky had been feeling, even if he'd become more adept lately at stifling his attraction. That said, he didn't want to offend Joe, who wouldn't even take money for the concert ticket. So, a few nights before the show, Nicky was officially introduced to the singer he would learn was nicknamed "the Boss."

Joe met Nicky at the door of his dorm room wearing jeans and a white V-neck undershirt. He was barefoot and his hair was damp and uncombed. "Sorry, just took a shower," he said, indicating his wet head. Nicky tried not to focus on his host as he entered. Joe pointed to a bean bag chair in the corner. "OK, pal, have a seat— and prepare for greatness." Nicky got swallowed up by the squashy chair as he dropped into it. There was no cool way to sit in the dumb thing. He glanced around the uncluttered room, walls bare save for a Cincinnati Reds pennant and a *Jaws* poster, which reminded Nicky that they'd never gone to see the movie as planned. A healthy pothos plant sat on Joe's desk, just beneath the window. A framed photo of Joe and, Nicky presumed, his brothers and parents, was perched beside the plant, as was a half-melted candle (the place smelled vaguely like vanilla). Fresh laundry was neatly stacked on the bed, waiting to be put away. It was an unremarkable room, and Nicky felt instantly at home in it.

Joe pushed aside the laundry, sat on the bed, and first gave Nicky the lowdown on Springsteen's three albums. He explained how, though the first two didn't get much airplay, they developed a kind of cult following. *Born to Run*, however, would be the artist's break-out album and the "astounding" title song was climbing the charts. Joe predicted this was the last time it would be easy to get tickets to one of the singer's shows. "You're watching music history, man," Joe declared with such infectious enthusiasm Nicky couldn't help but be won over. (Unlike Monty, who was so annoyingly superior about his music crush, Jerry Jeff Walker, that Nicky nearly had to leave the room when his records were on.)

Joe crossed to his turntable, which sat on a built-in bookshelf, and queued up what he considered the best songs from Springsteen's first two albums. Letting the tunes speak for themselves, he played Nicky "Blinded by the Light," "Spirit in the Night," and a rousing song called "Rosalita (Come Out Tonight)." So far, Nicky, hardly a music maven but he knew what he liked, was pretty damn impressed—and told Joe so.

"Just wait," Joe responded with one of his megawatt grins.

He then played Nicky his favorite cuts from *Born to Run*: the title tune (which *was* astounding), "Tenth Avenue Freeze-Out," and "Thunder Road," which sent chills up Nicky's spine. Joe then saved his personal favorite for last, a song he found so thrilling and pow-erful he would only listen to it with headphones—and wanted Nicky to do the same. So he placed the headset over Nicky's ears and intro-duced him to "She's the One," silently watching his friend's face as he experienced the special track for the first time.

When it was over, Nicky only had one word: "Wow."

"Would I lie to you?" Joe beamed again. With that simple, unequivocal response it was as if Nicky had justified Joe's entire existence. At least for that one musical hour in his dorm room.

Joe went on to deconstruct "She's the One," and how he thought Springsteen nailed the pain of falling for someone enthralling and beautiful but unattainable. Of wanting to believe in a lover so badly only to be deceived in the end. He rhapsodized about the song's drum and piano work and how, when combined, it sounded like two beating hearts. In that moment, Joe was deeper and more passionate than Nicky had ever seen him—and he felt an even greater appreciation for the guy.

When Joe finished his speech, he looked stirred, spent, self-conscious. "Sorry, I didn't mean to get carried away."

"No, I get it. It's an incredible song. They all were."

"Right? I can't wait to hear them live."

Nicky watched Joe, his hair now dry and fallen into place, as he returned the Springsteen albums to their covers and slipped them onto a shelf along with his other LPs. Nicky wondered if "She's the One" reminded Joe of Lori. Did he think she was "the one" for him but that he'd end up disappointed by her? Had he been disappointed by other girls? Joe didn't seem like a guy who got disappointed much. Maybe he just liked the song for the song.

And yet, Nicky found himself asking: "What did Lori think of 'She's the One'?"

Joe paused. "She asked if it reminded me of her."

OK, that was weird. "Does it?"

Joe broke into a grin. "Shit, man, I hope not."

That seemed as fair an answer as any.

SIXTEEN

THE BRUCE SPRINGSTEEN concert was life changing. At least that's how Nicky, Joe, and Lori, flying high after the electrifying three-hour show, all agreed it felt as they streamed out of the packed Orpheum Theatre. Sure, their seats weren't great, way up in the balcony of the giant old movie theater turned concert hall. But it was a nonstop party from start to finish as the Boss and his E Street Band played the best of their three albums. "Born to Run," "Rosalita," and, yes, "She's the One" brought the house down, while a medley of high-energy oldies sent the crowd out on an unbridled wave of joy. Nicky had a ball, especially sharing this watershed night with Joe and Lori. For the first time, he felt like they were an actual trio, basking in the magic of the music and the soul-satiating power of such an ecstatic, outsized experience.

As they headed up Tremont Street to catch the last trolley out of the Park Street station, ears still ringing with the thunderous sounds of the concert, Joe threw one arm around Lori, the other around Nicky, and they nearly danced their way to the T stop. They sang—loudly, badly, ardently—a mishmash of Springsteen lyrics, trying to remember every song he played. The raucousness continued on the trolley back to BU—the car was jammed with euphoric concertgoers—so much so that it resembled a kind of rock 'n' roll church on wheels.

Nicky, Lori, and Joe barreled past 700's fourth-floor security desk, flashing their laminated cards and singing "She's the One" as they pointed and bellowed at the startled young woman checking dorm IDs.

Landing in the lobby, still buzzing with residents returning from their Saturday night outings, Nicky wondered if the trio would now be splitting up: Nicky in one direction, Lori and Joe in another. He couldn't imagine his friends wouldn't have some post-concert cuddling in mind; they were clearly all too wired to even think about sleep. But Nicky's question was quickly answered when Joe invited them both back to his room for a little "Springsteen wind-down." Nicky was relieved not to be returning alone to his room, especially if his roommate might be there. (For the record, Monty and Sabrina had long patched up their little rift over his smoking; he was now down to a half-pack a day, and his—and Nicky's—lungs were the better for it.)

If Lori had any issue with Nicky joining them, she didn't show it. On the contrary, she happily clapped her hands and yelped, "Yay!" And they buoyantly made their way to the C-Tower elevators.

Joe's room felt even more intimate with three in the small space. But Joe, the good host that he was, lit the candle, set his desk lamp on low, turned his receiver onto album-rock station WCOZ-FM, and, voilà—it was comfort city.

"Maybe they'll play some Bruce in honor of the concert," Joe said, nodding toward the radio.

"Or—we could just put on an album," Lori suggested. "Why wait?"

"I don't know, with the radio, we could, like, guess which song of his they'll play next. See who's right."

Lori raised a provocative eyebrow. "And what does the winner get?"

Joe pulled out a fat joint. He waved it at the others with a sly look. "Some of this?" Nicky was surprised, didn't think of Joe as the pot type, per se. That is, someone with their own stash (if one joint a "stash" made) as opposed to one who just partook if offered (meet Nicky). It didn't matter to Nicky one way or the other; it seemed like an ideal time to get high, and he was there for it. Joe, seeing a responsive audience, lit the thick doob, took a deep toke, and passed it to Lori. She giggled, sucked in the smoke, and handed it off to Nicky, who did the same. In short order, they'd passed the joint around enough to decimate the thing and leave them feeling enjoyably loopy. And somehow all sitting on the floor. Meanwhile, they'd been listening to one song after another on the radio, but no Springsteen. Though it's possible they'd missed something.

"We should get a bong," announced Lori, as she leaned back against the bed.

Joe had a startled look. "Right now?"

"No, silly. Soon, whenever. They're more . . . what's the word? Official!"

The guys tried to process that. Finally, it dawned on Nicky: "I think you mean efficient."

Lori scrunched up her face, confused. "Isn't that what I said?"

Joe and Nicky traded a stumped look. Neither could remember for sure. Nicky's pal Pins had a bong that they'd sometimes smoked from and it was definitely a more . . . What was the word he'd just used? *Efficient!* Efficient high. Though he had to admit that joint just now was also super efficient. Nicky suddenly felt hugely relaxed and so . . . happy. Or was it the leftover joy still coursing through his veins from the concert? He got lost in his thoughts as he found himself gazing at the vanilla candle, its flickering flame casting shadows against the darkened window that resembled, what—A ghost? A cloud? An eagle? It didn't matter, it looked cool.

When he refocused, he turned and saw Joe and Lori pressed against the bean bag chair, their tongues entwined. Nicky thought they were being pretty quiet about it. About as quiet as two people could be who were making out five feet away. As if they felt Nicky's eyes on them, they stopped, pulled back, and each sent him a hazy smile. They started kissing again. Nicky couldn't stop watching. And that's when Lori drew away from Joe and motioned with her index finger for Nicky to come join them. He didn't know what in the world she could mean. Until she wiggled her finger again and flashed such a warm, loving, and wily look that, even in his current state, Nicky couldn't miss the message. And, if there was even the slightest uncertainty, Joe gave a welcoming nod that got Nicky off his feet and over to the bean bag chair. To do what, though, he was still unsure. Because the scenario that *was* running through his fuzzy head couldn't possibly be right.

Until it was.

Lori leaned in and kissed Nicky on the lips. She lingered there until Nicky kissed her back—as fully and deeply as he had soon after they first met. Lori raked her fingers through his hair and ran her free hand under his shirt. Nicky could feel himself getting hard, partly, he knew, because of Lori's moves and partly because Joe was watching him—calmly, closely, and, it seemed, intrigued. Lori then left Nicky and put her arms around Joe's broad shoulders, rubbing up against him, nuzzling his neck. Joe tilted down to reach her lips and they shared several long, heated kisses that had Nicky frozen in place until something so startling and near-otherworldly happened that Nicky could have been dreaming—and not just high and horny.

"Now *you* two," Lori told Nicky and Joe, wagging a finger between the two guys.

Nicky gazed at Lori, confused. "Now us two . . . What?" He looked at Joe for a clue, but there was none—just a sanguine stare on the stoned sophomore.

Lori nudged Nicky. "C'mon, you know you want to."

"Want to *what*?" he asked. And as soon as the words came out it was like someone whacked him with a sledgehammer. He realized what Lori meant, and it couldn't be even the tiniest bit possible. And, even if it was, how did *she* know that's what Nicky wanted—especially since *he* didn't know? Not exactly. Because attraction was one thing, but action was entirely something else.

The air was so filled with tension, anticipation, and late-teenage lust that none of them even registered that "Tenth Avenue Freeze-Out" was playing on the radio.

Lori crossed her arms and, with an impish grin, told the motionless guys, "That's OK, I can wait."

Though Nicky remained statue-still, Joe seemed to wake from his semi-stupor and grasp that he had a snap decision to make. If only to make Lori happy—or to meet her challenge. Or maybe because, at some improbably deep and curious level, he actually wanted to lay one on Nicky.

"Oh, what the fuck," Joe finally said. He grabbed Nicky in a bear hug and kissed him.

And, in one crazy and fleeting—and maybe weed-fueled—moment, Nicky held on to Joe's solid arm and kissed him back with a force that almost knocked the big guy backward. From the corner of Nicky's eye, he could see Lori watching them with the strangest mix of astonishment and delight. Nicky's trance then broke, and he lurched away from Joe, lost his footing, and landed with a thud on the bean bag chair.

"Now *that* was hot," said Lori.

From the look on Joe's face—more placid than pensive—Nicky couldn't gauge his reaction to what just happened. For Nicky's part, he felt both mortified and intoxicated. And a little out of his mind. Then Joe finally spoke.

"I think we made a mistake," he said with gravity.

Nicky felt his stomach sink. Of *course* he'd think what they did was a mistake! In what universe could he possibly think otherwise? Nicky, beside himself, but still awfully buzzed, was about to apologize—or at least say *something*—when he heard Joe's voice again.

"The joint was supposed to go to whoever guessed which Springsteen song they'd play!" Joe exclaimed.

Lori cocked her head. "That idea didn't make much sense, y'know. The doob was already yours—So *what* if you won? And if Nicky or I won, it's not like we wouldn't have shared with everyone. We should've come up with another prize."

All at once, they realized that Bruce was on the radio.

"Oh, my God! 'Tenth Avenue Freeze-Out'!" Lori shrieked.

They grooved to the tune, singing and dancing in place. And then it hit Nicky: *That* was the song he guessed. Lori had picked "Born to Run" and Joe went dark horse with "Backstreets." When he reminded them of that, they each whooped and high-fived Nicky. Joe added, "My man!" then pulled a second, smaller joint from a dresser drawer, and handed it over.

"You win. Yours to keep!" Joe said with a woozy smile.

Maybe he had an actual stash after all, Nicky thought, to no particular end. He thanked Joe, then waved the doobie in front of him and Lori. "Seconds, anyone?"

It was coming up on 3:00 a.m. and it was safe to say that no one was making very good decisions. And that included smoking more dope. Which they did anyway. And, though they were exhausted and completely out of it, they carried on a bunch of inexplicable conversations, laughed their heads off, laid waste to whatever Joe had that passed for food, and seemed to completely forget that, just an hour before, they'd all spent time in each other's mouths.

Until someone, Nicky couldn't remember who, suggested they all fool around again. And, even though Nicky felt like he was floating through most of it, he was still aware of how stupendously turned on he was. Certainly more than he'd ever been. By a mile.

What happened after that was a blur. But, when they all woke up much later that morning—Nicky draped over the bean bag chair, Lori and Joe passed out atop the bed—Nicky was floored to remember that he and Joe had both had sex with Lori. And, impossibly, each other.

Which meant that he'd finally lost his virginity. Twice.

SEVENTEEN

"**Where the hell** have *you* been?" asked Monty, sounding like some angry dad who'd waited up all night for his kid, when Nicky slinked back to their room around eleven. He was praying his roommate would be gone by then, maybe out with Sabrina on some Saturday morning jaunt. But no. He was sitting at his desk, cigarette smoldering in an ashtray, Jerry Jeff warbling about cows and broken hearts or whatever, textbooks open for some early-weekend studying. And a scowl on his neatly bearded face.

"I told you yesterday, we went to see Bruce Springsteen." Nicky pulled off his pea coat and sweater, tossed them on the bed. He checked his reflection in his dresser mirror. *Yikes!*

Monty agreed. "Jesus, you look like total crap. What was it, a fifteen-hour concert or something?" He eyed Nicky like a K-9 dog in search of drugs, then narrowed his gaze. "I think Nicky was a naughty boy. Am I right?"

The easy answer would have been: "You have no fucking idea." But since Nicky still only had a partial handle on the events of the last eight hours or so, it was too soon to leave himself open to Monty's surefire follow-up questions. For a self-serious cowboy, Monty liked his share of gossip, especially when it came to his floormates. *Well, not now, pardner!*

"Use your imagination," Nicky flippantly told him. His head was pounding, his eyes were bloodshot, and his mouth was like an ashtray made of sandpaper. He felt grungy, sticky, and a little dizzy, and probably would have just curled up on the floor in a ball if his stupid roommate wasn't there. He decided to take a long, hot shower instead.

"You went with Lori and Joe, right?" Monty asked, taking a drag off his Marlboro. Though he might as well have said "You *fucked* Lori and *blew* Joe" given his smarmy intonation (and he wouldn't have been far off). Or maybe Nicky was just feeling leftover paranoia. Christ, he smoked enough pot to make *six* people paranoid. Or maybe he was feeling a boatload of Catholic guilt and shame—and even fear—over how out of control he'd been. And, if he were being totally honest, over how much he may have enjoyed it and what it all may imply.

"Yeah. The concert was amazing," Nicky finally answered as he grabbed his shower gear. "I think even *you* would have liked it." He didn't mean to sound condescending; he was actually giving Monty the benefit of the doubt.

"The guy's OK," Monty conceded. "I've heard a couple of tracks on the radio."

"Since when do you listen to the radio?" Now *that* was meant to sound condescending. Nicky had taken his share of shit from Monty about what he called his "Top 40 radio taste," so turnabout was fair play.

"It might have been in Sabrina's room," Monty mumbled as he stubbed out his cigarette. God forbid it might have been on purpose. Like he would stoop to turn on a radio himself!

OK, enough. Nicky needed air—and soap and hot water—so off he went, leaving Monty with his textbooks and suspicious mind.

As Nicky stood in the shower, steamy water pelting his chest, he tried to replay what happened in Joe's room. It was a jumble of images and sensations, tastes and smells, sounds and motion. It was rapture and release. It was Lori's soft, blissful warmth and Joe's breathtaking solidness. Or was it? Nicky wished he had been more present, that he could've better judged his actions and reactions. Yet, if they weren't all so zonked, would they have ever crossed those fateful lines—much less together? And Nicky and *Joe*? How in the fuck?

The trio had been mostly silent when they woke up and slowly focused on where they were and what they'd done. There were no smug grins or sly stares. It was as if each of them were gauging the others' thoughts and feelings before committing to their own. A few things were evident: they weren't exactly proud of the evening's, uh, climactic activities, but they weren't sorry either. Still, it had definitely taken them off guard—to say the least. Any objective observer of the three, though, might say it couldn't have been a *total* shock. From the start, there were signs pointing to this moment—however and whenever they would get there.

Bit by bit, words became sentences, and Nicky, Lori, and Joe decided it'd be best to deconstruct their actions when they were clearer and perkier. They each went around quietly collecting random bits of clothing and food wrappers and neatening up the room. Joe cranked open the window, and Lori tucked in the bedspread. Nicky hand-swept corn chip crumbs off the bean bag chair. Nicky and Lori straightened themselves up as best they could, bid muted goodbyes to Joe, and stumbled out. They rode the elevator to 14A in silence. When they reached their floor, Lori gave Nicky a quick hug, said she'd see him later, and crossed to her room. Nicky stood there, watching her go. It felt like a lifetime since they'd been in the Orpheum Theatre watching the Boss tear it up.

Nicky didn't expect Joe to want to instantly discuss their experience. God knows Nicky didn't want to; he had his share of processing to do. But he *was* surprised that Lori—forthright, chatty, free-thinking Lori—didn't jump into postmortem mode, at least with Nicky. And yet, for as well as he knew her, he also knew she had a few mysterious corners (her hang-up with Joshua, for one). But who didn't, when you came right down to it? Nicky did—and Joe obviously did.

As Nicky began to shampoo, and the fog continued to lift, the sex he'd had with both Lori and Joe—as well as what, like some stoned pervert, he'd watched *them* do together—became sharper in his mind. And still, it seemed like an out-of-body experience—or, better yet, an experience with someone else's body. A double whammy out of some bisexual *Penthouse Forum* fantasy that bizarrely, mind-bogglingly, came to life. Speaking of which, was he? *Bisexual?* Was there even such a thing? Didn't you have to pick a side? In truth, he knew so much less about sex—real, live sex—and sexuality than most people who might've gotten themselves into such a sophisticated pickle.

Despite all the graphic, showboating, and too often clueless conversations he and his buddies Wally, Brad, and Pins had over the years about sex, Nicky could now admit he never really thought much about the mechanics of intercourse, much less the finer points of his role in it. If he was being completely truthful, he rarely thought much below the waist when it came to women. And whatever it was he may have felt toward men, he never considered what he would physically do about it, up close and personal. Early that morning, he experienced a crash course in all of it and, from what he could recall, most of what he did came pretty naturally. Whether he was any good at it was another story.

Back in his room, more revived and focused, Nicky realized he was starving. He couldn't remember the last thing he ate, but he knew it was crap (*Fritos? Twinkies?*). Yet the thought of going down to the dining hall and getting lunch made him queasy. So he had another thought.

He threw on his running clothes, told Monty he'd see him later, and was out on the Charles River Esplanade in a matter of minutes. It was chillier than the day before, but the late October sun was high and bright in the sky. There were whitecaps on the water from the bracing wind and more families and kids dotted the riverbank than usual. Nicky dispensed with any stretching exercises (coach Joe wouldn't be happy) and began to jog in long, measured strides toward an amphitheater far in the distance. He'd stop well before he reached it, as he and Joe always did, but at least it provided a focal point. *It's not the destination, it's the journey.* Isn't that what they say? Or maybe he'd seen it on a bumper sticker. He'd have to think about that.

In any case, Nicky was surprised at the energy he was able to summon, especially given how little sleep he'd had and the lack of fuel he'd consumed. Over the weeks he'd begun to match Joe in speed and endurance; Nicky's smaller, leaner frame seemed to give him an edge over Joe's bigger, brawnier body—at least when it came to running. Whatever, he had Joe to thank for the inspiration to get off his ass and get in some real exercise. Nicky wondered: if he'd been as motivated in high school, could he have actually developed his track skills beyond gym class? And then, in mid-thought, also like when he ran during gym class, his stomach suddenly rebelled— big time. He quickly detoured off the path and puked into a pair of scrubby bushes. It felt almost symbolic. He stood there a moment to collect himself, then took a long, cleansing drink from a nearby water fountain. Nicky, better now, eased onto a bench and popped a Wint-O-Green Life Saver he found buried in a sweatpants pocket. As Nicky gazed out at the river, lost in thought, he heard a familiar voice.

"Hey, there's no rest for the wicked, big guy!"

Nicky turned to face Joe, who was standing over him, grinning, jogging in place, cucumber cool. Like they hadn't just had the wildest night of their lives. Though maybe for Joe it hadn't been. Nicky was obviously missing some vital information.

"Is that what I am? Wicked?" asked Nicky. His eyebrow was slyly raised, but it was an earnest question.

"Depends how you define it." Joe dropped to the bench next to Nicky and gave his thigh a friendly slap.

Nicky eyed Joe, who'd clearly also just showered and shaved. He looked as sturdy and handsome as ever, and Nicky could feel the familiar stirring that had sent them both into overdrive just a few short hours before. It all still seemed so intensely surreal. Nicky looked away from Joe and back at the Charles. No rowers out today on the choppy water.

"So, hot shot, you running on your own now?" Joe asked.

"I guess I could ask you the same," Nicky tossed back, still facing the river.

"Actually, I knocked at your door to get you, but Monty said you'd already left. Then he looked at me kind of funny. It was a little weird."

"Oh, that's just his natural expression: everyone's guilty till proven innocent." Nicky turned to Joe, conceding, "He bugs the shit outta me, but he's not so bad. Just don't tell him I said so."

"Well, the guy must have *something*. That Sabrina's a sweetie."

Silence set in, and they both stared back out at the water. Nicky needed to talk but wasn't sure where to begin. Joe slapped Nicky's leg again and leaped up.

"C'mon, let's go!" he said, waving Nicky onto the running path. Then, seeing Nicky's pensive look, gently added, "We'll get into things later, OK?"

They did finally talk after they finished their run. (Nicky admitted to Joe he'd barfed and might need to take it easy, but their jog was surprisingly healing.) Joe stopped and faced Nicky as they reached the base of the Storrow Drive footbridge.

"So was that your first time?"

There were a few first times to address, so Nicky picked one. "What, doing it with another guy's girlfriend while he watched? Yeah, that was a first."

"I know. That was nuts."

Nicky lowered his voice. "More nuts than you and me getting it on?"

"That's actually what I was asking. If you've ever been with a guy before?"

Nicky shook his head in response, unsure whether to be embarrassed that it was his first experience with a guy—or that it was with a guy altogether. He decided to turn the tables. "What about you?" Nicky asked as they started up the footbridge.

"It's not like I talk about it or anything," Joe began. "I mean— *y'know*." He sent Nicky an atypically cautious look. "But, yeah, I've been with some dudes. A lot more women, but . . . look, I can't explain it. I don't, like, *pursue* it but . . . well, shit happens."

Of course it does, just look at you, Nicky thought, still shocked that someone like Joe could have a single gay bone in his hot body. "I don't get it," Nicky admitted. "Any of it, really."

"Maybe there's not that much to get. Maybe it's just—whatever gets you hard."

"OK, but it's got to be more than that. The world sure seems to think it is." Nicky didn't know a ton about the topic, but he knew guys "like that" were outcasts where he came from: targets of bullying, the butts of jokes. People spoken of in hushed tones and with rolled eyes. Someone's "bachelor" uncle or "different" cousin. "Artsy" types. Despite his vague—and not so vague—longings, Nicky had never thought of himself in anything close to those terms. But admittedly, he'd never looked any deeper than what his eyes took in. Until now.

"Sure, for some people it's like this—what's the word?—taboo," Joe responded. "This big deal. For me? It's just another way to get off." He gave his sexy nod to a pretty blonde bicycling toward them. She eyed him back. They always did.

Nicky wondered if he should take offense at Joe's comment—not that he could ever really be offended by the guy. But Nicky did what he did with Joe *because* of Joe, not for some random sexual experience. He could say the same for what happened with Lori, no matter how out of it he may have been at the time. At any rate, Nicky had to ask Joe what he'd already asked himself: "So, you'd say you're, like, what . . . bisexual?"

"I'm not a big fan of labels. Whatever, I try not to think about it."

"How can you not think about it?"

"I said, I *try* not to. Anyhow, what did the hippies say? If it feels good, do it? Right now, that sounds about right." Joe gave Nicky a fraternal shoulder punch as they exited the footbridge. "It's like, didn't you ever jerk off with any of your buddies when you were younger? You didn't get all serious about it—you just *did* it."

What?! Nicky could no sooner picture himself sitting around beating off with Wally, Brad, and Pins—or any other kid he knew— than he could see jumping off the Harvard Bridge. "Yeah, I can't say I ever did that," he informed Joe.

"Really? Maybe it's a Midwest thing. Though I doubt it," he said with a sly smile. As they turned up Comm Ave, Joe asked, "I have another question for you: Would you do it again? What we did?"

That caught Nicky short. Despite all the noise in his head, he hadn't considered if an encore with Joe was in the cards. Nicky assumed it was a one-time thing. A unicorn event brought on by too much dope and a side order of concert mania. He wondered what Joe wanted—or expected—to hear. Forget that, what did Nicky want? He glanced at his good-looking friend, recalling their heated encounter as best he could, taking in his faint scent of Aramis.

"Yeah, probably," Nicky answered as breezily as he could.

"Cool," said Joe. "Race you back to the dorm."

So Nicky did.

EIGHTEEN

WHEN NICKY RETURNED to his room from the run, he found a thick red rubber band twisted around the doorknob. That was Monty's alert that he was "occupied" with Sabrina and that 1406 was off-limits to his roommate until further notice. (It was also Nicky's signal should he ever choose to use it.) "Christ, it's two in the after-noon!" Nicky accidentally said aloud, as if the timetable for sex were restricted to late nights and the wee hours only.

"If the boat's a-rockin', don't come knockin'," said Chuck, who'd overheard Nicky's exclamation as he crossed to his and Ken's room two doors down.

Nicky didn't know if that was one of Chuck's frequent song-lyric responses or some sexual phrase he'd never heard of. But either way, he got the point.

"If you need a place to study, there's an open desk in our room—cub reporter Jimmy Olsen is out on assignment," Chuck told Nicky, wryly referring to Ken, who had just started writing for BU's *Daily Free Press*.

"Thanks, Chuck, but all my books are in there," Nicky answered, pointing to his currently impassable door. He also wanted to get out of his sweats and sneakers but that would obviously have to wait as well.

"In that case, want to watch *The Music Man*? It comes on at two thirty. It's, like, my favorite musical. My TV's only black and white, but the songs are still the same." Chuck struck a pose and sang something about a pool table and trouble in River City.

Nicky assumed it was from the movie, which he couldn't remember if he'd ever seen all the way through. "I think I'll pass, but thanks, Chuck." He almost said yes because Chuck looked a little lonely, but Nicky figured he'd be better off seeing if Lori was around. He felt kind of weird that he and Joe had discussed "it"—to whatever extent they actually had—before he and Lori could revisit their . . . what? Their three-way? Their three one-ways? The sheer impromptu craziness of those few hours?

"OK, well, watch out for the Wells Fargo wagon!" Chuck warned with a grin as he moved off for his room. Nicky liked Chuck, thought he was a decent guy and seemed really sincere, but half the time he had no idea what he was talking about. Much less singing about.

Lori was, in fact, in her room. Though it took her longer than usual to answer her door when Nicky knocked, like she had to run down a flight of stairs to get there. She admitted she'd been dozing for the past hour or so after taking a shower and drinking a cup of instant coffee. Her hair hung limply on her shoulders, still slightly damp; she was free of last night's makeup, party outfit, and, it seemed, free spirit. She looked, in a word, exhausted. Nicky felt a ripple of guilt and shame surge through him. And also worry: that he'd somehow ruined the unique and special friendship he'd developed with Lori. But his concern was misplaced. Yes, she was tired, but not angry or disappointed in Nicky. Or Joe. Or even herself.

"And you shouldn't be either," she told Nicky as they sat in their usual spots across from each other atop her bed. "I've wanted us to be together that way for as long as I've known you," she admitted, her unblemished face open and tipped up toward Nicky. "But I wasn't sure what you wanted, how you felt. I mean, yeah, we made out and whatever that first week, but most guys would have . . . what's the word? Persisted, I guess." She studied her long, tapered fingers.

"Well, I'm not like most guys," Nicky answered, sounding more defensive than jaunty, even if he was going for the latter. Yet, there was a lot more truth to his comment than he might have thought a mere twenty-four hours ago—before he had sex with his best friend and her boyfriend.

"You, my dear, are *not* like most guys. And that's why I'm crazy about you." Lori may have been trying, but she wasn't making this easier on Nicky who knew he was avoiding the elephant in the room—as well as the one clomping around his head.

Before he could respond again, she continued, "But if I'm being totally real here, the thought of being with you was less about sex and more about closeness." She paused and smiled for the first time since he'd walked into the room. "Not that I don't find you attractive. I think you know I do."

Nicky was about to ask why but didn't want to seem needy or obtuse. Instead, he repaid the compliment. "And I think you know I find *you* attractive," Nicky said, because he did. But there was also a knee-jerk quality to his reply. It felt a bit empty. He realized right then and there that he cared about Lori, that she was beautiful and kind and loving, but that he didn't have to sleep with her again. It was like, he *would*, but he'd also be OK if he didn't. He was pretty sure he knew why—and, apparently, so did Lori.

"But you find Joe more attractive," she said, looking Nicky straight in the eye, matter-of-factly, without judgment.

"Why do you say that?" He met her gaze, then added, "Does it have something to do with . . . what you and I did last night? Like, could you tell or something?"

Lori took Nicky's hand. "Oh, Nicky. Last night—this *morning*, whatever—was beautiful. Being with the both of you . . . well, it'll never happen again." She let go of Nicky's hand. "I was so wasted. We *all* were. So, I don't really remember all the specifics. But I *do* remember that you were completely . . ." Lori paused to find the right words as if knowing whatever she said would be imprinted in

Nicky's head forever. "Well, it was like you'd done it a lot. That's what I thought to myself."

Wow, that was a surprise. "Fooled you, huh?" They shared a warm smile. "But not about Joe, I guess." Nicky couldn't believe he was actually admitting his feelings about the guy. It was a relief to tell Lori, to be able to trust her just then. To trust her with such a sensitive and difficult and daring confession.

"At some level, I think I've always known." She smiled. "I can't say I blame you. Joe's a hunk and a half."

And then it was Nicky's turn at some intuition. "But he doesn't really do it for you, does he?"

Lori rose off the bed, picked up a brush from atop her dresser, gazed into the mirror, and started brushing out her long hair. "Why do *you* say that?" she finally asked.

Nicky sat up straighter, watched as Lori's hair regained its luster. "Because you never seem all that excited about him."

She turned from the mirror, looking almost apologetic. "Because honestly? He's not that exciting."

Was she talking about *Joe*? Because he was the most exciting guy Nicky had ever known. Though he also knew his definition of the word might be a little different from Lori's.

It was as if Lori could see the disappointment on Nicky's face, like a kid whose favorite superhero had just been criticized. She put down her hairbrush and gently sat back on the bed. "Joe is fun and sweet and, I think, a way more decent guy than most—present company excluded, of course." That made Nicky smile. "And, yeah, he *does* have that great face and body," she added with a sly grin. "But beyond all that he's kind of . . . predictable."

Now Nicky leaped off the bed. "Predictable? Really? Did you ever predict that he might be bisexual? Because I sure as hell didn't." Nicky didn't predict that he himself was whatever he was either, but he'd clearly been living in oblivion. He considered Lori to be a lot savvier than he was. And yet.

She looked up at Nicky, hovering above her. "I didn't mean predictable like that, though I can't say I was a thousand percent surprised. He talks about you an awful lot, y'know."

"He does?" Again, unpredictable. Nicky felt a buzz in his groin and flashed on Joe's chest and arms and . . .

"Besides," Lori continued, "I don't know if one dip in the man-on-man pool—especially while stoned out of your gourd—makes a guy bisexual."

That sounded fair and logical, but Nicky knew better, only because Joe had obviously revealed a truth about himself to Nicky that morning by the footbridge that he'd withheld from Lori—and understandably so. Not that Joe was bisexual, if that's what he was (*"I'm not a big fan of labels"*), but that he'd done stuff with other guys beyond Nicky. Knowing that Joe let him in on that particular slice of his private life made Nicky feel fleetingly superior and special. Until it began to feel hugely disloyal to know something so important about Lori's boyfriend that she didn't. Not that he could tell her and betray Joe's trust. Nicky wondered if it would make a difference to Lori either way; she seemed extraordinarily cool about—what did she call it?—*the man-on-man* of it all. Not to mention sleeping with two guys at once. Or at least one right after the other. He looked out the window, wondered what Joe was doing right now.

Lori rose and crossed to her shelf of LPs. As she flipped through a few albums, trying to decide which one to play, she turned and asked: "So how does it feel?"

"How does what feel?" Nicky replied, hoping no squishy Cat Stevens music was in the offing. Not now, anyway. There was enough soul-searching going on.

"To be bisexual." Lori slid Eric Clapton's *461 Ocean Boulevard* onto her turntable.

Nicky was starting to understand Joe's "no labels" thing. He turned away from the window. "What happened to 'one dip in the pool' and all that?"

"I was talking about Joe then, not you."

A song called "Motherless Children" began to play. Nicky didn't think he'd ever heard it, but he liked it. Lori sat in her desk chair. Nicky leaned against the windowsill, his arms crossed.

"What's the difference?" he asked. Lori stared patiently at Nicky, like she knew something he didn't. Nicky didn't know what to say so he took a stand. "I don't think I'm bisexual. I'm not even sure what it means. Y'know, beyond the obvious." The obvious *what*? What was he even talking about? Nicky glanced at Sabrina's lava lamp, the pinks morphing into reds and oranges. It was never the same, always changing.

Lori: "So then, what, you're gay?"

Nicky whipped his head around to face her. "Jesus, I'm not *gay*! What's wrong with you?" Bisexual was an unnerving enough thought. But gay? He was going to get married one day, have kids, coach Little League. Like every guy. Most guys. OK, most nongay guys. And maybe most non-bisexual guys, though who knew on that one.

"Don't get weird, I'm trying to help you!" Lori put her hands up in surrender.

"How is this helping me?"

Lori considered that for a moment, seemed a bit lost. Or maybe just overwhelmed. Or tired—so tired. She plugged in her hot pot and sighed. "Look, we don't have to talk about this. About any of this. Let's just put it to bed for now." Which, of course, made them both giggle. The giggles turned into guffaws. It was silly and cathartic and thankfully broke the rising tension.

"Want a cup of coffee?" Lori asked when they settled down, pointing to a squat jar of Taster's Choice.

"You wouldn't have any Swiss Miss, would you? Shelley had a bunch of it. Or at least she did awhile back."

"Would you rather hang out with Shelley?" Lori shot him a wry grin.

"I don't think so. She's been pretty quiet around me lately."

"That's because you broke her little Long Island heart."

"That's so not true. If anything, she backed away from *me*."

"Because she didn't think you were into her enough."

"Yeah, well," was all Nicky cared to say on the subject. "Anyway, it worked out for her OK, don't you think?"

Shelley had just started seeing some guy on 8A named Brent or Trent. They'd met in one of the 700 elevators when it broke down with them in it. Apparently, Shelley was claustrophobic, and this Brent or Trent went into full hero mode and talked her off the ledge until the elevator doors finally opened. (Shelley said they were stuck for twenty minutes but, turned out, it was more like five.)

"They've had a total of two dates, so no one's picking out china patterns just yet." Which was Lori's sneaky way of saying that Shelley still liked Nicky if he ever wanted to jump-start things—a long shot getting longer by the minute.

Nicky migrated back to the bed. Lori stayed in the chair, monitoring the hot pot. They were quiet for a bit until Lori broke the silence.

"College is a time for experimenting, right? Maybe you're just experimenting."

Nicky liked the sound of that. It was filled with leeway. "You think?"

"It's possible. And it's also possible you go both ways. Which, when you think about it, isn't the worst thing." Lori's face lit up with an impish grin. "Gives you double the chance for romance!"

"I doubt it's as simple as that."

Lori's smile faded. "Yeah, I know." She unplugged the boiling hot pot and spooned coffee crystals into a pair of flowered ceramic mugs. "I forget. Milk *and* sugar?"

"Just milk. I'm sweet enough as it is," Nicky retorted in tribute to his cranky dad, who always said that in jest. One of Stevie DeMarco's rare instances of self-awareness.

"I have to say, you don't seem too freaked out about having the hots for Joe." She pulled a milk carton from the mini-fridge and poured. "And, y'know, acting on it."

Nicky realized she was right. As bewildered as he was, he was handling it with . . . well, he was handling it. "I'm probably still in shock," he half-joked. They shared a careful laugh, both knowing, in the end, this was serious stuff.

Lori handed Nicky his coffee, and he nodded his thanks. "So

where does all this leave you and 'predictable' Joe?" he asked, still stunned over Lori's chosen adjective for the guy.

"I'm hoping exactly where we were." She sat back on the bed with her own steaming mug and eyed the baffled Nicky. "Don't look so surprised. I'm lucky to be seeing someone like Joe."

"But you said—"

"What I *said* was just an opinion. Not a deal breaker. There are worse things than predictability. And, I can be exciting enough for the both of us!" Lori's lips curled into a smile. "Plus, I don't know if you've noticed, but he smells really good."

Nicky thought it best not to admit he was aware of that, so he gave a vague half nod, half shrug and said, "Good, I'm really glad to hear that, Lori." And he was, because part of him just wanted things to go back to how they were before, when life was just a tad less complicated. He swallowed some instant coffee; it tasted like hot blandness.

Lori gazed into her mug, turned serious. "Though, while Joe and I *are* dating, I'd rather not have to compete with anyone for his attention, y'know . . . romantically." She looked up and eyed Nicky with love and a kind of steely resolve. Was she talking about attention to Joe from another woman—or from him?

The shudder that went through Nicky made him know that she meant him. And that she meant business.

NINETEEN

LEAVE IT TO Shelley and Chuck to be the ones to plan a 14A Halloween party. Nicky hadn't realized it, but the two of them had become buddy-buddy recently, bonding over what he had no idea except maybe a shared love of exuberance. It wasn't romantic, Nicky knew that much. (He didn't know what kind of woman he'd pair Chuck with but it wasn't Shelley.) Besides, Shelley was apparently getting cozier with Brent or Trent. And, according to Lori, who'd heard it from Sabrina by way of Julie (Pressman, not Elkins or Ohanian), after their last date they'd "semi-slept together." Nicky took this to mean a hand job for Brent-Trent *without* his pants on, but it was just a guess.

Anyway, most of 14A, at least all the freshmen (even cynical Monty), were excited about an All Hallows' Eve bash—it didn't hurt that the holiday fell on a Saturday—and spent the days leading up to it trying to outdo each other with costume ideas. Nicky, who'd always thought Halloween was a little stupid (was anyone *really* frightened by any of it—except the thought of kids eating candy collected from potentially sadistic strangers?), tried to get in the swing of it and faked enthusiasm for everyone else's enthusiasm. Still, once he found out that Lori had invited Joe, Nicky began looking forward to the night for real. It would be the one-week anniversary of their fateful fling—not that any celebrations of *that* would be in store.

The past week had been kind of a mindfuck for Nicky once the extent of his when-it-rains-it-pours virginity loss sunk in. (When he'd joked with Lori about being in shock, he didn't know just how true that was.) There was a ton to ponder, of course, things that made him feel happy and relieved but also discombobulated. Finally being with a woman—and passing the "performance" test— was hugely gratifying, no matter where it led. What he did with Joe, however, opened a Pandora's box of possibilities that worried the crap out of him. It also made his pulse race and his skin flush. He found himself slyly eyeing other guys—in the dorm, in his classes, in the library, on the street. He didn't know what he was looking for or what he would do if he found it, but he felt emboldened, freer. He received more outward response when he'd check out a passing woman—the coy smile, the approving nod, the shy head turn. And he was doing more of that now as well. Either way, Nicky began to believe that he had more to offer than he'd thought.

And it must have shown because even Monty, that sultan of self-absorption, took notice one night while he was polishing a pair of boots. "What's going on with you, man?" he asked, eyes fixed on Nicky, who was blithely humming "Bungle in the Jungle" as he lingered in front of his dresser mirror.

"What do you mean?" Nicky replied as he hand-combed his hair this way and that, thinking his long, loose curls were finally start- ing to work on him. They were looking cool with his mustache, which he was still amazed had come in so well. Even his biggish nose seemed to be fitting his face better. There was character to it, strength. (Forget that his mother had been telling him that his whole life; it finally made some sense.) He'd also noticed his legs and upper body had tightened up and gained some definition from all the running.

Monty grabbed a soft rag and began to massage the rough boot leather. "You act like you're either high half the time or you just found out some dead relative left you a million bucks."

"I wish. The second part."

"Did you get laid and not tell me? 'Cause that wouldn't be OK."

Nicky turned from the mirror. "I didn't realize we signed a contract." *I also didn't realize we were actually friends*, Nicky wanted to say. But maybe he'd misjudged that.

Monty looked hurt. "Whatever, dude." He returned to his boot polishing, silent.

Nicky felt bad, almost bad enough to fill Monty in on (some of) his adventures. But then he remembered that Monty rarely shared any intimate details of his and Sabrina's relationship, so the guilt quickly passed. Besides, no one in Nicky's life beyond Lori and Joe—and only because they'd been there—could ever know about his burgeoning secret side. End of story.

Strangely, or maybe not, Nicky had had no further conversation that week with either Lori or Joe involving sex—of any kind. And that included during three dinners, two lunches, one late-night Deli Haus visit with Lori, and an extra-long morning run along the Charles with Joe. It was almost as if Lori and Joe had made a pact to put the mini-orgy behind them and clean the slate. Or maybe there just wasn't much more to discuss. Nicky would beg to differ, but he wanted to seem cool about it all—or at best discreet. So, aside from a few unreturned verbal serves, he kept quiet on the subject and talked with them about everything but.

Meantime, Lori and Joe had had a couple of get-togethers without Nicky. So, they seemingly picked up where they'd left off, which was what Lori had said she wanted. And, apparently, it was also what Joe wanted. Nicky wondered if Joe were still talking to Lori about him, as she'd said, "an awful lot." And if he were, what it meant, if anything. It didn't matter; Joe was Lori's for now and, for Nicky, that was OK—it had to be.

THE HALLOWEEN PARTY was an unqualified hit. But that was mostly because, due to popular demand, it morphed into a three-floor bash, spreading up and down the stairwell from the all-female 13A to the all-male 15A. This commingling dramatically increased the odds of romantic success for the folks of 14A, if that were on anyone's agenda. If it weren't, it was still a great way to get to know people they may have only seen in the dining hall, in the elevators, or at the mailboxes. And, as costume parties always proved, it was easier to be yourself by pretending to be someone else. (Or, as in the case of many of the getups, some*thing* else.) Booze and weed helped.

Nicky hadn't put on a Halloween costume since his early trick-or-treating days when he wore the flimsy monster and superhero kinds that came in a store box. You'd end up seeing myriad versions of yourself going door-to-door, but at least those prefab guises took the guesswork out of dressing up. And really, who cared what you wore as long as you came home with twelve pounds of candy? But the stakes were higher now and Nicky had to—wanted to—come up with something clever.

Lori and Joe, who were going as Fred and Wilma Flintstone, invited Nicky to join them as Barney Rubble. At first, that sounded fun. But then Nicky realized he'd just end up dressing like Joe, who was bound to look way better than him in a loincloth—and who needed those comparisons? So, Nicky made up an excuse and went back to the drawing board. He thought about other TV characters (Herman Munster? Gomez Addams? Batman?), politicians (Abe Lincoln? Richard Nixon?), and musicians (Elton John? Alice Cooper? A Beatle?). But those kinds of transformations felt like a shitload of work; his interest in the event went just so far.

In the end, Nicky opted to go as a Woodstock-style hippie, once he was sure Sabrina, who was halfway there all the time anyway, had a different thought in mind. (She and Monty—or probably just Monty—decided to dress as a pair of country-western singers, far more of a leap for Sabrina than her Jerry Jeff-crazy boyfriend.) With the help of an old *Life* magazine that he dug up at Mugar Library, a visit to a Kenmore Square thrift shop, and some creativity he wasn't aware he had, Nicky showed up to the party looking like he had just fallen out of a flower-powered VW Microbus. Lori said he looked sexy, and Joe nodded at him in approval. Though, as Nicky predicted, it was those two, in their revealing cave-people duds, who truly turned heads, especially Nicky's. Looking at the beautiful couple, it was astounding to think he'd actually had sex with both of them.

Another pair who got its share of attention was Shelley and Chuck, who came as Bonnie and Clyde—only in reverse. Chuck made a fetching Bonnie in a blonde wig, tan beret, and a slouchy skirt-and-sweater set; Shelley had on a dark, three-piece men's suit, a white shirt and tie, and her hair tucked under a tall brown fedora. They both held plastic tommy guns and wore dastardly sneers. Two things instantly jumped out to Nicky: how at ease and confident Chuck seemed in women's clothes and that *he* was Shelley's partner for the night and not Brent or Trent. Had she and her new guy ended things before they'd barely started?

"We're young, we're in love, and we kill people," shouted Chuck, paraphrasing the *Bonnie and Clyde* movie poster. He struck a pose with Shelley, their guns hoisted high in the air. They didn't look as hot as Lori and Joe, but they sure were having a good time.

As was Nicky, who had downed two quick beers from a keg in the front hallway and felt loosened up before any weirdness could creep in.

Meanwhile, music blared from a stereo set up at the 14A elevators, with rotating "deejays" flipping albums and spinning old 45s, including themed hits like "Monster Mash," "Frankenstein," and "I Put a Spell on You." Partiers danced—or attempted to—wherever there was sufficient space, which became harder and harder to find.

Sabrina, seeing Nicky's hippie garb, ran back to her room and returned with a colorful string of love beads. She hung them around Nicky's neck to complete his groovy outfit.

"There, now you're perfect!" Sabrina enthused. Her hair was piled high, and she wore a jeans skirt, a sparkly denim jacket, and lots of lipstick and eye shadow. Nicky didn't know which country singer she looked like—if any—but it was a noble effort, clearly on Monty's behalf.

"Nicky's already perfect," Lori told her with a wink at Nicky. She and Joe had come up behind Nicky and Sabrina, beer cups in hand.

"Yeah, almost as perfect as me," Joe joked, sending Nicky a conspiratorial grin.

Nicky could feel himself blush. "I paid them to say that," he joked to Sabrina, who seemed to be assessing the Nicky-Joe-Lori dynamic. Nicky wondered if Lori had said anything to her roommate about their post-Springsteen activities.

A Western-hatted Monty found his way to his fellow country music star, and put a proprietary arm around her narrow waist. He was smoking a cigarette, but not as a costume prop. (Nicky wondered if it was part of his daily allotment or if Sabrina was even still enforcing that; she seemed unfazed.) Oh, and Monty had his guitar slung over his shoulder, which, if there were a contest, would have won him heaviest costume. He eyeballed Nicky.

"Somp'un tells me you don't like my kinda music, you hippie freak," Monty jeered with a pretty spot-on Southern drawl.

"You got that right," Nicky shot back with a grin. Monty was kidding, Nicky wasn't.

"You look cool," said Monty, back to his own voice. "I may have underestimated you."

Gee, talk about a backhanded compliment. "That makes two of us," said Nicky lightly, staring at Monty over tinted granny glasses.

"*Never* underestimate yourself, bud," Monty replied with gurulike authority. "Leave that to others."

Nicky wanted to tell his obtuse roommate that he meant he underestimated Monty—not himself. Even if both were actually true. But Monty and Sabrina had swept off by then, Monty's guitar banging people left and right as he went. Not that anyone noticed: the costumed crowd was getting sillier, rowdier, and drunker as the minutes ticked by. And that included Nicky, who found himself in a string of increasingly incoherent conversations with folks from his floor (including the three Julies, who were all dressed as Little Red Riding Hood) as well as people he didn't know from floors thirteen and fifteen—and likely wouldn't remember he ever spoke to.

One chat Nicky knew he would recall was with Chuck, aka Bonnie Parker, who had stashed his/her tommy gun somewhere and was double-fisting beer cups. Nicky commended Chuck on how well he was pulling off his gender-bending outfit.

"Yeah, why put yourself in a box, y'know?" Chuck said, with a knowing look. "Everyone needs to be who they are." It sounded a bit like Joe's "not a fan of labels" comment, if more thoughtful and committed. But was Chuck saying he liked wearing women's clothes or . . . what? Nicky was confused, so he decided to ask.

"Women's clothes?" Chuck replied with a raised eyebrow. "No." He indicated his costume. "This is just for fun. It was Shelley's idea, anyway. But it *is* fun." He slugged some beer. "Anyway, that's not my thing."

"What *is* your thing?" Nicky asked, unsure what possessed him to push it, aside from the beers that had relaxed his tongue.

Chuck eyed Nicky curiously, maybe cautiously. "Y'mean, aside from knowing the lyrics from every Stephen Sondheim musical?" Nicky shrugged; he only knew about the composer from Chuck's frequent gushing about him. Chuck backed up into a corner of the hallway, just out of earshot of the revelers; Nicky followed. Chuck studied him a beat.

"I don't know why, but I feel like I can trust you," he said quietly.

Nicky didn't know why either, but he'd recently learned the value of keeping a secret. "You can."

Chuck took a deep breath. His glossy red lips parted only enough to whisper: "I'm pretty sure I'm . . . not heterosexual."

All things considered, Nicky shouldn't have been surprised—yet he was. "Really?" Chuck nodded. "So . . . what, then? Are you gay?" Nicky spoke gently, tentatively. He might as well have added, "I'm asking for a friend."

"Look, no one knows. Except Shelley, I told her. And a few friends from home. Ken has no idea, though—unless he guessed it or something. And I'm still not sure why I told you." He stared at Nicky. "I hope we can still be friends."

That struck Nicky smack in the heart. How shitty that someone as nice as Chuck would have to even wonder that. But Nicky knew that's how it was. And it only reconfirmed that, not unlike Joe, he had to keep his personal life personal. He never wanted to have to ask anyone what Chuck had just asked him.

"Sure," Nicky told Chuck. And then, because he thought he saw a tear forming in Chuck's eye, added, "Thanks for telling me."

Chuck nodded again, appreciatively. He swiped at that tear with the back of his hand, then forced out a smile. "I better go find Clyde. He gets into way too much trouble without me." And Chuck disappeared into the crowd. If you can say that a six-foot-tall guy dressed like Faye Dunaway could disappear.

TWENTY

NICKY HAD DUCKED back into his room to change his shirt after some joker from 15A spilled an entire cup of beer on him. It wasn't on purpose, but the guy was totally crocked and literally walked right into Nicky, who now smelled like a brewery. Nicky switched into the thrift shop top he'd picked up as an alternate: a wide-collared paisley pullover that he'd worried might be too ugly even if that was kind of the idea. He stripped off the soaked shirt, wiped himself with a hand towel, then slipped on the paisley number. Still reeking of beer, he grabbed a can of Right Guard and sprayed it down his shirt and under his arms to mask the odor. He did a hair and mustache check in the mirror and was about to leave when there was a knock at the door. Nicky didn't know if some drunk bastard had just fallen against it or if he had a visitor. Wasn't everyone he knew in the hallways or the stairwells right now?

One of those people stood in the doorway when Nicky opened up. It was Fred Flintstone.

"Where's Wilma?" Nicky asked as Joe wobbled in.

"I don't know, I think I lost her." He'd clearly had a few too many but who hadn't by then?

"That's because there are so many women out there in a loincloth," Nicky deadpanned. He flipped the lock on the door more out of habit than necessity. Or so he thought.

"Mind if I sit down?" Joe asked as he plopped onto Nicky's bed. "I'm a little beat." He gazed across at Monty's side of the room. "Does Monty have, like, maid service or something? It's so fucking neat." Joe added, more to himself: "He doesn't *look* that neat."

"Yeah, he likes things just so. He gets pissed if I leave even a pair of socks on the floor. It's kind of a pain." Nicky wondered what Joe was doing there and if he was drunker than he seemed—or less so. His loincloth seemed to be covering less chest now, though Nicky couldn't tell how that happened. Joe caught him checking out his shoulders.

"Like what you see?" he asked, then grinned and flexed a bicep. Nicky looked off, embarrassed. He kind of wanted to get back to the party, or what was left of it. Somehow unexpectedly being alone around a bed with a semi-blitzed, half-naked Joe was a lot right now, even if the scenario *had* frequently crossed his mind the past week. In his fantasy, they got it on. In reality, all Nicky saw was Lori's angry, hurt, and disappointed face. And a giant STOP sign.

"Did you really lose Lori?" Nicky asked.

Joe didn't answer, just stared at Nicky. "You changed your shirt," he finally said.

"Yeah, some guy dumped his beer on me."

"Who was it? I'll punch his lights out!" Joe threw a lame punch at the air and almost fell off the bed. OK, he was maybe as drunk as he seemed.

"Relax, tiger, it was just an accident." Nicky cringed. *Tiger.* He couldn't believe he used that word. It was Joe's word—and sounded so much better out of his mouth. But Joe didn't seem to think so. His lips curled into a grin.

Joe leaned his head against the wall and looked like he was ready to conk out. Nicky didn't want him falling asleep in his room, didn't want to have to explain to Lori or Monty or whoever. Even if nothing to explain happened.

And then, as if someone plugged Joe in, he bolted up and off the bed, and stood in front of Nicky. Suddenly, they were nose to nose. Well, more like Nicky's nose to Joe's chin, but they were mere inches apart. Hippie to caveman. Joe swayed a bit as he eyed Nicky. Nicky, heart drumming, studied Joe: his stubbly face, crinkly eyes, the faint freckles on his nose, the pulsing vein in his neck—and felt the familiar pulling toward his handsome friend. Joe, decidedly in sync, took Nicky's head between his hands and drew him in for a kiss. Nicky tried to resist, if only out of duty to Lori, but, at that heated moment, his resolve didn't stand a chance.

Nicky tasted the bitter tang of beer, felt the firmness of Joe's jaw, as they locked lips and went exploring. Nicky grabbed Joe's broad, bare shoulders; Joe pushed up against Nicky's stiffening dick with his own responsive assets. Nicky knew what would happen next—what happened the last time with Joe—if he let it. And even though he was less drugged now and more conscious of his actions, he felt unable to control himself. And it seemed the same for Joe.

Until they heard the key in the door.

Nicky and Joe broke apart so fast it was like they'd been electrocuted. And, just as Monty and Sabrina were about to enter, the guys flew into separate spots—Joe sitting up on the bed, Nicky perched on his desk chair—and struck as innocent and casual expressions as their racing pulses would allow. Monty and Sabrina, a little drunk and giddy, looked startled to see Nicky and Joe and, it seemed, were trying to caption this picture. Nicky prayed he didn't have any beard burn on his flushed face.

Before Nicky or Joe could find words, Monty gave a sly cackle and said, "Sorry, guys, didn't realize the rubber band was on the doorknob."

Nicky got up, calmer now, and threw him a look. "Very funny. We were just leaving."

Joe also rose. "Yeah, I drank too much and had to crash for a minute. Door was open. So."

"Why was our door open?" Monty asked Nicky in a flinty tone, as if worried someone might've stolen a pair of his prized boots.

"Had to change my shirt. Who are you, Boston Police?"

"Just asking. It's my room, too," Monty said, backing down, maybe for Sabrina's benefit.

Sabrina cast a dubious look at Nicky and Joe. "If the door was open, why was it locked just now?"

Nicky never thought of Sabrina as the most aware chick on the planet, but this was definitely her Perry Mason moment. Before Nicky could concoct an excuse, Joe coolly jumped in: "I must've locked it. Force of habit. Like I said, I was pretty out of it."

"Are you OK now?" Sabrina asked, back to her kindly self.

"Yeah, I'm good. Thanks. Might even have one more beer left in me!" Joe flashed his most disarming grin. He could've sold sand in the Sahara.

"Have fun, you two," Nicky said to Monty and Sabrina as he and Joe made their exit.

Back in the front hallway, the party winding down, Nicky and Joe traded a look, one of relief mixed with satisfaction. And, of course, shared secrecy.

"I'd better go find Lori," Joe said, glancing around for his girlfriend.

"Look, Joe, I think we—"

Joe put up a hand. "Let's talk another time, OK?"

The elevator opened and a bunch of noisy folks in costume streamed out. A woman dressed like a sexy Catholic schoolgirl gave Joe the once-over. "Nice legs," she said, with a flirty smile.

"Thanks, back at you," Joe said, more politely than seductively. She eyed him with interest as she moved off with her friends. Joe turned to Nicky and shrugged his big shoulders: *What can you do?*

"Yeah, I know," Nicky said dryly, "you're irresistible." Which, let's face it, was true. And if anyone understood, it was Nicky. It may have been the only thing he truly understood about Joe. "Look, can I just ask you one question?"

"Nicky, really, like I said, can we—"

"Do you ever do this—what we did—when you're not drunk or high?" Nicky asked, quietly, carefully. They were suddenly alone at the elevators.

"Yeah, sure. Sometimes."

Nicky stared at him. Wanted more. Wanted a real answer. Joe could tell.

Joe looked around again. When he was sure they were still alone, he whispered, "Look, I know I kinda sloughed the whole thing off last time we talked. And I didn't mean to sound like a dick—but it's really complicated. I feel weird and guilty when I do it. I promise myself it's the last time. But then I do it again. And it feels great—until it doesn't."

That made a lot of sense to Nicky, and he told Joe so. He also told him what Lori said about not wanting to compete for Joe's attention, meaning, he assumed, affection. And how Nicky really didn't want to deceive his best friend, even though he just did.

But before Joe could respond, Lori swept up with the three Julies, all of whom seemed to have lost their red riding hoods. "There you are!" Lori said, flinging an arm around her cave husband. "I missed you!" She gave him a showy kiss. He returned it in kind. *Better to throw her off the scent*, Nicky thought. Or was Joe just really practiced in his duality? Nicky also thought the four women looked pretty out of it at this point—high on Halloween, among other things—or maybe everyone had just had enough. The stink of beer, pot, and sweat blanketed the hallway. The music had stopped, but the turntable still emptily spun, records strewn all around it. A ceiling light flickered eerily, a signal from the ghosts of 700 to call it a night.

"So, what happened to you guys?" Lori asked, fixing her glassy eyes on Nicky and Joe. There was nothing suspicious in her voice, more like a concerned mom keeping track of her family.

"Oh, Nicky and I got roped into a game of beer pong upstairs," Joe answered without skipping a beat. Nicky was impressed by his instant creativity (and, again, wondered how often he had to put it to use).

"What's beer pong?" asked Julie Ohanian.

"It's like ping pong with beer. And cups and stuff," Nicky swiftly replied as if he'd invented the thing. "It's stupid," he added, for color. The women seemed convinced.

"OK, well, I think this Flintstone is ready for Bedrock," Lori punned off the TV show's fictional town.

Joe pulled her in for a sideways hug. "Good one, Wilma."

And suddenly, Nicky was left alone by the elevators—the Julies scattering to their respective rooms and Joe following Lori to hers. Nicky wondered how long Sabrina would be with Monty; Nicky was sleeping in his own bed tonight no matter what.

A FEW NIGHTS later, over 11:00 p.m. eggs and coffee at Deli Haus, Lori told Nicky that she and Joe didn't sleep together after the Halloween party, even though Sabrina had never returned from Nicky and Monty's room. (The couple was conked out by the time Nicky got back—no rubber band was on the doorknob—so he just crawled into bed and hoped for silence. Which, luckily, he received.) Nicky didn't ask Lori why she and Joe had a chaste sleepover or why she felt the need to tell him about it, beyond the fact that she told him so many things. (Nicky had given up on *not* being Lori's sounding board; she was, despite some select omissions, his as well.) He just nodded in understanding and signaled the waitress for a second coffee refill.

It took a circuitous path for Lori to get there—a rehash of the Halloween party ("Oh, and if you're wondering why Brent wasn't there with Shelley, his great-aunt died and he had to go home for the funeral"), another diatribe against her creative writing professor ("I think he thinks the crueler he is, the better the chance I'll sleep with him"), and an update on her parents' divorce ("They're still fighting over the house—and our dog")—but she finally landed on the big news.

"And, oh, guess what?" she said, spreading jam on her wheat toast, "Joshua's visiting this weekend." Her look was neutral, hard to read.

"Wait, visiting *you*? Here? What for?"

"He said a Princeton friend was driving up to Boston to drop off a car or something, so he thought he'd tag along."

Nicky processed this as he swallowed the last of his cheese omelet. "I'm confused. I thought you told him not to come to Boston, that you didn't want to see him, and that you were happily dating someone else. I think most of that's a quote."

"I did. But he's coming whether I'm going to see him or not, so it's different."

"What are you talking about? He wouldn't be driving all this way if you weren't here."

Lori sighed, studied her plate. "I knew I shouldn't have told you."

"You knew you couldn't *not* tell me."

"That's true," she admitted, looking up with a wry half smile.

Nicky wanted to back out of this discussion, knowing Lori would do whatever she wanted—or thought she wanted—no matter what he said. But he couldn't help himself. "Where's he staying?" Nicky asked tightly.

Lori paused, then: "I don't know, we didn't get that far." Nicky shot her a dubious glare. She visibly squirmed. "Well, he's not gonna stay in a hotel. That'd be ridiculous. And expensive."

"What about the guy he's driving up with? Where's he staying?"

"With his parents. Out in the suburbs. He's from here." Which was Lori's way of saying Joshua would be staying with her.

"What about Sabrina?"

"Stop asking questions, OK? I wouldn't be surprised if Joshua changed his mind and didn't show up at all." Which she and Nicky both knew would not be the case.

"Fine, whatever. But I'm allowed one more question," Nicky asserted. Lori didn't argue.

"What about Joe? Did you tell him yet?" he asked.

"I just found out myself," Lori said, dipping a toast crust into her over-easy egg yolk. "But I will. I mean, of course I will." She chewed the soppy crust and added, "He'll be fine about it. He'll understand."

"Yeah? What makes you say that?"

"If I can understand the fact that he likes to be with the occasional guy, I'm sure he can deal with my ex coming for a strictly platonic visit." Before Nicky could reply, she looked squarely at him and said, "Which it will be."

Nicky had a few more questions, but let them go. He wanted to be a good, supportive friend but also wanted to protect her. And maybe even Joe.

THAT FRIDAY NIGHT, sometime after Joshua's unseen arrival earlier that day, Nicky and Joe took the T to a second-run theater in nearby Brookline and finally saw *Jaws* again. Nicky thought it was as good as the first time, maybe even better. Though that could be because, afterward, they went back to Joe's room. And what happened was anything but platonic.

TWENTY-ONE

Today

LUNCH WAS SCHEDULED for twelve thirty at a place called
the Kenmore, a pub-eatery located, of course, in Kenmore Square.
Despite some enthusiastic Yelp reviews, Nick didn't know if the
food would be any good; the online menu showed the standard bar
offerings: burgers, fish tacos, chicken wings, nachos. The Kenmore's
website dubbed the fare "elevated" and "locally sourced." Just what
the world needed: elevated chicken wings. The menu also featured
craft and artisan beers, cleverly named cocktails, and a modest wine
list.

Not that it mattered. Nick didn't pick the spot located at
476 Commonwealth Avenue for the food. He chose it because it was
the site of the old Deli Haus, where Nick had had about a thousand
late-night drinks and snacks over the three years in which he'd lived
in dorms near Kenmore Square. (His senior year he shared an apartment on upper Comm Ave in Brighton, though still often found his
way to the beloved diner.) And even though Deli Haus had been
more Nick and Lori's place than Nick and Joe's, he couldn't resist the
"for old times' sake" of it all. And it was as close as he could get to

eating somewhere that was around when he was a student since, as best he could tell, none of his BU-area haunts from back then still existed.

Nick was running late, so instead of walking as he'd planned, he took the T two stops, from Copley Square to Kenmore Square. It still seemed like a fairly safe and efficient form of travel—and riding it was such a blast from the past. He flashed on the last-trains-out he'd taken so many weekend nights in college, coming back from bars and movies and concerts, as well as parties on other campuses. Looking around at his fellow passengers now, it seemed like the usual week-day mix of businesspeople, students, senior citizens (*Yikes, was he considered one?*), lone wolves, and a few skeevy types. In that regard, it hadn't changed so much from the old days, just a more diverse sea of faces and lots more tattoos (and not just on the younger riders).

Once out in Kenmore Square, Nicky felt a crisscross of familiar pangs. Sure, it looked different—better, slicker, some might say; gentrified beyond a doubt—and, like Deli Haus, the businesses had all changed. So many of the structures, too. But there was the Citgo sign, now an official Boston landmark (*Wasn't it considered kind of tacky back in the day?*), looming high above him, blinking LEDs where there once was neon. The sign was everyone's trusty guide back to Kenmore Square and the BU campus, especially at night. Nicky knew it sounded dramatic, but it was like seeing an old friend.

Speaking of old friends, he was just minutes away from his reunion with Joe O'Rourke, the object of his anxiety. Nick hadn't seen Joe for decades, had had little communication from him beyond the occasional Like on Facebook and a two-word annual birthday greeting. (Joe was essentially a social media ghost: never posted, only observed, and used an ageless avatar as a profile photo.) Nick sent him an email now and then with updates on his life, work, family, health, and so on. Nothing in great detail but enough to offer a sense of Nick's changing world over the many years. Joe would respond with something brief and upbeat but impersonal; he let on little about himself or the day-to-day of things. What Nick did know was that Joe became a successful controller for a string of midsize companies—apparel, insurance, medical—and moved from city to city as his jobs required. He had no children, as far as Nick was aware, and had a series of romantic relationships (again, few details), including one early, three-year marriage that was, apparently, complicated.

About a month ago, out of the blue, Joe had emailed Nick that he would be traveling from his current home of Charlotte, North Carolina, to Boston in late September for his nephew's wedding (his second marriage, as it happened) and asked if Nick might have any interest in meeting up with him "where it all began." You could've knocked Nick over with a Q-tip. He'd probably asked Joe three dozen times over the decades to get together for a visit—either at Nick's in LA or wherever Joe was living at the time—but would never receive a response. Not even an "I'll let you know." Nick never pushed it, would just try again in his next email, usually many months later. But it was always in vain. He did sometimes wonder if Joe—outgoing, charming, beautiful Joe—had become a loner or, worse, an eccentric. After all, everyone gets at least a *little* quirky as they age, so it was possible. Even for a onetime golden god.

When Nick reached the Kenmore, he could feel the smile spread across his face. The entrance, still several steps down from the sidewalk, looked about as no-frills as Deli Haus's once did, yet a welcoming feel remained. What he wouldn't give to snap his fingers and be back sitting across from college-era Lori inside that divey old diner, listening to stories about her dating life, the profs she loved and hated, the endless wranglings of her parents' divorce, and all the other things—from the profound to the profoundly silly—that they shared over plates of cheap eggs and bottomless cups of coffee.

He also wished she could be there today with him and Joe—what a kick that would be! But he'd have to settle for Joe alone. Wait, "settle?" Hardly. As antsy as Nick was, he couldn't wait to lay eyes once again on the man who changed everything so many years ago.

Nick took a seat at one of the high pub tables against the Kenmore's back wall and, awaiting Joe's arrival, felt his heart race. Just like it did that thrilling first semester at BU.

TWENTY-TWO

<u>1975</u>

Despite Lori's prediction, Joe didn't exactly "understand" why she was spending the weekend—any part of it—with the ex-boyfriend who'd caused her so much angst. "Either she's done with the guy or she's not," Joe said to Nicky on the ride over to Brookline to see *Jaws*. "And if she's not, that's cool, but I'm not sure what it says about her and me." He faced Nicky. "What do you think?"

What could he say? "If I had to guess, I think she has unfinished business with Joshua. And, who knows, maybe if she can deal with him face-to-face, she can finally get rid of the jerk." When Nicky saw that Joe didn't look convinced (and understandably so, Nicky was just making shit up), he added, "And maybe *then* she'll be able to commit more to you."

"That's a lotta maybes, son," Joe said as he stared out the trolley window.

"What if they really *don't* sleep together? Would that make you feel better?"

Joe turned to Nicky with an incredulous look. "Don't be naïve."

"But she said—"

"I know what she *said*. I'm just being real here."

Nicky wasn't being naïve. He, too, doubted Lori's willpower, if not her intentions. There *was* something malleable about her. But he wanted Lori and Joe to stay together, to continue what they'd started, and to keep their trio with Nicky going as well. He felt weirdly secure in their little bubble and didn't want it to burst.

Still, it didn't completely surprise Nicky that Joe put the moves on him when they returned to his room for a beer after the movie. Watching *Jaws* seemed to recharge Joe, return him to his more cheery, optimistic, energetic self. He didn't mention Lori again the entire trip back to 700, nor for the rest of the night. At some level, Nicky couldn't help but wonder if Joe's advances toward him were a reaction to Lori's weekend visitor; a bit of passive-aggressive retaliation. Or was it, as Joe had bluntly first explained his interest in guys, just "another way to get off"? Nicky never considered Joe a petty or vindictive person. Far from it, in fact. He seemed too relaxed, too even-keeled to get all that worked up about most things. For Nicky, he was just genial "Joe Hello" from that first day in the elevator (with, OK, maybe a few surprises up his sleeve); not some manipulative, self-absorbed dude with an agenda. He hoped he was reading his friend right.

Nicky wasn't proud of his lack of self-control around Joe, especially when here he was questioning Lori's resolve with Joshua. (Not to mention his unspoken "noncompete" pact with Lori that he'd embarrassingly blown to bits.) He may not have known exactly what he was doing in this mostly uncharted territory, but Nicky found himself so drawn to Joe that, frankly, all bets were off. And this time, the sex—sober, aware, deliberate, consensual—confirmed for Nicky that he enjoyed it and wanted more. That being with a man was terrifying, but not horrifying. Anything but. And that, despite his Catholic upbringing, he wouldn't burst into flames or be struck by lightning because of his actions. Not that he'd be shouting any of this from the rooftops. That hadn't changed—couldn't change.

He also learned things about his body that he never knew—frankly never thought about—as well as a lot about someone else's body. Which isn't to say Nicky's limited experiences with the opposite sex weren't also physically enlightening; making it with Lori just the one time was definitely instructive, baked as he may have been. No matter, Nicky still had questions for himself *and* for Joe, now more than ever. But, after about an hour's worth of urgent, athletic bone-jumping, as they were unwinding in bed, Joe had a question for Nicky.

"Are you OK?" he asked with concern.

Nicky was moved. He sat up. "Yeah, thanks. I'm more than OK. This was great."

"OK, good. I'm glad. And yeah, it was pretty great." Joe rose and slipped on his briefs, which had landed on the floor along with the rest of his and Nicky's clothes.

Nicky watched admiringly as Joe got into his jeans and threw on a T-shirt. Joe turned, caught Nicky's gaze, and flashed a knowing grin. "OK, tiger, enough for tonight. I still want to get in some studying."

Tiger. That word still got to Nicky. He didn't want to go yet but didn't want to seem needy. So, he steeled himself, jumped out of bed, and gathered his clothes. Joe turned on a light and lowered the radio—album-rock station WBCN-FM, which he'd had on high to muffle any incriminating sounds—as Nicky started dressing.

"How about you?" he asked Joe. "Do you still feel 'weird and guilty'? Y'know, about all this?"

Joe considered that. "Not really. Actually, I feel . . ." He mulled some more. "Maybe it has something to do with you."

Nicky felt his face redden as he buttoned his shirt. "Yeah? Like how?" He wasn't fishing for a compliment; he was genuinely curious.

"Maybe because we were already friends. Most of the other times have been with strangers, or guys I barely knew."

"Except the kids you used to jerk off with," Nicky said drolly. He still had a hard time imagining that.

A faraway look crossed Joe's face as he straightened out the messy bed covers. "We didn't know what we were doing back then, but it was fucking exciting."

"I'll bet you knew exactly what you were doing."

Joe gave an inscrutable shrug and sat back on the bed. "Then, little by little, everyone started dating girls. And then *that* was exciting."

"Did you have a lot of girlfriends?"

Joe raised an eyebrow. "Do you really want to talk about that now?"

Nicky finished tying his sneakers. "Not really. But I *do* have one more question."

"Shoot."

He wasn't going to ask, but he needed to know. "Was tonight about Lori in any way?"

Joe weighed that. "Like what? Revenge? For hanging out with her ex?" Nicky gave a small nod. "There are simpler ways to get back at someone. Don't you think?"

Now Nicky wasn't sure what to think. "So . . . is that a no?"

Joe hunched forward on the bed, looking earnest. "Nicky, tonight was about you and me. About having some fun." He added, his tone hardening, "And look, I know you worry about Lori. About her feelings. About hurting your friendship. And I get it. I'd never want to hurt her either. But trust me, she's tougher than she seems."

Nicky didn't know about that last part but had to let it go. He eyed Joe as he started for the door and wondered: If he'd just slept with a woman, wouldn't he give her a kiss goodbye? A nice hug at least? This was all so strange. Hot, but strange. "Well, I'll see ya," Nicky finally said with a half wave.

"Hey, want to run in the morning? Meet me out front, like, ten?"

It was too tiring to think about just then but, of course, Nicky said yes. He was barely out the door but couldn't wait to see the guy again. He hoped he wasn't going insane.

UNBEKNOWNST TO NICKY or Lori, Monty and Sabrina had taken off that Friday afternoon for an impromptu weekend on Cape Cod to celebrate their two-month anniversary, a milestone Nicky would have never seen coming for the seemingly mismatched pair.

He didn't discover the note Monty had left for him until after midnight when he returned from Joe's; Lori found Sabrina's message (written in hot pink marker on their door pad) around dinnertime, just before Joshua's arrival. Though it was good news for Nicky—a whole weekend without the ol' buckaroo!—it was an awkward surprise for Lori. She was counting on Sabrina's overnight presence to thwart any romantic shenanigans Joshua might have in mind. (Sabrina had promised Lori she'd sleep in their room both nights in solidarity; she'd obviously had her own share of dick boyfriends.) It turned out Lori was more serious about a hands-off visit with Joshua than Nicky or Joe had given her credit for. And that Sabrina was less reliable than Lori had expected, though, in fairness, the getaway, Lori would later learn, was a last-minute surprise from Monty.

All by way of saying that, while Joshua was reportedly a total gentleman his first night alone with Lori, he turned full-on octopus their second night together, and sweet-talked the susceptible Lori into a "one more for the road"–style sexual sendoff.

"I hate myself," she told Nicky at Deli Haus that Sunday night during a weekend postmortem. She was scarfing a cheeseburger and fries which, to Nicky, didn't seem like a good sign for the always-weight-watching Lori. "I am such a loser. Such a spineless fucking marshmallow."

According to Lori, she and Joshua had a perfectly fine Saturday, calmly talking through their past issues while sightseeing around Boston: Copley Square, the Public Garden, the Freedom Trail (they were particularly impressed with the State House and the Old North Church), Chinatown, and the Italian North End. Joshua apologized profusely for breaking up with her, said it was selfish and short-sighted and that he wished they could start over but understood if they couldn't.

"He said, 'If I were you, I don't know if *I'd* go back with me,'" related Lori. "Which I think was one of the most honest things he's ever said."

Nicky took a guess: "And also made you think for a minute that maybe you *could* get back together?"

"*Less* than a minute. Five seconds, maybe." Lori dipped a fry in ketchup and swallowed it blissfully. "An apology—a sincere one—is very sexy, in case you weren't aware."

He was not aware, but he was also just figuring out what actually *was* sexy to him. "I'll keep that in mind," Nicky said, as he buttered a bagel. He hadn't had a bagel since he'd left Long Island and felt nostalgic for one. This one tasted like round bread.

"And that was it," said Lori. "End of his charm offensive to get me back. The whole rest of the day—we had a great dinner at the Union Oyster House, by the way—it was like being with an old friend. Until we got back to the room and it was like being with an old *boy*friend. Who was hell-bent on giving it one last college try."

"So to speak."

"Ha. Yeah. So, before I knew it, everything I ever loved about the guy came rushing back, and . . . there we were. And when it was over, I was angry. So angry. At him—but mostly at myself. I did exactly what I swore I wouldn't." She gazed into her food, a tear welling.

Nicky put down his bagel. Lori looked miserable. And maybe rightly so. She'd abandoned her own best instincts. She was blinded by emotion and lust and self-indulgence. And she may have hurt someone else in the process. Which was pretty much what Nicky had done by connecting with Joe on Friday night. Realizing that he was hardly one to pass judgment, Nicky searched for a response that would be kind and supportive but also cover his own ass.

"We're only human," Nicky finally said, purposely including himself—or maybe the world at large—in that equation.

"Then I'm a shitty human," Lori said. She took a huge bite of burger as if for emphasis.

That didn't sound to Nicky like someone tougher than she seemed. Or was Joe right? Would she bounce back quickly and return to her regularly scheduled life? Because they became such fast friends, Nicky sometimes felt like he'd known Lori for so much longer than he had, maybe so much better than he did. But that could be deceiving. Because how well do we really know anyone?

How well does anyone know me? Nicky thought. *How well do I even know myself?*

Which made him think about Joe again—and where he factored into Lori's remorse. "Are you worried about how Joe would feel if he found out?" he asked.

Lori stopped mid-swallow. "How's he going to find out?" she asked, her words muffled by meat.

"When you *tell* him, maybe?" Nicky knew he was treading on thin ice. Not by recommending she be honest with Joe, but by forcing himself to be honest with Lori *about* Joe. Unless that's what he subconsciously—or not so subconsciously—wanted, he needed to back out of this part of the conversation, like, yesterday.

Lori sucked up a strawful of Tab, which was apparently her meal's one low-cal concession. "Oh, I thought you meant when *you* tell him." Nicky couldn't tell if she was serious. Her face was blank.

"Why would *I* tell him?"

"Not on purpose, Nicky, come *on*! But you two are close. It could slip out. On a run—or when you're just hanging out." She pushed aside her half-finished plate. Nicky could swear she put a spin on the words *hanging out*, though that was probably just the hearing of a guilty man.

He chewed on his bagel and considered his next move, but still knew he should change the subject. And yet . . . "I'm not going to tell Joe. I wouldn't do that to you—or him, to be honest." Nicky paused, realizing why Lori was talking around this. "But you're not going to tell him either, are you?"

Lori cast her eyes at the table and quietly shook her head. Because it was now confirmed: she *wasn't* tougher than she seemed. She might even be more fragile. Not the "spineless fucking marshmallow" she called herself, but not as self-possessed as Nicky once thought—and Joe still seemed to think. That didn't make Nicky think any less of her. He meant what he'd said about being only human, and not just as his own personal escape hatch.

Nicky completed his thought aloud: "Because you don't want to hurt Joe—and you also don't want to risk losing him." Again, he could have been speaking for himself. Just substitute "Lori" for "Joe" and "her" for "him."

"Of course. But mostly I'm embarrassed." Lori looked like she might tear up again, but it passed, and she slid her burger plate back in front of her. "And just so we're clear, I hate lying."

So did Nicky. So much. But there was a lot at stake. And, where Joe was concerned, Nicky knew he wasn't exactly thinking straight, no pun intended. "I know that," he told Lori. "But, like I said, your secret's safe with me. If you still want it to be."

She reached across the table; put her hand over his. "Thanks, friend. And thanks for understanding."

As Lori picked up her burger and took another healthy bite, Nicky asked, "By the way, you never said: How did you leave things with Joshua?"

She chewed and swallowed. "I told him to have a nice life."

"And that was that?"

"I think so. Yeah." She didn't sound entirely settled—or convincing. Nicky shot her a dubious look. She sighed and said, "You *met* him, Nicky. I think you can see what I'm up against."

Nicky did meet Joshua. Lori had brought him by the day before for a quick intro. He was surprisingly friendly and talkative, warm even. And his pictures hadn't done him justice—or maybe he'd changed a lot since they'd been taken. Joshua was solid, like Joe, and about as tall, but leaner, more tapered. He was prep-school handsome, with a knowing smile and kind of glinty, blue-green eyes. His dark, straight hair was loose and shortish, and he ran his hand through it a lot, which Nicky found appealing. Nicky wondered if he came from money; he gave off that vibe. Nicky definitely saw what Lori was "up against," though he still would've taken Joe by a mile. And he told her.

"Maybe," Lori said, pointing a French fry at Nicky. "But they couldn't be more different." As she popped the fry in her mouth, a blob of ketchup dripped down her chin. Nicky reflexively leaned across and dabbed her face with his napkin. Their eyes met and, in that split second, anyone could have seen the singular affection between them—if not the complications.

"I haven't even asked," Lori realized, "how was *your* weekend?"

"Pretty good. Saw *Jaws* again, worked on my econ paper, blew your boyfriend." Nicky didn't say any of that, of course, just shrugged and answered, "Not bad." It would have to do for now.

TWENTY-THREE

"How's my baby boy?" Nicky's mom asked after his dad handed her the phone during their weekly Sunday night phone call. Except it was Monday because Nicky forgot to call them the night before. They weren't as upset about that as he thought they'd be, especially after Monty, who'd picked up when they'd called looking for Nicky, had told his parents Nicky was "out with a girl." A date or that he'd just been hit by a bus were probably the only two excuses for blowing off the call that would have flown with Stevie and Rose. Forget that the "girl" was Lori, who Nicky had already made clear was just his friend; they heard what they wanted and already couldn't wait to meet her parents.

Rose still referred to Nicky as her baby boy, even though he was barely a year younger than his brother and far from her youngest child. "You'll *always* be my baby boy," she told him when, at around twelve, he asked her why she still called him that. His father called him Nicky or son—terms of endearment were not his thing. Nor was small talk. Thus, during these Sunday night phone chats, he'd ask Nicky thirty seconds of perfunctory questions, then say, "I'll put your mother on." After a lightning round of queries about Nicky's health, eating and laundry habits, roommate, and "girlfriend," Rose would speed through as much news about his relatives, the neighborhood, and her part-time bookkeeping job as she could pack into the fifteen minutes Stevie allowed her. (Nicky was certain his frugal father stood there with a stopwatch.) Fortunately, his little sisters were usually in bed by call time, or they'd burn up another quarter hour prattling on about their trivia-laden tween lives, interchangeably named friends, and favorite new TV shows. (Nicky liked talking to Cindy and Donna the best: they were so sweetly self-absorbed they never asked him anything about himself.)

On this call, however, Rose had business to discuss. Thanksgiving business. As in, when was Nicky coming home? Could he get a ride or would he have to fly (and, if so, shouldn't he have gotten his plane ticket already)? And wouldn't it be wonderful if his girlfriend could spend the holiday with them on Long Island? "But it's just an idea, honey," she tacked on.

Thanksgiving. It was less than three weeks away but Nicky, caught up in his BU cocoon, had given it barely a thought, even though he'd heard snippets of other folks' holiday plans in passing. *Wait, didn't Monty mention he was bringing Sabrina to Pittsburgh for Turkey Day, or was she bringing him to New York—or neither?* In fact, the thought of leaving Boston at all was hugely unsettling. Though some people had already darted home for a long weekend in October, Nicky had happily stayed back in the dorm. If he didn't have to be with his family for Thanksgiving, would he even leave then? He had undergone so many changes in the last few months that it was as if he no longer belonged in Franklin Square. Little, boring, predictable Franklin Square. (Or at least that's how it was seeming from afar.) It's not that he didn't miss his family, he did . . . sort of. And it'd be great to hang out with Brad, Wally, and Pins, even if he felt disconnected from them, too.

It was strange and a little scary that he felt so comfortable away from everything he'd always known. The freedom he'd had to be himself—or whoever he was becoming—since that shaky first day at 700 had been cumulatively intoxicating, without him fully realizing it. And leaving Joe and Lori, even for five days, seemed like an eternity. But Nicky had gotten so used to everyone—Shelley and Chuck and Ken and Sabrina and their RA, Valerie (to whom you were supposed to be able to tell anything in confidence but she had kind of a big mouth), as well as so many others on his floor, in the dorm, and in his classes. Hell, he'd even miss Monty, whose posey, curmudgeonly ways Nicky had begun to better accept.

Nicky bit the bullet and told his mother that he had no plan yet for Thanksgiving but would make one within the next day and let her know. Given that it would require another phone conversation, likely within twenty-four hours, he heard his dad say "Enough, Rose," and she obediently hung up before much in the way of local or family news could be shared. Nicky wondered how his very different parents ever ended up marrying, then realized from his own recent experiences that chemistry and attraction were truly random and mysterious things.

As Nicky began worrying about Thanksgiving in earnest, a funny thing happened. The next morning, instead of running (it was getting cold out there!), Joe asked Nicky if he wanted to go for a workout at Case Gym. Nicky had yet to visit West Campus—short of passing by it on the T en route to Allston and Brighton—and had no classes until the afternoon, so he figured, Why not? He'd never lifted weights in his life and didn't know much except that it could further improve his already improving body. And that working out had definitely made its mark on Joe. So Nicky threw on some approximation of workout clothes—and his pea coat over them—and off they went.

The weight room at Case Gym was pretty vast and well stocked with what looked like every kind of dumbbell and barbell, along with benches, pullies, racks, and other instruments of potential torture that might have intimidated Nicky had he not been there with workout veteran Joe. The space was fairly empty, save a few grunting, iron-pumping football players (Go, Terriers!) who made Joe look puny. Joe offered to take Nicky through a lighter, somewhat abridged version of his usual workout that would cover each of the main muscle groups. He explained how he normally did a split routine: chest, shoulders, and triceps one day; legs, back, and biceps another. Today they'd work a little of each. Nicky was open to whatever, mostly because it meant close proximity to Joe. He could already feel himself getting horny for the guy as Joe stripped down to gym shorts and a too-small T-shirt. Nicky tried not to be unnerved by it (Jesus, he'd seen him—*had* him—buck naked and then some, shouldn't he be used to his presence by now?) but rather enjoy the transporting, heart-racing feeling. *This is just a phase,* Nicky told himself, *a passing thing. Another way to get off.* Isn't that all it was for Joe?

As for that "funny thing," after about thirty minutes of bench presses, arm curls, and shoulder raises—Joe's workout coaching was as clear as his Econ 101 tutoring, and Nicky was quickly getting the hang of it—Joe brought up Thanksgiving.

"OK, so *this* sucks," he began, as he returned a pair of dumb-bells to their rack. "I was planning to go back to Cincinnati for Thanksgiving, but my parents just decided to spend it in, of all fuck-ing places, Glasgow."

"They're going to Scotland?"

"What? Oh, yeah, no—Glasgow, *Kentucky*. My aunt and uncle and mess of cousins live there. I haven't been there since I was ten." Joe grabbed a pair of fifty-pound weights and hauled them to an incline bench.

"And, what sucks is you weren't invited?" Nicky guessed.

"No, what sucks is I *was* invited." Joe sat back on the low-slung bench and lifted the weights straight above his head. "See, you bring the weights up, then slowly down to either side of your chest," Joe explained, demonstrating. "Then hold for a few seconds, and lift them up again." Joe banged out a set of ten presses and then dropped the weights on the rubber-matted floor with a thud. "I'd first have to fly to Cincinnati, then drive with my family, like, three frickin' hours to Glasgow." He leaped off the bench, pointed to the weight rack. "Grab a pair of twenties—no, fifteens—and *you* try it."

"Couldn't you fly directly there? Meet them?" Nicky asked, crossing for the dumbbells.

"Sure, if I wanted to change planes four times—then drive a whole bunch more. But that's not really the point. If I'm going back to Cincinnati, I want to stay in Cincinnati. See my friends, do fun stuff with my little brothers, hang out with my mom, enjoy the city. Not be stuck for four days in the middle of nowhere. All due respect to my Aunt Dorothy and Uncle Carl, who are nice people."

Weights in hand, Nicky settled onto the incline bench. This didn't sound like kind, easygoing Joe. He realized that Joe mentioned spending time with his mom and brothers but not his dad. It also occurred to Nicky that Kentucky sounded like the end of the world (is that farther than the middle of nowhere?), but that was from someone who'd never been south of Washington, D.C., or west of Pennsylvania.

"OK, try for eight reps," Coach Joe instructed Nicky. Joe stood behind the bench to guide Nicky up with the weights—*and catch them if they fell*, Nicky thought. Which made him aware, once again, how safe he felt around Joe. He wondered if that was part of the attraction—and if it was, was that weird? *Any weirder than having the hots for another guy?*

Nicky copied Joe and lifted the weights up, then down in an arc to each side. The weights weren't that heavy (he was secretly glad Joe suggested the lighter ones), but the movement was a bit awkward. Joe grabbed him under his elbows and helped guide the weights.

"That's it—and down in one smooth motion," Joe told him. Nicky liked the feel of Joe's hands on his arms, the closeness, and the faint, spicy scent of Aramis that, by now, seemed permanently attached to him. "Good, you got it," Joe said after Nicky finished. A couple of jocks on side-by-side bench presses grunted noisily as they tried to outlift each other.

"But what really gets to me," Joe said, as he reclaimed his place on the incline press, "is that my parents made these plans without even asking me first—and then just assumed I'd go with them." He lifted the fifties like they were Nicky's fifteens and started another set.

"Yeah, that does suck," Nicky agreed, watching Joe's chest and shoulders flex as he worked the dumbbells. Nicky knew his parents might do exactly what Joe's did, just substitute Cranston, Rhode Island (that's where Nicky had family), for Glasgow, Kentucky. "So do you have to go?"

"If I want to spend Thanksgiving with my family, yeah," Joe said as he pushed out his last fly. He sat up on the bench, took a breath. "Though my mom said I don't *have* to go if I don't want, that we'd make up for it at Christmastime. She was weirdly cool about it."

"What about your dad?"

"We haven't talked about it, but it's my mom's side of the family so he wouldn't care as much. Plus, he'd save money on a plane ticket." Joe eyeballed the room, deciding on the next exercise. A few more jock types showed up and jumped on the multi-station Universal machine. Weights clattered. Joe waved Nicky toward another unit. "Let's do some seated rows. Work your back."

Nicky liked the weight room—the rubbery smell, slightly still air, and sunlight that peeked through a bank of high, narrow windows. It felt strangely cozy, kind of sealed off and private. The word *safe* returned to mind.

Joe sat on the row machine's low, flat bench, grabbed a pair of handles attached to a weight stack, and pulled them toward himself, slowly and evenly. "Most important thing here is to keep your back straight, don't hunch forward to meet the weights."

"So, what'll you do if you don't go to Kentucky?"

"Stay here, I guess. Get some work done. Take it easy. The dorm stays open, mostly for the international students." Joe drew the weight pulley in toward his midsection; looked graceful, in total control.

Nicky had a crazy idea. So crazy he didn't know if he could even speak it. But before he could stop himself, he blurted out, "Wanna come home with me for Thanksgiving?" Joe stopped in mid-pull, looking up at him in shock. Now Nicky knew the idea not only was crazy, but it was stupid and irresponsible. He was cringing inside, his stomach knotting like a pretzel. Until:

"Really? You'd do that for me?" Joe asked, with almost childlike wonder.

Nicky wasn't sure he'd heard right. Was he misreading Joe's reaction? He could feel his gut relax. "Uh, yeah," Nicky answered. "Why not? I mean, what're you gonna have for Thanksgiving? A hot turkey sandwich at Deli Haus?" Nicky smiled and Joe returned it.

"OK, well, if it's cool with your parents, I'm there! Wow, thanks, Nicky."

Nicky had no idea if his parents would be "cool" with a holiday visitor who wasn't a girlfriend, but it was too late now—Nicky was in it. *Fuck, what if they say no?* He then flashed on Joe sleeping three feet away on the foldaway cot in his bedroom. That seemed way too close for comfort. That is, if Joe still had any interest in fooling around with him. For all Nicky knew, after their steamy Saturday night, Joe may have decided to go back to women full time. And maybe Nicky should, too. Speed up the "phase." Get out before anything bad happened because, really, no good would come of this part of his and Joe's friendship—if the underlying panic he was increasingly feeling was any indication.

Joe, still smiling, knocked out another couple of reps on the seated row, then jumped up and made way for Nicky to go again. As Nicky settled back into the bench and grabbed the pulleys, he realized he'd completely forgotten about something. Or, rather, some*one*.

"What about Lori?" he asked. "What if she wants you to go back to New Jersey with her?" Forget about the fact that Joe and Lori hadn't spoken since Joshua set foot in 700—and that Nicky and Joe hadn't talked about her again since Joshua left. It seemed worth bringing up.

Joe simply shrugged and raised his hands in response. Something told Nicky that Joe knew what Lori had done with Joshua without even being told. Or maybe he just preferred the thought of Thanksgiving with Nicky. (*Seriously?*) No matter what, Nicky would talk to Lori about it later.

That night, Nicky called his parents and asked about bringing Joe with him to Long Island. There was silence on the other end

(Nicky imagined Stevie and Rose trading a baffled look) until his mom asked, "What about your girlfriend?"

Nicky sighed. "Mom, I told you: Lori's not my girlfriend, she's just a friend who's a girl. A woman. And Joe's my friend, too, and his family's going away without him."

More silence from Franklin Square, and more imagined confusion from Stevie and Rose. "He'll have to sleep in your bedroom," Nicky finally heard his mom say. "Grandma's going to be on the pull-out in the den."

"Grandma's spending the weekend?" Nicky assumed she was talking about his grandma Carmela, his dad's mom. She could be warm and lovable but had become kind of a loose cannon after her beloved husband, Alfonse—Stevie's father—died suddenly of a heart attack three years ago. It was like she lost her censoring device along with her better half. She wasn't senile or anything—she was usually quite shrewd and perceptive—you just never knew what might come tumbling out of her mouth.

"You got a problem with that?" Stevie called into the phone.

"What? No! Of course not! I can't wait to see Grandma." It would actually be a plus. Grandma Carmela was the only person his dad was afraid of—it went back a ways, Nicky gathered—and Stevie was usually on his best behavior around her. It was a sight to behold.

Rose wanted to keep chatting but Stevie said, "Say goodnight, Rose," and they were over and out. Nicky thought about that Carly Simon song, "Anticipation," and was glad he still had a few weeks to go before what would surely be a Thanksgiving weekend to remember—for better or worse.

TWENTY-FOUR

A RESPECTABLE FORTY-EIGHT hours after Joshua departed from BU, Joe and Lori finally spoke again over an early dinner at the student union. According to Lori, who tracked down Nicky in the 700 study lounge afterward, Joe was his usual easygoing self. He didn't ask her a thing about Joshua beyond if they'd had a nice weekend; Lori offered nothing back except that it had been "fine and emotionally uneventful," which was BS, but she was trying to move on. Joe asked Lori to go indoor roller skating the next night and she said yes even though she hadn't skated since her ninth birthday party. They then made out for ten minutes outside the union before returning to the dorm. The world was apparently back on its axis. Nicky was, for all intents and purposes, relieved, mostly because he didn't have to lie—at least at that very moment.

As for Thanksgiving, Lori thought it was cool that Joe was spending it with Nicky.

"And you're not, like, I don't know . . . jealous or annoyed or anything?" Nicky asked her as they stood in the hallway outside the study lounge.

"What? No, I'm happy he's got somewhere to go," Lori answered, sliding to the floor and resting her head against the wall. "I couldn't take him to Cherry Hill. It's gonna be a shitshow."

"Your parents?" Nicky joined her on the floor. The linoleum was hard and cold.

"They each want me to spend Thanksgiving with them—my mom at our house, my dad in his new apartment. Which is kind of a depressing place. Plus, my dad said he has 'somebody he'd like me to meet,' which I'm sure means he's started dating someone. Which also means my mom will be unbearable because of it. Talk about jealous *and* annoyed!" Lori took a breath, studied a chip in her nail polish. "I wouldn't want to bring Joe into any of that, would you?"

Nicky shook his head, though he knew Long Island might be a gamble as well—because his parents *were* together and his grandma was a chatterbox and his sisters could be annoying. He had no idea what to expect of Richie, who would definitely wonder why someone like Joe was friends with Nicky, something Nicky still often wondered himself. Not that he'd bring any of that up to Lori: her family issues were tougher than his right now, and she was pretty much on her own with them.

They sat in silence as a few folks wandered into the lounge, textbooks in hand. One of them, a good-looking guy with wire rims and shoulder-length hair, said a familiar "Hey, you," to Lori as he passed, to which she responded, "Hey, back."

"Do you know him?" Nicky asked her.

"Not a clue, but I like the hair," she answered, with a sly eyebrow raise. Another pensive beat and: "Joe's parents are idiots, y'know, for going without him. He obviously didn't learn his good manners from them."

"He says nice things about his mom, but not a lot about his dad."

"All I know about his father is that he's a cop—and that he's kind of a hard-ass."

"A detective, actually." Nicky wondered how much he "detected" about his oldest son.

"Which means he *started* as a cop, right?"

"I don't know how it works. But Joe seems more like the son of a gym teacher or something."

Lori studied Nicky, then gently asked, "So how *are* you feeling about your buddy Joe these days?"

Nicky froze. Then defrosted. "In what way?"

Lori sent him a knowing, almost tender look. He was unprepared to discuss this now, much less there, sitting on the hallway floor. He so desperately wanted to talk to Lori for real about Joe but was afraid that once he got started, he wouldn't stop before incriminating them both. In the same way Nicky wondered if Joe had an instinctive sense about Lori and Joshua, did Lori subconsciously know about him and Joe? And if, despite her warning that she didn't want to romantically compete for Joe, was Lori no longer that adamant about it? Then the biggest question: How much did she *really* care about Joe?

"Somehow or other we've become really good friends," Nicky finally answered, feeling himself starting to cave. It was like slipping on ice and trying to right oneself, hoping no one would notice. "What happened between him and me that time was just . . . what it was." Which said nothing, but Lori seemed to accept it.

Her look turned needy. "So . . . would you say you're better friends with Joe now than me?"

Is that all she wanted to know? Who was the better friend?

"You are number one, Conover," Nicky said, resting his head on her shoulder, suddenly sleepy. He meant what he said. Something told Nicky he'd know Lori forever—if he didn't mess it up.

But she wasn't done. "Do you think much about what *we* did— what you and I did that night?" It was as if they hadn't already talked about that part so soon after it happened. Like their sexual recap that day, which Nicky thought had covered a lot of ground, was only half the conversation.

"Of course, I do," Nicky told her. "How could I not?" Which was true. He thought about it often. Less often than he thought about what he did—was doing?—with Joe. But it was a defining moment and he was beginning to wonder if he shouldn't try to repeat it. Not with Lori, but, well . . . someone. At some time. If he was going to be bisexual, he might as well *be* bisexual. That was a big "if" though, and it hurt his head just to think about it.

Lori pulled back from Nicky, looking touched. "I do too," she said and ran a hand through his curls. "And y'know what's weird? The more time goes by, the better I remember it. Like we weren't as stoned as we actually were."

"Same here," he realized. "Or maybe we're just remembering what we want to remember." He grabbed his books and stood, his ass aching from the hard floor.

"That'd be OK, too," Lori answered philosophically, rising as well. Her face broke into a smile. "So! For the first time in ages today, someone told me I looked like 'that girl from *The Partridge Family*.' I was starting to think I'd lost my whole Susan Dey thing." She added drolly, "I mean, *then* what would I do?"

"First thing I thought that day in the elevator: Laurie Partridge."

"Know what I thought when I first saw *you*?" Lori asked, with a devilish grin.

"'Who's this dweeby freshman I hope I never have to see again?'"

"Literally, *to* the word," she said, deadpan, without further comment. Nicky assumed—hoped, anyway—she was kidding. "Wanna get high, then go to Deli Haus?" she asked, breaking into a disarming smile.

Who could say no to that?

AS FOR THAT PANIC Nicky had been experiencing, it came and went, though generally lingered when he thought too deeply about his personal and romantic—and yes, sexual—future. But what was he supposed to do? There were times when Nicky felt like he was floating through life—somebody else's life, at that—and decisions would somehow be made for him. Other times, things felt frighteningly real and deeply precarious. His dreams of late had been, in a word, wacko.

He decided to hole away one class-free afternoon at Mugar Library with a pile of books on human sexuality, particularly human homosexuality. (Bisexuality didn't seem to exist on Mugar's shelves; maybe it didn't exist at all.) The more he read, the more confused he became. There was so much contradictory information from book to book—the older the book, the more contradictory—that it was hard to figure out where he, Nicky DeMarco, fit into the whole sexuality thing. He even looked through *Everything You Always Wanted to Know About Sex* (*But Were Afraid to Ask)*, a book that seemed so forbidden when he was growing up that Nicky's heart pounded just opening the well-worn Mugar Library copy. But even to a novice like Nicky, its chapter on homosexuality seemed so twisted and negative that he stopped reading midway through. Nicky may not have known where he stood on the subject (except for how great being with Joe felt—no book talked about *that*), but he had a feeling reading too much about it was a recipe for emotional disaster.

If only Nicky knew someone else like him. Someone he could confide in. Or at least ask a few stealthy questions. Someone discreet, careful. Other than Joe, that is, who didn't seem to want to discuss the subject any more than was necessary (and maybe wasn't objective enough when he *did* talk about it). And then it hit Nicky: *Chuck*. But he broke out in a sweat and shook off the idea. No, he'd have to go this alone for now, play it out, make his own mistakes.

Except, coincidence or not, that night in the dining hall, Nicky found himself sharing a table with Ken, Chuck, and Elena, a friend of Ken's from his Journalism 101 class. Over 700's version of Chinese food (it was a rare "theme night"), Ken and Elena got into a prickly debate about the Watergate scandal and President Ford's pardon of Nixon. (Ken was against, Elena pro, but not because she was any fan of the disgraced ex-president.) Nicky tried to keep up with their back-and-forth but was painfully underinformed about politics so it became futile. Chuck glazed over about three minutes in and spent most of the dinner shooting Nicky eye rolls and humming to himself. Nicky couldn't swear it, but he was pretty sure he recognized "Chim Chim Cher-ee" from *Mary Poppins*.

The Watergate debate ended in a draw and, after everyone opened their fortune cookies (three of the four said the same thankless thing: Life is short, enjoy it), Ken and Elena left to quiz each other for the next day's JO 101 test on, appropriately enough, writing obituaries. Chuck mimed an enormous yawn, patting his hand against his mouth.

"I know," said Nicky. "But they're into all that stuff."

"To say the least," Chuck said, finishing a Pepsi. "Ken's a decent roommate, but he can be really intense. And, I don't know if you've noticed, but I've stopped getting into any debates with him. About anything. Too exhausting. It's easier to just agree or be neutral." Chuck rattled the ice cubes left in his soda glass.

While Chuck was talking, Nicky was deciding whether to have the chat with him that he'd briefly considered and as quickly dismissed. He didn't have to let anything on, just ask questions, and see where it went. Chuck was a bit doofy at times, but he also seemed smart and, in some ways, oddly confident. And Nicky remembered how moved he was when Chuck asked if they could still be friends after coming out to him. (*That's what it was called, right?*) Suddenly, it seemed like the right time to do this. And the right place, as they were stuck away in a corner, no one else within earshot.

Nicky asked Chuck if he wanted coffee—he did—and when they returned to the table, steaming cups in tow, said, "Chuck, do you mind if I ask you something?"

"I don't know, should I?" he answered in jest. But when he saw Nicky was serious, Chuck sobered, leaned in a bit, and said, "Sure, what's up?"

Nicky almost backed out again but, instead, swallowed some coffee and, in his best casual voice, asked, "OK . . . remember when you said you didn't think you were heterosexual? How did you know?"

Chuck seemed taken aback by Nicky's question. He lowered his voice. "I was a little drunk when we talked about it that night."

"That's OK. You don't have to get into it again if you don't want to." Nicky *knew* this might be a bad idea, could feel himself deflating. "I know it's pretty personal." Yes, he did.

"Yeah, well." Chuck took a hit of coffee and looked off. "How did I *know*?" he finally answered. "Probably when I was nine and had this weird, I don't know what you'd call it . . . crush, I guess, on my day-camp counselor. Roger. He was this big, blond, muscly type, maybe eighteen—our age now, which is kind of amazing. He was really strong, always picking us kids up and hurling us in the pool, letting us ride on his shoulders, that kind of thing. He was so much fun. We all loved the guy . . . though, I guess, some more than others." Chuck stopped and studied Nicky. "Are you sure you're OK hearing about this?"

"I asked, didn't I?" Nicky shrugged. As the words fell out of his mouth, he realized Chuck could rightly reply, "Yeah, and why *did* you?" Thankfully, he just went on with his story.

"So, after that, I became hyper-aware of other guys—older guys like Roger, not kids my age or anything," Chuck carefully explained. "I didn't know what it meant or why, it just . . . was. A few years later I started watching old Hercules and Tarzan movies on TV when I was home alone and I would—" He let the memory hang in midair, his face reddening. "You get the point."

Nicky did and he didn't. Chuck seemed like he was conscious of other guys way earlier than Nicky, who was, like, sixteen before he took notice of his wrestler classmate, Larry. But what was it about them both being drawn to bigger, stronger dudes? Was that a coincidence . . . or a symptom? (On another note, Nicky was pretty sure he'd never seen a Hercules movie in his life; the occasional muscle magazine, maybe. What did *that* mean?)

Before Nicky could respond about "the point," Chuck brightened and asked, "Hey, y'know who kind of reminds me of Roger? My old camp counselor?" Nicky shrugged, couldn't begin to guess. "Joe," Chuck said, finishing off his coffee.

"Joe who?" Nicky asked, truly not making the connection.

"*Your* Joe." Chuck lowered his voice again. "Your hot friend."

"Oh." Then, in a weird mirror image of his conversation with Lori, Nicky asked, "You think he's hot?"

Chuck looked at Nicky like he had two heads—neither of which had a brain. "Yeah, Nicky, he's hot. Trust me."

Nicky nodded, pretending to make sense of that. He felt like an idiot, a dishonest one at that. But it paved the way for his next question: "Have you ever done anything? With, y'know, another guy?"

Chuck sighed theatrically. "Nothing I'm proud of. But, to borrow the old song title, someday my prince will come. He held up an imaginary cigar and, in his best Groucho Marx voice, added, "If *I* have anything to do with it."

The song and the double entendre went over Nicky's head, mostly because he was already on to his next question. And, since he knew it had to be his last, lest he overplay his hand, he made it a big one: "If you *are* gay, What do you think the rest of your life will be like?"

Chuck's cackle made Nicky recoil. Chuck took off his aviators, rubbed his eyes, put the glasses back on and, still smiling, eyed his interrogator. "Who the hell knows? It's like me asking you: 'If you *are* straight, What do you think the rest of *your* life will be like?'"

Nicky wondered if Chuck was questioning whether Nicky was, in fact, straight. It made him want to fess up. To share his actual experiences, perceptions, fears, and joys instead of using Chuck to make himself feel better—or clearer. But the moment had passed; it would have to wait. And maybe that was OK. "Yeah, I see what you mean," Nicky told Chuck. "One day at a time, huh?"

Chuck shrugged. "Que será será." Catching Nicky's blank stare, Chuck translated: "What will be will be?" More staring. "Like Doris Day? From *The Man Who Knew Too Much*? The Alfred Hitchcock movie?"

"I know who Doris Day is," Nicky eventually said. "*And* Alfred Hitchcock."

"Well, thank God for that!" Chuck said with a sly wink. His face went serious. "I appreciate you asking about all this, Nicky." He quietly added, "It's good to talk about it."

Nicky couldn't disagree.

TWENTY-FIVE

NICKY AND JOE ended up catching a Thanksgiving ride to Long Island with a floormate of Joe's who, coincidentally, was from Hewlett Harbor, around twenty minutes south of Franklin Square. Stuart, the driver, a sophomore like Joe, must've had money because (a) Hewlett Harbor was a much ritzier place than Franklin Square and (b) he had a car—a nice one at that: a 1974 Pontiac GTO—which was something most BU students didn't have unless they lived off campus. Way off campus. He dressed well, too, and was wearing designer jeans (were those creases?), a print Huk-A-Poo nylon shirt, and a thin gold chain around his neck, all under a black leather coat. Oh, and his perfectly styled hair didn't move the entire trip. Nicky thought he had to be uncomfortable all duded up like that, crammed behind the wheel of his compact car for four hours. Maybe he wanted to look good for his parents when he showed up—or he was stopping at a disco before going home. Either way, it seemed like a lot of trouble.

Holly, a high school friend of Stuart's and another BU sophomore, rode shotgun, and slept for much of the trip, waking up only long enough to check the time or reapply her makeup. She, like Stuart, seemed friendly enough, but didn't talk much and kept mixing up Nicky's and Joe's names. Stuart and Joe chatted about music and cars and the others on their floor, but Nicky could tell Joe was being more polite than interested. As people, they were clearly worlds apart.

There were long stretches of the ride without any conversation, which was fine by Nicky, who was enjoying the jumble of FM stations that popped up (they must have heard Jigsaw's "Sky High" twenty times) and sharing the tight back seat with Joe. Now and then, Nicky could feel Joe's sneakered foot against his or Joe's hand grazing his leg. Whether intentional or not it gave Nicky a surge and the closeness made him feel safe and warm. Nicky wondered if Stuart had any inkling about Joe's secret side, though Joe had assured him that no one on his floor had any reason to suspect a thing. All they knew was that he had a girlfriend, had dated lots of other women, flirted with the rest, and was a cool, considerate, stand-up guy. They also knew Nicky was his freshman friend and that they sometimes studied, ran, or ate a meal together, like Joe might with anyone. Still, a bunch of times throughout the trip, Nicky could swear he saw Stuart checking out his backseat passengers in his rearview mirror.

One bathroom stop in East Hartford, two stretches of sleet along the 91 South, a traffic jam getting on the 695, and a wrong turn off the Hempstead Turnpike exit later, Stuart delivered Nicky and Joe to 777 Willow Road, also known as Chez DeMarco. They were just in time for dinner on this Thanksgiving eve. Nicky hoped his mother had made her famous lasagna.

"Door-to-door service," Stuart announced brightly as he pulled up in front of the modest, celery-green shingled ranch house. Nicky thought it was classy of the guy to drop them off, even if Franklin Square *was* on his way. And all for only the five bucks apiece he'd asked Nicky and Joe to chip in for gas.

It was already dark out, but, with the front porch light ablaze, Nicky could see the skeleton of their giant maple tree. Who raked its leaves this fall in his absence? His mom's old Ford Falcon was parked at the curb; his father's newer Plymouth Duster, the car

Nicky learned to drive in, filled the driveway. Nicky felt an unexpected flood of nostalgia as he stared at the familiar house. Was it his imagination or did it look smaller than he remembered?

As soon as Nicky and Joe exited the car (no easy task from the two-door's narrow back seat), Cindy and Donna, wearing only sweaters and skirts, came barreling out the front door screaming Nicky's name. He swept his excited sisters up in his arms as Joe grabbed his and Nicky's bags from Stuart's trunk. Nicky was overwhelmed—in a good way—by Cindy and Donna's joyous greeting. The girls prattled away with such high-pitched enthusiasm he could barely make out their bubbly words. Nicky turned and waved goodbye to Stuart and Holly as the GTO took off down the block.

"Girls, get back in here. You're gonna freeze your rear ends off!" yelled Rose from the doorway. She grabbed a coat and her daughters' parkas and ran out to join her kids at the curb. Rose nearly pushed Cindy and Donna out of the way to get to Nicky. She hugged her younger son like he'd been lost at sea.

"Oh, my God, Nicky, look at you!" Rose studied him under the light of the street lamp. "Look at that *mustache*! You look five years older! And *so* handsome." She turned and took in the vision that was Joe. "And, wow, talk about handsome!"

"You, Mrs. DeMarco, are too kind," he said, flashing her a full-toothed, Joe Hello smile that could have melted an igloo. "Thank you so much for having me in your home for the holiday." He went to shake Rose's hand, but she swatted it aside and moved in for a hug. Not as big as the one she gave Nicky, but pretty significant for a stranger.

"Call me Rose, sweetie," she said, pulling back to give Joe another once-over. "And it's our pleasure. No one should be alone for Thanksgiving."

Donna, who looked like she'd lost weight since summer, stood eagerly next to Cindy awaiting an introduction to Joe. Nicky proudly aimed a hand at him and said, "Girls, this is my friend, Joe O'Rourke. Joe—meet Cindy and Donna."

Another big smile. "Hello there, ladies. Happy to meet you." Joe turned to Nicky, eyes cartoonishly wide. "Nicky, you never *told* me what gorgeous sisters you have," he said with a conspiratorial side-wink. Cindy and Donna squealed like the preteens they were and raced—embarrassed and thrilled—back into the house.

Rose, Nicky, and Joe traded smiles. "Where's Pop?" Nicky asked his mom, as he took his suitcase from Joe.

"Inside, where it's warm. Like a normal person." She pulled her coat around her and started up the front path. "C'mon, Nicky, he can't wait to see you."

Nicky wanted to ask "Really?" but knew that wasn't fair. His father never showed much emotion (except when he was pissed) but, Nicky knew, loved his kids to death. He just wasn't an easy guy to access; maybe Nicky hadn't been either.

They entered the living room to find Stevie stoking a stack of blazing logs in the fireplace. Cindy and Donna were crouched at his side, entranced by the flames. "Stevie, look who's here!" Rose bel-lowed. Nicky winced, had forgotten how loudly all the DeMarcos spoke.

Nicky's dad turned from the mantel to face him and Joe. He gazed at Nicky as if trying to figure out what was different about him. He broke into an uncharacteristic smile. "You gonna just stand there or come give your old man a hug?" He opened his arms to Nicky—another unusual gesture for Stevie. Maybe he'd had a few beers.

"Hey, Pop," Nicky said as he hugged his father. It wasn't a natural fit like it was with his mom, but he suspected that's how it was with most fathers and sons. He'd have to remember to ask Joe if Detective O'Rourke was a hugger. Given what little Nicky knew of Joe's dad he highly doubted it. He glanced around the living room, at the bro-cade-covered couch, nubby club chairs, gold shag carpeting, and wall of framed family photos, weirdly comforted to see that nothing had changed in his absence. Only *he* was allowed to change, right?

"How about that mustache?" Rose said to Stevie, with a nod toward Nicky's wooly upper lip. Nicky felt like a science exhibit; he sent Joe an eye roll. "And that hair—gorgeous!" Rose proudly ruffled her son's long curls. "I hope that girlfriend of yours knows what she's got." Nicky didn't correct her—too much trouble so soon—and, this time, shrugged helplessly at Joe, who seemed to get it.

Donna turned from the fireplace, her eyes wide. "Does your mustache tickle when you kiss your *girlfriend*?" she asked impishly. Cindy joined the laughter and the two sisters got all sing-songy about the word *girlfriend*.

Stevie seemed less impressed by Nicky's hair, facial and otherwise. "Wouldn't kill you to take a haircut while you're home," he told his son. "*And* a shave. I'm sure Sal & Vin's will be open Friday," Stevie added, referring to a local barber shop that Nicky and his brother had gone to their whole lives. Before Nicky could respond—not that he was going to—Stevie set his sights on Joe. "You could get a trim too, y'know, while you're here," he said, then extended a hand. "You must be the friend."

"No, genius, he's the cab driver," wisecracked Rose. "He's waiting for a tip." She turned to Joe. "Can you believe he actually holds a responsible job?"

Joe smiled politely, introduced himself to Stevie, and heartily shook his hand. Nicky could tell that Joe would nimbly survive the DeMarcos like the cool orientation leader that he was.

"That's some handshake you got there, pal," Stevie said, extracting his hand from Joe's. "You work out or something?" He assessed Joe, who had taken off his coat and wore a snug V-neck sweater over a white T-shirt.

"Couple of times a week, actually. Nicky, too, lately." He hooked a thumb at Nicky. "This one's a beast with the weights." Joe shot his friend a fraternal grin.

Stevie whirled back and eyeballed Nicky. "I *knew* you put on a few pounds." Then he turned, shot Joe a dry grin. "Most this one ever lifted was his ass out of the chair." Cindy and Donna started giggling again: their father said *ass*. Stevie shot the girls a look that said "Enough!" and they muzzled it. He turned to check on the fireplace. The others dropped into seats almost in unison.

"By the way, I know Richie's not flying in till tomorrow, but where's Grandma?" Nicky asked, hoping to shift the attention off him and Joe. Plus, he was curious. Had she changed her mind about the weekend? Someone had to keep Stevie in line; he knew his dad's current chipper state couldn't last.

Stevie poked at a smoldering log, and a plume of embers shot out. "She's coming out in the morning." He spun around to face Nicky. "Maybe you and Joe here could pick her up—she'll be on the eleven twenty-nine. Don't be late."

"Uh, sure, OK," Nicky replied to his dad's half-question/half-command. He turned to Joe. "I can give you the grand tour of Franklin Square on the way to the train station."

"Sounds good."

"Don't get too excited," Nicky said with a grin. "It'll take about eight minutes."

Stevie dropped onto the couch next to Rose, his face darkening. "What's the matter, city boy? We too small-time for you now?"

Rose jabbed her husband. "Stevie, behave."

"Yeah, c'mon. Don't get all sensitive, Pop. I was just joking." Nicky tried to keep it light, if only for Joe's sake. But he sensed the cloud forming even sooner than expected.

Rose jumped in with a diversionary tactic; Nicky could recognize them a mile away. "OK, kids—and husbands—dinner will be ready in about fifteen minutes. Hope everyone's hungry!" She smiled and turned to her son. "I made your favorite."

"Lasagna?" he asked hopefully.

She looked confused. "Wait, *that's* your favorite?" He nodded, equally puzzled. "I thought it was my chicken parm with ziti?"

"Actually, that's Richie's favorite." Nicky saw Rose's eager face fall. "But it's great, too, Mom." He faced Joe and emphatically told him, "She makes the *best* chicken parmesan." Rose brightened again.

"Love it. Can't wait!" said Joe, matching Nicky's urgent positivity. In the absence of Richie, the family's usual peacekeeper, Nicky was grateful for Joe's diplomatic presence.

He'd been home fifteen minutes and was already wiped out.

NICKY ALERTED JOE that dinner would be a kind of preview of the next day's Thanksgiving meal, only with fewer people. That is, massive amounts of excellent food, lots of loud cross talk and blunt questions, Cindy and Donna's giddy bickering, and Rose and Stevie agreeing to disagree on almost everything. But Joe seemed unfazed and, once at the table, easily settled in. He continued his charm offensive, told funny tales of past Thanksgivings, and wowed the family, even the skeptical Stevie. Joe ate for three, which couldn't have thrilled Rose more, acted kidlike with Cindy and Donna, and, for the umpteenth time, made Nicky feel honored to have him as a friend. And more than a little turned on.

Rose was shocked to learn that Lori was Joe's girlfriend, not Nicky's (he finally corrected his mom), and spent the rest of the meal trying to figure that one out. Rose had many good qualities but often saw things through, well, rose-colored glasses, which, Nicky thought, may explain how she had stuck it out with Stevie all these years. Joe went chapter and verse on how terrific Lori was and what an awesome friend she was to Nicky, who was basically responsible for her and Joe getting together.

"So where are *you* in the dating department?" Stevie asked his son, peering over his Rheingold bottle.

"Beating 'em off with a stick, that's where he is," Joe wildly misinformed the table before Nicky could stumble through a real answer. Nicky wanted to kiss him (in thanks!) right then and there—the guy was truly a god among men. Rose and Stevie looked, for once, speechless, though that didn't last long.

"Well, I'm not surprised, with that face!" Nicky's mother unobjectively pointed out. "But, honey, why didn't you tell us any of this?"

Joe apparently wasn't letting Nicky screw this up. "Oh, you know Nicky, he's kinda shy about all that stuff. Which, of course, is like catnip to the ladies." Joe cheerfully cuffed Nicky's shoulder. Nicky was, again, awed by Joe's support—and how he dug up the word catnip. Rose looked thoroughly tickled about Nicky's "booming" social life. At this point, Cindy and Donna looked bored.

Stevie finished his beer and plunked the bottle down. "OK,

Romeo, but remember, you're there to get an education—and not just *that* kind."

"Got it, Pop." He should only know the kind of education Nicky *was* getting.

Nicky lay awake in his old bed that night, gazing out into the dark, as Joe sawed logs on the cot nearby. Nicky wanted to sneak over and climb in next to Joe, to feel his firm, warm body against his, take in his familiar scent, and bask in the sense of security—since day one, really—that he always felt around him. And tonight, at dinner, was Joe at his protective best. When Nicky thanked him for it later, Joe shrugged and smiled: "It's what I do." Though Nicky wondered if he meant "It's what I *have* to do," as in: he wasn't just protecting Nicky.

Nicky stayed in his own bed that night—for every obvious reason. But as he was finally falling asleep, an insane thought crossed his mind: *What if I'm falling in love with Joe?* No, it wasn't even remotely possible. Not in Nicky's world. Sex with a guy was crazy enough, but love? He'd have to come up with another word.

He wondered if one had yet to be invented.

TWENTY-SIX

AFTER BREAKFAST AND before Grandma Carmela's train was due in from Forest Hills, Nicky took Joe on the promised tour of his hometown. It was a crisp, sunny Thanksgiving morning, with the temperature hovering around fifty, and, driving around in Stevie's Duster, Franklin Square looked especially bright and inviting. Or was it exactly as it had always been and Nicky had missed the place more than he wanted to admit? Narrating as they went, Nicky showed Joe his elementary school, which was just up the street from his house, followed by Valley Stream North High—a combo junior high and high school—a handful of blocks away. They wound their way through a maze of residential streets till they landed on busy Franklin Avenue, where Nicky turned right. He drove past the Carvel ice cream stand, the Franklin Bowl, and the sprawling Pathmark supermarket, followed by dozens of other smaller stores, gas stations, and neighborhood restaurants up to the intersection of Hempstead Turnpike. Nicky swung a left onto the wider commercial stretch and passed the Franklin Theatre where he saw his first movie—*101 Dalmatians*—and hundreds after that, including many with friends or on dates throughout high school. He kept going until they hit the next town, Elmont, then hung a U-turn and pointed the Duster in the direction of the Long Island Railroad station.

"Well, that's Franklin Square," Nicky said in conclusion. "Thrill a minute, huh?"

"I don't know, seems like a nice place to grow up. Reminds me a little of where I'm from—only more cars."

"More cars than Cincinnati?"

"Actually, we live just outside Cincinnati, across the river. Erlanger, Kentucky."

"Kentucky?" It conjured up images of horse farms, Colonel Sanders, and Civil War monuments. "So, you're really a Southern boy? No wonder you've got such good manners."

"Ha! No, our part of Kentucky is more North than South. And, as far as my so-called manners, my dad drummed them into me and my brothers. Not the worst thing, I guess."

Nicky glanced at Joe, his parka open, hair still shower-damp, in need of a shave. He felt his breath shorten, his skin flush, as it so often did when looking at Joe. He wished he could take his hand or touch his face or have some physical contact. Just like he felt the night before. But he was in Franklin Square, where, unlike big-city Boston, the possibilities were fewer. Life here had limits and constructs and rules. Under his parents' roof, in his father's car, on the streets where he grew up, he wasn't free to be himself, to explore his dimensions, to take those mighty leaps. Not if he ever wanted to return. That much he knew for sure.

As they made their way toward the train station in Stewart Manor, one town over from Franklin Square, "Born to Run" began to play on WPLJ-FM, Nicky's favorite local station. Hearing those thrilling, unmistakable opening chords catapulted Nicky back to that night of the concert—and everything that followed. He felt such a rush of feeling that it was all he could do to not break down and cry for that evening's spectacular tangle of events. It must've triggered something in Joe as well because he did what Nicky had only thought about: he silently reached over and squeezed Nicky's arm. It almost caused Nicky to swerve out of his lane, but he didn't, nor did Joe remove his hand. It was a strange, tender, lovely moment, and they each seemingly chose not to ruin it with any discussion—even if the gesture cried out for it. They just listened to Springsteen sing his heart out about mansions of glory and suicide machines. And then, as if of one mind, Nicky and Joe spontaneously sang along, joining their voices in a rousing "*O-oh!*" Joe removed his hand from Nicky's arm, and they let the heart-pounding tune careen to its conclusion. When it was over, it was like they'd driven through an invisible curtain and come out the other side of it united, free, empowered.

Joe turned to Nicky and beamed as if he had written the song himself. "I'm really happy to be here with you right now," he said, locking eyes with his friend.

There were so many things Nicky wanted to say—to do—but he kept his response safe and simple. "Me too," he said, then pulled up to the train station with three minutes to spare.

Upon meeting Joe, Grandma Carmela proclaimed that if she were fifty-seven years younger, she'd be all over him "like a cheap suit." (How she came to that exact number went unquestioned.) She was otherwise a total lady, and Nicky was excited to see her. But he also knew that these days, she was always just one glass of rosé away from becoming Grandma Unplugged.

ROSE OUTDID HERSELF with the Thanksgiving meal and, as predicted, it was an impressive and unruly feast. Nicky was surprised at how happy he was to see Richie, and not just because he was on his best behavior around Franny. (That she broke with her own family tradition to spend the day with the DeMarcos won her about a million points with Stevie and Rose.) Richie and Joe got on like a house on fire, bonding over sports and Springsteen—unbeknownst to Nicky, Richie had become a fan. Stevie had carved the giant turkey within an inch of its life and, as he did every year, plunked a drumstick on each of his son's plates before they were snapped up by anyone else. (It was one of those dad-ly gestures that made Nicky think his father's grumpy routine was partly an act.) Meantime, Rose had whipped together a lasagna as "an alternative or a side dish," but Nicky knew it was to make up for last night's favorite-meal mix-up. There were also two kinds of sweet potatoes, Italian green beans, garlic bread, and a Jell-O, fruit, and marshmallow concoction called *ambrosia*. Once everyone sat down and all the platters and bowls and trays and dishes were in place, you couldn't fit a paper clip on the table.

"OK, everyone," Grandma Carmela began, shouting above the noisy eaters, "let's talk turkey."

Rose turned to her, looking worried. "Oh, no, it's not too dry, is it?"

"What? No, honey, it's delicious. I mean talk *turkey*, brass tacks, *la verità*—the truth." All other yakking stopped cold. A wary silence filled the room. Carmela raised her empty wine glass and motioned to the bottle at Stevie's side. "But first, do the honors, would you, Stevie?"

As Stevie leaned across and hesitantly poured red wine into his mother's glass, Nicky whispered to Joe, "Here we go."

Carmela hoisted her glass in the air. "*Alla famiglia!*" she announced to the table, then took a healthy swallow of the vino.

"*Alla famiglia!*" everyone responded, raising their glasses and toasting whoever was in reach. Joe merrily clinked his glass with Nicky on his one side, and Franny on the other, then leaned across to tap Cindy and Donna's soda cups. The girls giggled, enjoying their handsome visitor's special attention.

"We have so much to be thankful for at this table," Carmela continued. "I just wish my Alfonse could still be here to see it." She looked heavenward and signed herself. "We miss you every day, *caro mio*," she said, a tear in her eye, then took another hit of wine.

Nicky glanced around to see everyone caught between trying to respect Grandpa Alfonse's memory and desperate to return to the mountain of food on their plates. He spied Donna trying to silently chew a forkful of sweet potatoes. Could see Rose anxiously gauging the waning temperature of the food. It was an exercise in all-around restraint, something the DeMarco clan was not known for.

"Now, for the truth!" Carmela declared.

Stevie, who was obviously having second thoughts, gently suggested, "Ma, maybe let's enjoy Rose's food first? Save your questions for dessert?"

Carmela shot Stevie a look that could slice meat. "Who's telling you not to eat?" She swept an arm around the table. "Go ahead, people. Eat! *Mangia!*" There was a collective clatter as everyone dove back into their food. "But there's things I want to know!" She turned to Richie. "Let's start with you." She indicated Franny with her wine glass. "And you." Franny froze in her seat. "How long have you two been a couple?" Carmela asked.

Richie: "Five years."

Franny: "And two months."

"So, basta! When's the wedding already?" Carmela asked—no, demanded.

"Grandma, we're nineteen," Richie gently reminded her.

"Yeah? I was seventeen and your grandfather was eighteen when *we* got married."

Rose, a forkful of turkey in hand, stepped into the fray. "Mom, that was a long time ago. No one gets married that young anymore."

"I don't really think it's even legal," Franny added, though she didn't sound very sure.

"Oh, of course it is!" Carmela insisted, draining her wine glass.

Nicky knew this truth game could only go one way: downhill. And, it seemed, so did Stevie, who wisely tried to change the subject. "Rose, these green beans are terrific. Did you do something different this year?" Not that anyone was listening to him.

Carmela looked squarely at Richie and Franny. "All I'm saying is, I'm an old woman. My days on this earth are numbered. I want to live to see my favorite grandson get married. And maybe have a few children. Three would be nice."

Richie and Franny visibly squirmed. And somehow, Carmela's "favorite grandson" remark went over everyone's head—including that of her apparently *not*-favorite grandson. Nine-year-old Cindy, however, caught that particular fly ball.

"Grandma, you're not supposed to have a favorite grandchild," she informed Carmela, her mouth full of food. "We're *all* supposed to be your favorites."

Carmela was unruffled. "Did I say 'favorite,' sweetheart? I must've meant oldest." Moving on, she pointed a finger at Nicky. "OK, Mister Mustache, now you." She burned her gaze at Nicky, who thought he saw a kind of paranormal glint in her eyes. Just what he needed.

"Go ahead, Grandma. Ask away," Nicky said, steeling himself for the inevitable embarrassment. He continued eating in case he wouldn't feel like it when she was done.

Carmela raised her fork like a scepter and asked, "When are *you* going to bring home a girl for your old grandma to meet?" She was really pushing the "old" thing.

Before Nicky could concoct an answer, Stevie unexpectedly jumped in. "I wouldn't worry about it, Ma," he chuckled. "Joe here says Nicky's got himself a harem up there to choose from." He waggled a thumb in the general direction of Boston. Or the garage.

"Is that so?" Carmela shot a dubious look Nicky's way, then dipped her fork in a slab of ambrosia.

Richie nearly choked on his garlic bread. "A harem? *Nicky?* Since when?" He stared at his brother. "Why didn't you tell me? I mean, how many times did I ask you about the BU women?"

All eyes were on Nicky. "Once," he replied. "Which is how many times you've called me since we left for school." And he'd been feeling so good about seeing his brother today, too.

"Yeah? I don't remember *your* calls, little brother," said Richie with his eleven-month-older indignance. Franny sent him a look that read: "Relax." He slumped back and gave a small, obedient nod. Nicky felt only slightly vindicated; he'd really meant to call Richie more.

"And yet," Carmela picked up her train of thought, "he brings along his big, gorgeous friend here." She flapped a hand between Nicky and Joe. "Which is very nice, don't get me wrong, but . . . well, makes an old lady wonder, that's all." Seemingly finished and awaiting a response, she inhaled the jiggly ambrosia.

Nicky wasn't sure what his grandmother was getting at nor what she expected to hear. But the way the others went on with their noisy eating and talking, it seemed as if they didn't care—or simply didn't want to encourage her. Still, Carmela's words rattled Nicky, like she'd intuited something both vague and specific. Or maybe he was just being paranoid. He realized he had to say something, if only to defend Joe's presence. Even if Joe, who was chowing down like he was going to the electric chair, seemed unfazed.

"I love you, Grandma. Thanks for worrying about me, OK?"

She looked up from her plate and, with a faraway smile, said, "I always will, Nicky." Which seemed to put a button on the inquiry. At least for now. If she had questions for anyone else, she'd apparently forgotten them.

The rest of the meal was filled with high-spirited taunts, bad jokes, old DeMarco family stories, and political clashes. (Stevie still insisted Nixon was innocent and that the Vietnam War had been justified; arguments ensued.) Cindy and Donna sang the sultry song "Pillow Talk," but when they got to its orgasmic moans (which they had no idea were sexual—just thought were funny) Stevie shouted "What the hell?!" and stopped them cold. The girls launched into the safer, if equally annoying "Kung Fu Fighting" instead. Seconds and thirds of food were taken and, by the time everyone sat down in the den to finish dessert (homemade pumpkin pie and bakery cannoli) and watch the Rams trounce the Lions, no one could move. Literally.

Through it all, Nicky could tell he was a better version of himself around Joe and hoped his family could see that too. For a stretch, he even forgot about the daring, insanely thrilling things he and Joe had done together. And when he remembered, he wanted to do them all over again. Things that, sitting in his childhood home, seemed as if they'd happened in an alternate universe.

That night, before they fell asleep, Joe told Nicky how lucky he was to have the family he did, flaws and all. "Your parents are real, man, and Grandma's a trip," he said. "There's a lotta big love here."

Nicky was moved by the observation. It made him see his clan a bit differently.

Joe went on to explain how his own family was so much more formal and uptight. How his dad was a control freak and his mom was passive. How his teenage brothers, much as they looked up to and relied on Joe when they were younger, were becoming more like their father—rigid, competitive, and superior—instead of their gentler mother. Joe got along with his dad, mostly because he was capable and compliant, learning at an early age how to cover his tracks whenever he did something he knew his father—and by extension, his mother—wouldn't approve of. Which was a lot.

Nicky wasn't that surprised; he knew Joe's dad was a tough nut. But he *was* amazed at just how different Joe seemed from the family he described (whereas Nicky was more like all the parts of his parents and siblings put together than he cared to admit). How does that happen?

"Easy," Joe said to the dark. "I decided a long time ago that, if I were going to be happy, I had to be the opposite of my parents. It didn't mean I didn't love and respect them—because I do—but there was a better person inside me that needed to get out. I kind of figured out how to have it both ways, I guess."

Nicky took that in. "Y'mean, like doing it with men *and* women?" he whispered. It came out sarcastic, but he meant it seriously.

Joe, ever the cool cat, gave a low chuckle. "Yeah, something like that."

TWENTY-SEVEN

THE NEXT TWO days flew by, a whirlwind of leftovers (re-served by Rose in every possible configuration), hanging out in and around the house, group TV watching, keeping Grandma in check (she was good by day, dicey at night), and all the DeMarcos doing their best to interact as peacefully and patiently as the group knew how. Everyone continued to glom onto the good-natured Joe and, at one point, Nicky worried Richie would try to swoop in and make him his new best friend. When Nicky mentioned this to Joe, he said, "I like your brother, but he's a little too tightly wound, y'know?" Nicky *did* know and was relieved someone else saw it too.

Friday night, Nicky, Joe, Richie, and Franny went to see the movie *One Flew Over the Cuckoo's Nest*. When they invited Stevie and Rose to come along, Stevie said, with his usual finesse, "If I want to spend time in a nuthouse, I can just stay here." Rose gave her smart-aleck husband a playful smack and told the kids to go have fun. Which they did. They thought the movie was amazing and that Jack Nicholson ruled, but that Nurse Ratched stole the show. After, they went to a diner, ate pancakes, drank loads of coffee, played their window-table's jukebox, and laughed about the DeMarco family. In another dimension, Nicky would have considered it a really successful double date.

Saturday afternoon, Nicky and Joe met up with his buddies Wally, Brad, and Pins on the field at North High for a game of touch football. Richie was going to join them but, at the last minute, agreed to go shopping with Franny, so Brad's younger brother, Lewis, filled in.

Nicky felt strange being back on high school grounds with his three old friends who, frankly, all paled in comparison with Joe—but then most people did. For all the time Nicky had spent with Wally, Brad, and Pins over the years, seeing them again now was a bit of a—Nicky tried to find the right word—*letdown* kept coming to mind. They hugged and joked when they first saw each other, but, at least for Nicky, it felt like a piece was missing. Sure, it was a happy reunion, and, for a while, it felt like the old days. They all gave Nicky shit for his way-longer hair and serious mustache; Wally told Nicky he looked like "the world's nerdiest stud," whatever that meant. Brad asked Nicky if he'd "gained weight or something," that he looked "bigger." Nicky said he and Joe had been working out, which made Pins, who hated exercise like the plague, literally step away from Nicky.

Nicky's first impression upon laying eyes on the guys was that they didn't look any different. Wally's hair drooped a bit longer over his forehead, Brad's hair was a little shorter, and Pins had grown a sparse beard. But they were essentially as he'd left them. (Who *did* look different was sixteen-year-old Lewis, who must've shot up four inches since the summer.)

Wally, Brad, and Pins were a bit cool to Joe, trying to get a handle on him, and not instantly succumbing to his formidable looks and charm. It was clear they didn't see Nicky—the Nicky they thought they knew—with a friend so outwardly out of his league. He wanted to tell them that it was OK, that he often wondered that himself. But then it hit him, maybe for the first time, that he wasn't wondering that anymore. That he and Joe may look and act differently and may be from different worlds, but had become more equal than Nicky had ever thought possible. Was it that Wally, Brad, and Pins now felt *less* equal to Nicky? That he'd been friends with these not especially hip, popular, attractive, or brainy guys for so long because that's how *he* felt? He felt guilty thinking that, thinking he was maybe outgrowing them as Richie had with some of his friends once he left for college. It happened. Nicky also knew that Joe had "happened"—and Lori and his other new college friends, too—and his world had dramatically opened up. And then, of course, there was all that "experimenting" he'd been doing . . .

These thoughts kept popping up through the football game and during beers that followed at Rusty's, a corner bar in nearby Malverne. Joe entertained Wally, Brad, and Pins (the underage Lewis was sent home) with stories about some all-night frat party he'd gone to the year before where there were four women for every guy and everyone ended up naked after playing drunken strip poker. Nicky was almost certain Joe, a wicked gleam in his eye, was making up this wild tale as he went along to keep Nicky's friends entertained—which they were, in spades—so Nicky wouldn't have to. It helped Nicky relax (that and the three beers) and, by the time the afternoon was over, he felt better about his buddies as well as himself. Wally, Brad, and Pins promised to visit Nicky and Joe in Boston sometime next semester, though Nicky had a feeling that once the beer wore off the trio would forget all about it.

Driving home, Joe confessed that the story was fiction though he *had* been to a frat party once where he got so drunk that he woke up the next morning in a hallway closet wearing nothing but an American flag.

"Were you standing at attention?" Nicky asked with a sly smirk.

"Maybe if you were there I would have been," he answered just as slyly. But then his face turned serious, even vulnerable. He looked as if he was about to say something more but couldn't. Just like Nicky still couldn't express exactly how he felt about Joe—to himself or anyone else. The feelings remained too big, too bewildering, to ponder. Which isn't to say they weren't always on his mind. And, he felt at that moment, maybe also on Joe's.

"ARE YOU SURE you're OK?" Nicky asked Lori when he and Joe called her that night. "You sound a little weird." She was with her mom at the house in Cherry Hill after staying for two nights with her dad in his "grim" apartment nearby. She'd caved and had Thanksgiving dinner with him and his new girlfriend (yep, Lori guessed that one right), a TWA flight attendant named Annette, and Annette's elderly widowed father, who cracked lame jokes and smelled like mothballs. It sounded like enough to put anyone in a foul mood.

"Yeah, I'm alright," Lori answered unconvincingly, with no trace of her usual chipper energy. "It's just been a long four days. I can't fucking wait to be back in Boston."

"We miss you, Lori," Joe told her. He was on the extension phone in the front hallway, while Nicky spoke from the kitchen. Nicky missed her, too, but realized that he and Joe had barely brought her up the whole weekend. He suddenly felt like a shitty friend.

"Yeah, so much!" Nicky added, maybe a bit too enthusiastically. He gazed at the many years of family photos affixed to the fridge. It was a carnival of changing hairstyles.

There was a pause on Lori's end of the line. "Thanks, guys."

"How's your mom?" Nicky asked, wondering if that might be the cause of Lori's distress. After all, she'd predicted her mother might react badly to news of her dad's new girlfriend.

"Yeah, how's she doing?" Joe leaped in.

"She's sad, but trying to keep it together," Lori answered in a faraway voice. She sounded as glum as her mother apparently felt.

Nicky flashed on Lori's mom from that first day in the dorm elevator. How pretty and pleasant she seemed, happy to be seeing her daughter begin a new life chapter—while her own life had recently fallen apart.

"Look, I should go," Lori said. "My mom's in the den watching TV and I want to keep her company."

They said their goodbyes, and Nicky felt a twinge in the pit of his stomach. Something was definitely going on with Lori. Not that he would have asked her with Joe on the line, but he wondered if she'd seen Joshua that weekend and if that had messed her up somehow.

Joe saw Nicky's concern as he bounded in from the hallway. "Don't worry, pal," he said in his most soothing voice. "She'll be fine once we all get back. You'll see."

Nicky nodded, hoping Joe was right. He figured they'd find out soon enough.

It was 1:00 a.m. by the time Nicky and Joe went to bed. They'd stayed up in the kitchen scarfing late-night snacks and talking with Richie, who'd returned around midnight from Franny's house. He popped open a beer and revealed that he and Franny had sex that night while her parents were out and had the house to themselves. Nicky wasn't sure if Richie was telling them this to boast or to seem cool or because he actually thought they'd care, but he went into a surprising amount of detail that would have mortified the sweetly reserved Franny.

It left Nicky feeling jealous that Richie could crow about the sex he had with Franny, while Nicky had to keep the bliss he'd experienced with Joe a secret. It also left Nicky feeling extraordinarily horny, something he'd worked hard to suppress while under his parents' roof. And, though Joe acted blasé about Richie's bonking report, Nicky imagined he was feeling equally revved up.

Good guess. Once it was lights out for Nicky and Joe, there was a palpable sexual tension in the air. The guys were stretched out side by side—Nicky in his narrow bed, Joe on the wiggly cot—separated by just a few feet of floor space. It was a chasm that, for the last three nights, had felt like a hundred miles to Nicky. But no longer. He got up, carefully opened his bedroom door, and listened for any sounds or stirring from the other bedrooms or the den where Grandma Carmela was sleeping. It was as still as a tomb.

"What are you doing?" Joe whispered.

"Ssh, nothing," Nicky whispered back. He quietly closed the door, took a giant breath, leaned down over the cot, and kissed Joe.

Joe reflexively, eagerly kissed Nicky back. "Are you fucking crazy?" he whispered, as he grabbed the back of Nicky's head and pulled him deeper into him.

"Looks that way," Nicky murmured, keenly aware he had zero control over his actions.

Joe quietly found his way to his feet and put his arms around Nicky and, now face-to-face, they began to feverishly make out. Nicky ran a hand under Joe's T-shirt and felt his warm, hard chest. His heart raced and his knees weakened. Joe pulled Nicky's T-shirt up over his head, flung it off, then whipped his own shirt off as well. The guys reconnected, skin to skin, mouth to mouth. Nicky felt like he was in a fog—a delicious, intoxicating, blinding fog. He had no idea where this was going to go, but he was going there. And apparently so was Joe, who slid his hand down Nicky's belly and into his briefs, grabbing hold of Nicky's stiff joint.

Just as Nicky let out a low, ecstatic moan, the ceiling light burst on and it was as if all time froze—and maybe hell along with it—as he and Joe turned to see Grandma Carmela. She was standing in the doorway in her floral nightgown, mouth agape, eyes the size of dinner plates, right hand clutching her chest. Nicky thought he would drop dead right then and there but was afraid his grandma would beat him to it. He didn't know if it was the bright light or some optical illusion but her face actually looked blue. And for once, she was utterly speechless.

As were Nicky and Joe, who grabbed their T-shirts off the floor, threw them on, and bolted to opposite sides of the room. If Nicky could have jumped out the window, he would have. He then realized there was still a large, unmistakable bulge in his briefs that he prayed Carmela was too shocked—or blind—to see. As if it would matter: his life was officially over.

"I . . . thought this was the bathroom, I was half asleep," Carmela finally croaked out when she regained her voice. Her eyes had found their way back into their sockets, and she was slowly backing out of the doorway.

"It's. Next. Door," Nicky haltingly said, his throat like a vice, as he pointed to his right. Like she didn't already know that. She mechanically nodded anyway.

Joe hadn't left the corner, just stood there like a statue—a mortified, terrified statue—arms crossed over his chest. Nicky had never seen his laid-back friend looking anywhere near so flipped out. And for good reason.

And without another word, Carmela closed the door behind her, and the entire unthinkable episode was over. Or had it just begun?

Nicky slapped shut the overhead light Carmela had switched on. He needed to be plunged back into darkness, didn't want to see Joe's anguished face again. Didn't want Joe seeing his.

"This is *so* bad," Joe whispered to Nicky from across the room.

"I know," Nicky whispered back. He faced the wall, his back to Joe, as his mind flew through the possible ways this nightmare might play out—one result worse than the next. On the other hand, by some miracle of biblical proportions, no one else in the house had been awakened by Carmela's intrusion. So, for this very second, what happened was between Nicky, Joe, and his mouthy, erratic, deeply Catholic, seventy-eight-year-old Italian grandma. He had to head this off at the pass before anyone else found out. Tell her she didn't see what she saw. That she was dreaming! Or hallucinating! Or losing her mind!

Joe was right: this was *so* bad. Even worse.

Nicky felt a hand on his shoulder. He turned around to see Joe, whose distraught face had settled into something calmer and more contemplative. Or maybe he was just plain dazed.

"I'm so sorry," Nicky said in a pained whisper.

"It's my fault, too." He spoke in a low, measured tone. "But why didn't you lock the door first?"

Good question, except: "There *is* no lock. My parents never allowed them in our bedrooms." None of the kids ever questioned Stevie and Rose's lack of trust in them, just took it for granted, and tried to play it safe when an adult was home. Until now.

Joe nodded, clearly weighing worst-case scenarios. "What should we do?" he finally asked. That startled Nicky; Joe usually had the answer to everything. He'd been Nicky's guide and protector from the jump, but this crisis was almost beyond rational thought.

"I'm going to talk to her before she can tell anyone." Not that he'd put it past Carmela to wake up his parents and raise holy hell. All, however, still seemed quiet outside Nicky's room.

Joe considered the wisdom of Nicky's plan, and then asked, "Should I come with you?"

Much as he wanted Joe by his side, something told Nicky that this was a one-man job.

TWENTY-EIGHT

THE RIDE BACK to Boston was, to put it mildly, somber. At least for Nicky and Joe, who were still in shock and distress over Grandma Carmela's 1:00 a.m. invasion. Thankfully, Stuart picked them up at 9:00 a.m. to get a jump on traffic. So there was less than an hour for Nicky and Joe to be around the DeMarcos and any potential fallout—of which there was gratefully none. So far.

That's because Nicky *did* end up talking to his grandmother about what she'd walked in on. He found her sitting silently on the edge of the den pullout couch, staring into the dark, and clutching the same strand of rosary beads she'd had for as long as Nicky could remember. She didn't look up as he entered, mumbling prayer-like sounds to herself. Nicky quietly shut the den door behind him and gingerly sat next to her on the open sofa bed. After a few moments, she went silent and Nicky, stomach knotted, heart hammering, managed to speak.

But only one word came out: "Grandma."

He tried to continue but was a blank. No combination of words was making sense in his head. He was fatally lost in alien territory. Carmela, however, was able to deliver a speech.

"Nicky. My sweet Nicky," she began. *So far so good*, he thought and felt his heart rate slow. "I've loved you dearly since the day you were born. You were always such a good boy. The apple of your grandma's eye." She vacantly rubbed the rosary beads between her fingers. Nicky wanted to ask if he was more "eye apple" than his brother given her slip about Richie being her favorite, but it seemed wildly irrelevant just then.

She continued: "And I'll *always* love you, honey, because that's what grandmas do. I want you to know that."

Deeper relief set in. Nicky was blown away by her generous response. He wished Joe *had* come in with him; he'd be equally shocked.

Carmela grabbed Nicky's hand and squeezed it hard. So hard that he let out a little yelp. Still clenching his hand, she pushed her face into Nicky's and said, in a gravelly whisper, "But I also want you to know something else: You, my darling grandson, are going straight to hell. Do not pass Go. Do not collect two hundred dollars! If— *if* you continue down this path of sin and wickedness." She added, "Remember: hell is not His choice; it's yours."

She let go of Nicky's hand and pushed it away so hard he nearly fell off the mattress. Carmela was still glaring at him when he regained his balance. Nicky couldn't have predicted his grandma's exact response, but the whole "hell" thing was still a surprise. So was the *I'll always love you because that's what grandmas do* bit. (And where in the world did that Monopoly reference come from?) He was at a loss.

Nicky remembered why he came to see her to begin with: to beg, plead, and grovel. He gained some semblance of composure, and, in a low, even, unequivocal voice said, "Grandma, look, you can't tell Mom or Dad—or anyone *anywhere* about this." He grabbed her hand again, looked her square in her unforgiving, black-brown eyes, and added, "Please, Grandma. You have to promise me." Nicky stared at Carmela until she was forced to answer.

"OK," she said. "But you have to promise *me* something."

"What is it, Grandma? Anything." He felt a surge of blind optimism.

"That you'll never, ever, *ever* again do what you were doing in there. That you'll find a nice girl one day, get married, and have lots of babies. Make your grandma proud."

Nicky would have said anything to get out of that room in one piece, which is exactly what he did. "You got it, Grandma. I promise."

Now would Carmela keep hers?

That's what Joe wanted to know when Nicky tiptoed back in from the den.

"I'm gonna go with yes," he said, because he had to believe that. And so did Joe.

Though Nicky and Joe kept up happy faces for the unsuspecting DeMarco clan in that hour before leaving Franklin Square (Carmela wisely decided to sleep in, so there were no awkward goodbyes—a good sign, Nicky thought), once they were in Stuart's car, they both retreated into their heads. There was no anger between them, but some quiet—some distance—was apparently needed. And what better than a four-hour car ride to accomplish that?

Helping matters, Holly had flown back to Boston the day before, so Joe grabbed her place up front and Nicky was happy to have the whole back seat to himself. Stuart talked all the way out of New York State—his gabbing was like welcome white noise—then let the sounds of FM radio fill the space. They briefly picked up a country music station somewhere outside Hartford and damn if a Jerry Jeff Walker song Nicky recognized from one of Monty's albums wasn't on in all its twangy glory. He'd have to tell his roommate about that when he got back.

From his vantage point in the rear seat, Nicky watched Joe, who spent much of the trip gazing out the passenger window. Even back and side views of his strapping friend still sent a rush through Nicky. He could only imagine what was going through Joe's mind; he knew what was going through his own head, and it was stressful and complicated and more than a little sad.

About an hour from Boston, Stuart pulled off the highway to gas up the GTO and use the station's bathroom. While he was out of the car, Joe turned to Nicky and, with a conflicted yet decisive look, said, "I think you should start dating women again. I think you need a girlfriend. And I think I need to start paying more attention to mine." He held Nicky's gaze, then faced front again. Nicky didn't respond, didn't quite know what to say, but understood what Joe meant. It didn't mean they needed to end their friendship, but maybe take a break from the, well, hornier parts of it. At least that's how Nicky interpreted it—*wanted* to interpret it. More than anything, he was just glad Joe was talking again.

"I get it," Nicky finally answered. He *did* get it. And he also didn't. He felt like he was walking a tightrope, one that could upend his entire life at any given moment if he wasn't hypercautious. Still, like anyone crossing an actual tightrope, he needed to take it one step at a time.

Stuart pulled up in front of 700 around 2:00 p.m. after hitting a traffic snarl coming into Boston. Nicky didn't think he'd ever been so happy to see a building in his life. And from the look on Joe's face, he was feeling the same. They were back in the unreal world.

Nicky and Joe exchanged a quick goodbye at the mailboxes before leaving for their respective floors. There was so much more to say, but it would have to wait. Still, Joe thanked Nicky for the weekend and for making him feel "like an honorary DeMarco." Nicky hoped Joe would ask him to go running the next morning or to Case Gym for a workout, but he didn't. Maybe that was just as well. Nicky watched Joe walk off to the C Tower elevators and felt his heart sink just a little.

Back in his room and with Monty not yet returned from Pittsburgh (or had he gone to Manhattan with Sabrina?), Nicky unpacked and called his parents. They asked—well, ordered—him to phone as soon as he got in, so they'd know he arrived safely. "Don't wait till after eleven when it's cheap," Rose told him, confirming she meant business. As he dialed the number he'd known his whole life, it hit him that if Carmela had spilled the beans, he'd instantly hear it in his mom or dad's tone, whoever picked up. But before he could agonize any further, his mother's familiar—and seemingly happy—voice was on the line.

Just to be sure, Nicky asked if Grandma Carmela had gone back to Queens and if she was OK. He stared out the window at Comm Ave and held his breath.

"Yeah, she took the noon train. And, come to think of it, she did seem a little strange," Rose said, then added, with a laugh, "but, I guess, no stranger than usual." Nicky felt relief cascade through his body. "She said the two of you had a very nice talk last night."

Nicky gulped. "We did? Uh, yeah, we did, I guess." His mouth went dry. "It was late, so we didn't really talk for long." *Just hang up the phone! Now!*

"How's Joe? Is he alright?" Rose asked.

Hang. Up. The. Phone! "Uh, why? Any reason he shouldn't be?"

"Just asking. What a wonderful young man. And so easy on the eyes, if you know what that means." He did know what that meant. *Too well* he wanted to tell her. And not for nothing, that comment sounded a little creepy coming from his fifty-year-old mother about a nineteen-year-old guy. Even if it *was* Joe. *OK*, now *hang up!*

"Wait," Rose said, "let me put your father on." *Argh!*

Luckily, Stevie said all of ten words, six of which were "Don't forget what I told you," and hung up. Nicky didn't remember what his dad had told him that weekend, but as long as it wasn't "Don't fuck other men," he was in the clear.

Nicky, exhausted, lay down on his bed and conked out until Monty arrived an hour later. He *had* gone back to Pittsburgh—and not with Sabrina; she went home to Manhattan. Nicky was surprisingly happy to see him, and Monty was thrilled that Nicky had heard Jerry Jeff on the radio en route to Boston. Inspired, Monty played Nicky "Amie" by a country-rock band named Pure Prairie League, a song that seemed to bridge both of their musical tastes. Monty considered that a win, and Nicky couldn't disagree. He was so grateful to be back.

Lori arrived back from Cherry Hill around dinnertime and

summoned Nicky to her room. That she phoned from across the hall instead of coming by should have been a tip-off to, well, something, but Nicky was so excited to see her that he almost tripped on the way out his door. When he got to Lori's room, he was surprised to see Joe sitting in her desk chair. He looked as confused as Nicky, though Nicky couldn't deny the little zing he got from seeing Joe again so soon.

Nicky gave Lori a happy hug and, though she felt a bit stiff in his arms, she held on. He pulled back and studied her. She looked weary, her eyes ringed from, what, lack of sleep? There was none of her usual shimmery, fresh-as-a-daisy aura; dark had seemingly replaced light. Spending a holiday weekend with her divorcing parents really must have taken its toll.

Two words landed on Nicky and Joe like an anvil.

"I'm pregnant," Lori said.

No lead-in, no chitchat, just the facts. No wonder Lori looked so miserable—and sounded so weird on the phone the previous night. Nicky's notion that maybe Joshua had caused her weekend gloom led to a more startling thought: Was her ex the father? That idea, hatched before Nicky even paused to do the math, was summarily axed.

"It's one of yours," Lori told them with bleak certainty, then plopped onto her bed.

Nicky was flabbergasted, his brain exploding. It couldn't possibly be his! He and Lori only did it once—and pretty quickly at that! If it was anyone's, it was Joe's. They'd been together *way* more times!

That was apparently Joe's first thought as well, given his look of total, irrevocable dread. That is, until both guys' heads stopped spinning and they remembered (tenth-grade health class, anyone?) that, when it came to conception, it was quality, not quantity. And, as Lori, who was far better versed in the basics, was quick to confirm, based on her cycle, all signs pointed to the night (or early morning) of their "three-way stupid-a-thon."

Oh, sure, now she called it that! Nicky could never regret that experience, no matter what. Then again, he wasn't the pregnant one. "Besides," she grudgingly added, "we didn't use anything that night—if you two happen to remember—because we were all so fucked up. It was my one time rolling the dice like that—and pow! It's like, I don't know, the anti-lottery or something."

Joe asked Lori the question that was as offensive as it was inevitable: "Are you *sure* there was no one else?" His words hung in the air, filled with implication.

If her facial reaction were a painting it could have been titled *Laurie Partridge Breathes Fire*. But Nicky knew her flared eyes and indignant stare were just for show. And that if Lori's calculations were correct—which he believed they were—then the Joshua part was irrelevant anyway. At least at this very moment.

Lori's angry look receded, and she answered Joe with a tight nod. He nodded back with what read like either acceptance or retreat. Or maybe both.

Now it was Nicky's turn to piss off Lori.

"But how do you *know* that you're pregnant?" he asked, cringing as each dopey word came out. The thought that he could be a dad by the time he was nineteen was right up there on the I'm-fucked meter with Grandma Carmela catching him with Joe's hand down his shorts. Talk about a one-two punch.

"Don't be an idiot, Nicky," Lori lashed back, then hugged the little stuffed bear that she kept atop her bed. Nicky shrank back and sullenly dropped into Sabrina's desk chair.

Perhaps realizing she maybe *did* owe the guys a few more details, Lori sighed and said, "By Thanksgiving Day I was four days late—I'm never late!—and I started feeling all kinds of strange. I was queasy, my boobs ached, I was peeing a lot, and things started tasting weird. Next day, I snuck away to this free clinic and took a test."

Nicky felt terrible—and a little sick to his stomach. "I'm so sorry you had to go through that alone, Lori," he said. She narrowed her gaze at him, maybe rethinking the "idiot" label.

Joe began pacing, looking purposeful. "So, what are we going to do?"

Lori tossed the stuffed bear aside and sat up taller. "Well, I don't know what you two are doing, but tomorrow I'm going to look for a place."

Nicky asked, "A place?"

Lori shot him an impatient look. "A place to take care of it."

Joe stopped in his tracks. "Whoa! Y'mean, take *care* take care of it?"

"It's legal now—in case you didn't know," Lori snarled. She might have sounded tough, but she looked petrified. And so did Joe.

Nicky was scared, sure, but mostly just numb. He stared at the lava lamp on Sabrina's desk. Like some message in a bottle, the swirling colors were light pink and powder blue: one for a baby girl, one for a boy. But the shades quickly blended into a pastel purple—and disappeared out of sight. It was all too much to fathom.

The door opened, and Sabrina pushed through, suitcase in tow, floral knapsack slung over her shoulder. She took in the tense-looking trio. "OK, so what did I miss?"

TWENTY-NINE

Today

NICK ROSE FROM the table as Joe filled the Kenmore's doorway, his imposing frame backlit by the sun like some action-movie hero arriving to save the planet. As Joe reached Nick, his hand extended for a shake, he flashed that thousand-watt smile that seemed only barely dimmed over so many years. Nick's heart leaped as he grabbed hold of Joe's hand, pulling him in for a hug. He felt the same as he once did: strong and easy and comforting, if maybe a bit softer. And damn if Nick didn't take in the familiar smell of Aramis; he couldn't believe they still made it, much less that Joe still wore it. That scent alone catapulted Nick back fifty years to a time when he knew so little and learned so much. And right now, that time felt like an hour ago.

"Look at you!" Joe boomed, his voice lower than Nicky remembered, as he stood back to assess his old friend. "Exactly the same!"

"Yeah, I wouldn't say 'exactly,'" Nick said with a wry grin. He also couldn't say *exactly* the same for Joe, who was still big and attractive with a twinkle in his gray-green eyes. But what were once effortless good looks had become looks on which less and less effort had seemingly been expended. His hair, like Nick's, was mostly gray, but thinner and shapeless. His skin had the crinkles and crevices and spottiness of someone who'd ditched the sunscreen long ago. His clothes—worn loafers, faded tan khakis, and a loose, short-sleeved cotton polo shirt under an unzipped nylon jacket—felt random and dated. No matter, Nick felt instantly drawn to Joe, who remained, in his eye, as appealing as ever. Clearly old habits die hard.

They sat across from each other on the pub table stools, silly grins plastered on their faces. The place was filling up with the lunch crowd, and Nick could feel the noise level rise around them. Maybe it was just the space, whose general contours hadn't much changed since the '70s, but he was happily reminded of those busy, buzzy late nights at Deli Haus. It made Nick once again think about Lori and how she should have been there with them.

"Nicky, I can't believe it's actually you," Joe said, a wondrous look on his face. He peeled off his jacket and laid it across his lap. Nick couldn't help but glance at Joe's forearms, still one of his best features.

He smiled. "No one's called me Nicky since college."

"Sorry, you'll always be Nicky to me."

It startled—and moved—Nick to think that he was still anything to Joe, given his evasiveness and downright ghosting over the years. "It took awhile, but I even got my parents to call me Nick," he told Joe. "*That* was a mountain to climb!" One of several with them.

A platter of those famous chicken wings whisked by. Nick realized how hungry he was. He reflexively picked up the menu and then put it down. He gazed at Joe; it truly was astounding to see him after all that time. So much he had to ask, so much he wanted to know. He wasn't sure where to begin. Or, frankly, even how. It had seemed a lot easier before Joe sat down. Then a song came over the sound system that couldn't have been more perfect.

"'Born to *fucking* Run,'" said Joe, with an ear-to-ear grin.

"Are you kidding me? Tell the truth: Did you plan this?" Nick joked. Joe kept smiling, lost in the legendary tune. "Hey, you know what I think of whenever I hear this?" Nick asked.

"No, but I know what *I* always think of: Thanksgiving morning, 1975. Driving around your neighborhood and singing the shit out of this song when it came on the radio." Joe cocked his head in the direction of the speakers. "Then picking up your grandma at the train station."

That was Nick's go-to memory exactly. And it shocked him to think it was also Joe's. Again, that almost fifty Thanksgivings later, he still thought about Nick in any kind of detail. Did Joe also remember how he leaned over and squeezed Nick's arm when the song came on? Nick did. He also recalled almost swerving off the road at Joe's touch. He was putty around the guy so much of the time back then. It was embarrassing to think about now, but also kind of sweet. God, they had been young.

"Grandma Carmela," Nick said, shaking his head with a bemused grin. "I can still see the look on her face when she walked in on us."

"Craziest moment of my life," Joe said, then realized, "Well, definitely in the top three."

As Nick picked up his menu, he snuck a glance at Joe, who was scanning the pub food offerings. Nick had been with a lot of men since Joe: some great, some less great, some fleeting, some longer term, and one he even married. But he always found himself comparing every one of them—fairly or not—with the man sitting across from him. Joe didn't deserve that place, that elevation. Not really. But being with him now reminded Nick why. Or as Lori had once said, "Be careful who you lose your virginity to."

"There's a whole lot of bacon and barbecue sauce on this menu, isn't there?" Joe asked, an eyebrow raised.

"Well, I think you know we're not here for the five-star rating."

Joe smiled and looked around the place. "I know. It's so wild to be here. But this was really your and Lori's spot."

Lori. "When would you say was the last time you saw her?" Nick asked.

"Oh, God, I don't know." Joe put down his menu and thought for a moment. "Probably 1988 or '89, when I was working in Baltimore. She was there for a psychology conference. We got *so* drunk." Nick shot him a devious grin. "Nothing happened," Joe told him, looking a bit contrite. "I mean, that ship had long sailed."

Yes, it had. Nick nodded wistfully. He thought about the last time he had seen Lori. Then remembered the time before that. "She visited me in LA about five years ago. She stopped overnight on the way to Hawaii. Still looked like Laurie Partridge. Well, maybe her mother, but still so beautiful—inside and out." Nick remembered that's how Lori described Joe when they first started dating. And how it wasn't quite the compliment that it seemed. But Nick meant it. It was always how he felt about her.

"It's great that you kept in touch," Joe said, still scanning the menu.

"Not as much as I wished we had, but we did our best, I guess." Nick paused, then pointedly added, "It takes work, y'know."

"I haven't been much of a friend all these years, have I?" Joe asked, eyes downcast, message obviously received. Their waiter passed by. Joe gave him the "one-minute" sign, which Nick took as an opening to respond to Joe's question—with a question.

"Why is that?"

Joe paused, meeting Nick's gaze. "Because it was easier not to."

"Born to Run" ended and a Taylor Swift song began. *Didn't that say it all?* Nick thought dryly as he mulled Joe's enigmatic response. It seemed like a trap door just waiting to be opened. *So much to ask, so much to know.* What the hell. No time like the present.

"I'm listening. If you want to explain," Nick said gently.

Joe considered that, then: "Let's get some food first, OK?"

At least it wasn't a no. Nick flagged the waiter.

THIRTY

<u>*1975*</u>

THE FLORENCE CRITTENTON Home was located in a mostly residential area of Brighton, a twenty-minute bus ride from Kenmore Square. Lori had picked the place out of Boston's four available outpatient facilities after she discovered it was the state's first licensed abortion clinic and, before that, had been around some fifty years housing unwed mothers. Still, she took Nicky with her to see the site in person before making her final decision—about which clinic to use, not the procedure itself. That part she seemed resigned to.

When Nicky asked Lori why she didn't ask Joe to join them she said that she had flipped a coin and Nicky "won." That sounded evasive, but he didn't press her on it. She'd been mostly uncommunicative since Sunday night's announcement; he was just glad she was talking to him at all. Joe had absented himself from Nicky's life the past few days: no invites to run or work out. (Nicky bundled up and jogged along the Charles by himself Monday morning—it was cold and lonely and felt appropriately punishing.)

Lori was quiet on the bus ride to Oak Square, a peaceful spot north of Brighton's more congested, student-heavy section around

Comm Ave. About halfway through the trip, Lori heaved a big sigh and said, "I never, ever expected to be in this position, and I feel so completely idiotic and irresponsible."

"It's not your fault," Nicky said.

She turned to face him. "Really? Whose fault is it then? Yours?"

He was silent. *Wasn't it kind of?* He was obviously too stoned and stupid that night to think to ask if Lori was on the pill or anything. But everything had happened so fast, so heatedly, hadn't it? Nicky wondered about Joe's role in all this. *Wait—Joe had already slept with Lori. The issue of birth control must've come up before that night, no?*

"Ultimately, I'm the one in charge of my own body—not you, Joe, or any other guy," Lori continued. "And I failed myself." She turned and gazed out the window as they veered north toward Oak Square.

Soon after, they got off the bus and walked the few blocks to the clinic at 10 Perthshire Road. It was cold and murky out; a storm was fittingly in the forecast. They both huddled into their parkas as a bitter wind pushed them forward. Nicky kept his mouth shut, knew there was nothing right he could say to Lori now—if ever again.

The Crittenton facility was a large brick, slate, and wood structure that reminded Nicky of a Lego house—well, a classy Lego house— in which the builder kept adding wings and turrets and arches and gables until there was nowhere left to expand. Lori said it looked enchanted as they gaped at the sprawling place, but then realized that was a weird way to describe what was basically a longtime home for "wayward girls."

"I guess I'm just a 'wayward girl,'" she joked, darkly. Nicky felt mildly heartened—it was her first stab at humor since they'd boarded the bus. A flicker of the Lori he knew and adored and hoped would fully return when this ordeal was over.

"Do you want to go in?" Nicky gingerly asked, knowing there was just so much she could learn about the place from the outside, pleasant and well maintained though it seemed.

Lori hesitated, her face a map of doubt and worry. Nicky could only imagine how frightened she must feel. "I don't know," she finally answered, a warble in her voice.

"Well, you should probably look around. Maybe talk to someone? Get a sense of the place?" Nicky had no real idea what he was suggesting but was trying to do his part—whatever that was. He wished Joe was with them; he'd know what to do. Then it struck Nicky: Did Joe know where Lori was right now? Had they even spoken since Sunday night? Nicky was about to ask when Lori straightened up and looked decisive.

"I'm going in," she told him.

"Should I go with you?"

Lori shook her head. "Just wait out here, OK? I'll be quick." And, before Nicky could respond, she was walking up the home's front steps and ringing the doorbell. He watched as the door opened, and Lori disappeared inside. As if on cue, the sky darkened, and a wintry chill ran up Nicky's spine. He wondered if he should go in after her, make sure she was safe; thought how she shouldn't be alone in that strange, rambling place. But he decided to respect her wishes and stayed put.

As Nicky paced the sidewalk in front of the clinic, he thought back on what Lori called their "three-way stupid-a-thon": the bonds it forged, the crucial shifts it caused, and the thorny, odds-defying result of their tryst. He thought about the muted state of his and Lori's friendship right now and how lost she seemed. He then reconsidered where he stood with Joe, and his suggestion that Nicky start dating women again. Was that the advice of a guy who was "taking a breather," as Nicky first thought, or someone backing away from a life-changing force? And was he asking Nicky to do the same—for *both* of their sakes? Strangely, the Carmela intrusion seemed to rattle Joe and crystalize things for him more than it did for Nicky—and she was *his* grandma! For Nicky, it felt like a bullet dodged, a neon sign to proceed with greater caution and not to end what he'd only started to explore. But was Joe right and did Nicky just have his head up his ass?

Snow flurries began to fall. Nicky pulled up his parka hood and zipped the jacket as high as it would go. Damn, it was getting cold. *How long would Lori be in there, anyway?* He sat on a stone bench on the home's damp front lawn and waited. And waited. About twenty minutes later, as Nicky was about to go inside and find Lori, a young, short-haired woman, wearing only a wool cardigan over a blouse and skirt, hustled out of the building. She told him that Lori was in an exam room and probably wouldn't be out for two hours.

"What?!" he asked, leaping off the bench. "She was just going in to look around."

"Well, all I know is that she's seeing a doctor now and should be having the procedure shortly." The woman, whose plastic nametag read Dawnette, didn't look much older than Lori. She wrapped the sweater tightly around her narrow frame as bits of snow landed on her nose. "Are you the father?"

Nicky wasn't sure how to answer that. He didn't want Lori to appear, well, irresponsible, but figured she wasn't the clinic's first patient to be a bit fuzzy about the paternity issue. He met Dawnette's soulful brown eyes and told her the truth: "Maybe."

Her face remained judgment-free. "You're welcome to get out of the cold and wait in the reception area. Or you can come back in a few hours. Either way, you won't be able to see her until she's recovered." Dawnette said that last word gently, almost reverently.

Nicky was still shocked that Lori was having the surgery right then and there and wondered if that had been a snap decision or her plan all along. "What do most . . . fathers do?" he asked, stumbling on the "F" word.

"Most fathers aren't here to begin with." She wiped the flurries off her chin with the back of her sleeve. "Whatever you're comfortable with."

"If I come inside, is there any way I can, I don't know . . . help?" He didn't know what he was asking but thought it might help him decide.

Dawnette looked bemused, was clearly new to that question. "Not really, no." Nicky still didn't move. She indicated the bench. "Why don't you sit here a bit and think about it, OK?" Then, nodding toward the house, kindly added, "Just ring the buzzer."

Nicky watched her vanish back into the clinic as the flurries became full-on snowflakes. The bench was looking slick and less welcoming, but something stopped him from waiting inside just yet, especially if he couldn't be with Lori. It also made no sense to go back to BU only to have to return to Oak Square an hour or so later. He checked his watch: 3:20. Nicky wondered if he should call Joe on the off chance he'd be in his room. He had a right to know what was going on. Unless Lori really *didn't* want him there, though Nicky couldn't imagine why.

Unsure if they'd let him use the phone in the clinic, Nicky burrowed into his parka and walked back in the direction of the bus stop, where he remembered passing a corner diner. He figured they'd have a pay phone, as well as some hot coffee he could warm up with and kill some time. The snow, heavier now, was sticking to the sidewalk and trees, and Nicky hoped the roads wouldn't be too bad by the time they took the bus back to Kenmore Square. The thought of riding a bus—a lurching, exhaust-belching, stranger-packed bus— seemed like something Lori shouldn't be subjected to after an ordeal that, Nicky guessed, would leave her woozy and worn out. Maybe, when she was ready, he could call a cab.

He pulled his wallet from his jeans pocket and counted a total of three single-dollar bills. He didn't know what a taxi would cost, but it had to be more than that. Plus, he needed money for coffee and maybe a muffin or something, as he was starved. He didn't know how much cash Lori had on her, but it was a good bet whatever she had would go to pay for the procedure. (*It wasn't, like, free or anything, right?*) Plus, he couldn't ask *her* to spring for a cab, not after all this. Shit, he could take at least some responsibility here! Then again, so could Joe—if he could be located. Which Nicky tried to do as soon as he entered Sam's Diner, a small, old-timey place, and was directed to a pay phone next to the restrooms. But Joe's phone rang and rang, and Nicky finally hung up, retrieved his dime, and took a seat at the empty counter.

A waitress who reminded Nicky of Nurse Ratched, but without the starched white uniform, gave him a suspicious look and slid a menu his way. "You're too late for lunch and too early for dinner, so good luck," she said in a thick Boston accent. She stared at Nicky as if daring him to order.

"Just coffee for now," he said. "Oh, and do you have any muffins?"

Nurse Ratched's twin sister scowled. "All we got left is corn." *Cahn.*

Nicky wondered if he told this joy machine that his friend was having an abortion just up the road and he was starting to freak out, would she be any nicer to him? It was hardly worth chancing, so he agreed to the muffin, which turned out to be so dry it could have been made of sand. Luckily, the coffee was decent, and he had three cups of it while he watched the clock and waited to call Joe again.

When half an hour had passed, Nicky returned to the pay phone and dialed Joe once more but, again, the phone just rang. Nicky was about to hang up when Joe breathlessly answered.

"'lo?!" he asked.

"It's Nicky."

It took Joe a moment. "Nicky. Oh. Hi. Sorry, I just ran from the elevator, heard the phone ringing, and I—"

"I'm in Brighton. With Lori. Well, not with her this second but— she's having it done now." A spindly guy, eighty if he were a day, exited the men's room. Which was strange since Nicky had been the only customer in the diner. Where did this old fella come from?

"Now?" Joe shouted. "What happened? Is she OK?" Joe's voice was ragged, strained, not his usual smooth cadence. "Why didn't anyone tell me?"

Nicky didn't know what to say, hadn't thought through this conversation, so decided to be honest. "I don't know, Joe, it wasn't planned—at least I don't think it was—we just came to look at the place and—"

"Where is it? I should be there! Shouldn't I be there?"

"I don't think there are any real rules, but I'd like you to be here."

Nicky gave Joe the clinic's address, told him how to get there, and offered to meet him at the bus stop. He also told him to bring cab fare for the trip home. Joe didn't question that, just hung up without a goodbye. Nicky felt a little better now—and a little worse.

Make that a lot worse. He ran into the men's room and threw up in the sink.

Instead of returning to his seat, Nicky dropped a buck on the counter, then speed-walked out of the diner and into the frosty twilight. Though Nicky's stomach felt sour, he decided to roam around Oak Square until Joe arrived at the bus stop. It flickered across his mind to phone his parents just to hear their familiar voices. But he realized he'd have to call collect, which would wig them out, and really, What could he say to them now anyway? So he just kept walking. And walking. Until he found himself back at the bus stop right as Joe was stepping off the number 57 from Kenmore Square. Nicky felt such a pang in his chest at the sight of his friend that he almost cried. He didn't give a shit what Joe or any passersby thought and hugged the guy like he'd just returned from the dead. If Joe seemed overwhelmed by Nicky's intensity he didn't let on, just hugged him back.

"Are you alright, pal?" Joe asked, as he pulled away and eyed Nicky's anxious face.

"Better now." Nicky wanted to ask why Joe hadn't spoken to him since Sunday night's revelation but let it go. They could discuss their relationship another time. Now it was about Lori.

Walking to the Florence Crittenton Home, Nicky filled Joe in on whatever details about the place and the procedure he knew—which were admittedly few. He also reassured him that Lori inviting Nicky over Joe was totally random; Joe tried not to act offended but probably was. But, like Nicky, his concern for Lori's well-being seemed to eclipse any personal, bigger-picture feelings he might have been having just then.

As they turned the corner that led to the clinic, the snow tapering off to a slight mist, Lori emerged from the front door zipping up her parka. She stopped short at the sight of the guys—who froze in their tracks as well.

"They said you'd be waiting inside for me," Lori said to Nicky, pulling a dark wool hat over her head. She looked on the verge of tears.

"I'm sorry, I really am, but they said it would be a few hours and I went to the diner and had coffee and then called Joe and I walked around and then waited to meet him at the bus. Are you OK?" Nicky nervously spilled out. He took Lori in from top to bottom, relieved that she was standing on her two feet and, except for looking pale and sad, seemed to be alright. Whatever "alright" was supposed to look like after what she'd just been through.

Joe went to Lori and put his arms around her in a tight hug. She didn't seem to have the energy or inclination to return it, just patted his shoulder with one hand until he broke away. "I wish I knew you were doing this today," he told her. "I would have been here from the start."

"I wish I knew I was doing it, too, but . . ." She drifted off, then regained her train of thought. "Can we just go home?"

Just as Nicky said he'd call them a cab, a taxi pulled up, and Lori explained she'd already ordered one. Joe immediately offered to pay for it, and neither Nicky nor Lori protested. They all piled in the back seat, and Joe directed the driver to 700. Not another word was spoken. It would have to wait until Lori was ready.

THIRTY-ONE

LORI MAY NOT have been ready to talk yet, but someone else was.

When Nicky returned from Brighton with Lori and Joe, they each quietly, awkwardly went their own way, with understanding nods but no hugs or promises to meet up again later. Nicky felt sad and wistful for their earlier days and weeks together, well before the Thanksgiving weekend had presented its startling pair of curveballs. Hopefully, things would look brighter in the morning.

As for one of those curveballs, Nicky had continued to trust that his grandmother would take his secret—their secret—to her grave. Call it naïve, overly optimistic, or just plain blockheaded, but he simply couldn't imagine her getting out the words to tell anyone what she had seen that night in his bedroom. And maybe, just maybe, she'd feel that if she *did* talk about it, it might actually make it true; if she stayed silent, it might all go away. Nicky knew she was just superstitious enough to believe that. Plus, he did promise he'd get back on the straight and narrow, and wasn't that all Carmela wanted? Or did she somehow sense that was just lip service?

Nicky would be proven flat wrong in his assumptions when, around eight o'clock that night, his father called. This caused an ear-splitting alarm bell to go off in Nicky's head. His father *never* phoned him; Rose would always place the call and then, at some point, Stevie would briefly hop on. Nicky's first thought was that someone was dead. He didn't know that someone could be him.

"Nicholas, it's your father." Stevie's words came booming through the earpiece. Nicky's chest pounded. He could only remember his dad calling him "Nicholas" once: when he was ten and accidentally pitched a softball through their kitchen window. Stevie had taken away Nicky's TV privileges for a month.

"Where's Mom?" Nicky asked, fearful and confused.

"That doesn't matter. I just got an insane phone call from your grandmother."

Nicky could feel his throat close up, his skin flush. He prayed he was wrong, but knew in the pit of his twisting gut where this was going. He felt dizzy and weak. He leaned against his dresser, the phone cord stretched to its limit.

"Insane . . . how?" Nicky asked with whatever was left of his voice. He shut his eyes and clenched his teeth, grateful at least that Monty wasn't there to witness this.

"She said when you were here last week, she walked in on you and your friend Joe . . ." Stevie trailed off, clearly unsure how to put this—or, Nicky thought, so disgusted that he couldn't get the words out. But his father regained his verbal footing and added, "doing it."

That seemed like a pretty juvenile description for a man in his fifties but Nicky appreciated his brevity. "Doing . . . what?" he asked, suddenly aware there might be a path out of this mess.

Stevie's words came out so strained that a gun could have been pointed at his head. "Jerking each other off."

"What?! That's totally crazy!" Well, it *was* somewhat crazy—only Joe had been jerking Nicky off.

"That's just what I told your father!" Rose blurted. She'd apparently been listening in on the extension phone.

"Mom?"

"I said, 'Stevie, your mother has gotten a little nutty. You *know* that. You can't believe everything she says these days."

Nicky saw a potential life preserver being tossed his way and grabbed it. "Mom's right, Pop. Why else would Grandma say something like that? I mean, where in the world would that even come from?" Then added, "Jesus!" for some authentic disbelief. He held his breath. Was there a chance in hell his tough, cynical father would buy this? Then again, it hit Nicky, why wouldn't he? Stevie had no reason to question his son's sexuality—that Nicky knew of, anyway.

That hope was short lived. "She said you made her swear not to tell anyone," Stevie told his son. There was a steeliness to his words, an anger that Nicky had only heard on rare occasions. And on those occasions, the guy never backed down.

"Stevie, now *you're* sounding crazy," Rose said. "Besides, you heard what Joe said: that Nicky had a harem after him. A harem is made up of women!"

"Shut up, Rose. I know what a harem is! I want to hear from Nicky." There was dead silence. At least he was back to calling him Nicky.

Nicky didn't know what else to say—he was still astonished that Carmela had betrayed him. But he remained sure of one thing: he could never tell his parents the truth. Because when it came to who he was, what it meant, and where he was going, he didn't really know the truth. And frankly, he was as surprised as anyone that he was on this journey. Maybe he should just double down on the "harem" bit. Oh, and tell his father he may have gotten Lori pregnant. That would make the old man proud.

"Dad, if you want to believe Grandma, go for it, OK? I have studying to do," Nicky said with a distinct tinge of *I won't dignify this crap with any further discussion.* He hoped it was convincing.

Rose responded for her husband: "Honey, go study. Do what you have to do. And forget about this silly call, OK?" Nicky couldn't have appreciated his mother more.

"Happy to. Thanks, Ma." Nicky paused for his father to say something. When he didn't, Nicky asked, "Anything else, Dad?"

"Just this: I find out your grandmother saw what she saw, and you don't set foot in my house ever again. Got that?"

"Stevie! What the hell is wrong with you?" Rose shouted. "Nicky, don't listen to him. Your father's just upset about Grandma. Doesn't want to face the fact that she's losing it. Maybe already lost it." Rose took a breath and said, "We'll call you Sunday night, OK, baby?"

Nicky's hand trembled as he put the receiver back on the hook. He knew this was far from over and that all he'd done was slap a Band-Aid on an open gash. His grandma may have gotten loopier, but she wasn't completely around the bend and, he suspected, would bring the subject up again—and again—with his parents and who knows who else? (*Please, please don't tell Richie*, Nicky thought, and then wondered if he already knew.) Sure, Nicky's "situation" was a lot to dump on an old lady and he could only imagine how much space it was taking up in her mercurial head. And he was sorry for that. But the consequences of her indiscretion were too great. And Nicky believed his father's threat about locking his son out of the house—and, it would seem, out of his life.

NICKY BARELY SLEPT that night, imagining all the worst-case scenarios. He could see Stevie becoming obsessed with this story, which could conceivably morph into something exponentially worse with each retelling. Even if Nicky could prove he was innocent—which, of course, he wasn't—the vision would stick in his father's mind. And also maybe the minds of whomever else would eventually hear about it, until all anyone would see when they thought of Nicky was what a pervert he was. Their word, not his!

And yet, through all his harrowing, ticking-bomb thoughts, Nicky never considered cutting it off with Joe, even if that seemed to be where Joe was headed with him. Why? Because, pure and simple, Nicky was in love with the guy. It was an absurd, astonishing, frightening, dangerous, inconceivable notion, but that's where he landed. He also doubted if Joe could ever truly return the feeling—even if that kind of thing, for two guys like them, were remotely possible.

Nicky stumbled through his morning classes (finals were terrifyingly around the corner and he couldn't be less prepared) and returned to 700 just as the dining hall opened for lunch. He hadn't eaten since that awful corn muffin at Sam's Diner—like twenty hours ago!—and was ravenous. He grabbed a tray and piled it high with pasta salad, tuna salad, chicken salad, and salad-salad; an onion bulkie, two cups of coffee, and a powdered doughnut, and sat at a corner table facing the wall. Nicky got lost in his mega-lunch, eating his troubles away, when he saw a pair of familiar hands plunk down a tray across from him. He looked up to see Joe standing there in a pair of navy cords and a checked flannel shirt open over a white, waffle-knit thermal. His hair was combed back and shower damp, his face freshly shaved. Aramis wafted. He looked outstanding.

"Mind if I join you?" Joe asked tentatively.

"Sure, sit. I've wanted to talk to you," Nicky said. "I mean, really talk to you."

"I know. Me too," Joe said, settling into a chair. "I guess I've just needed some, I don't know . . . time alone or something."

Nicky looked around; the tables closest to theirs were empty. There was some privacy—for now. "Have you spoken to Lori?"

"Not yet. You?"

Nicky shook his head. "I hope she's OK. Yesterday was a weird fucking day."

"Especially for her." Joe examined the burger beneath his bun. Satisfied, he took a huge bite. "You look like shit, by the way," he told Nicky as he chewed.

Nicky swallowed a hunk of chicken salad. "Didn't sleep much last night," he answered. He didn't plan on getting into it just then but ended up recounting the whole miserable phone conversation with his parents. Nicky felt better telling Joe—telling *someone*—and sharing the burden, but he could see that it instantly blew Joe's mind.

"What did they say about *me*?" he asked, panic on his face. It seemed like an odd first question to ask.

Nicky thought for a second. What *did* they say? "Not much, I don't think. It was basically about, 'Was my grandmother hallucinating or just acting crazy?'" *Or was she clear as a bell?*

Joe's shoulders relaxed. "So they don't think I tried to corrupt you or anything, right?"

If it wasn't such a serious moment, Nicky would have laughed out loud. Sweet, sexy, laid-back Joe wouldn't corrupt a fly. And as if Nicky wasn't a totally willing—if sometimes confused—participant. "Like I said, you didn't come up. Except that my grandma walked in on *us*. Or that she *said* she did."

"Which you denied."

"I kind of threw her under the bus, but, yeah, of course I denied it. Forcefully." When Nicky thought about it, he was probably more indignant than forceful. And he never really told his parents, in so many words, that he and Joe didn't do the alleged deed. But he still thought he put on a convincing show. For what that may be worth.

"OK," Joe said, "but do you think your dad would really do what he said? If he found out for sure it was true?"

"Yeah, I do," Nicky answered. He pictured a return to his child-hood home only to find the locks changed. Nicky tried to shake the image. He vacantly spread tuna on his onion roll.

A table of four filled up next to Nicky and Joe. Joe eyed the group, then lowered his voice. "OK, but you don't think your father would, like, try to call *my* father to get to the bottom of this, do you?"

Nicky mulled that as he bit into his sandwich. Joe's question seemed far fetched but not totally off the charts. *Shit, that would be some phone call*, Nicky thought. He tried to put Joe's—and his—worry to rest. "How in the world would my father find your father's phone number?"

"He'd force you to get it from *me* and give it to *him*! Would you put it past him? I've met your dad; he's no pushover."

That all made more sense than Nicky cared to acknowledge. "Joe—no one's calling anyone's father."

Nicky and Joe silently ate for a moment. Ken and Chuck passed with their lunch trays. They nodded at Nicky as if they were about to join him. Then, maybe sensing something was up, moved on to another table.

Nicky finally asked Joe the burning question. "So where does this leave us?"

"Us?" Joe studied his plate.

"You said that I should date women, and you should focus on Lori. Fine, but what did that mean exactly?"

Joe considered his words. "Nicky, look, the thing with your grandma was upsetting enough. But now that your parents are involved, it's out of control! It's like this big, flashing warning sign: we don't stop, we could blow up our entire lives."

"Joe, my parents aren't *involved*, they're just—"

Joe raised a hand to stop him. "Nicky, we can't be friends. We can't be anything anymore," he declared in a clenched whisper. "I'm sorry but . . . we just can't."

Although Nicky had more or less predicted Joe's answer, hearing it aloud and in such resolute terms was crushing. Still, he had to ask: "OK, but why we can't at least stay friends?" Really, who just gives up a best friend?

Joe studied Nicky a beat. "Let's go outside," he said, bolting up with his tray. Nicky grabbed his own tray and followed.

Nothing more was said as Nicky and Joe exited 700, crossed Comm Ave and the Storrow Drive footbridge, and landed on the Charles River Esplanade. They'd booked from the dorm so fast that neither thought to grab jackets. But it was a sunny, weirdly mild December day (did it really snow yesterday?) so that didn't stop them. They began walking along the jogging path.

"OK," Joe started, seemingly calmer now, "do you *really* not know why I can't just be friends with you?" Something accusing in his voice unsettled Nicky, clawed at his stomach.

"If I knew that, I'd still be inside enjoying my lunch." He didn't mean to sound flip, but he both did and didn't want to hear Joe's answer. A cool gust came up off the Charles and blew right through Nicky's BU sweatshirt.

Joe took a deep breath. "Nicky, look, I've been with a lot of guys over time, but never more than once. That was the deal I made with myself."

"Deal?"

"Agreement, promise, whatever. That the sex would be fast, in secret, and no repeats."

"Just another way to get off?" Now Nicky meant to sound flip.

Joe visibly flinched at his own words. He looked away from Nicky and out at the river. It was free of rowboats, crew season long over. "It wasn't like that with you," Joe said.

Nicky was struck by the word *wasn't*, its finality. "What was it like?" he asked, with a lingering touch of snideness. He had never felt defensive with Joe until now.

Joe stopped in his tracks, face flushed, eyes moist, his usual cool vanished. "Nicky, fuck—do I have to spell it out? I'm really into you, man. And I don't want to be. I *can't* be. It's taken everything I have to hold myself back from jumping you every single time we're alone." Joe wiped his eyes with the back of his hand. He turned away, embarrassed. He'd never looked more appealing to Nicky than at that very moment.

Nicky could feel his heart bursting—and breaking. He wanted to wrap his arms around Joe and tell him that he loved him. He wanted to say that everything would be OK and that they could figure it all out—together. But he didn't. He somehow knew that nothing he could do or say would change Joe's mind. And Nicky, feeling a sudden, uncharacteristic surge of self-possession—the kind he had long admired in Joe—realized he didn't want to have to beg or try to persuade someone to be with him, as a friend *or* a lover.

He put a hand on Joe's shoulder. "Thanks for saying all that. Now I understand." And, before any more tears were shed or feelings proclaimed, they walked silently back to campus.

THIRTY-TWO

NICKY SPENT THE rest of the day—two classes, a study session at Mugar library, and dinner at the Student Union with, of all people, Shelley, whom he ran into on the plaza as he was entering the building—in a haze. Which, for him, was like a daze, but more functional. He was able to get himself from place to place, correctly answer a few questions in class, exchange hellos with other students, absorb the chapters he revisited in his econ textbook, and get through an entire meal with the chatty Shelley without her needing to ask, "Is anything wrong, Nicky?" (Not that he could tell you what they talked about over their taco salads, but he's pretty sure she mentioned breaking up with Trent or Brent. If she was fishing for Nicky's romantic attention, the bait went untaken.)

What happened earlier with Joe, despite Nicky's stoic, self-assured acceptance of his friend's exit from his daily life, left him with an aching hole in his heart and soul. Hence, the haze, which kept him at a gauzy distance from things as he processed (fixated on?) that talk with Joe: how pained the guy seemed and how shocked Nicky was to hear how Joe truly felt about him.

Nicky never imagined that Joe was anywhere near as hooked on him as he was on Joe. He certainly never got the feeling that Joe struggled to keep his hands off him. Maybe that was because Nicky never felt he was as hot as Joe—in any way—so, really, who was more irresistible? Which isn't to say that because of Joe, Nicky hadn't become more confident about his looks and vibe, not to mention his knack in the sack. Still, Joe was a ten (ask anyone), which would always be a few points above Nicky—and most guys out there. What Nicky now realized, though, was that Joe didn't feel or act like a ten, which may have been one of the many things that made him so compelling to men *and* women.

More importantly, he also realized that Joe may have been even more confounded—and terrified of—his sexuality than Nicky. That could be because Nicky was so new to it all and had such a kind-hearted guide in Joe that he'd been happily—and hornily—swept up in the whirlwind. Sure, he still wasn't sharing his secret with anyone but Joe (and Lori, who at least knew as much as she'd witnessed) and he absolutely had to keep his family at bay. But whereas Joe seemed determined to give up sex with guys (Could he?), Nicky now felt like he had to keep exploring. And that might include playing both sides of the field and seeing where it led, even if he might never repeat how he felt with Joe. Amazingly, he'd stopped seeing his future in such fixed or preset terms. Maybe that was the downside of being a golden boy like Joe—there was an expected life track with no room for error. But what could you do when your inside didn't match your outside? It was a shitload to take in.

Between his haze, exhaustion, and general gloom about Joe, Nicky just wanted to be alone. Which, of course, was easier said than done when you lived in a packed dorm, on a floor where most every-one was in each other's business, and with a roommate who always seemed to be there when you least wanted him—and rarely when you did. Tonight was no exception as Nicky entered his room to find Monty encased in a cloud of cigarette smoke, Jerry Jeff Walker blaring on the stereo, lounging on his bed in only a pair of tighty whities, textbook open in his lap. He looked content as a clam and, Nicky had to admit, not unsexy. Still, he wished Monty wasn't around, and it must have shown on his face.

"Who shit in your spaghetti?" Monty asked as he blew smoke rings into the murky air.

Nicky bristled. "Would you say that if I wasn't Italian?"

"Relax, it's just an expression."

"Well, I've never heard it." Nicky stared in the mirror. He *did* look like someone who'd found a turd in his dinner.

Monty stubbed out his cigarette. "OK, I'll rephrase that. You look like someone who just lost his best friend. Better?"

Actually, worse. Nicky turned from the mirror. "It's a long story."

"I've got time." Monty stuck his hand down his shorts and scratched his balls. Nicky pretended not to watch.

"Yeah? Where's Sabrina?"

"Study lounge. Aesthetics paper due tomorrow. Could be an all-nighter." Scratch, scratch.

"That why you're smoking up a storm?" Nicky nodded toward Monty's brimming ashtray. Monty shrugged, pulled his hand off his dick. "Are you back to a pack a day?"

"I think we were talking about *you*. You've been weird—weird*er*—since Thanksgiving."

Nicky said nothing, just eyed Monty as he languorously stretched his arms over his head. He wished he didn't find his roommate's lean, hairy chest such an eyeful. Nicky spun away, plopped into his desk chair, and faced the wall. He riffled through his stack of textbooks, as if Monty would be gone when he turned back around. The Jerry Jeff album ended, followed by a hiss. God, the silence was beautiful. Not that it lasted long.

"What's going on with Lori?" Monty asked with unusual care in his voice.

"What do you mean?" Nicky still faced the wall.

Monty got up and sat on the edge of Nicky's bed, next to his desk. "Sabrina said she's been kind of under the weather. And not saying much."

"That sounds about right." Nicky wanted to go to sleep. It was only nine, but it felt like 3:00 a.m. He thumbed through a chapter in his ethical reasoning text but it was all a blur.

Monty scooched closer to Nicky; he smelled like a pack of Marlboros. "Dude, let it out. *Did* you lose your best friend?" Nicky realized he meant Lori, not his *other* best friend, the one he did recently lose. If that made Lori Nicky's number one again, he knew he needed to get back to being a better friend. And that started with helping her out of her justifiable funk and maybe even laying a few truths on her.

NICKY KNOCKED ON Lori's door, gently at first, then louder when there was no answer. He heard stirring inside, but the door remained closed. He didn't want to intrude on her solitude—he certainly knew how *that* felt—but wanted to be sure she didn't slip too deeply into the melancholy she had to be feeling. He wondered when she'd last eaten, if at all. The Julie who was Shelley's roommate (*Elkins!*) passed as Nicky banged on Lori's door.

"Everything OK, Nicky?" she asked. Nicky knew he probably looked a bit wild eyed. He relaxed his stance as best he could.

"Have you seen Lori? Do you know if she's in there?"

"No idea. I don't think I've seen her since . . . yesterday morning? Maybe?" Now Julie looked worried. She pushed in front of Nicky and pounded on Lori's door. "Lori, it's Julie. Elkins. If you're in there, would you open up?" Nicky didn't know why Lori would open for Julie and not him. Then he realized he'd never announced himself when he knocked. He'd make a great cop.

The door opened, and Lori stood there, bleary-eyed, hair askew, in a knee-length crimson T-shirt that read *Cherry Hill High School East*. She eyeballed her visitors. "Is this an intervention?" she asked with a trace of her old wryness.

"Do you need one?" Julie earnestly replied.

Lori sighed. "Hardly. I'm fine. Thanks for the concern."

Julie looked from Lori to Nicky and back, seemingly convinced.

"OK, well, I'll leave you to it, then." And she moved off down the hallway.

"Can I come in?" Nicky asked. Lori moved out of the doorway to let him through, then closed the door behind them.

"I was asleep," she explained. "It's kind of all I've been doing."

"Have you eaten?"

Lori thought about that. "I don't think so." She looked in the mirror. "Ugh," she declared.

"Get dressed," Nicky told her. "There's an omelet with your name on it." He didn't know about Lori, but he was feeling better already.

TWENTY MINUTES LATER they were sitting at their favorite table at Deli Haus: the last booth in the back right-hand corner. Lori was demolishing a Swiss cheese omelet with hash browns and rye toast; Nicky ditched his usual scrambled eggs for a tuna melt, and they were both on their second cup of coffee.

"Oh my God, I had no idea how hungry I was," said Lori. "The thought of food was, like—no way. And now I can't eat it fast enough." She'd regained color in her cheeks and a lilt in her speech.

"Be careful," Nicky warned. "You don't want to, I don't know, shock your system."

Lori paused, her fork poised in the air. "After yesterday's shock to my system, this is nothing." She dug back into her omelet.

"How *are* you feeling? I mean, did it hurt? *Does* it hurt?"

"Oh, Nicky." Lori sighed, shook her head. "It was horrible. I mean, they numbed me up so it wasn't that painful—more, like, some weird sensations. Since then, I've had cramps and dizziness and stuff, but what it really fucks up is your head. I mean, the whole idea is just a mindblower. Like you're playing God or something. Defying nature." She stared into her coffee cup. "I don't know, I'm just glad it's over."

Nicky tried to carefully digest her words before responding. He chewed extralong on his sandwich to buy time. Finally, he swallowed. "Can I ask you a question?"

"Sure," Lori shrugged. "I probably owe you a few answers. And I'm sorry if I've been so out of it and angry and emotional all week. But, well . . . it's been a lot."

"I know. And I hope I haven't done or said anything too stupid. I mean, honestly? I've felt way over my head with all this. I've learned more about . . . your *procedure* in the last few days than I have in my entire life."

"Yeah? That makes two of us." Lori signaled the waitress for a coffee refill, then turned back to Nicky. "So, what do you want to know?"

"OK, well, don't take this the wrong way, but did you ever think about, y'know . . . not doing it?"

"Not doing what?" Then she realized. "Oh, right." She paused as the waitress arrived and topped off her coffee cup. "The night I found out, I actually dreamt that I *had* the baby and that you and Joe and I all lived together with her—it was a girl—in a house at the Jersey Shore. Wildwood, which I really like. And we were no longer in college. At least I don't think we were. Anyway, it was all sort of perfect, and we were so happy. But then I woke up smiling and, for a second, it seemed like, 'How great would *that* be?' And then I realized the dream made no sense and that keeping the baby, at least for me—right now—was just a totally irrational thought. Sad as it made me feel to think that." Lori poured milk into her coffee, took a long sip. "Does that answer your question?"

He nodded; her answer was as good as any. Plus, it was a cool dream. He knew that Catholics were against abortion (he was sure Grandma Carmela would have a few choice words about it) and probably lots of other groups were too. But he also knew that no one should tell anyone else how to live their life. That applied to Nicky's transformation as well—and the future roads he might take. He'd have to remember that.

They ate quietly, pensively for a minute. Nicky watched as a couple, maybe his parents' age, took an adjacent table and picked up their menus. You didn't often see older people here later at night, and he wondered what brought them in. What brought them together to begin with? Everyone had their stories.

Lori pushed away her plate mid-omelet. "I hit the wall. Too much too soon, I think."

"I'd never say 'I told you so,'" he said, saying just that. They shared a smile.

"Of course you wouldn't." Lori drank some ice water and settled back in her seat. "I'm sick of talking about me; let's talk about you. What's going on?"

Nicky was desperate to tell her everything: about him and Joe, the Grandma Carmela saga, his parents' nerve-wracking phone call, and even a few of the high points of his Thanksgiving weekend (which had gotten lost amid the more dramatic developments). He had wanted to be truthful with her, right? To be the honest friend she deserved, even if, he knew, it might mean losing that friend because of it. He'd tamped down his guilty feelings in the service of his own satisfaction for way too long. But before he could open up to her, there was something he needed to know.

"Can I ask you another question?"

Lori peered at him. "Why are you being all formal? It's me. Ask away."

"Where are you with Joe?"

"I don't know. Where are *you* with Joe?"

He paused. "How do you mean?"

"I think you know what I mean. Even if you don't think I actually know."

Nicky put down his sandwich and gathered his thoughts. He still wanted to be real with Lori, but suddenly it seemed disloyal to Joe. That is, if Joe and Lori were going to have any kind of future. Nicky wouldn't be shocked if Lori had guessed what had been going on between the guys; she was nothing if not intuitive. But she could also be a bit pie-in-the-sky, often seeing what she wanted to see. What did she want to see when it came to her boys?

He glanced at the older couple next to them. They were chatting happily, laughing. The man took the woman's hand; she blushed like a teenager. Nicky decided that they'd met at BU in, what, the 1940s? Both became professors and lived in some nice brownstone in the

Back Bay. Maybe facing the river where Nicky and Joe ran.

Nicky didn't realize that in taking his time to respond to Lori she became impatient, decided to go first, and informed him of her status with Joe: they were over.

"I think I spent more time seeing him through your eyes than mine," Lori said. "I mean, he couldn't have been sweeter and more attentive when we were together. And, of course, that face and body are, well . . . I don't have to tell *you*." Nicky fidgeted, felt like he was sitting in an X-ray machine instead of a dining booth. She went on: "I liked having sex with him, and I think he enjoyed it, too. But I also sort of felt like he was going through the motions. Doing what he thought was expected of him, instead of what might really float his boat."

"So why did you keep dating him?"

Lori nibbled at her toast. "You're gonna think I'm a freak."

"I won't think you're a freak." *If you don't think* I'm *a freak.*

"Because it was another way to be close to you." She paused for his reaction. When there was none, she kept going. "I know how you feel about him, and I know how I feel about you, so . . . I don't know. What's that called, a win-win?"

It sounded more like a lose-lose to Nicky, but her reasoning was so poignant, so genuine, it brought a lump to his throat. He didn't know what to say, so Lori said it for him.

"I love you, Nicky, and I'm so grateful to have you as a friend. I just wish it could be more." She blinked away a tear. So did Nicky. The sounds around them faded.

"What if it *could* be more?" Nicky asked like a guy who wasn't in love with another guy.

Lori sniffled back more tears. "What if it could? Until the next Joe comes along and turns your head. Where would that leave us? It wouldn't be fair to me—and it wouldn't be fair to you." She tried to swallow more coffee but couldn't and set her cup back down.

"For what it's worth, whatever was going on between me and Joe won't be going on anymore." Now it was Lori's turn not to react. "He doesn't even want to be friends."

"Really? Why not?"

"I'm apparently too much of a 'distraction' to be around. If you get my drift." He almost had to laugh. "I never thought I'd be accused of *that*."

"You, sir, are a major distraction. So get used to it."

Nicky rolled his eyes. "Oh, please." He went back to work on his tuna melt.

Because the cat was so far out of the bag anyway, Nicky went on to tell Lori about the Thanksgiving debacle and its fraught aftermath. And how on some level he was scared shitless about what could happen and, on another level, less deterred than he would have ever imagined.

After she pulled her jaw up off the table and exclaimed "Holy shit!" she told Nicky, "That's because you've grown about ten years in the last three months." She flashed her first full-on, old Lori smile in days. "I'd like to think I had at least *something* to do with it."

Nicky matched her grin. He had his best friend back.

"How did you know?" he asked as they walked back to 700. Though the day had warmed up, the night was December cold. Nicky hunkered into his parka.

"What? About the secret life of Nicky and Joe?"

"I wanted to tell you but obviously *didn't* want to tell you. I knew it was the wrong thing to do, especially after what you said about not wanting any competition, but . . . anyway, I didn't want you to hate me."

"Oh, sweetie, I could never hate you." Lori locked her arm in Nicky's as they passed the Kenmore Square Cinema. A Marx Brothers double feature was playing. Nicky had never seen any of their movies but heard they were really funny.

"Good to know," he said with another smile. "But how *did* you know? Did Joe tell you?" He couldn't picture Joe saying anything to her but had to ask.

"He didn't have to," she said and left it there. Nicky didn't press her on it. It didn't matter, he was just glad it was out in the open.

They came upon New England Music City. Amazingly, the *Born to Run* display was still up in the window. Nicky and Lori stopped and gazed at it.

"That was one crazy night, huh?" Nicky asked.

"Unforgettable," she agreed.

THIRTY-THREE

Today

"Do you remember what I said when we . . . it seems strange to say 'broke up,' but I guess, in a way, that's what it was?" Joe asked Nick, midway through his second Sam Adams. Nick had only had one beer so far, but the drinks definitely helped. It had taken them a bit to find their long-lost rhythm.

"Not verbatim," Nick said, "but I remember the gist of it." He drained his Corona bottle and offered a puckish grin. "Something to the effect that I was so irresistible you couldn't keep your big hands off of me, so you had to shut the whole thing down." Nick tried to keep it light, but Joe's face went serious.

"You have no idea how difficult that was," he said like it was yesterday and not fifty years ago.

"Joe, I was there, remember?" Nick gently replied as the waiter arrived with their meals: a turkey burger and roasted sweet potatoes for Nick, and Caesar salad with chicken for Joe. Nick ordered a second Corona; Joe declined another.

When the waiter took off, Joe gazed at Nick. "I sometimes wonder what would have happened if I'd said 'fuck it' and we just kept doing what we were doing. But more . . . for real. As, y'know—a couple."

"A 'couple'? In 1975? At *BU*?"

"OK, maybe a secret couple. Closeted, stealthy, whatever."

Nick considered him. "You really *have* thought about this."

"And you haven't?" The sly, infinitely sexy smile that Nick remembered all too well flashed on Joe's face.

"Of course I've *thought* about it. More than I'd like to admit. For longer than I'd like to admit." Nick studied his burger plate. "And when you did that, it totally sucked. I tried to move on, get you out of my system—the best that a smitten, eighteen-year-old kid could. But it took awhile. You were a tough act to follow, my friend." Nick cut the hefty burger in half, took a bite.

"I let down so many people back then. Starting with you and Lori."

"Beneath that sweet, mellow, gorgeous exterior was a first-rate heartbreaker."

"Not so 'sweet.'" Joe assessed his salad, poured the extra side of dressing on it.

"So you admit you were gorgeous."

"I'll admit I was better-looking then than I am now."

Nick stabbed at a sweet potato. "Who isn't?"

"Relatively speaking? You." That smile again. Joe dug into his salad.

"Flattery will get you everywhere."

"Good to know."

They turned self-conscious, focused on their food. Were they just flirting? How did *that* happen? And so quickly. Flirting with Joe was not on Nick's agenda—if anything, the opposite. Besides, for all Nick knew, Joe had some live-in girlfriend waiting for him back in Charlotte and Nick had been his last foray into "the dark side." Joe knew more about Nick, assuming he actually read the emails he'd sent over the years. Or at least enough to know that Nick and Henry had split five years ago after twelve years of marriage (ten together before that) and since he'd never mentioned a subsequent husband—or anyone else long term for that matter—that he might be available. But for what, for fuck's sake?

"Anyway," Joe finally said, between salad bites, "to get back to the answer I started to give to your original question—"

"Which was what again?" Nick joked.

"Basically, why I've been such a shitty friend."

"Did I say 'shitty'? If I did, I meant 'shifty.'" Which was another joke, though if shifty were a synonym for elusive (*was it?*), there was some truth there. Joe half-grinned at Nick's reply, then swallowed the rest of his Sam Adams. Nick realized he'd never received his second Corona. Maybe he didn't really need it.

Joe set his empty beer bottle on the table. "To your credit, you didn't say either word. But I was trying to explain how in the same way I backed out of our friendship at school because I didn't want to be tempted by you—and yes, you fucker, you *were* irresistible—I also kept my distance afterward for the same reason."

Nick had figured as much—it was less hurtful than thinking Joe simply didn't care—but was surprised to hear him admit it. He was also surprised that they were getting into such deep territory so quickly. But Joe clearly had a lot to get off his chest and had been waiting a long time to do so. And, though Nick really hadn't known what to expect, it was truly exciting to see Joe after so long. He didn't exactly feel eighteen again, but he was definitely awash with nostalgia. Nick pushed his plate toward him.

"Roasted sweet potato? They're good."

"Sure." Joe snapped one up with his fork, gave it a try. "Tasty," he declared. "Anyway, I knew that being close to you, even long distance, would bring up too much stuff for me. Stuff that I'd kept successfully stashed away and didn't want to unleash again. That's what I meant when I said it was easier not to be friends." Nick nodded in understanding if not agreement; two roads diverged in a wood, and Joe took the one more traveled by—as people do. Maybe more traveled back then than now, but still.

The waiter rushed over with Nick's Corona. "Sorry, man, I forgot about this. It's on the house, OK?"

"Wow, can't say no to that," Nick told him, then added, with a two-finger salute, "Thanks." Nick tipped his beer bottle at Joe, took a swig; was glad it had appeared after all.

Joe continued, "But, look, all that aside, it was great getting your letters and your emails and hearing about your life—the life you were living that I ran from. The life I never had the strength or confidence to try. At least not out in the open, for the whole world to see. And by the time I *was* ready . . . well, it was too late."

That was a lot to take in, but hardly the first time Nick had heard a story like that. More from the generation before his, but still many from guys around his age. Men who, no matter what they felt inside, opted for the kind of life they grew up around. The life they thought they were supposed to have. The accepted, more traditional, and, in some ways, less complicated life. But for too many, maybe like Joe, the choice proved *more* complicated and wreaked its share of collateral damage.

"It's funny," Nick said, "back then I always thought of you as the strong and confident one. From the second I saw you in that elevator, all smiley and cool and godlike."

"Oh, please."

"Don't 'oh, please' me. It's the truth." Nick drank more beer and studied Joe. He could still see the impressive young man he'd adored in the face and body of the older, more wistful, maybe less remarkable guy eating lunch across from him. Even after today, he'd probably always see and think of Joe as he first knew him—so emblazoned was he in his heart and mind—and always feel that familiar stirring. There were worse crosses to bear.

"*You* were the strong and confident one," Joe said. "You just didn't know it at first."

"I didn't know a lot of things."

"Maybe, but you were a quick learner."

"I had a good teacher."

Were they bantering or flirting again? wondered Nick, or were those really the same things? This time, though, the guys didn't look away from each other but, instead, shared a sly smile.

"What are we doing?" Joe asked, eyes narrowing.

"Swinging down memory lane," answered Nick. "I mean, isn't that why we met up again after a hundred years?" He took a few bites of his burger; had almost forgotten it was there.

Joe watched Nick as he ate a last forkful of salad. "So far, I'm enjoying the trip. You?"

Nick didn't have to think about it. "I am. Most of all, I appreciate your honesty."

"I guess if you wait long enough, anything can happen."

"Maybe, but you're wrong about one thing."

"Only *one*? I'm batting a lot better than I thought."

"It's never too late. To live the life you want," said Nick. "If you really want it." He raised his beer bottle in toast to Joe, took a long and satisfying swig. Couldn't remember the last time he'd had two adult beverages at lunchtime. What the hell, it was a special day.

THIRTY-FOUR

<u>1975</u>

"NICKY, WHAT THE actual fuck?!" exploded Richie when Nicky picked up the phone. No preamble, no niceties, no brotherly concern. And the last thing Nicky needed at eleven o'clock at night while he was cramming for his finals on this last week of the semester. His stomach dropped as soon as he heard Richie's crazed voice—he instantly knew what he was yelling about. "Is it true?"

"Is what true?" Nicky asked, buying time until he could invent a suitable answer. As much as he figured their father might bring Richie into this at some point, Nicky had hoped restraint or discretion would win out. Who was he kidding? It was as inevitable as his grandma blabbing to his dad. Nicky came from compulsive people; he had to remember not to become one of them. Fortunately, Monty had just left the room to take a shower so Nicky was free to discuss this—or he could just deny it all and hang up. Why did he even answer the phone?

"Are you . . . I don't even know how to say this . . ." Richie lowered his voice. "Into guys?"

Nicky didn't know how long he could play dumb but he'd find

241

out. "What are you talking about?" He gazed at Monty's side of the room, still so neat after all these weeks. Maybe he came from compulsive people too.

"Nicky, stop it, you know exactly what I'm talking about. Dad called and told me what Grandma told him, then asked me if I knew anything about it."

Jesus, Grandma. "And what did *you* say?"

"I said I didn't. Know anything. But, honestly—and I didn't want to mention this over Thanksgiving—you and Joe seemed . . . I don't know, I've seen you with your friends your whole life and this was different." He paused. "Franny thought so, too."

Oh, she did, did she? Nicky had the urge to tell Richie the truth. Sure, maybe temper it a little (*Yeah, Joe and I fooled around once, so what? Didn't you ever jerk off with your friends when you were younger? Don't be so uptight!*) and let him deal with it however he wanted. But that urge quickly passed, and Nicky decided to say as little as he could—but still say something.

"I never thought you were paying such close attention." He stared at the mirror. On the one hand, he was impressed with the mustache he'd grown. It made him look older and maybe a little tougher— or cooler. Went with his new, more substantial build. On the other hand, he wondered if he should just shave it off before he left for Christmas.

Richie sighed. "I'm your big brother, for God's sake, of course I've been paying attention. I care what happens to you, you idiot."

"Isn't that the pot calling the kettle an idiot?" Nicky joked—sort of—still stalling until Richie would maybe get bored and hang up.

"I don't know what that means, but you're avoiding the issue."

"The issue is that Grandma Carmela is losing it, and Dad is trying to cover for her by making it seem like she's this sharp tack— and turning it on his son, which is fucking insane." And in case that wasn't persuasive enough, Nicky added, "I don't know what Grandma thinks she saw but, trust me, she was hallucinating."

How did Nicky think for even a second that he could be honest with Richie? He'd committed to hiding this from his family, and he needed to stick to that. They'd never get it—Nicky still wasn't even sure *he* did—and it would only cause pain and anguish. He glanced back at the mirror. He was keeping the damn mustache.

There was a stretch of uncomfortable silence on Richie's side of the line. Nicky had said all he was going to; it was up to his brother to respond. Which he finally did.

"Nicky, look, I don't know what Grandma did or didn't see or what's going on in Dad's thick head. But if there's ever anything you need to talk to me about, I'm here for you. And so is Franny. I'm not the enemy."

"I never said you were." *I just thought it.*

"Cool. OK, I guess I'll see you back home next week. We'll hang out."

"Sounds good." And maybe it did. Nicky's heart had resumed its regular beat.

Just as he hung up, Monty returned from his shower. Towel wrapped around his waist, Wella Balsam bottle in one hand, dopp kit in the other. He smelled of shampoo instead of tobacco, his floppy hair shiny, conditioned, and blow dried. It struck Nicky that as much as he liked the bigness of Joe, he could also get used to a smaller guy like Monty. The thought—or maybe the view—was giving Nicky a semi.

"What are *you* looking at?" Monty asked suspiciously as he whipped off his towel and gave his body a final rubdown.

Nicky felt more exposed than his roommate. "Get over yourself, Monty."

Monty broke into a grin as he stepped into a pair of briefs. "You sure I shouldn't tell Sabrina she's got competition?"

Nicky turned away, returning to his desk. "Tell her whatever you want." He sat, reopened his econ textbook.

"Jesus, relax, man, I'm just messing with you. Didn't mean to strike a chord."

Nicky gazed at the book's highlighted passages. He knew he was overreacting and why. He was acting stupid and defensive. If he got a little zing from seeing Monty in the buff, so what? Monty seemed to care a lot less than he did; he *was* just joking with Nicky. Whatever way—ways—Nicky decided to romantically travel, he needed to own it, at least to himself. And not knock out well-meaning people in the process.

Nicky turned around to see Monty lounging on his bed in briefs and an *Allegheny Folk Festival '74* T-shirt. He was fishing around for a cigarette. "So, speaking of Sabrina, things still good between you two?" Nicky hoped the question didn't seem too olive-branchy.

Monty found his Marlboro pack and tapped out a cig. "You *would* ask me about her while I'm about to grab a smoke."

"Wow, now who's striking a chord?"

Monty gave a reluctant grin, flicked open his lighter. "OK, got me there." He lit his Marlboro, took an extra-long drag. So much for that shampoo smell. "Actually, Sab and I have been fighting a lot lately. Mostly about my smoking."

"That you're back to a pack a day or that you smoke at all?"

"That I don't have enough respect for her to do what she's asking."

"You're not purposely trying to disrespect her, right? You're just hooked on cigarettes."

"She thinks I should be hooked on her *more*." He flicked his butt into an ashtray. "What can I do? My little cowgirl's a post-hippie vegetarian with a strong moral and ethical compass and a surprisingly strong spine for such a gentle chick. And me? I guess I'm just a dirtbag."

"You said it, not me," Nicky joked, which made Monty cackle. He may have been a bit eccentric and contrary, but Monty was no dirtbag. In his weird way, he was kind of a classy guy. Nicky never thought he'd think that but suddenly did. "So, what's it gonna be: smoking or Sabrina?"

Monty sat up, pensive. "Well, I don't want to quit—or frankly even cut back. But I also don't want to lose her." He crushed out what was left of his cigarette. "I may not be the world's most-experienced guy, but I know this: women like Sabrina don't come around every day. At least not for an oddball like me. So, whatever I have to do or say, I'm not gonna let her get away." He leaped off the bed and moved to his desk. "Enough of this deep-talk shit, I gotta study." He snapped on his lamp, flipped open a trio of textbooks, and settled into his chair.

That little speech was a lot for Nicky to unpack, which he tried to do as he returned to his own late-night studying. First, there were Monty's two surprise confessions: that he wasn't the player Nicky may have thought—or that he might have had others think—and that he considered himself an oddball. That's some serious honesty, whether he meant it that way or not. Second, and more important, was his commitment to doing whatever was necessary to hold on to Sabrina. Even if it might mean giving up his beloved cigarette habit. In other words, if you care about someone enough, you move heaven and earth to make it work. It may not have been the most novel philosophy, but it sure spoke to Nicky in light of recent events.

Joe clearly cared about Nicky, maybe too much for him to handle. And even if Nicky wasn't going to push him into continuing their relationship, he wondered if he'd too easily given in to Joe's fear and guilt. Yes, Nicky had worried about the highwire act of it all and knew the risks. But he now felt they needed to finish what they'd started—or at least take it to a more natural conclusion—rather than always wonder what might have been. The how, when, and where had to be figured out, but one thing was certain: he had only one week to act before they left for Christmas vacation. If only those stupid finals weren't there to get in the way.

Nicky plugged in his hot pot to make some instant coffee. It was going to be a long night.

NOT ALL OF Nicky's finals were read-'em-and-weep sit-down tests. His economics and psych classes had written exams, but both his ethical reasoning and career management profs assigned term papers. Like everyone, he had his work cut out for him, though some folks seemed more worried than others. Monty was acting pretty cool about it all, as were Ken and Chuck and even Sabrina, who, as a philosophy major was, well, philosophical about the outcome.

Lori was nervous, mainly because she'd been derailed by her terrible week both before and after surgery, and was now desperately playing catch-up. Shelley, too, convinced that she was a lousy test taker (and none of her finals were papers) was in general freakout mode. Nicky fell somewhere between anxious and semi-confident—much like his usual personal demeanor—but wasn't leaving anything to chance. He wanted good first-semester grades for his own satisfaction, sure, but also to show his parents, especially his dad, that their investment in his education wasn't going down any drains.

It hit Nicky that, if he and Joe were still friends, he would have asked him for help prepping for finals, just like Joe had coached him in the past. Joe would never have refused—he was all about getting good grades. (After all, wasn't he committed to a 3.5 GPA or it was back to Kentucky?) But what about now? Would Joe make an exception to his Nicky boycott if he knew he needed a hand acing his tests? Just when he'd thought that finals week might screw up his plan to fix things with Joe, Nicky realized he had the perfect excuse to reconnect.

Then an astonishing thing happened. The next day, Nicky was deciding the best way to approach Joe for study help. He knew he had to have his ducks in order—that is, figure out specifically which subjects he needed a hand with and, within those, the exact areas—so his ask would seem legit and not just some ploy to make Joe pay attention. After dinner, Nicky was ready to make his move and knock on Joe's door. But as he was walking to the 14A elevator to make his way to C Tower, he was intercepted by Shelley. She looked a bit frantic, but also weirdly appealing in a messy bun, tortoise-shell glasses, and a blue, man-tailored shirt, half unbuttoned and hanging down over a pair of footless red tights. Her small, neat toenails were painted bright pink. She grabbed onto Nicky's arms so tightly he thought she was going to faint.

"Shelley, what's wrong?"

"Nicky, I'm dying!" *Dy-ink.*

"What? What are you talking about?" Her nails were digging

through his T-shirt and into his upper arms. He removed her hands from his flesh but held on to them. She was trembling.

"You're shaking."

"I'm just so scared. I've been studying and studying and, it's like the more I study the less I'm remembering. I'm gonna flunk every final, I just know it."

He squeezed her hands. "Shelley, you're not gonna flunk any-thing. You've had a really good semester, right?" She shrugged, tears in her eyes. "You've got yourself all worked up. Maybe you should take a break. Put the books down for the night. Go back to your room and relax. Or watch TV. Or go have a few drinks. You'll feel better in the morning." He realized he was still holding her hands—they were steady again—and gently let go.

Shelley wiped her tears and took a deep swallow. "A drink sounds good." She eyed Nicky, shyly. "I have beer in my fridge. Join me for one?"

A beer with Shelley was about the last thing on Nicky's schedule just then. He was itching to get to Joe and was kind of in now-or-never mode. But Shelley looked so needy and fragile and adrift that he couldn't say no. He glanced at his watch: 9:05. He could have a quick beer with her, make sure she was OK, then exit by nine thirty. That would still give him plenty of time to track down Joe and make his case. He followed Shelley back to her room.

He'd forgotten just how purple the place was (*did she always have that lavender shag rug?*) and it seemed like there were quite a few more pillows and stuffed animals around, though maybe not. Nicky sat on her bed as Shelley handed him a cold bottle of Schlitz. It wasn't the brand he would have pegged her for until she revealed it was her dad's favorite and she grew up watching him drink it. "A lot of it," she added, without further explanation. She grabbed a bottle for herself and joined Nicky on her bed.

"To passing our finals," she said, clinking her bottle against Nicky's.

"With flying colors," he added. The comment, or maybe that first gulp of the beer, seemed to settle Shelley. She sat back against a pillow and heaved a satisfied sigh.

"Thank you, Nicky," she said, "I feel so much better." *Beh-tah.* "Do you think I was having like a panic attack?"

He thought for a second. "I don't really know what a panic attack looks like, but I guess it's possible."

She took another gulp of beer, stifled a little belch. "I make myself crazy sometimes."

"Who doesn't?" he said, mainly to make her feel better. He swallowed more of the Schlitz and thought it was pretty good. He was getting a nice little buzz.

Apparently, so was Shelley because without warning she whipped off her glasses, moved into Nicky, and kissed him. Nicky was startled: he really thought they'd gotten past all that. Besides, there was a guy he was hoping to make out with soon if things went right, which made the moment feel ridiculously out of whack. And yet he could feel himself getting into it, responding to her soft lips and creamy skin and gentle touch. She seemed more proactive, more assured now than the last time they'd landed in this clinch; maybe she'd learned a few things with Brent or Trent. Their mouths were active, open, exploring. Shelley's hand slid down to Nicky's crotch and massaged the hardness. He slipped a hand inside her open shirt and cupped her breast, which sent a tingle up his spine. It must've had a similar effect on Shelley because she moaned. And, before a word could be said, clothes were coming off, pillows and stuffed animals were being flung out of the way, and Nicky was inside her but not before asking if she was using anything because he'd learned that lesson the hard way. She gasped out the letters I-U-D as she best positioned herself for entry. It was over almost as quickly as it began and left the two floormates breathless. And, at least one of them, more than a tad conflicted. Hint: it wasn't Shelley, though she did turn shy and quiet as they dressed.

"Oh my God," she finally said when they were back in their clothes. "That was . . ."

"Unexpected?"

"Yeah. That's the word. Even though we got halfway there that one time."

Nicky watched her. She looked a bit wobbly. "Are you OK?"

"I think so. A little calmer than when I ran into you. And also a little embarrassed."

He reached for her hand. "You have nothing to be embarrassed about."

Shelley smiled. "Thanks." She pointed to their half-empty beer bottles. "Wanna finish those and, I don't know, *not* talk about what just happened?"

It was Nicky's turn to smile. "I should probably get going." Plus, his head was swimming, and he wasn't sure he could put many more words together.

Shelley leaned in and kissed his cheek. "You're one of the good ones, Nicky."

"You, too, Shelley." And he meant it, just not in the way she might have hoped.

THIRTY-FIVE

NICKY NEVER MADE it to Joe's room that night, nor did he get much more work done. After about a half hour back at his desk, he got too antsy, so he threw on his parka and a scarf and went out for a walk. It was cold but clear and Kenmore Square was unusually quiet for 11:00 p.m. on a weeknight, which made the perfect backdrop for Nicky to be alone with his dizzying thoughts.

As he passed all the stores, bars, clubs, restaurants, and other hangouts that had become so comfortably familiar, Nicky flashed back on his impromptu tryst with Shelley and the strange knot of feelings it created. From a purely mechanical standpoint, Nicky got turned on by Shelley—or at least the situation—more than enough to do his part. He didn't have to think about it, it just happened. In the same way it had happened that night with Lori. He was young; it was exciting; he reacted. But how did it really feel? Not just, as Joe might have put it, as another way to get off, but in the bigger picture?

The sensations felt great, but he'd be lying if he said he wasn't thinking as much about Joe during it all as he was about Shelley. To be brutally honest, *more* about Joe—and maybe also Monty and the handful of other guys around campus who'd made him look twice. When he was with Joe, he experienced an electrifying rush that sent him into another dimension. He felt more earthbound with Shelley—and even Lori that time—and less swept away. True, he'd spent more physical time with Joe, and they'd done relatively more "things" together. It wasn't a contest, but he could tell the difference. And he had a growing idea which side might ultimately win out.

Nicky turned around at Mass Ave and walked back into Kenmore Square, his thoughts clearer and more focused. So much so that he started thinking about his career management paper and how he would have to barrel his way through it. It was kind of a bullshit subject and, though he'd done OK in the course so far, he hadn't taken it seriously enough. But with a solid final grade, he could nab an A- for the semester. He was ready to put in the effort. Starting tomorrow.

As he passed the Kenmore Square Cinema, the theater was letting out and he found himself amid a trickle of exiting moviegoers. Nicky glanced up at the marquee. It was the Marx Brothers again, this time *At the Circus* and *Horse Feathers*. When he looked back down, he was facing Chuck, who seemed happily surprised to see him.

"Hey, were you in there?" Chuck asked. "I didn't see you."

"No, just out for a walk." Nicky nodded toward the theater. "Any good?"

"The Marx Brothers are always good. If you like that kind of humor, which I do. My favorite is *Animal Crackers*. Ever see it?"

Nicky didn't want to say that he'd never even heard of it, so he just shook his head.

"It's fucking hilarious. Margaret Dumont always cracks me up." Off Nicky's blank look, Chuck gently explained, "Oh, she's in all their movies. A lot of them, anyway."

They started walking toward the corner of Beacon Street. The wind had come up, and the cold with it. Chuck said, "I was going to end my 'date for one' with baklava at Aegean Fare. Wanna join?"

Nicky was beat and wanted to get back to 700. But he felt like the guy could maybe use a friend. Who couldn't? "What's baklava?"

"Only the dessert of the gods," Chuck grinned and waved him on. "Come on, my treat."

Aegean Fare was less cozy and more brightly lit than Deli Haus, but Nicky liked the friendly vibe as he and Chuck sat at a table by the window. As they awaited their baklava and Greek coffee, Chuck explained that he was up to speed on his studying and needed a comedy break, hence the Marx Brothers double bill.

"I've never gone to the movies alone," Nicky confessed. "Is that weird?"

"It would be for me. But I think it's already been established I'm not like everyone else," Chuck said, neatening the sugar packets in their chrome caddy.

Nicky knew what he meant but didn't want to think of himself in those terms: as an "other." It made him sad to think that Chuck, who was a really decent guy, might feel that alienated. Though he understood.

A waitress served their dessert and Chuck lustfully eyed the layered, crispy-looking triangle. "Dig in, my friend," he told Nicky as he stuck his fork into the baklava's flaky crust. Nicky followed suit and found the sweet, chewy pastry as good as advertised.

"Excellent," he told Chuck.

Chuck struck a pose and said, in a theatrical voice, "Stick with me, kid." He rolled his eyes. "I know: half Humphrey Bogart, half Mae West." Chuck peered at Nicky and, before he could ask, Nicky jumped in.

"Yes, I *know* who they are," he said with mock impatience.

Chuck raised his hands, clapped three times. "Congratulations."

"So, what do I win?"

"My undying respect." Chuck grinned, sipped his coffee. "Now tell me, young man, what were you doing walking around Kenmore Square alone at eleven thirty at night?"

Nicky swallowed another bite of baklava. When it came to ethnic desserts, he was still a cannoli guy. "I just needed to get out of the dorm. And think about stuff."

"Yeah? What kind of stuff?"

Nicky paused and considered unloading on Chuck, but chickened out. "I don't know. Some personal shit."

Chuck put down his fork, raised an eyebrow. "Is it romantic?"

OK, here was Nicky's opening again—how many more would he have? Especially before he left for Long Island? (He'd already decided that, despite Richie's "I'm here for you" speech, his family remained a no-go for any confession.) Nicky looked around the now mostly empty restaurant, then back at Chuck. Felt safe. He knew he couldn't name names—Chuck was pals with Shelley, it wasn't Nicky's place to out Joe, and he always felt protective of Lori—but figured he could get his point across. And maybe get some perspective that wasn't in a book.

Nicky's heart began to race—and not because of the strong Greek coffee. He took one last bite of baklava and steeled himself. "You have to swear not to tell anyone." He leaned in. "And I mean *no* one."

Chuck's eyes widened and, in a loud stage whisper, he asked, "Nicky, did you kill somebody?"

Nicky surprised himself with a guffaw, breaking the tension. "How'd you guess?"

"It's written all over that cute face of yours." Chuck winced, embarrassed. "Sorry, that just came out."

"Don't apologize. I can take a compliment." Which, Nicky realized, was not something he'd always done well. But positive reinforcement was, well . . . reinforcing. He studied Chuck, really for the first time. Behind the aviator glasses and brainy veneer was a nice-looking guy with welcoming eyes, a head of obedient dark hair, straight white teeth, and good shoulders. He wondered how many people—male or female—looked right past Chuck and on to someone more instantly alluring, cool, or self-possessed.

"Well, anything less than murder can't be *that* bad. What is it?" asked Chuck.

So, with buoyant Greek music playing faintly from tinny speakers, Nicky told him. In broader strokes than he might have liked, but the gist was that he'd slept with a few women and one man since he'd been at BU, and he felt like he might be leaning toward guys.

He didn't explain why, just left it open ended, in process, which it was. Oh, and he didn't mention that he'd fallen in love—if that was an accurate description.

Several silent moments ticked by. Nicky shifted in his seat. Chuck took off his glasses, rubbed his eyes as he'd done before, and composed his thoughts. He slipped his glasses back on, gazed at Nicky, and nodded as if in understanding.

"Wow, OK." Chuck drained his coffee cup. "Is that why you asked me about *my* deal that time at dinner?"

"Maybe. A little. Though I *was* genuinely interested." Nicky wondered if his reveal had been a bad idea. Not that he could close that door now.

Chuck looked squarely at Nicky. "Was it with your friend Joe? Because if it was, I'd say that was the score of the century."

Nicky was holding fast. No names. No mention of anyone's pregnancy. Or allegiances. The specifics were less important than the general concept; the conundrum of it all. He answered with a shrug. Let Chuck think what he wanted, he would anyway. And, yeah, being with Joe *was* the score of the century. But it would be a greater triumph if he could revive things with him. Which he would try to do tomorrow—or later that day, as it was now well past midnight.

The waitress returned with the check. Chuck swiped it from her hands before Nicky could protest. "I told you: it's on me." He winked at Nicky. "Your story was more than worth it."

"So . . . are you surprised?"

"Are *you*?"

"Not when I *really* look back on the last few years, I guess." He told Chuck about his fixation on Larry Marquez and the other tell-tale signs. "If I'm surprised about anything it's the fact that I actually had the balls to go through with it."

"*Balls* being the operative word." Chuck grinned, pulled a five-dollar bill from his wallet, and laid it atop the check. "Look, here's what I know: we're all human and complicated and filled with contradictions. Straight, gay. Black, white. Male, female. And everything in between. But strangely, I think most big life decisions are made for us." He collected a few stray baklava crumbs with his fork.

Nicky took in Chuck's words. They were profound and perceptive for someone their age. Chuck had obviously thought a lot about this, for a lot longer than Nicky had. It was impressive. And he told Chuck that.

"It's amazing how much you can learn from show tunes," Chuck drolly replied. "Especially when so many were written by gay men—in *or* out of the closet."

It was late and time to wrap up, even if they'd only just scratched the surface. Why *did* Nicky open up to Chuck at that very moment? What was he looking for or hoping to hear? Did he want Chuck to feel less alone—or Nicky? If there were some kind of answer or validation he was searching for, he didn't get it. Yet.

"I'm a little jealous, y'know," Chuck said.

"Of me? How?"

"OK, maybe jealous is the wrong word. But I feel inspired." Chuck's eyes lit up. He pushed aside his plate and leaned across the table. "You're living your life. Taking chances. Jumping into the deep end of the pool. And yeah, I know you're scared. Or confused. Or overwhelmed. Or all of the above. And there are tons of reasons to feel that way. But you have so much more strength than you know."

"Really? It doesn't feel like it."

"Take it from someone who's been stuck in the proverbial mud. You are officially my hero. And don't let anyone tell you otherwise."

No one had ever called Nicky a hero. He was not the hero type. Chuck's words gave him pause. His mind churned as a Greek instrumental tinkled over the sound system. He felt emboldened; oddly proud of his actions, tricky and impulsive as they may have been. But he also felt as if Chuck was selling himself short. And that somehow seemed wrong.

"Thanks for saying that, Chuck, really." A realization hit him. "But you may have inspired me, too."

"Me?"

"Yeah, that night at the Halloween party."

Chuck looked skeptical. "Why, because I went as Bonnie instead of Clyde? Men have been dressing up like women since Shakespeare's day, probably before that. It was just performative."

Jesus, where did Chuck get these words? "No, because of what you said. Something about not putting ourselves in a box. That we all need to be who we are."

Chuck shrugged. "I was just talking in code."

"Until you weren't. You told me your truth that night and that was cool. And brave. You're kind of a pioneer."

"Pioneer?" Chuck gave a rueful laugh. "Then how come I haven't even been able to talk to any guys I like—y'know, *like* like—since I've been here?" He glanced away, fiddled again with the sugar packets. "Except for maybe you."

Chuck looked back at Nicky. They locked eyes. Nicky felt a tingle fly up his chest, the kind he so often experienced around Joe. It wasn't as strong or as blinding, but it was there. Chuck melted into a shy, endearing smile. No quip or rejoinder—or song lyric—required.

As a few diners made their exit, a group of four students noisily entered. Nicky rose. "We should probably get going."

Chuck stood as well. "Thanks for the company, Nicky."

"Thanks again for the dessert. And the conversation."

They exited into the now-colder night, huddled into their jackets. "Let's hang out more next semester, OK?" Chuck said as they walked off toward the dorm. "There are a few . . . bars in town I've been too chicken to check out. Alone, that is."

Nicky got his drift. "Sure, let's do it," he said, intrigued. Even as his mind wandered back to Joe—and his last-ditch plan to win him back.

THIRTY-SIX

TODAY

AFTER LUNCH, NICK and Joe walked up Comm Ave to the BU campus, whose already significant footprint had startlingly grown over the years. Like so much else Nick had seen of Boston since his arrival, the area's one constant was change. The layout of the vast university was still recognizable. But its 1970s design had been so imprinted in his brain that the renovations—and innovations— were jarring. Sure, he'd read about these new buildings, property conversions, and, especially, the many donor-named facilities in BU's alumni magazine. But seeing them up close and personal was something else. Unlike his more sanguine expectations, Nick now felt more like a visitor from another galaxy than someone who was coming home. Even so, he decided to just appreciate his alma mater's progress and savor the visit.

So what if the old Howard Johnson's Motor Lodge, where everyone's visiting families stayed back in the day, was now a BU-owned dorm, affectionately known as HoJo? And did it matter if the School of Management, from which Nicky had graduated, had relocated to a massive brick and concrete, 1990s-built edifice and later renamed the Questrom School of Business? And what of the newish glass and steel, nineteen-story behemoth further up the street called the Center for Computing & Data Sciences? Designed to look like a giant stack of books, was it over the top or a remarkable feat of state-of-the-art construction? Who's to say?

On it went as Nick and Joe moved up Comm Ave, mixing in—though not blending in—with the streams of swift, eager students crisscrossing in and out of various buildings and up and down the expansive street. Among the better changes was how much more eclectic the student body seemed fifty years later: a vital reflection of the world around them. One place that looked about the same was dear old 700 Comm Ave, rechristened Warren Towers the second year Nicky lived there—and called that ever since. Businesses lined the soaring dorm's ground floor, starting with a ubiquitous Starbucks on its easternmost corner followed by a sushi joint, a juice bar, and a convenience store. Neither Nick nor Joe could recall what shops were there back in the '70s until Nick remembered a spot, where the juicery now stood, that only sold cheesecake. Its name remained a mystery though the guys agreed that, today, the menu would have to include gluten-free, sugar-free, and dairy-free choices.

"Aka fun-free," Joe snarked. This led him to reveal he was pre-diabetic, took statins for his cholesterol, and had "turbulent" blood pressure. "And don't even ask how often I get up to pee every night," he added with an eye roll.

Nick joked, "That's because you're so much older than me." But he knew it was less about age and self-care and more about luck—genetic and otherwise. Yet, as if Nick needed another reminder, it underscored how much time had passed and how the vitality and invincibility of youth went by like a shot.

As they strolled up Comm Ave, past the relatively—and reassuringly—unchanged exteriors of the College of Arts & Sciences (in Nick's day, the College of Liberal Arts), Marsh Chapel, the sprawling Marsh Plaza, Mugar Library, and the George Sherman Student Union, Joe peppered Nick with questions about his marriage to Henry. He wanted to know what brought them together (laughter and lust), what split them apart (Henry's late-breaking wandering eye), if they remained friends (not exactly), about the son they adopted together early on (Dylan, now twenty-three, a UCLA research assistant and all-around awesome dude), if Nick had dated many—or any—women after college (two until he went full homo), and his current romantic status (open but selective).

Joe nodded pensively at each answer, passing no verbal judgment or observation. Nick wondered if there were any specific reasons for his questions beyond general, respectful interest. Was he gauging Nick's openness to a possible advance—one more hot hookup for old times' sake? Or was Joe comparing—and contrasting—the arc of Nick's gay, adult life to his own semistraight, if maybe less emotionally eventful existence? Nick could have asked him outright but chose to wait. There was so much else he wanted to know.

Nick got his turn as they made their way to the grassy knoll behind Marsh Plaza nicknamed BU Beach. It was a parklike expanse across from the river, where students used to hang out, study, relax, sunbathe, or toss around a Frisbee. And from the looks of it on that fine fall afternoon, they still did. In droves. The place always had a warm, festive air, and being there could feel like a little vacation from the city campus. Nick never spent much time there his first semester. He usually opted for the less-populated Esplanade several long blocks up when a getaway was in order. And, of course, back then, the Esplanade made Nick think of Joe and the time they shared jogging and getting to know each other. Just as it did again that very morning.

They found a spot on the lawn in the shade of a broad Scarlet oak. As they sat, Nick noticed how gingerly Joe lowered himself to the ground. It reminded him of the deliberate way his friend Ramón moved before he had his knee surgery; maybe that was in Joe's future. Nick didn't think of himself as Superman in any way, but he was struck again by how Joe, once such a stellar physical specimen, had become a mere mortal so many years later. It shouldn't have surprised him—even the greatest athletes lost their vigor eventually. Still, it made Nick wistful for the past. And uneasy about the future.

"OK, so what about you?" Nick asked as they settled into the sloping stretch of grass. He watched as a pair of attractive girls, seemingly deep in conversation, passed a few yards away. They broke into a conspiratorial giggle. One of them—tallish, lithe, shoulder-length, straight hair—reminded Nick of Lori. Until she didn't.

Joe gave a sideways grin, anticipating Nick's inevitable probing. "What *about* me?"

"I mean, I know where you've lived and worked, but not much about your . . . private life all these years."

"If you want to know who I've slept with, just ask."

Nick laughed. "You make it sound so sordid." A Frisbee zipped past. A tall young guy in a BU sweatshirt ran after it and grabbed the disc with a long, outstretched arm. Made it look so easy. He glanced at Nick and Joe, gave a friendly nod, and jogged off.

"He probably thinks we're visiting our grandkids," said Joe with a dry smile.

"I'd rather he think we're professors. On a class break."

"Knock yourself out." Joe leaned back against the oak tree and stretched out his legs.

"Anyway, about your sex partners."

"Now *you* make it sound so sordid."

"Was it?" They were bantering again. Nick didn't mean to be provocative and yet . . .

Joe raised an eyebrow. "Well, I assume you want to know about the men."

"Have there been that many?"

"Define 'that many.'"

"We've been around a long time, Joe. Things add up."

Joe grinned like he was holding back some delicious prize. "Not a ton," he finally said, bringing his knees to his chest. "For the most part, it's been a struggle."

"OK, good," Nick said, crisscrossing his legs.

"*Good?* I said it's been a struggle!"

"*Good* that we're finally getting somewhere."

Joe gazed off into the distance. A quartet of students were talking animatedly as they bounded across the grass. "Were we ever really that young?" he asked Nick.

Nick peered at him. "Is that a rhetorical question?"

"No, just stupid and self-pitying." Joe broke into a smile. "I'm joking. OK, details!"

Joe, if still not one to overshare, gave Nick a speedy overview of his romantic life over the years. The long and short of it was that he'd had his share of low-key hookups with men, though kept a "straight face" for most of that time. He stopped cold when the AIDS pandemic hit in the 1980s (Nicky could relate, big time), keeping to himself until the early '90s when safer sex became common practice. But by then he focused mainly on women. That's because he was getting to that age where he'd have to put up or shut up about his sexuality, and enough people—from his family to his friends and coworkers—were starting to wonder why he wasn't married (uh, to a woman) and starting a family. And it was around that time, while back living in Cincinnati near his parents and brothers, that he met Nina, a pretty, divorced veterinarian. They started dating and, within the year (just shy of his thirty-sixth birthday), got married, and Joe became not only a husband but a stepfather—to Ethan, Nina's son from her first marriage. They were a happy little group for several years (yes, the sex between Joe and Nina was satisfying enough) until her reformed ex wooed her back, and she wanted to reunite her family unit.

"Maybe she never loved me enough or, at some level, guessed at my flexible nature," said Joe. "But I didn't fight it and let her go. I missed being a stepdad more than a husband and would take Ethan to a movie or a ball game now and then until I took a new job in Pittsburgh."

"Pittsburgh! You could have looked up my old roommate, Monty—remember him?"

Joe tried to conjure him up. "The wannabe cowboy?"

"Exactly! He and Sabrina got married right after college and had three daughters. Did you know we lived together junior year, too? At Shelton Hall?"

Joe shook his head. He'd been long gone from BU by then. At the end of Joe's sophomore year, his father was involved in a police department scandal. He lost his job and a bunch of savings in legal fees, and Joe had to finish college at Ohio State through a work-study program. Nick felt bad for Joe at the time but was secretly relieved at the forced distance between them. If Nick were to guess, Joe likely felt the same.

Joe continued sweeping through his personal history: in the years after Nina, he had short-term things with a succession of women (including one who was married and one who was bisexual), until he pretty much lost interest in the ladies for good. But it didn't send him back into the arms of many men. That is, until a while later when he had a quiet, six-month fling with a coworker until the guy wanted Joe to move in. Even if out gay relationships had become so much more accepted and routine over the decades, Joe still couldn't make the leap. He'd always be a cop's son from Kentucky. And, as he'd said back at the Kenmore, at a certain point he felt it was too late. For him, anyway.

"And now you know as much as I do," Joe concluded.

Nick doubted that but was appreciative. "Thanks for telling me all that."

"Thanks for being interested," Joe replied without irony.

Nick leaned back on his arms. "So, then you're OK with the whole 'lone wolf' thing?"

Joe thought for a beat. "Truth? I don't have the patience or energy now for much else. I can do what I want when I want. I don't have to kill myself looking good on the off—*off*—chance I'll have to get naked with some stranger. Don't have to get all tangled up in somebody's complicated life. Especially at our age, know what I mean?" He thought for a moment. "So, yeah, I guess I'm good."

Nick didn't believe him for a second—or maybe didn't want to. He still wanted him to be Joe Hello, the golden boy with the rad body and the sexy smile and the shining future. And maybe so did Joe.

"Y'know, *pretty* good," Joe backtracked, more convincing now.

He stood. "My ass is too old to sit on the ground this long. Let's walk, OK?"

They crossed BU Beach, taking in its swath of seemingly carefree students. Nick thought about Tyler, the kid from Emerson he met that morning. How he, too, first looked carefree, yet was anything but. Nick then recalled his panic attack and how much calmer he now felt. Had he really been that anxious about seeing Joe? Or returning to Boston in general? Either way, it seemed silly in retrospect—though not at the time. Isn't that how it always was?

"Are you disappointed?" Joe asked as they walked back through Marsh Plaza and onto Comm Ave.

"In BU? No. I mean, yeah, a lot's different now but—"

"I meant, in *me.*"

Nick stopped cold and looked at Joe. He seemed fragile, his armor visibly cracking. It saddened Nick that Joe would ask. And that his response, if he chose to voice it, might be yes.

"Are you kidding? It's so great to see you!" Nick said with a dash of forced enthusiasm.

"Nice way to avoid an answer, pal." Joe flashed another sidelong grin.

At least he's smiling now, Nick thought as they resumed walking, retracing their steps toward Kenmore Square. Joe was awaiting the truth, so Nick complied.

"I think you know I had you up on the world's tallest pedestal back then. I don't anymore. But that says more about me than you." That seemed fair. And honest. Enough.

Joe seemed satisfied. Enough. "Well, I'm anything but disappointed in you. Not that I expected to be." He paused, reflectively. "Not that you're asking."

That brought a lump to Nick's throat. "Thank you. But I've done a lot wrong in my day." He managed a wan smile. "Just ask my parents. Oh, wait—you can't. But you get my point."

"How did they react when they found out?"

"That I was gay? Well, remember, I always had the Grandma Carmela incident hanging over me. So they couldn't say my news was a total shock. Still, they reacted like most old-school Italian Catholics. At first, it was like I'd died. And then, little by little, I was resurrected."

"Like Jesus," Joe quipped. "But with a better barber."

Nick laughed out loud. "My mom came around first, then, astoundingly, my father. It was touch-and-go but, in the end, they referred to Henry as their 'third son.' And they were crazy about Dylan. They lived to see us marry but not split, which was good. You know how the Catholics can be about divorce. Even now."

They passed the Computer & Data Sciences building again. It looked even more massive from this angle. Perspectives shift. That much was clear.

"Well, you should be proud of yourself, Nicky. You did good."

"Thanks, but I really wish you'd call me Nick."

"OK, Nicky." Joe shot him a grin. And suddenly there was a spring in his step. "Let's hit the Esplanade. Like the old days."

Nick didn't have the heart to tell him he'd already run there that morning. So off they went.

THIRTY-SEVEN

<u>1975</u>

NICKY HOPED HE'D bump into Joe in the dining hall, where he could "casually" ask if they could study together that night. He had a whole speech ready, filled with just enough anxiety and terror to make Joe believe he seriously needed help preparing for his finals, now only a few days off. But lunchtime came and went without a sighting and Nicky, undeterred, decided to knock on Joe's door later that day. But that wouldn't be necessary as, leaving the dining hall en route to the A-Tower elevators, Nicky ran into Joe at the mailboxes. If that was a good sign, he'd take it.

Joe was his usual relaxed, captivating self, looking like a magazine model in jeans, desert boots, and a thick, cable-knit crewneck sweater. Nicky was so happy to see him, for a second he forgot he'd been dumped. He quickly remembered, slapped on a "worried" look, and made his pitch. But not before making it clear that his request for a few hours of tutoring was strictly business. Joe hesitated, then said to meet him in his room at eight o'clock. It took all of Nicky's self-control not to burst into an ecstatic grin. And to manage his expectations because, let's not forget, Joe had been pretty darn clear about why he couldn't be friends with Nicky—or even around him.

That night, after an upbeat dinner with Lori, during which he'd kept mum about his evening plans, Nicky showered, shaved, and dressed for maximum appeal. Monty blew into their room as Nicky was carefully trimming his mustache. He shot Nicky a strange look, grabbed a textbook and his smokes (he still hadn't quit), and, thankfully, left again without a word. Nicky gazed into the mirror above his dresser, liked what he saw. He was ready to do battle.

Nicky knocked on Joe's door, but there was no answer. He checked his watch: 8:06. It's not like he was early. Nicky panicked; Did Joe get cold feet? Did he just plain forget? This was Nicky's last chance and it was slipping away. *Fuck!*

As he stalked the 10A hallway hoping to find Joe, he ran into their Thanksgiving-weekend driver, Stuart, who was exiting his room.

"Stuart, hey, have you seen Joe?" Nicky tried to sound offhand.

"Oh, hi, Nicky. Nope, haven't seen the big stud all day."

The big stud? "Is that what you call him?"

"Wouldn't you?" Stuart flashed a sly grin and moved off.

Nicky couldn't disagree but wondered how Stuart meant it. Whatever, Joe had clearly kept his "secret" secret. It made Nicky feel a tad invisible which, in this case, was probably a good thing. He stopped thinking and hustled back toward Joe's door, where he found him entering his room with a six-pack of Michelob. Joe turned and smiled.

"Hey, were you waiting for me? Thought I'd run out and grab us some beers in case we went late."

Nicky, encouraged, followed Joe inside, and shut the door behind them. Joe set the six-pack down, then peeled off his parka to reveal the same jeans and sweater he'd been wearing earlier. Unlike Nicky, he hadn't changed for the occasion. Not that he knew there *was* an occasion. He still looked great. He handed Nicky a beer and grabbed one for himself.

"To acing our finals," Joe said, hoisting his brew in a toast.

Nicky clinked his bottle and took a fortifying slug. He studied Joe for any sign of discomfort or weirdness but there was none. At least that he could see.

Joe took a seat at his desk. "So, what's first? Where do you need the most help?" He eyed Nicky standing there. "Wait, where are your books?"

Oh, shit! Nicky had completely spaced on bringing any textbooks, notebooks, or even a pad and pen. He'd been so wrapped up in his real mission that he'd forgotten the fake one. This was going to be a disaster; his stomach told him so. Joe's face settled into realization.

"You didn't come here to study, did you?" He didn't seem annoyed as much as confused.

"No. I came to talk." Nicky swallowed more beer. Hoped Joe would do the same, maybe help keep things mellow.

"Is that why you shaved?"

Nicky reflexively touched his cheek. "How did you know that?"

"Because when I saw you at the mailboxes, you had like a three-day growth."

Not that he'd been looking. Nicky pondered his next move. He had about an eighth of a second to decide.

He motioned to Joe. "Can we sit?"

Joe shook his head. They both knew that sitting might lead to something more horizontal.

Nicky sighed. "Fine. We'll stand." He gathered his thoughts, steeled himself, and told Joe the truth as he knew it. "It comes down to this. I love you. And maybe I can't define exactly what that means because I've never said it to anyone before. But it's as close to what I'm feeling as I can put into words." He took a breath, waited for a response, even some physical cue. But Joe didn't move, just stared at him impassively. So Nicky kept going because, at that point, Why the hell not? "And, yeah, it's crazy and complicated and probably dangerous. But I don't want to give up on you yet. And I have the feeling that, no matter what you've said, you don't want me to either." He gave a smile and added, "I mean, c'mon, who notices how often another guy shaves?"

Joe still said nothing. Finally, he moved in gently, pressed an open palm against Nicky's chest, and held it there. Nicky could feel his heart beating beneath Joe's hand. He watched his eyes. Joe's look—passionate, pained, resigned—was filled with more words than he ever could have spoken. And seemed to say it all.

Nicky remembered Monty's words about Sabrina. *Whatever I have to do or say, I'm not gonna let her get away.* And though that inspired Nicky at the time, he now realized that the situations were different. Maybe so much more than he'd ever understood. And that he wasn't giving up on Joe—he was letting go.

But Joe let go first as he removed his hand from Nicky's chest, kissed his forehead, and wished him good luck on his finals.

"You, too," Nicky told him. "I'll see you around."

Going down in the empty A-Tower elevator, Nicky felt no resentment or anger toward Joe, but toward the world at large. Maybe one day guys like Nicky and Joe would have a real shot at togetherness. At happiness. At acceptance. At something remotely resembling equality. Till then, Nicky knew, like the advice he'd given Chuck that night in the dining hall, it was one day at a time.

NICKY DIDN'T ACE his finals, that much he knew. He wouldn't learn his actual grades until he returned in January. But he felt pretty sure that, between the written tests and term papers, he did well enough to avoid any issues with his parents and to give him the confidence to take on the next semester. Nicky found it kind of amazing that he got through his coursework given all the dramas, detours, and diversions he'd experienced since September. But he learned that he was a stronger, more capable, more self-assured guy than he'd ever imagined. It only took being thrown into the deep end of the pool to learn how to swim—so to speak. What would the rest of his freshman year bring? More of the same, yet also less of the same—if Nicky had to predict. But really, who could predict much of anything in life, especially when you're still figuring out who you're supposed to be?

The dorm cleared out for the holiday mostly over two days, the Friday and Saturday before Christmas. Nicky was grabbing a ride back to Long Island again with Stuart, who couldn't leave till Saturday at noon. So, as one of the last folks to vacate 14A, Nicky had plenty of time to hang with and say goodbye to his closest floormates.

That included Monty, who was going back to Manhattan with Sabrina. They planned to spend a week in the city with her family, then take the train to Pittsburgh to stay with Monty's parents for New Year's. It was a ten-hour ride, which they thought sounded romantic; Nicky thought it sounded deadly. He'd be surprised if they didn't just stay in New York the whole time and fly back to Boston on January second. That was also the day Monty had committed to quit smoking for good. Start the year with a clean slate—and cleaner lungs. Nicky, for one, could not wait.

Shelley, like Nicky, was returning to Long Island. She planned to work at her dad's accounting office for the week to make a few bucks. She was a little self-conscious around Nicky after their last rendezvous, so, ever since, he tried to act as friendly and natural as possible. It seemed to work, because she eventually loosened up, started talking a blue streak again, and even got a bit handsy with him at times—but in a totally endearing way. They talked about meeting up for a drink or a movie over the holiday, given how close they lived to each other. Nicky hoped they could make it happen, especially if he was missing his BU pals, which he had a feeling he would.

Chuck and Ken were taking the train together back to New York City. Ken was going to see if he could spend a few days hanging around the *New York Times* newsroom, soaking up some atmosphere, and maybe even doing some free grunt work. After writing for the *Daily Free Press*, he was more compelled than ever to become the next Woodward or Bernstein—or both. Chuck had already ordered tickets to a bunch of Broadway shows, mostly musicals of course, and one drama, a revival of *The Glass Menagerie*. He invited Nicky to come into Manhattan and join him for one—or to just walk around the city and see the sights. Nicky said he just might do it, and Chuck was thrilled. He'd thought about Chuck a lot since their night at Aegean Fare and, well, now that he was single again, who knows?

Lori and her dad were flying to Miami to visit her grandparents, who spent winters there. Her mom gave Lori the go-ahead, as long as she was back in time to spend a few days with her before returning to school. She broke down and told her mother about being pregnant, though omitted exactly how—and by whom—she ended up that way. Her mom didn't press for details or offer any lectures, just reacted with love and concern. They both agreed to maybe not tell her father just yet, if ever.

"I think I definitely underestimated my mom," Lori said over one last late-night session at Deli Haus before she and Nicky left for the break. "But this divorce is really making her see the world a little differently."

"Maybe if you judge her less, she'll judge *you* less."

"When did you become such a guru?" Lori asked, buttering her toast.

"Oh, just an acute observer of humanity," Nicky said, repeating how she described herself at the start of their friendship. He grinned. "I think I heard that phrase somewhere."

"Well, whoever said that must be a genius."

"Yeah, turns out she's a pretty smart gal."

Lori bit into her toast, looked a bit defeated. "Not *that* smart."

They stared into their plates, silent for a moment. Nicky looked up. "How are you feeling? Y'know, since the . . ." He trailed off. Why was that such a difficult word? Did it make the act that much more real, that much more troubling?

Lori met his earnest gaze. "I'm feeling OK. Back to normal, I think." She traced the rim of her coffee cup, gave a small, appreciative smile. "Thanks for asking."

Nicky reached across and took her hand. "Do you wish that night never happened?"

Lori put her free hand atop his. "I wish I'd been less wasted and more careful. But no, it was an amazing night. And it brought us all together in a way that could never happen again." She considered her words. "*Should* never happen again."

"That sounds about right. On all counts."

They shared a knowing smile and returned to their plates.

"Of course, there is the bigger question in all this," Lori said.

"What's that?"

"What would Laurie Partridge do?"

"Oh, that's easy. Sing a song and go to a commercial."

"Ha! I'll have to try that sometime."

The waiter stopped by, coffee pot in hand. They each took refills.

Nicky pushed aside his egg plate. "So, here's another big question." He leaned into Lori. "Think you'll be seeing Joshua when you're back in Cherry Hill?" As far as he knew they hadn't spoken in weeks, maybe not since he visited her at BU. But given how coy she'd so often been about her ex—and her currently unattached state—it seemed like a fair question.

"No, I will not," Lori categorically declared. "That is completely and totally over." They locked eyes. "And don't look at me that way. This time I mean it. D-O-N-E." She swept her hand across the air in an erasure motion. Nicky believed her.

"Now *I* have a question," she said. "Are you and Joe still a no-go?"

"Unfortunately, yes. But not for my lack of trying."

She nodded; no further explanation was needed. "What a beautiful, complicated guy. It'll be interesting to see what happens to him."

"He may surprise us. We *all* may surprise us," Nicky said.

"My God, let's hope so."

The next day, at noon on the dot, an icy chill in the air, Stuart pulled his GTO up in front of 700. He hopped out and popped the trunk for his sole passenger. Nicky tossed in his suitcase and a duffle bag full of laundry he could do at home. Nothing like a free washing machine.

As Nicky opened the passenger door, he glanced across at the T platform and spotted Joe, baggage in hand, boarding a trolley.

A connecting train would get him to Logan Airport. Nicky watched as Joe took a window seat. As if he could feel Nicky's stare, Joe turned, gazed out, and their eyes locked. Nicky raised a hand in hello. Joe did the same, then pressed his palm flat against the window. The trolley issued its trademark wheeze and set off down Comm Ave.

Nicky, his heart still a bit broken, climbed into the GTO and settled in for the long drive home.

THIRTY-EIGHT

TODAY

THE LATE AFTERNOON sun glinted off the Charles River as Nick and Joe walked the path they'd once jogged on with happily competitive spirit. An autumn chill had come up off the water and, unlike that morning's warmish breeze, Nick felt it creeping up his bones. Joe zipped up the jacket that had earlier seemed unneeded but was now the wise choice. Nick rolled down his shirtsleeves and buried his hands in his pockets.

Outside he was cold, but inside he was glowing. The whole afternoon was proving a steady march toward a new and mutual understanding between a pair of onetime friends and lovers. Nick and Joe were so forever joined by that fleeting, if seminal slice of their late-teenage lives that, despite the passing decades, they still spoke a language uniquely their own. Their words might sound familiar to the casual listener (and, on the surface, even to Nick and Joe), but the subtext was pinpointedly private. Nick could feel Joe slowly drifting into his psyche and, he could only assume, Joe felt the same.

Despite the kaleidoscope of topics they'd covered these past hours, the guys had discussed little of consequence about Lori.

They'd talked about her, and around her, but, at least for Nick, it was hard not to feel her presence looming at most every turn. He'd hoped Joe would ask more about Lori, want to hear about that last time Nick saw her. On the other hand, maybe Joe felt it was too personal, too intrusive, too . . . sacred, and was waiting for Nick to bring it up. If that was the case, now seemed as good a time as any. So, as they approached the spot where he'd had his morning mini-meltdown, with the Hatch Shell in distant view, Nick told Joe about Lori's last months. How she'd lived. And how she'd died.

He told him about Lori's husband, Pete, a handsome, five-years-younger graphic artist she met on the eve of her thirty-eighth birthday and married six months later. How they'd quickly had two daughters, Mariah and Carly, who, as young women, each looked so much like their mother it made Nick cry. How Lori worked as a psychologist in the same Cherry Hill high school for more than thirty years and said she loved every minute of it. How, the year after she retired, the tumor that appeared during a random checkup at first proved treatable and, within six months, not at all. And how Nick spent an unforgettable weekend with Lori and her family in Cherry Hill about a month before she started hospice care. She never really changed much over time, remaining the lovely, witty, reflective, caring, and intuitive woman they'd both first met at BU. Nick would miss her always.

Joe listened in rapt silence as Nick told his story. Neither had realized how far they'd walked until they came upon the stairs to the Harvard Bridge. The sun was beginning its descent, and the temperature had continued to drop. The guys stopped, looked at each other.

"Wow. I mean, I knew. But not really. Not the details," Joe said.

"You should've answered my email. I would have told you more."

Joe stared off at the river. "I didn't know what to say."

"How about 'I'm so sorry you lost your friend of forty-four years'?"

Joe sat on a bench at the foot of the stairs. "I lied, you know," Joe admitted.

"About what, exactly?"

"About what I think of when I hear 'Born to Run.' Yeah, I think of you and me driving around your hometown that Thanksgiving, listening to the radio. But I usually *first* think of that night of the concert. That magical first time we all saw Bruce." Joe paused, took in a breath, lost in reverie. "And the crazy shit that the three of us did after. We were so fucking high. And so damn fearless." He wiped the tear he could no longer hold back. "What happened to us, Nicky?"

Nick took a bracing breath and sat next to Joe. "Life happened to us. Like it happens to everyone. We're nothing special, y'know." He gazed at his old friend. "I mean, maybe we were. For a brief, shining moment. But it doesn't last. It can't. Otherwise, we'd never know what real life feels like."

Joe turned to him. "Are you saying what you and I had wasn't real?"

Nick's face melted into a smile. "Oh, no. Just the opposite. That was as real as it gets. As pure as it gets. *That* was our brief, shining moment."

Joe watched Nick. He looked chilled. Joe took off his jacket and handed it over. "Here, put this on."

Nick hesitated, then took the jacket. He slipped into it and instantly warmed up. He looked at Joe's bare arms. "Now aren't *you* cold?"

Joe thought for a second. "Not really, no." He smiled wryly. "Actually, it's invigorating."

Nick grinned. "You're so full of shit."

He returned the smile. "Only sometimes."

They watched the sky over the river slowly darken yet brighten at the same time: its cobalt blue and wispy gray clouds giving way to streaks of pink, orange, and violet. A final crew team whisked into view, then, just as quickly, sped down the Charles and out of sight.

"Do you think we could find something real again?" Joe asked, still gazing out at the rippled water.

"Real again as in . . . what?"

Joe turned and faced Nick. "As in us."

Nick hadn't quite known what to expect from the day, but this wasn't it. Or was it? Was there a part of him—that hopeful, dreamy, sentimental side—that wondered if he and Joe weren't somehow destined to finish what they'd started, no matter how much time had passed? Or maybe because of it? That despite his resistance to get sucked back into the Joe of it all, deep down that was what he'd been wishing for since he arrived in Boston? Better yet, from the minute they first planned their reunion? So much happened between them at BU and yet, in the scheme of things, so little. Maybe just enough to be haunted by, but without shutting off any new possibilities.

All the same, Nick honestly didn't know what to say. So he said just that.

"So, it's not a no, then?" Joe asked hopefully.

Nick glanced at Joe's tantalizing forearms. Took in his sturdy shoulders, the pale freckles that still spread across his nose, and the tiny cleft that remained in his squarish chin. Fifty years melted away. They were back in Joe's dorm room, two young guys discovering each other—and themselves. But, as they say, that was then and this was now.

"Is that what you really want? At this point in your life?" Nick asked. *Is it what I really want at this point in my life?*

"If not now, when?" Joe answered without hesitation. "You said it yourself: it's never too late to live the life you want." His eyes widened and his head tilted like an eager, curious pup. An almost seventy-year-old pup.

Nick gazed at a pair of college-age guys in sweats jogging past, their heads up, shoulders back. They looked purposeful, focused, in sync. And swift. So swift. Were they friends? Teammates? Lovers? Nick felt a pang of regret—and longing.

Joe watched with Nick as the joggers vanished around a curve in the path. Still staring forward, Joe put an arm around Nick's shoulders and drew him in. Nick didn't resist, perhaps welcomed the closeness, took in the fading scent of Joe's Aramis and the near-ghostlike feel of his touch. He felt his resolve wither and his heart expand. *OK, not so fast*, he thought.

Nick faced Joe. "What happened to 'I can do what I want when I want'? About not getting—What did you call it?—'tangled up in somebody's complicated life?'"

"Maybe 'what I want, when I want' is to be with you. And, for the record, I wouldn't be getting tangled up in just *anyone's* complicated life."

Nick sighed, appropriately disarmed. "I guess it's not really *that* complicated. At this point, anyway."

"And it's not like I don't have my share of baggage," Joe said. "I think that's pretty clear."

"Oh, it's flashing like the Citgo sign," Nick joked, more than conscious of the potential red flags.

Joe smiled, then went silent. They were both aware this was not something to be done lightly, if maybe at all.

"How would it work?" Nick wondered aloud. "You in Charlotte, me in LA?"

"I don't know, Nick. But we're both in Boston now. We can start here."

Nick. Finally. His pulse quickened, and his throat went dry. "I thought you had a wedding to go to."

"That's not till Sunday. And I'm sure I can bring a date."

"A date. Really." *Hmm.*

The sky's pinks and purples were fading to black as the afternoon came to its definitive end. They watched the sun sink out of sight and plunge the city into twilight. There was nothing left to do but take a step toward the future. Of which there was increasingly less. It could be one night. Or one weekend. Or the rest of their lives. How would they ever know if that first September day in the 700 elevator was truly meant to be—or just a random encounter with a finite expiration date? Was it their destiny or just a fleeting, singular moment in time?

Nick leaned in and kissed Joe, who returned it with depth and urgency and joy. The river and the esplanade and the Boston skyline fell away around them as fifty years came rushing back like a torrent. A welcome, terrifying, intoxicating torrent.

It could be the start of a new chapter or the end of an old one.

There was only one way to find out.

ACKNOWLEDGMENTS

IT WAS GREAT fun digging back into my memories of college life to write *Please Come to Boston,* even if my actual freshman year at Boston University was far less dramatic, romantic, and adventurous than Nicky's. Still, while this isn't my story per se, it's a kind of idealized version of what might have been had I been further ahead of the game than I was at the time—and if fate had dealt a remarkably different hand. Not that I would have been even remotely ready to jump on to that particular thrill ride; I reserved that for my far more intrepid main character.

All by way of giving thanks to BU, the bridge that it served—both socially, emotionally, and intellectually—to my adulthood, and to my many college friends, floormates, classmates, and others who show up in small, subtle, and amalgamized ways here (though you may not be who you think!). I will say, however, that Nicky, Lori, and especially Joe are almost entirely fictional concoctions; I wish I had actually known them.

While I'm on BU, I'd also like to single out a few of my professors whose contributions to my future I could never have guessed at the time: journalism profs Jeremiah V. Murphy and Gary Woonteiler, whom I hold almost wholly responsible for my ability to write—I hope—a clean, well-structured sentence (all that obit writing paid off!); cinema profs Roger Manvell, George Bluestone, and Arnold Baskin for opening my mind to the possibilities of film, its history and construction; and my many English lit professors, who helped me realize my strengths and, more importantly, my weaknesses as a reader and an interpreter of the written word.

From today's BU, a shout-out to executive staffers Colin Riley and Michael Ciarlante, who helped confirm various school facts, past and present (yes, you *could* smoke and drink in the dorms in 1975!), and kindly directed me to the campus resources I needed during pre-publication. Thank you, as well, to Marc Chalufour and Joel Brown of *Bostonia* magazine for their attention and support.

Appreciation also to my eternal pal Mark Feldman, whom I met so long ago at BU. He not only offered his ace marketing skills to assist with the launch of this book, but also helped me recall several obscure factoids of life at BU and, particularly, of 700 Comm Ave, where we both lived for an overlapping year. Let's always keep making each other laugh. And, of course, to his wife, Barbara, who first entered the picture while Mark and I were in college, and has been another wonderful part of the equation ever since.

To Debbie (Wolensky) Orrio and Laura (Markowitz) Miller, who have also remained among my most cherished BU friends: I love you both. And to Robin (Rubinstein) Hutner, who brightened my college days, made me a Springsteen fan, and was a dear friend for decades after. You are deeply missed.

If the physical writing of a novel is a mainly solitary effort, getting that novel out into the world is anything but. So big thanks and hugs go out to my early readers (you know who you are!) who offered heaps of encouragement and invaluable input before the selling process began.

Gratitude also to Allison Mann at Hadleigh House Publishing, who continued her streak as an unflagging cheerleader, creative ally, discerning voice, and generous friend. For the third time, my editor, Kate Ankofski, made me look like a better writer than I am and, again, has proven a fine collaborator. Cheers also to Amanda Pisani for her eagle-eyed proofreading skills and to Susan Walter, Ken Pisani, and W. Bruce Cameron for their accomplished perspectives and writerly inspiration.

Though it goes without saying, I will say it anyway: to my family, fellow authors, work cohorts, and other friends and partners in this crazy journey of life and career, I couldn't have done it without you. Nor would I have wanted to. I've been blessed with much love and support and am well aware of how fortunate I have been. I hope I've been able to adequately return the many kindnesses I've been shown.

My sister, Lynn Rosenberg, has been my lifelong champion, and it's been fun to share our writing journeys these last years, especially as she created her own campus-inspired novel, *Never My Love.* Everyone should have a sibling as caring and connected as I do.

And finally, to Bill, who has brought more joy and solace to my life than I could have ever imagined all those years ago when I was trying to figure it all out. There's a lot to be said for living your authentic life—whatever it takes to get there.

ABOUT GARY GOLDSTEIN

GARY GOLDSTEIN is an award-winning writer for film, TV, and the theatre, with more than 30 produced screen and stage credits. His first novel, the romantic comedy *The Last Birthday Party*, won an IBPA Benjamin Franklin Award for Excellence in Fiction. Goldstein's second novel, the family drama *The Mother I Never Had*, was named one of the "Must-Read Books of Fall 2022" by *Town & Country* magazine. He has also been a contributing arts writer for the *L.A. Times* since 2007. A New York native and yes, Boston University graduate, Goldstein lives in Los Angeles with his husband, Bill, and their camera-ready Labrador retriever, Bella.

You can follow Goldstein on X (Twitter) and Instagram @GaryGoldsteinLA, and at facebook.com/GaryGoldsteinLAauthor. More info/contact via his website: GaryGoldsteinLA.com.

PLEASE COME TO BOSTON BOOK CLUB QUESTIONS

1. If you went to college, what's your most vivid memory of your first day on campus? Who was the first meaningful person you met?

2. It took Nicky leaving home to realize he needed to explore his sexuality, overwhelming as it was. What part of yourself did you explore when you were on your own for the first time?

3. We may not realize it in our teens or twenties, but, as we get older, having longtime friends with whom we share a deep history can be particularly special. Talk about one of your oldest friends, how you met, and how you sustained the relationship over the years.

4. No matter one's sexuality, most people have ended up in a romantic situation, at one time or another, with what might be considered an unlikely partner. Whether it works out in the long run can be another "unlikely" story. Tell yours.

5. Once Nicky starts to seriously consider his attraction to Joe, he realizes that those feelings were not without precedent—even if, pre-Joe, he'd never truly recognized them. Did you find it credible, even for the times, that he'd never previously put two and two together?

6. Joe seems like the ideal man in so many ways, yet Lori never fully embraces him. Still, she seems to carry a torch for the imperfect Joshua. Why do you think that is? What might she actually be looking for in a partner?

7. Along those lines, Lori and Nicky, for a few key reasons, never really get past the friend stage. If Nicky were straight, Do you think they would have become a real couple? Or would they always have been destined for friendship?

8. Nicky logically feels coming out to his family, in any way, would be unthinkable. And, as he tells Joe years later, it was a no-go for a long time. Given the era and his family, what do you think might have happened if Nicky had opened up to them soon after the "Grandma incident?"

9. Okay, spill, you lifelong heteros: While in high school or college (or that age), did you ever romantically or sexually "experiment" with someone of the same sex? How did it happen and what was it like? Did you find it emotionally derailing in some way or surprisingly gratifying?

10. Nick and Joe's present-day reunion leaves a door open for a future together. Talk about the kind of relationship they might enjoy after all these years if they were finally able to give it a go. What might be some of the upsides—and downsides?

www.ingramcontent.com/pod-product-compliance
Lightning Source LLC
Chambersburg PA
CBHW022114310726
48972CB00007B/2027